In the Company of My Sistahs

In the Company of My Sistahs

ANGIE DANIELS

KENSINGTON PUBLISHING CORP.

DAFINA BOOKS are published by

Kensington Publishing Corp.
850 Third Avenue
New York, NY 10022

ISBN 0-7394-6493-0

Printed in the United States of America

This book is dedicated to the members of
In the Company of My Sisters book club in Dover, Delaware.
Shouts out to Sharon, Latasha, Melissa, Toni,
Tamara, Sherri, Beverly, Avonda, Cecelia, and Antynea.
Thanks for all of the weekends loaded with calories.

Acknowledgments

To my son Mark Kelly, I love you. Mama wants you to know that we all make mistakes, what's important is that we learn from them. You are truly a wonderful young man.

To my friends Tonya Hill, Ja'net Daniels, Norma Rhodes, and Kim Ashcraft for spending several fun-filled days with my sister, Arlynda and me in Jamaica. Thanks for just being yourselves thus making this book possible.

To all the members of *angiedaniels@yahoogroups.com* for your continued love and support.

I love to hear from my readers. Please drop me a line at angie@angie daniels.com.

Chapter I

RENEE

"What the hell do you mean you can't find your birth certificate?"

"I thought it was in my desk drawer, but when I looked a few minutes ago, it wasn't there."

I took a deep breath, drawing on the lessons bestowed upon me. *Patience is a virtue* is right up there with *do unto others as you want done unto you.* Shit, I've been flunking both for years.

"Why the hell did you wait until it's time to leave to look for your damn birth certificate?"

"I thought I had it," Nadine mumbled.

See, this is a prime example as to why I have very few female friends—because they are either catty or doing some stupid shit, like losing a damn birth certificate.

I told my sister Lisa this wasn't going to work, but she refused to hear me. So listen to what I am about to tell you. Four women can't spend a week in Jamaica together.

Nadine, who I'm on the phone with now, is a notorious procrastinator. I've been telling her big titty behind for almost three months that she needed a birth certificate. I even went as far as to instruct her to put the damn thing in her suitcase so she wouldn't forget it.

Now she wants to call me just as we're getting ready to roll down to St. Louis to say she can't find the damn thing.

"Renee, what am I going to do?" I heard her say.

"I don't know what you're going to do, 'cause I told your ass!" What she needed was a miracle and my name sho' in the hell wasn't Helen Keller.

Glancing over at the digital clock on my nightstand, I noticed it was already after five and rolled my eyes. "If you had taken the time to look for it an hour ago you could've ran downtown to Vital Statistics and picked up another copy."

"What time they close?"

"They closed five minutes ago! See, that's why I don't fool with you." Breathing heavily into the receiver, I tried counting to five but that shit wasn't working. I had problems of my own. My ex-husband was supposed to have picked up his kids at one o'clock. As usual his tired ass was late.

You know what? I ain't got time for this shit.

"My advice to you is to keep looking and call me back." Without bothering to say good-bye, I punched END on the cordless phone, then tossed it onto my bed. I wasn't even about to worry about her right now.

Besides, Nadine ain't even my friend. She's my sister Lisa's home-girl.

It doesn't matter that Nadine and I used to blow spit bubbles together or the fact that her funky-ass feet used to be in my face when she slept at the bottom of my bed. So what if I used to fart and pin her ass to the mattress so she had no choice but to smell it. None of that shit counts. She's still Lisa's friend, not mine. I just hang with Nadine from time to time 'cause she doesn't have too many friends. After my sister moved to Texas her ass was acting all lonely and shit, so I felt sorry for her. But regardless of how you want to look at it, Nadine ain't my friend. She's Lisa's homegirl.

With her dilemma still fresh on the brain, I reached under my bed, pulled out my suitcase and decided that after all that ranting and raving I better make sure my passport hadn't expired. I believe it's good for ten years. My second husband was in the Army, and we lived overseas, but that's another story.

I found it between my vibrator and a box of magnum-size condoms (hey, a sistah's gotta be prepared) and just as I thought, my passport was still good for another two years. I tossed it into my purse and reached for my deodorant on the dresser.

Hearing footsteps coming down the hall, I looked up to find my thirteen-year-old daughter, Tamara, entering my room, followed by our schnauzer, Nikki.

"Mom, you need some help?" she asked me as she took a seat on my bed.

I shook my head. "No, Princess. Are you all packed?"

"Yes, Mom."

"You got your toothbrush?"

"Yes, Mom."

"Plenty of clean underwear?"

"Mom," she groaned, "you already asked me that this morning!"

"And I'm going to keep on asking, smart-ass," I retorted. Who the hell does she think she's talking to? I don't know what's wrong with kids today. If I had spoken to my mother that way she would've knocked my ass clear into next week.

Nikki jumped on top of my open suitcase. Spoiled-ass dog. "Get down, Nikki," I ordered. Luckily, she obeyed and jumped down, taking a seat near my daughter's feet; otherwise I would've thrown my shoe at her. Don't get me wrong. I love my dog. We all do. She's been in our family for almost nine years, and I consider her part of the family. Nevertheless, her ass is spoiled. Have you ever heard of a dog that sleeps in the bed under the covers with her head on a pillow? *Rotten.*

I looked over in time to see Tamara reach into my suitcase and pull out a size-ten bikini I found on clearance at Wal-Mart.

She turned up her nose. "Mom, I hope you ain't wearing this."

"Shoot! I don't know why not."

"'Cause, your stomach is too big."

"Whatever," I mumbled as I snatched it from her hand. I don't care how big my stomach is, not this week, anyway.

All four of us agreed that whatever happens in Jamaica, stays in Jamaica. So if I want to wear a bikini and show my childbearing stretch marks, then that's my damn business. I will never see any of those people again. Besides, my stomach ain't that bad. I'm the stomach-crunch queen. I just have a little pooch, nothing more . . . well, maybe a little more, but not that much. Nevertheless, after two kids, I still look good. Smooth caramel skin, hazel eyes, small firm breasts (my shit don't sag), big legs, and a phat ass—*ssshittt*, you better ask somebody.

I put the bikini back in my suitcase and took a quick inventory of its contents. I had a swimsuit for all five days with flip-flops and butt wraps to match. There were also sundresses, tops, and shorts. Yes, you better believe this sistah was prepared. "Princess, can you go get my blue-jean shorts out the dryer?"

"Aw'ight." She slid off the bed. "Come on, Nikki." On command, her dog rose and happily followed her down the hall.

Before she got too far, I called after her. "Before you do that, go call your dad." The sorry bastard.

I'm sorry. I'm probably coming off as a bitch and I apologize. I just have a lot on my mind these days. A great deal of stress. When I get back from Jamaica, I have to make what I consider one of the biggest decisions of my life. I have been putting it off for months and time has finally run out.

By the time I inventoried my suitcase, my phone rang. I looked down at my caller ID and saw it was my girl Kayla Sparks.

"Whassup," I greeted.

She smacked her lips as she spoke. "Gurl, Nadine says she can't find her birth certificate."

"I know, she already called and told me."

"What's she going to do?"

"I don't know what she's gonna do. I've been telling her the same damn thing for weeks and it went in one ear and out the other."

"She's ridiculous."

I clicked my tongue. "Tell me something I don't already know."

Obviously there wasn't shit else she could tell me that I didn't already know, because she changed the subject.

"I've already dropped Kenya and Asia off at my mom's. My bags are packed and I'm ready to go."

"So am I. That is, as soon as Mario's sorry ass gets here."

"How much spending money you taking?" Kayla asked.

"Not much. My car insurance was due. I got enough to cover my half of the room and buy everyone a gift."

Kayla paused a second too long. "I thought you were paying for our rooms with your credit card," she finally said.

"Excuse me? I *reserved* our rooms on my credit card. You need to *pay* for your half of the room when you get there." My statement was followed by another long pause. *Uh-oh, not another one.* I lowered onto the bed. "You do have money for your room, right?"

"No-o-o. I thought you were paying for them and we were paying you back later."

"Y'all are fucked up! I'm not First National Bank. I specifically said I would hold the rooms on my card. I never said shit about paying for them."

"You're silly." Kayla had the nerve to sound appalled.

"No, y'all bitches are crazy," I spat. My other line beeped. "Hold on." I clicked over. My older sister Lisa was calling me from her cell phone. She and her husband Michael arrived from Texas last week and have been staying with his parents.

"Hey, you ready?" she asked.

"Almost. I got Kayla on the other line, but check this shit out. Nadine called; she can't find her birth certificate."

"What?" Lisa screamed. "Just the other day she told me she had it."

"Well, she lost it. The way her house looks I ain't the least bit surprised." It was no secret Nadine's house was a damn pig sty. She saves every doggone thing she gets her hands on because she's afraid to throw anything away. I tried once to help her organize her shit. Even brought over a paper shredder, but she refused to part with anything. Which was fine with me because I don't have to sleep there. However, I did tell her nasty ass not to even think about inviting me over again until she cleaned her damn house.

"Man, this is unbelievable," I heard Lisa say.

"You right. She called right after Vital Statistics closed."

"If she had bothered to look yesterday, she could have gone down with me."

"I know. To top it off, Kayla thought I was paying for both rooms with my credit card and y'all were paying me back at a later date."

"Damn, both my girls are trippin'."

"Hell yeah, they're trippin'." Especially since my credit card was maxed out. Shit, I couldn't even use it to pay for my own half of the room. "You ready to roll?"

Lisa cleared her throat. "Actually, I was calling 'cause Michael wants me to spend the evening with him. I'ma go to the boat tonight."

"Bitch, whatever! You gonna end up missing the plane."

"No, I won't. You know I get up that early anyway."

"Uh-huh," I returned with straight attitude. My sister owns a bakery in San Antonio and yeah, she does get up early, but that's beside the point. The four of us had made plans for the evening that obviously now had changed. Leave it to some damn man to rain on my parade. "Yeah, whatever."

"What's wrong with you?" Lisa asked.

"I need some dick. I'll call you back." I clicked back over to the other line in time to hear Kayla's pissed-off sigh through the receiver. "Ho, don't even try to get no attitude, 'cause you're always putting me on hold." Returning to the problem at hand, I asked, "So, do you have money or what?"

She sighed again. "Yeah, I just got paid. I was going to put my house note in the mail before we left but I guess it can wait until I get back."

"It's gonna have to. I'll have a check waiting for me when I get back. So, if you need me to spot you a few bucks then, I can help you out. I just don't have it this week."

"Cool." Kayla sounded pleased by my offer. I don't have a problem loaning her money as long as her broke ass remembers to pay me back.

I heard my kids fighting in the other room. "Girl, I'll call you when I'm on my way. In the meantime, see if you can help Nadine."

I hung up and made it down the hall and into the living room in time to catch my sixteen-year-old son hitting his sister upside the head with a pillow. "Y'all are trippin'! You know this room is off limits."

"Mom, Quinton started it!" Tamara screamed.

"No, I didn't!" he countered.

"I don't care who started it. Just get out of my living room. Now!"

My kids know when I ain't playing, because they scrambled down the hall to their rooms. I picked the throw pillows off the floor and put them back on my cream-colored Italian leather couch.

I love my living room set. It took every dime of my income tax return but it was worth it. With beige carpeting on the floor and runners to protect it, my children knew the living room was for company only.

I was checking my plants to make sure they had enough water, when I heard a car pull up in my driveway. Peeking through taupe mini blinds, I saw my ex-husband Mario's raggedy blue Cavalier. About damn time.

"Mama, Daddy's here!" Tamara screamed from her room.

"I know," I returned. I waited until he knocked before I opened the door and gave him my best negro-you're-late stare.

"Sorry, I had car trouble." He was dressed in his faded blue jeans and a white t-shirt, smelling like motor oil.

I stepped aside so he could enter. He moved over to the couch I just fluffed, and—*oh no he didn't*—dropped his funky ass onto my cushions.

His eyes traveled around the room. "I see you've been decorating."

"Always."

He draped his arm across the back of my couch. "Yeah, I miss this old house. We should still be doin' all this together."

Oh, Lord, here we go again. Mario and I have been divorced for almost twelve years but every time he comes around he wants to talk about what we coulda, shoulda been if we had stayed together. I don't feel like hearing that shit today.

"Hey, Dad." My daughter came bouncing into the living room, flopped down on my couch next to him, and planted a kiss on his cheek.

"Hey, girl." He smiled down at her.

Tamara's a daddy's girl. She sees him only one weekend a month but to her, he does no wrong. They look just alike. They have the same dark eyes covered by thick bushy eyebrows and long black lashes. Mario was a tenderoni back in the day. He's just short as hell. I don't know why I used to have a thing for short men.

Quinton came into the living room, carrying a tote bag over his shoulder. I smiled because my son is handsome and destined to be a heartbreaker. Already six feet, he got his height from my side of the family. He is always dressed nicely. If it doesn't have a designer label, he ain't wearing it, which is why I made his spoiled ass get a job this summer. As I said before, my name ain't First National Bank.

"Look at them gym shoes." My ex-husband was referring to my son's one-hundred-dollar Nikes.

"We put your child support to good use," I snorted.

"Must be nice. I can only afford Wal-Mart. I ain't got it like that."

"Whatever," I mumbled under my breath. He was about to go into his long spiel about how poor he was.

"Shoot, I ain't got a pot to piss in or a window to throw it out of."

What did I tell you? Mario's got my daughter feeling so sorry for him she asked me to give him back his child support. Has she lost her damn mind?

Mario rose. "Let's go, kids. Renee, make sure you bring me back some of that Jamaican rum."

Yeah, whatever. I gave both of my kids a hug and a kiss, made sure Mario had the number to the hotel in case of an emergency, then pushed them and Nikki out the door.

I straightened the couch again, then moved to the bathroom. After a quick shower, I was ready to get my vacation started. Tamara never did bring me my shorts. I went down to the basement and pulled them out the dryer. I double checked the doors and windows to make sure they were secure, then raced back up the steps to grab the phone.

It was Nadine.

"Did you find it?" I asked.

"No. I must have thrown it away when I cleaned my room last week." She sounded frustrated, but I didn't have time to be feeling sorry for her. Nadine ain't never bothered to clean her house before, so why start now?

"I don't know what to tell you," I said with probably a little less feeling than I should have. Hey, it's been a long day and my ass is horny.

"I think I might have one at my parents' house."

"In Kansas City?" That was almost a two-hour drive.

"Yeah, I'm waiting for them to call me back. If so, I guess I'll drive there and back tonight and leave for St. Louis in the morning."

"That's fine. Lisa and Michael are spending the night at the boat. She's getting dicked tonight, so I won't see her until the morning either. Just meet us at the Waffle House." I hung up and went to my room to get dressed. Getting some dick didn't sound like a bad idea.

I have a hook-up in St. Louis that I visit whenever I'm in town. Vince is a real kind of brotha. What you see is what you get. He lives in one of those old historical homes in the city that is in such bad shape, it needs to be either restored or torn down. He drives on the back of a garbage truck and is broke, but what the hell. I don't want his money. Just his dick. We met at a nightclub six months ago and just by the way he gyrated his hips I knew he could fuck. Maybe I'll call him when I get to St. Louis. Maybe I won't. He knows I'm coming tonight so maybe I'll wait and see if he calls first.

Thirty minutes later, I was rolling down the road in my black Camry with Mariah's new CD blasting through my speakers. I rolled down my window, allowing the warm July breeze to toss my braids. I needed a drink.

My cell phone rang. I reached for it and noticed that the number had been blocked. When I'm at home I ignore blocked or anonymous callers because nine times out of ten, it's either a telemarketer or a damn bill collector. Now my cell phone, that's a different story altogether. The first thing that comes to mind is somebody is playing on my dime.

"Hello?"

"Yeah, is this Renee Moore?"

"Who wants to know?" I asked with straight sistah girl attitude.

"Ricky Johnson's wife, that's who."

Uh-uh. No the bitch didn't. She doesn't know my ass from the damn man on the moon. So how the hell she gonna call me talking crazy?

"*Excuse me?* I know you ain't calling my phone talking slick." The tone of my voice told her whatever my words didn't, because she didn't say shit. "What can I do for you?"

Finally, she sucked her teeth. "I want to know why my man's been calling you."

"Why don't you ask your man?"

"I did and he says y'all been discussing business."

You know, one thing that burns me up is a lying-ass nigga. First off, I met Ricky's ass last week at this club that ain't no more than a juke joint. Now, I ain't gonna lie. The brotha is fine. Berry black skin, wavy hair, tall, and one helluva dresser. I didn't waste any time getting his attention and before the end of the night, we had exchanged cell phone numbers. Now I might not remember everything that slick mothafucka told me, but one thing I do know, he told me his ass wasn't married.

I rudely laughed in her ear. "Okay, so if he already gave you an answer, then why the hell you calling me?"

"Because I don't believe him."

"Then that sounds like a personal problem."

"No, it ain't no problem 'cause all I need to know is what the hell y'all were talking about; then I'm gonna whoop somebody's ass."

I thought the shit was funny so I started laughing again. "Bitch, you know what? First off, you must be hard up for a man because there ain't no way in hell I would be calling some female's number I found on my man's caller ID, trying to find out what he's been up to. Secondly, the only ass you're gonna whoop tonight is his. So unless you want me to hang the fuck up, I advise you to come correct."

She then had the nerve to laugh. "Damn, girl, your ass is hard. You have to excuse me 'cause right now I'm feeling some kind of way. Me and Ricky been together ten years so I have a lot of time invested in this relationship."

"Yeah, and it's obvious you make a habit of checking his phone."

"Shit, I pay the damn bill."

Stupid wench. "Girlfriend, let me school you. You need to check Ricky's punk ass instead of wasting my damn time. 'Cause by you calling me all you're doing is letting me know the dick is good. I mean why else would you be checking his every move? Now, first off, one sistah to another, your man told me he wasn't married. And one thing I don't do is mess with another sistah's husband. Secondly, the only business he and I had to discuss was me getting some dick. However, since I am in such a good mood, I'll do you a favor, and leave his ass alone. In return, do me a favor . . . both y'all mothafuckas lose my damn number." I clicked END and lowered the phone onto my lap. That bitch had to be ugly—why else would she be running after some trifling negro. Or maybe as I said before, Ricky's got some good dick.

I reached for my cell phone again and called Kayla to tell her I was on my way, then I stopped by the ATM and withdrew enough cash to last me a week. Five minutes later, I pulled into her driveway.

Kayla was standing on the porch, with her suitcase in front of her feet, waiting. She was dressed in her usual black pants and white t-shirt. She is a big woman with a really pretty face, and tall enough to be a model if she was a dozen dress sizes smaller. She has a cute upturned nose, big green eyes, and a dazzling white smile. Her skin is so beige she could almost pass for white if it wasn't for her nappy-ass hair.

We met during college. I was attending night classes and she was in several of them. Somehow, like oil and vinegar, we mixed. I'm wild as hell, while Kayla is one of those who travels the straight and narrow, living her life according to the good book. She is the type of woman to be married. Instead, she has two girls with different baby's daddies that she has to track down every six months for child support payments.

"Hey, girl," she greeted. She put her suitcase in my backseat. As she climbed onto the seat beside me, I complimented her on the ten straight-back cornrows she had secured with a hair tie.

"Your hair looks good."

"So does yours." Kayla reached out and fingered one of my braids. "I can't believe she was able to braid your hair."

"I didn't even." Her cousin Danita did my hair. You can't go to Jamaica with a curling iron. The humidity is a bitch. I have always worn one of those Halle Berry haircuts, so my hair is only *that* long. But I've been growing it out for almost four months for this occasion. Danita had to pinch, and damn that shit hurt. My hair was so tight that I had fucking Chinese eyes. But I refused to take them out. I just took the pain and two days of severe headaches. It's a shame the things women have to go through to look beautiful.

"Where's Lisa?" Kayla asked as I was pulling out of the driveway.

"She's at the casino with Michael. We'll see her in the morning."

"This is ridiculous! We were supposed to go to St. Louis, get a room, and hang out at the club before leaving for Jamaica in the morning."

"So, what's the problem?" I asked even though I knew good and damn well what she was getting at.

"There ain't no one but us. How are we gonna kick it if it's just us?"

I glanced over at her holy ass wondering why she was tripping. Kayla wouldn't have done anything but sat in a corner all night sipping on a virgin daiquiri, telling every brotha who tried to step to her that they needed Jesus in their life.

"You know what," I finally said as I made a U-turn in the middle of the road. "We are going to Tropical Liquors. I'm gettin' me a frozen Long Island Tea, and you a daiquiri, then we're rollin' out. When we get to St. Louis, I'm droppin' your ass off at the hotel."

"Where're you going?" Kayla asked.

"I'm going to get me some dick."

Chapter 2

KAYLA

Shortly after Renee left, Kayla moved to the bathroom to run herself a bath. She slipped out of her shoes, then reached into her tote bag for her Calgon. She needed to be taken away. As soon as she adjusted the water temperature, she took a seat on one of the full-size beds and reached for the phone. Digging into her purse, she removed her calling card and placed a long distance call, then hung up. By the time she pulled her pajamas from her suitcase the phone rang.

She grabbed it on the first ring. "Hello?"

"I see you made it safely," said a deep baritone voice.

"What happened to you this afternoon? I thought you were coming to see me before I left."

"I couldn't get away."

"Leroy, I'm so sick of hearing that excuse. When are you going to tell her the truth?" Kayla huffed.

There was a long pause before she finally heard him say, "I promise to tell her before you get back from Jamaica."

Kayla grinned, pleased at his response. She had been waiting almost two years for this day to come. "I miss you already."

"I miss you too, baby. I'll see you when you get back."

"All right." Kayla was still smiling long after she hung up the phone. Reverend Leroy Brown would soon be hers.

Sinking down into the tub of steaming hot water, she sighed. Oh, it felt good, although having some of Leroy's good loving before she left would have been even better.

Closing her eyes, she affected a dreamy expression. Renee thought she was sweet and innocent. If she knew Kayla was having an affair with a married man, she would probably shit her pants. Kayla giggled at her secret before her expression sobered.

She never set out to fall in love with Reverend Brown. It just happened.

Kayla had been an active member of Mt. Carmel Baptist Church for almost a decade and during that time she had seen them go through several different pastors.

Reverend Green, a young man straight out of the sanctuary, preferred to spend his evenings visiting the single women of the church, making sure all their *needs* were met. He didn't last five months before the elders of the church ran him out.

Reverend Hollis came to them from another church. He preached on Sundays and fornicated the other six days. He could be found in every strip club in the city. The deacons knew, but what could they do without implicating themselves? It wasn't until Hollis started taking the church's money and tossing those dollars across the stage that they finally had the grounds to dismiss him.

When Reverend Leroy Brown, his wife Darlene, and their four adorable children came to Mt. Carmel, the congregation's prayers were finally answered. He could preach a sermon that made you want to stand up and shout. He could also talk his congregation into filling the offering plate. It wasn't long before word got around about his ministry, and their congregation increased tremendously.

Kayla took an instant liking to him because Leroy reminded her so much of her grandfather. Reverend Sparks led a large Baptist church in Baton Rouge, Louisiana. Everyone admired him and she always felt so proud knowing she was his favorite granddaughter. At ten she vowed to marry a man just like him.

Leroy was a tall man, dark as melted chocolate and just as smooth. Kayla was willing to head any committee he needed, just to be near him. She didn't try to fall in love with him, and even tried to deny it for as long as she could; however, on one particular night there was no getting around it.

It was Wednesday night and they had just finished Bible study. Mrs. Brown had stayed at home because their son Tyree had a bit of a cold. Kayla said good-bye to everyone and was halfway to her car when her four-year-old daughter Asia cried that she needed to go to the bathroom.

"Girl, why didn't you say something earlier?" Kayla scolded, wishing that she had left Asia with her older sister, who had stayed home to complete a paper for school.

"I didn't have to go then." Asia dancing with her legs clamped tightly together, Kayla grabbed her hand and pulled her back to the church and down the stairs to the ladies' room. As quickly as Kayla could get Asia to wash her hands and dry them off on a paper towel they were back up the stairs and out the door just as Reverend Brown was locking it.

He gave her a warm smile. "Sister Sparks, I didn't know anyone was still here."

"Sorry, Asia had to make a pit stop."

"No problem." He smiled.

Reverend Brown was such a patient man. She had seen it many times when the women of the church were ranting and raving about one thing or another. He always seemed so calm and laid back that he made you feel guilty for acting a fool.

"How's school coming along?" he asked as he walked them down the dirt road to her car.

"Fine, just fine. I should be graduating in December."

"Good. Very good. I'm proud of you."

"Thank you." Her hands were shaking. She hadn't even known that he knew she was taking evening college classes. Did that mean he had been asking about her? She was so nervous she thought she would throw up the lasagna she'd had for dinner.

Kayla waved as the last car pulled away from the church. There was now no one but Kayla, Asia, and Reverend Brown.

They continued walking in companionable silence. It was a wonderful evening. The sky was full of stars and there was a slight warm breeze, a clear indicator that spring was almost over and summer was quickly on its way.

When they reached her car, Leroy turned to her. "Well, Sister, I guess we'll see you at church on Sunday."

She nodded, nervously, not sure what else to do. Fumbling, she reached into her pocket and removed her keys. He opened the back door and helped Asia in.

"Thanks, Reverend Brown." Kayla had just reached down to open her door when his hand slipped over hers. She raised her eyes to meet his sexy brown eyes.

"Call me Leroy." The words slipped off his tongue like melted butter.

"A-all right, Leroy." She couldn't have looked away even if she had wanted to.

"Please tell me if I'm wrong but I get the feeling that you're attracted to me."

His statement startled her. How had he known?

As if he could read her mind, his thick lips curled confidently as he spoke, "I've seen the way you look at me."

She was embarrassed. The Lord was certain to strike her down for thinking such things! Before she could think of something to say, his thumb began to caress the back of her hand. "Reverend, I—"

He held up a hand. "Ever since I met you I've wanted to get to know you better. But because I'm married and a man of God, I knew it was wrong." He hesitated a moment. "But things have changed. I have tried for years to make my wife happy and it seems no matter what I do, it's never good enough. I've tried to convince her to go to counseling but she refuses. We don't even sleep together anymore." He reached up and grazed her smooth cheek with his fingertips. "I know this is probably totally out of line but I'd like to get to know you better."

Speechless, Kayla looked up at him, eyes wide as saucers. For almost a year she had dreamed about this exact moment when Reverend Brown would confess his love. Now that she finally had his interest, she didn't know what to say or do.

So she panicked.

Heart pounding a mile a minute, Kayla hopped in her car and sped away as fast as she could. As much as she wanted him, adultery was wrong, and she knew it. She had to stay strong. But with all the pain and heartache that she had experienced in the last fifteen years of her life, she didn't want to be strong. She wanted to be held and her heartache to be replaced with love.

Reverend Brown called her every night for a week before she finally gave in and met him for dinner at a small restaurant thirty miles away. She listened to him talk about his wife's refusal to make love to him, and the way she belittled him in front of her friends. On Sunday, Kayla saw the first lady of the church in a new light. By the second week, Leroy was sending her flowers at work.

One Friday night, he called and asked her to go with him the following evening to Macon, Missouri, where he was visiting a church. Without hesitation, Kayla dropped her girls off with her mother Saturday afternoon and waited for Leroy to pick her up. After waiting for almost two hours, he called to say that he had finally asked his wife for a divorce and all hell had broken loose. He went on to say that he was already in Macon and was too upset to attend the Saturday evening program. However, he had checked into a Motel 6 and could use her company.

Kayla threw her suitcase in the trunk of her beat-up Cutlass Supreme and made the twenty-minute drive to the hotel on the outskirts of the city. The entire time she cursed Darlene Brown for letting a good man like Leroy slip through her fingers. Nevertheless, Kayla was thankful that she was there to pick up the pieces.

She parked around back then walked to room 2B and knocked. Leroy peeked through a crack in the door and made sure no one was looking before he let her in. As soon as he closed the door, he pulled her into his arms and held her tight.

"Thank you for coming. I could use your strength right now."

I should be thanking you, she thought as she returned the embrace. His heart was pounding just as hard as hers. Leroy could have chosen any woman to spend his evening with and he had chosen her.

He pulled back, breathing hard, eyes dark with longing. Then, without warning, he leaned forward and pressed his lips to hers.

Those big juicy lips stole her breath away. His kiss was long and gentle. Without thinking, she gave into the kiss, the sweep of his tongue, the strong arms that held her.

Breaking the kiss, Leroy stared down into her eyes. "Forgive me, Lord, for what I am feeling for this lady is wrong," he prayed while waiting for some sign of resistance.

Kayla swallowed. Seeing the tears falling from his eyes, she ignored the inner voice telling her it was wrong. It was only right that she be there to comfort him.

"I want to be with you, and as soon as I can, I'm going to do right by you." His hand then came down to cup her left breast. The contact almost brought her to her knees. He fondled her nipple while his lips nipped at her neck.

Oh, heaven help me!

She wasn't sure when he unbuttoned her blouse or removed her bra. All she knew was that she was laying across the bed watching him slip off his pants, followed by his silk boxers. She stared down at his penis standing proud. Her smile faltered slightly before she reminded herself, it isn't the size of the ship but the motion of the ocean.

Lying down beside her, Leroy commenced to licking and sucking her in all the right places until she was begging for more.

It wasn't until he entered her that Kayla thought maybe she was making a mistake. But when the words *I love you* slipped from his tongue, right or wrong no longer mattered. Only how good he made her feel.

Shifting in the tub, Kayla's mind returned to the present.

"Lord, please forgive me. I know what I am doing is wrong but I can't help myself. I love him so much." How could something that felt so right be wrong? That was a question she had been asking herself for almost two years.

Chapter 3

RENEE

"Hey, baby." Vince embraced me and gave me a deep wet kiss that got my juices flowing. "I was hoping you'd come and see Big Daddy before you left."

I pulled back to stare up at his sable face. "There was no way I was going to leave without getting me some."

"I thought all women went to Jamaica searching for the big bamboo," he said playfully.

I hooked my fingers in his belt buckle and pulled him against me. "I got my big bamboo right here." I reached into his pants and stroked his long, hard dick. The act made my coochie pulsate.

Going up to his room, we quickly removed our clothes. I lay across the bed, legs spread wide while staring over at him glistening with baby oil. Oh, hell yeah, Vince is hung. When you got dick, you got dicked. He has never asked me to suck his thing, but he sho' the hell knows how to lick my shit. However, tonight I wasn't in the mood for foreplay; I wanted to fuck, plain and simple, and Vince was just the man for the job.

"Roll your ass over."

He didn't need to ask me twice. I rolled on my stomach and got up on all four. He knew how I liked it. Doggy style. Vince slipped on a condom, then positioned himself between my legs and slid all nine inches into my coochie with one push. As he stroked in and out, I held onto the headboard. My coochie was so wet, it was making farting noises.

"How you like it, baby?"

"I like it."

He slapped me hard across my ass. "I can't hear you."

"I love that shit!" I screamed. I was willing to say whatever the hell he wanted to hear as long as he didn't stop. The shit was off the chain. Vince continued to pump while I pushed my ass back to meet his strokes. I wanted all of him inside, filling me to capacity. I could feel his balls slapping against my ass. That shit felt so damn good I reached down between my legs and stroked them.

"Damn, you've got some good shit!" he moaned. Vince grabbed my hips and pushed all the way in, then slid all the way out and back in again. That shit was driving me crazy and he knew it. I screamed, not caring who heard me.

A few minutes later he flipped me onto my back and with my legs on his shoulders he drove in again. He pumped fiercely until I came. Once I was satisfied, he came too.

Breathing hard, I decided I better take a quick nap. With Vince, round one was only the beginning.

Chapter 4

NADINE

Nadine was just walking down the stairs when she heard the horn blow. Opening the front door, she signaled to the airport limo driver that she would be right out, then moved to the kitchen, where her eighteen-year-old son was having breakfast.

"Jay, I'm leaving."

"All right," he murmured while chewing on a Pop-Tart. "Have a good trip."

"Thanks." She leaned over and gave him a kiss, then reached for her purse. "Carry my bag out."

He reached for her large suitcase in the hall and rolled it outside.

Nadine took one more look around to make sure she wasn't forgetting anything.

This would be her first trip since her divorce.

She had been so busy working and going to school that there hadn't been much time for anything else. She deserved this trip, she told herself, even though she kept thinking that she could have spent the money on new carpeting for her house. But at thirty-nine, she needed this. In the last six months the only excitement she'd had in her life was when she had time to watch television.

She was short, ten pounds overweight, and disgusted with her life. She vowed that after she had passed the bar, she was going to make a major change in her life. She just wasn't sure yet what it was going to be.

What about Jordan?

Nadine shook her head and reached for her purse. She wasn't ready to think about that, at least not until she got back from Jamaica. However, despite her intentions, she felt a tightness in her chest just thinking about the two of them lying in each other's arms. Of all the men she'd encountered in her lifetime, why did she have to fall in love with Jordan?

It was impossible for the two of them to be together. Her friends and family would never understand. They would judge her and talk about her behind her back. She shook her head. No, Columbia was too small. Rumors could destroy a person. She had seen it happen before. Nope. Their relationship was over. She would have to find a way to move on. She hoped five days of baking in the hot sun would be a good start. With Renee running around bitching and talking shit, she didn't have to worry about being bored. Nope. The trip was the perfect time for her to move on with her life. She was confident that by the time she left that island, Jordan was going to be the furthest thing from her mind.

With renewed determination Nadine swung her purse strap over her shoulder and moved toward the door. Yep. If she had to screw every man on the island she was determined to get Jordan out of her system once and for all.

Chapter 5

LISA

Michael Miller hugged his wife a second time before they pulled apart. "You sure you're up to this?" he asked.

Lisa looked up at him, touched by his warm heart and genuine concern. He was a wonderful man. She couldn't have picked a better husband. "I'm fine," she reassured him. "Really I am. I have my medicines."

He didn't look convinced. "I just wish you could have done this here."

"I know. But you know as well as I do, Renee is going to go off and be ready to kick my ass, so I might as well break the news to her where she has nowhere else to go with our friends around."

He nodded, knowingly. They had been going over this same scenario for several months and no matter how or where it was done, he knew no way was going to be easy.

"I love you," he told her.

"I know. I love you too." Her eyes clouded with tears and if he didn't leave soon she was going to be a nervous wreck. "Be good."

"You know I will."

Yes, she had trained him well. He was a good husband and provider. What was he going to do if she didn't pull through the surgery? She hated the thought of him being alone. Her one disappointment was that she had never given him a child. If there was still a chance that she could conceive, she would. But now it was too late.

Biting her bottom lip, she gave him one final hug and moved away. She then stood on the steps of the Waffle House as he pulled out of the lot and waved.

Glancing through the window she found Kayla and Renee already inside. They waved and she waved back. Wiping her eyes, she moved toward the door.

It had been her idea for the trip to Jamaica. What had started out as just her and Renee later included Kayla and Nadine. They had known one another for years. She loved them all. They were her family. Which was why she thought a trip was the best way to break the news. Her life was about to change.

Chapter 6

RENEE

Ilooked up the second my sister stepped through the door. "About time. Girl, I thought you were going to miss the plane."

Lisa gave Kayla a quick hug, then took a seat on the bench beside her. "Puhleeze. You know Michael had to get him a piece before he would let me out the bed this morning."

"I know that right," I mumbled more to myself than anyone else. Vince's performance had been outstanding. He rocked my world until the wee hours of the morning, then carried me out onto the balcony, where he fucked me some more. I'm certain I saw that nosy-ass Mrs. Byrd next door peeking out her window. Shit, I didn't care. If she got her rocks off in the process, I'm glad to have been of service.

"Where's Nadine?" Lisa asked as she reached for a menu.

I rolled my eyes and glanced over at Kayla, who dropped her head with laughter.

I sucked my teeth. "Girl, I'm not going to even go there. Let's just say Nadine had better have that birth certificate or she is going to be one sad-ass puppy."

My sister's eyes grew wide. "She better. She's my roommate and I'll be damned if I am going to pay for a room by myself."

"I hadn't thought about that," I mumbled as I studied her face.

Before last week, I hadn't seen Lisa since my kids and I visited her and Michael during spring break. One thing I noticed, she looked more tired than usual. Dark circles shadowed her chestnut eyes. I think she has been working too many hours, but the other day, when I asked her, she said it was nothing to worry about.

She and I looked like sisters except that Lisa is the color of dark toast and a few pounds heavier than me. She wears her hair cut so low, she almost resembles India.Arie. The first time I saw her new hairstyle, I freaked out. I thought she looked like a bald-headed boy and asked her what the hell she was thinking. Lisa said she was tired of long hair and wanted to try something different. After a while the look grew on me. Not everyone has the right-shaped head to shave their head. My sister, however, does. Unlike this dude I used to date. I don't know why every brotha wants to look like Michael Jordan. This cat had so many dents in his dome you would have sworn someone had beat him upside his head with a baseball bat.

Our waitress arrived with my coffee and Lisa also asked for a cup, then glanced down at her watch. "What time is Nadine supposed to be here?"

Kayla simply shrugged her shoulders. I, on the other hand, always have something to say.

"Girl, I don't know why you even invited that crazy-ass girl. She's gonna miss the plane."

Lisa rolled her eyes. "Hooker, that's your friend, too. Don't even try and play."

Kayla chuckled.

"Whatever," I mumbled against the rim of my coffee cup.

My sister hates for anybody to talk about Nadine. She is always defending her. I don't know if Lisa has noticed, but Nadine is grown and no longer needs my sister to fight her battles. I remember in high school, whenever someone was ready to beat that midget down for running her damn mouth, Lisa was always there telling them they had to get through her first. They also knew if they messed with my sister then they had to deal with me. *Shiit*, you better ask somebody. I may be three years younger, but this sistah ain't no joke.

"Here she comes now," Kayla said as the waitress returned to fill Lisa's mug.

I turned in the direction of Kayla's gaze to find Nadine getting out of an airport shuttle. "What the hell she got on?" I asked my sister.

Lisa shrugged and reached for her coffee. "You know Nadine only has clothes for work and church."

"So which is that?" She had on a long winter-white dress that buttoned down the front with long sheer sleeves.

Lisa gave me a long hard stare. "Promise me you're going to be nice."

My sister knows that once I get started, it is close to impossible to get me to stop. I snorted a response.

I stared out the window, sipping my coffee and pouting like a little girl. I can see right now, Lisa plans to spend the entire week reprimanding me. I know she's the big sister, but damn, can a sistah at least have a little fun? I am on vacation, after all.

"Renee!" I heard someone calling my name, interrupting my thoughts.

"Damn. What?"

"What the hell are you thinking about?" Nadine asked as she lowered onto the seat beside me.

"Don't worry about it."

"She spent the night with Vince," Kayla offered.

Lisa blew the air out of her cheeks. "And you was trying to talk about me getting some."

"And?" I challenged. "Shoot, Big Daddy was on point last night. I needed something to tide me over for a few days."

"Girl, please, we all know your ass is going on a dick hunt the minute we touch down in Jamaica," Nadine said.

I glanced at her out the corners of my eyes. "Bitch, don't hate 'cause your shit has shriveled up and died."

"Nah, I just ain't ho'ing like you," she retorted in fun.

My temper flared. "Fuck you."

My sister glanced over at the couple to our right, who were giving us funny looks. "Can we all just get along?" she whispered.

I rolled my eyes. "That's your girl talking crazy, looking like Grandma Moses in that dress."

Nadine laughed, then reached over and playfully nudged me on the arm.

See, that's her problem. Every time I look around she has to put her hands on me. I can't stand for a woman to touch me. Nadine is either playing too much or getting on my damn nerves. "Lisa, get your friend before I hurt her."

"Girl, you know you love me." She slapped my hand. See, I told you she likes to touch all the time. Damn! She was already getting on my nerves.

Seeing that goofy smile on her face, I knew she was trying hard to be my friend. I know I can be a bitch at times. But that's just me. I don't understand why people take what I say personally. I'm just me. But being that my sister says that her girl is sensitive, then I guess I'll try to be nice. Remember, I said I would try.

"Did you get your birth certificate?" I asked.

"Yes, I did." Nadine eagerly pulled the document from her purse and handed it to me.

I unfolded it and stared down at it for several blank seconds before looking up and asking, "What the hell is this?"

Nadine had the audacity to look at me as if I was crazy. "My hospital birth certificate."

"Look at this shit." I passed the piece of paper around, allowing both Lisa and Kayla a chance to see what I was talking about.

"What is this, Nadine?" Lisa asked. She appeared to be the only one concerned. I think she's just afraid that she is going to have to pay for that room by herself; otherwise, she probably wouldn't care either. Nah, I take that back. She would still have cared because that's just the way my sister is.

I snorted rudely. "Girl, do you know what this is? This is the sheet of paper the nurse fills out when you are born that goes in your hospital record. That thing ain't worth the paper it was printed on."

"Yes, it is. I called your Aunt Lori last night and asked."

Okay, so now she's trying to call me crazy. I know my aunt didn't tell her that paper was any good.

My aunt is the travel agent who actually booked this crazy-ass trip. It was only after my father called and told my sister that he still had Holiday Inn vouchers to be used before the end of the year. He bought these vouchers five years ago, which enables him to stay at Holiday Inns around the world for half the price. So Lisa jumped at the chance, had my stepmother book us two rooms, and called my aunt to arrange airfare. From day one, my aunt has been hounding us to make sure that we had either a passport or a birth certificate. That sheet of paper in Nadine's hand is neither.

I rolled my eyes. "You know what, you would have been better off bringing your expired passport with you."

"I did." She reached into her purse again. "See?"

"Then do yourself a favor and give them that because they are going to laugh at you when you show them that crusty-ass sheet of paper."

I looked up at the waitress standing over our table ready to take our orders. I was suddenly very hungry. "Let's hurry up and eat so we can get to the airport. Because of Nadine we are going to need a little extra time."

I love the Waffle House. There ain't nothing better than pecan waffles. Well . . . maybe some dick, but I've already had some of that.

Two hours later, I parked my car in long-term parking. We moved to the center of the lot and stood with our bags, waiting for a shuttle. Our plane was scheduled for departure at nine. It was barely seven o'clock and already the humidity proved today was going to be a scorcher.

The shuttle arrived and we lined up, anxious to get to the airport and get this trip started.

"Let me get that for you," the driver said as he climbed off the shuttle.

"Thank you." I smiled up at the toothless man and climbed on-board fully aware that he was watching my ass. The rest of them climbed on behind me. I took a seat in a long row in the back. Lisa and Kayla sat to the right of me. Nadine took the seat beside me and released a burp that smelled like day-old collard greens.

"Damn, gurl. That shit stinks!" Fanning my hand, I rose and moved to another seat, trying to get away from her funky behind.

She did it again, then started cracking up. "Sorry, I think I ate too much. My stomach is starting to hurt."

"Don't be farting," I warned.

Kayla waved both hands in the air like she was testifying in church. "Lord have mercy! Nadine and I drove to the mall last week and her stinky behind farted all the way there."

I rolled my eyes. "Shit, she can't help it. Nadine just stanks."

Nadine held up her middle finger and the three of us howled in laughter.

"Renee, you got a lot of nerves," Lisa chimed in.

I sucked my teeth. "Girl, ain't no shame in my game. If I leave it in, my heart might stop."

"Ain't you nothing," Kayla piped in.

Nadine laughed.

"That's probably why we get along so well." I winked over at Nadine. "If you got to go you got to go."

Nadine reached over and gave me a high five and a knowing smile. "I know that's right." She started laughing again and I started laughing along with her. The others had no choice but to join in.

Even if I talk shit, Nadine and I do have a few things in common. As a matter of fact, let me take a moment and give her her props. Nadine is one sistah who always has my back.

I remember when I was short on cash, bouncing checks from here to the East Coast. I didn't have to ask and Nadine offered me the money. She didn't ask when I was planning to pay her back or anything. I like that about her. Okay, I just said something good about her. But she still ain't my friend.

Chapter 7

NADINE

"Do you have any other forms of ID?" the agent asked as she handed Nadine back the useless document.

Nadine looked down at her purse. She could already hear Renee saying, "I told you so."

"I have an expired passport." She handed it to the lady.

The blonde nodded. "This will do. You are going to have to wait a few minutes while I type up some paperwork for you to sign."

Nadine nodded, feeling relieved as the agent moved behind a counter. She took a seat and watched the woman's fingers fly across the keyboard as she typed.

Typing had never been one of Nadine's strong points. While she was married, if she ever needed anything important done, she'd asked her husband's secretary to help her. Carla had definitely been an asset. At least that's what Nadine had thought before she had decided to come home from work early one afternoon.

It had to have been about three years ago. Around the time she was working as a paralegal.

She remembered being worried because her husband, Arthur, hadn't touched her in weeks. She told herself it was because she was going to law school and trying to also work part-time. Her husband worked second shift. When they did have time they were usually too tired for sex. But deep down she believed it was because she wasn't trying hard enough to find the time. That last year, she had felt like something had been missing.

During the beginning of their twelve-year marriage, even when they were busy they always found time for sex. In the bathroom. On the kitchen counter. On the floor in front of the fireplace. They made the most of their time together, especially on the weekends. Before her son was born they would even hide out at a hotel all weekend, making love and ordering room service.

Those were the days and she had wanted it back. Her mind had begun to wander into areas that she didn't care to explore and suddenly she panicked and wanted her marriage to be everything it used to be. That's why while on her way to work one morning, while thinking about her husband still lying in bed home alone, she decided to call in sick. Nadine then pulled into the nearest Wal-Mart and rushed inside. She grabbed a cart and moved to the lingerie section, where she picked out a sexy teddy that could barely contain her breasts. She then moved to the health and beauty, where she bought a box of Summer's Eve and a bottle of mango-scented body lotion. Arthur always said he loved when she smelled good enough to eat. As soon as the cashier put Nadine's purchases in a bag, Nadine rushed into the handicapped bathroom stall, where she douched, rubbed lotion all over her body, and slipped into the teddy. She then slid back into her black three-inch pumps and long black trench. With her suit stuffed into the bag, she exited the building and chuckled all the way to the car. On the drive home, she swung by a small diner and ordered breakfast for two and carried out two Styrofoam containers.

When she reached their subdivision, Nadine drove around the block and pulled onto her street. In order for her return to be a surprise, she parked in front of the house next door. She quietly slipped through the side door, slid out of the coat, then took a deep breath as she reached for the Styrofoam containers and sashayed up toward their room. As soon as she hit the top step she heard the moans and frowned. Arthur knew how much she hated him watching dirty movies. But as she moved down the hall, she decided maybe this was one time they could watch a movie together. With the return of her smile, she swung her wide hips into their bedroom.

She froze when she spotted her husband between some blond bitch's legs.

"What the fuck!"

The two of them jumped and she realized it was his secretary, Carla. The two couldn't shield their naked bodies fast enough.

"Hold on, I got something for both y'all asses." She tossed the first container of food at blondie. The second hit the headboard above Arthur's head.

"Damn, Nadine, hold up!"

"Nah, you hold up!" She grabbed Carla by her ponytail before she could run out the door and sent her naked ass flying across the room. Nadine then moved over to the closet, reached into a box on the shelf, and removed a .38.

"Nadine, now you trippin'!" Arthur shouted.

"Trippin', I'll show yo ass trippin'." She fired a shot and blew out the television. Arthur jumped back onto the bed. Carla was crouched down in a corner, scrambled eggs hanging from her eyelids.

"Please, I'm sorry," she begged with snot running from her nose.

"Get your ass out my house, now!" Nadine ordered.

Carla reached for her clothes.

"Uh-uh! No clothes. You bold enough to fuck my husband in my house, then you're bold enough to run your lily-white ass out that door."

Carla didn't give the idea a second thought as she dashed out the room. Arthur tried to run behind her. Nadine cocked the gun. "Not you."

He held up his hands, pleading with his eyes. "Come on, baby, I made a mistake."

"And what mistake was that. Getting caught?"

"No, trying to mess around."

Nadine lifted her right hand and pointed the gun at his face. "Oh, you're right. You made a mistake. You didn't even have enough respect for me to use a condom."

"It just happened."

"Carla just happened to be laying butt naked in my bed with your dick buried inside her pussy. You must think I'm some kinda fool. Now get your punk-ass up!" she screamed. He quickly moved to his feet. "Now move your ass downstairs."

Arthur was shaking. "Damn, at least let me put on some clothes."

Her voice was as cold as ice. "You shoulda thought about that before you disrespect me. Now get to stepping."

He decided to play tough. "I ain't going no damn where."

Nadine didn't realize she had fired another shot until she heard him scream.

"You shot me in the ass!"

She gave a hysterical laugh. "Next time I'm aiming for your head. Now move!" She made him crawl down the driveway. The entire time he pleaded and begged for his life. He was halfway up the street, leaving behind a trail of blood, before the police arrived.

Arthur and his ho pressed charges. Luckily for Nadine, one of the lawyers at her law firm was able to get her off on a temporary insanity plea.

"You okay?" Lisa asked, nudging her from her thoughts.

Nadine blinked, pushed the images aside, then laughed self-consciously. "Yeah, everything's fine. I should be ready in a few minutes."

Lisa smiled, looking pleased by her response, then turned to join the others.

Nadine allowed her eyes to travel over to the agent who was completing her paperwork and found herself admiring her delicate features. Realizing what she was doing, she released a frustrated breath. She didn't realize how badly she needed this trip until now. First her marriage. Now this. She crossed her legs as the things she preferred not to think about pushed to the surface.

Jordan Justice.

If anyone had told her she would have fallen for Jordan she would have never believed it. She allowed herself to get caught up and tangled in a web. Now she was so in love she couldn't think straight. That was why she had to let go. That was why they'd had a heated argument two nights ago that ended in her tossing a priceless piece across the room, causing it to shatter into hundreds of little pieces.

Jordan wanted to live together. To let the whole world know that they were in love. Only Nadine couldn't bring herself to do it because deep down inside she still had not found a way to accept their relationship. Guilt overwhelmed her every time she thought about it because Jordan had a wonderful heart and was a good person, yet Nadine could not accept that she was in love with another woman.

Chapter 8

RENEE

As the plane prepared for takeoff, I fastened my seatbelt and closed my eyes.

"I thought you were going to read."

I opened one eye, glanced at Kayla, who was sitting next to me, then shut it again. "I changed my mind. I suddenly feel worn out."

"That's because Vince had your legs in the air all night. I bet you didn't get any sleep."

I laughed. "True that."

Kayla pursed her lips with disapproval. "You know, you need Jesus in your life."

I yawned. "I can't argue with you there." I turned my head toward the window and folded my arms across my chest. I was pleased that Kayla got the hint I was done talking.

One thing I can say about the girl, is that she is right. I do need Jesus. Maybe then I could make some sense of my life. Maybe even figure out where I am headed.

For the umpteenth time I asked myself how the hell I got myself into another mess. Sometimes I do the dumbest things, then sit back and think, *what the hell did I do?* If it wasn't for common sense I wouldn't have any sense at all.

It wasn't like my parents raised no fool. My stepfather didn't take no mess. He was quick to clock a sistah upside her head. He was one of those who whooped your ass first and asked questions later. There were many times I got my behind beat for something that Lisa or my younger brother, Andre, had done. All he had to say was, "Well, you probably needed it anyway."

My mother was a softy. In my opinion she wasn't what I would call a bad parent, even though she never bothered to talk to my ass about any important shit, like sex, for instance.

To this day I remember the only discussion we'd ever had on the subject of sex. I had to have been around nine. My girlfriends and I had been in the school playground around the block, playing kick-ball, when my mama pulled up in a 1968 Rambler and told me to get in the car.

She glared at the older boys sitting on the school steps, smoking cigarettes, then over at me. "Keep your fast ass out that school play-ground!" she yelled as she screeched away from the parking spot. "Do you know what can happen to little girls?"

I slumped down in the seat and shook my head.

"They rape little girls. Do you know what rape is?"

"No, Mama," I whispered.

"It's when a boy sticks his penis inside a girl's vagina."

With that said she pulled the car in front of our house and got out. We never had that discussion again. I spent that night staring at my clit trying to figure out how a boy's ding-a-ling would fit in there. That shit haunted me for years until I discovered I had another hole. I just wished it had been before I was lying across the floor with my legs spread open and Wayne Williams's skinny ass lying between them.

Even after that I still was stupid and naïve when it came to men and sex. I found myself with one after another, searching for some-thing I never found.

It has taken me thirty-six years and three marriages before I have finally come to the realization that I love the idea of being in love. Now, stay with me a moment as I try to explain.

Almost every time I meet a man, I allow myself to get so wrapped up in the physical and emotional aspects of the initial relationship that I find myself saying "he's the one" long before I have even learned my partner's middle name. I have dated men and before the first month is over, I discover we are already living together. Then, when I finally come down from the clouds, I realize I can't even stand his ass.

I think a lot of it originated from the fact that I never knew my real father. My mother had never married him and when I turned five she married my stepfather. They were together for almost ten years, and no matter how hard I tried, I never felt loved or accepted by him. Once I got older, I drew the conclusion I was just part of the package deal. At the time he had no other choice but to deal with my ass.

I held on to my virginity until I was sixteen years old before I started looking for love in all the wrong places. I ended up losing it to a high school basketball star on a dare. "Wayne Wonder" was what they called him. I thought he was the finest thing to hit Hickman High School. When he asked me if I wanted a ride home from school I was so excited I practically peed on myself before I managed to say "yes." On the way he asked if I'd like to see his new house, and being the dummy that I was, I said "sure." We weren't in his place five minutes before he managed to talk my panties off. With the help of a jar of Vaseline and to the tunes of the DeBarges's "Time Will Reveal," he popped my cherry. The next day, Wayne couldn't even remember my name.

After that I tried to find acceptance any way I could, and along came Morgan Brown. We both ran track. One afternoon it was raining so hard, we were forced to run down the school's corridors instead. He and I were running and talking about Michael Jackson's *Thriller* video when he asked could he talk to me in private. Being the dummy that I was, again I agreed, and as soon as we hit the next corner, he pulled me into the boys' bathroom with him. He led me to the last stall where he leaned me against the wall and stuck my hand inside his pants. His thing was so big that like a damn fool, I screamed. I thought it was a pet snake. Shit, how was I to know dicks came in all sizes. Up until that point, the only ones I'd seen was my little brother's and Wayne's and neither was worth sitting down and writing about in my diary. Anyway, he whipped his dick out so I could take a closer look. Curiously, I reached down and touched it as it grew right before my eyes. Morgan was about to teach me what a hand job was when the bathroom door swung open. Scared it was our coach, I slid down into a squatting position on the floor, near the toilet, hoping that I wouldn't be seen. Ryan and Vernon, better known as Dumb and Dumber, pushed opened the stall door to find Morgan with his pants down and his dick only inches away from my mouth. By the next day, I had been labeled the super headhunter.

When you get a bad reputation there ain't shit you can do but live through the nightmare. Boys were then interested in me because they believed the things they heard. Even with all of the rumors floating around, I still found myself willing to do just about anything just to be accepted, to feel loved.

I remember I would meet a guy that I really liked and thought he liked me enough to look past the rumors. But as soon as he caught wind of who I was, to my disappointment, he ended the relationship. Several other disappointments after that left me feeling used and abused.

Then I met Mario.

He was the first man who couldn't care less what anyone said. To me he was heaven sent. I thought I had found my knight in shining armor. It wasn't long before I realized how crazy and possessive he was. If he even thought I was with another man he went off and even hit me upside my head a couple of times. But instead of ending the relationship I tried harder to please him. I was so naïve and stupid that I let him dictate my life. At age sixteen, we were already practically living together. I wasn't allowed to hang out with my friends; instead I was at his apartment making him dinner and washing his stanky-ass drawers.

My junior year I ended up pregnant, and was excited that I would finally have someone to love. I lost the baby during my twelfth week and ended up in a deep depression. It was a blessing in disguise; I just didn't realize it at the time.

I married Mario when I was eighteen. I was pregnant again and scared. I didn't know what to do. My mother had run off somewhere and all I had was my grandmother, who was as old fashioned as it got. My grandmother insisted that Mario marry me and he did one month before Quinton was born.

With me dressed in a red polka dot dress that looked like a circus tent, we were married in my grandmother's living room with my cousin and her boyfriend as our witness. I cried the whole time but I went through with it because I didn't want to disappoint my grandmother. Afterwards we drank grape Kool-Aid and ate tuna fish sandwiches.

When Quinton was born, I poured my heart into my child. Three years later Tamara was born and at that point, I decided that I had had enough of the abuse and wanted something more if not for myself then for my children. So I put Mario's ass out. It was a struggle, but I endured.

At twenty-four, I finally learned how to drive; then came the drinking. Soon I was back to having one man after another, looking for love all over again.

I met my second husband on my twenty-seventh birthday. I went to Fort Leonard Wood with my cousin Danielle. Troy Harris was a high-yellow brotha who instantly became attached to me and my kids. I don't know what it is about a brotha in uniform but it turned me the fuck on. Troy was only in Missouri three months for school but by the time he was ready to return to Panama, he proposed. I looked past his insecurities, and I looked past the cheap-ass wedding ring he bought from Wal-Mart. All I could think about was that he was taking me away from my dead-ass town to another country to live on a military installation. We knew each other exactly six months before we were married in the basement of my house in front of fifty of my friends. I knew something wasn't right but I did it anyway.

I quit my job and hopped on a plane, eager to start my new life. It took another six months before I realized that I had married a liar. We drove each other crazy and after being dogged for so many years, it was my turn to dog. By the time we returned to the States our relationship was over. He went to Arkansas and I went back home.

I had several more relationships afterwards with me allowing one man to move in after a month and believing I was in love. And after one too many failed relationships, including two sperm donors whose seeds I deposited at the nearest Planned Parenthood, I met John Moore.

I was working part-time at a nightclub—it's a long story so I won't get into it right now—but I will say that he asked for my number. And like I did with everyone else who asked, I gave it to him.

My phone used to ring so much that I used to ask myself why did I give my phone number out to people I wasn't even interested in. However, if I went one day without receiving a call, I would become depressed and feel unwanted.

Anyway, he called and asked me out, and with me working two jobs, not to mention my busy social calendar, I was eventually able to fit him in. We went out to dinner, and even though I found him to be a very nice guy, he was too nice. He was the type of man who'd give you everything, and he fell in love faster than I ever did. I tried to ignore his calls, but he was persistent. Eventually I let him take me out again, and after dinner I felt so lightheaded, he insisted on following me home. I wasn't too happy about that because I didn't want him to know where I lived. He not only followed me home, but he made sure I made it into the house. He came back the next morning while I was asleep and shoveled the snow from my driveway. I had no choice but to invite him in for breakfast. The kids took a quick liking to him and he convinced me to let him take us out for pizza. How can you tell a child no to Chuck E. Cheese?

After that it was hard to get rid of him. He popped over all the time, even if it was just to drop off McDonald's. Within a month he had grown on me. I began to realize that he was not like the other men. He was lonely and desperately wanted a family of his own. But the difference was he didn't want to share what I already had, he wanted to give me something I didn't already have. He didn't want to move in with me, he wanted me to live with him. He didn't want to use up my hot water. He wanted to pay the damn bill.

I knew even before he proposed that he was going to ask me. When my sister told him that if he wanted me, he had better put a ring on my finger quick, he took that shit to heart. He and Lisa went to the mall and together they picked out a one-carat princess-cut diamond. The next night, John took the kids and me out to dinner and proposed to all three of us. My kids were excited and I was in shock. I didn't know what I wanted to say but before I realized it, I was saying yes. He didn't even give me a chance to change my mind, because if he had, I definitely would have said, "hell no!" Instead he rushed my ass off to the justice of the peace, and a week later, I was Mrs. John Moore.

I quit my job and he let me stay home and pursue my career as a writer. I have to admit it was wonderful staying home and being there when my kids got home from school. I bought cookbooks and started planning meals. John let me handle the household finances and he never questioned any financial decisions I made. For almost an entire year I enjoyed being a housewife. Then summer rolled around and I started spending the weekends hanging out with my girls, meeting men my age. John is fifteen years older than me, and extremely overweight. I began to question why I married a man that I wasn't even attracted to. The sex wasn't good and I started to question if it was ever good because so many times before I had convinced myself sex didn't really matter. All that mattered was what he was able to do for me and it was a helluva lot more than any of them other tired ass mothafuckas had been able to do. But after a while I began to ask myself, if he wasn't supporting me and I had a job would we be together, and I kept coming up with the answer. Hell no! I began to dread him touching me. I looked forward to him working second shift.

When John was offered a job in another state, I was excited and came up with the decision that he go ahead of us and prepare for us to come, while in the back of my mind I knew I had no intention of following. At first John flew home every other weekend to visit, then eventually it became less and less. Being away from him was like a breath of fresh air. Unfortunately, a year has passed and two weeks ago, John gave me an ultimatum. The kids and I either join him in Delaware before school starts or we need to consider ending our relationship.

I've had several extramarital relationships during the year but nothing worth ending my marriage over. I found myself asking, what am I looking for? Was I looking for a fairy tale? What is it going to take to make Renee happy?

Now time had run out, and I have one week left to figure it out.

Chapter 9

RENEE

When I woke up my neck was stiff from sleeping the wrong way most of the plane ride. However, as soon as I glanced out the window, pain was the farthest thing from my mind. All I cared about was the magnificent sight below: turquoise waters and miles of lush green land.

I was one of the first to depart the plane. As soon as I stuck my head out the door, I knew we were in Jamaica. Black folk was everywhere. Unlike in the States, instead of using a ramp that leads directly into the airport terminal, we departed off the plane outside. I felt like I had just stepped into a furnace as the heat radiated around me. It was hot. But none of that seemed to matter. I was just excited to be there. And the big smiles on all of our faces proved that.

My Jamaican sistahs and brothas, glistening with sweat. Their skin ranged in colors and was startling against their radiant white smiles. As we descended the stairs onto Jamaican land they waved and welcomed us to Jamaica, and we all waved and thanked them.

We moved through the small airport, listening to the musical lilt of island accents that floated around the building. The language was lively and my excitement rose as I moved through the door.

We were directed toward an air-conditioned coach bus that would take us to the Holiday Inn. I moved to locate our bags as two fine brothas loaded them at the bottom of the bus.

Nadine nudged me in my side, and I for once didn't mind her touching me and nudged her back. We both grinned like two fools at a brotha with legs the size of tree trunks. And he was boy-legged. Ain't nothing better than a boy-legged brotha. In my years of experience, I discovered it ain't the size of his hands or his feet. It was how much room he needed to accommodate his package. A boy-legged brother required a great deal of room. He was definitely a Mandingo. Just the way I like them.

Lisa came up behind us. "Come on, you two, before the bus leaves without y'all."

I rolled my eyes. "Damn, Lisa, you're missing the sights."

"I'm not missing shit," she said as she moved to the door and climbed the stairs. "I might be married but I'm far from blind. Don't worry, you'll see more than enough of that this week."

"I sure hope so."

"I know that's right, girl!" Nadine said. She and I jumped in the air and screamed with excitement as we high-fived. This trip was already starting off on the right foot.

I boarded the bus and took a seat beside Kayla, who was reading *The Daily Word,* while Nadine and Lisa found a seat near the back of the bus.

I waited until Kayla closed the small book before I spoke. "I'm hungry. I hope we aren't too far from the hotel." My pecan waffles were nothing but a memory.

Kayla reached into her purse and pulled out a bag of trail mix. "Here, eat some of this. I think I heard someone say we have a half-hour drive."

I eagerly poured myself a handful. I have never been big on squirrel food but right now I was too hungry to care.

While we chomped on fruits and nuts, I glanced around at all of the faces. The bus had quickly filled with eager white folks.

"As soon as we get to the hotel I'm getting myself a drink."

"Me too," Kayla chimed in.

I twisted my lips in a frown. "You mean a glass of Kool-Aid, right?"

"You know it."

I shook my head and stared across at her holier-than-thou ass. Kayla likes to act like she doesn't remember the way the two of us used to roll up to Fort Leonard Wood. For years, we both had a thing for servicemen. Fort "Lost in the Woods" is a training post, so soldiers from all over would come down and take classes for several weeks, then return to their duty station. Every couple of months we'd drive down to meet us someone special, then let him wine and dine, and throw our legs over his shoulders. I think things changed for Kayla when she met this guy named Carter Drake. I have to admit he was fine. Taller than her, skin like a chocolate bar, and he had the sexiest smile. If she hadn't gotten to him first, I definitely would have hopped on his ass. However, he made it clear the first night we met him and his boy Chico—who was ugly as hell—he had a thing for big women.

Carter drove down to see Kayla every weekend, and every weekend she catered to all his needs in and out of the bedroom. He told her he loved her and promised that when he returned to California— where he was currently stationed—he would send for her.

Kayla was strung out over the brotha. She would spend hours talking about marrying him and spending her life traveling around the world with him. She was so excited, and I was happy for her. Then the negro left and she never heard from him again. She tried to hide her pain but I knew she was hurt. I was hurt for her. After that she started spending all her spare time at church, and never wanted to go down to Fort Leonard Wood again. About that time I had already met husband number two, so I didn't have a reason to make the trip. Then after the shit that brotha did to me I was through with servicemen myself. Like I said before, I'll save that story for another time. That fool is a book all by itself.

I popped a few more nuts into my mouth, then closed the bag. My throat was dry and the soda machine inside the "no frills" airport was broken. Unlike in our American airport terminals there weren't concession stands all around to satisfy your eating pleasure.

I breathed a sigh of relief when the driver finally stepped onto the bus and welcomed us all to Jamaica.

"How far are we from the hotel?" I blurted out because a sistah needed to know.

"About twenty minutes. But I'll try to get you there as quickly as possible." He then chuckled like he knew something I didn't know.

Shit, I heard about the way Jamaicans drove, and *quickly* didn't sound like such a good idea. "Take your time," I suggested. Several others nodded their heads in agreement. Apparently, they'd heard the same thing I had.

He winked. "No problem, mon."

I swung my head around. "Did he just call me a man?"

Kayla covered her mouth and laughed. "Girl, you are silly. He said 'mon', not 'man'. You know, that's what the Jamaicans say."

"Oh, yeah." I'm glad she clarified that shit.

The driver turned on some uplifting reggae music as he pulled away from the airport and we glanced out the window while trying to snap pictures of the scenes around us. So far Jamaica looked poverty stricken. Shacks, clotheslines with dingy drawers hanging, and a bunch of malnourished-looking dogs. There were also numerous primitive-looking hotels. I hope to hell that we weren't staying in any shit like that. I wasn't worried. My father and his new wife had invited Lisa and my brother down to join them on several occasions when they visited Jamaica. It was an invitation that had never been extended to me. That shit used to hurt. Eventually I just brushed my shoulders off.

As we moved farther from the airport we started seeing cows and something that looked like goats. There were old brothas sitting out on the curb, playing dominos. Shit, I shot up half my roll of film on the drive over.

Finally we reached the tourist area of Montego Bay, and it was like stepping into the twilight zone. It was like going from black and white to Technicolor. We passed shopping strips and merchants on the side of the road and made mental notes to stop and patronize each and every one. I wanted a large wooden giraffe. Last year I had my basement remodeled and was working on an entire jungle theme. Big silk plants, face carvings, and animal paintings. There was a mile and a half of hotels and all-inclusive resorts surrounded by white sand beaches.

The driver made a left at the end of the block and pulled into a wide circular drive in front of our hotel. I couldn't wait to get off that bus but there was this fat woman in front of me, moving like a turtle. When Kayla and I finally got off the bus, we waited for Lisa and Nadine. Two men rushed from inside the hotel and began unloading the bags from the bus.

Lisa stepped off smiling. "Welcome to the Holiday Inn Sun Spree. You're going to love this place."

I guess she would know since this is the only place she's ever stayed on the island. Glancing around at the well-tended grounds dotted with tall green palm trees, hibiscus, and other tropical flora, I had to agree it was paradise for sure.

"Come on—let's check in," I said. I was actually anxious to get out of the heat. It wasn't until we stepped inside that I realized the lobby had no doors or windows. It was all open air, spacious and relaxing. I stepped across the Aztec marble floor over toward the front desk. From the far left Calypso music could be heard, which made me want to kick up my heels and dance the night away.

There was an excursion desk up front as well as a place to rent a car. After watching them crazy-ass Jamaicans drive down the highway, renting a car wasn't even an option. I don't think my nerves could take it. If someone cut me off, I'd have to climb out my car and cuss his ass out. Since I'm supposed to be on vacation, I didn't need the unnecessary stress.

In the center of the lobby was a large indoor fountain surrounded by a profusion of tropical foliage in brilliant colors of pink, green, and blue. As we walked past it the cool water sprinkled against my damp skin. As hot as I was, I could have jumped in head first. Before I could stick my hand in, the smell of barbecue meat hit my nose. I glanced out the back of the hotel, which was also open, and could see people standing in front of little straw huts, ordering drinks in their bikini-clad bodies.

Suddenly I couldn't wait to join in.

A cute pecan-colored woman with dimples stood behind the desk. Her name tag read, LESLIE.

"Welcome. Checking in?" she greeted with a smile.

I nodded, finding her smile contagious. "Yes. We have two rooms reserved under Lisa Miller and Renee Moore."

While she punched in the names, we glanced around the lobby. I noticed a buffet to the far right of the fountain, where the staff was preparing for lunch.

"Yes, I have your reservations here," Leslie said, drawing our attention. "That will be one-fifty a night for seven nights."

All four of us swung around at the same time. Of course I was the first one to speak. "Excuse me. How much did you say?"

She gave me another sweet smile that was now wearing my nerves. "One-fifty per night."

"Oh, hell, naw!"

Lisa dropped a hand to my arm, silencing me, and stepped up to the counter. "I'm sorry, that's not right. Our rooms should be seventy-five a night."

Leslie shook her head and looked at Lisa like she was crazy. "I'm sorry, but we don't book rooms at that price."

I glanced at Kayla, who looked ready to puke on herself, while Nadine was reaching into her purse for her credit card.

I leaned across the counter and cleared my throat. "Leslie, we ain't crazy. I specifically spoke with my father and he said our rooms were seventy-five dollars a night. So I advise you to go and get your manager, now!" Leslie scurried inside an office behind the desk.

I was one minute away from getting ghetto, so hopefully this was going to be easily resolved.

I slammed my palm against the countertop. "That bitch is trippin'!"

Lisa gave me one of those looks. "Be nice."

I rolled my eyes, then glanced over at Nadine and Kayla, who were both mumbling under their breath. All I heard were the words "ghetto" and "embarrassing."

"If y'all heifers want to pay the full inflated rate you go right ahead, 'cause I ain't paying a dime over the amount that was quoted to me."

"Dang, why you always got to be so loud?" Kayla started making "tsk" sounds with her teeth while Nadine struggled to keep a straight face.

"You would want to shut up and let me handle this." Her broke ass has got a lot of nerve, especially since up until the point I had corrected her ass, she had thought I was paying for her room. She didn't even have enough to pay the reduced rate let alone the buck fifty. So the best thing for her to do was to shut the hell up and let me handle things.

"Here we go," I heard Nadine mumble. She was obviously pissed off.

"You would want to shut up, too."

"Lord, give me strength," Lisa whispered, then sighed.

I know times like this she would rather disown me. Maybe I am a little too loud at times but being quiet never gets you anywhere. Believe me, I know.

I remember when I was a freshman in high school, our neighbor agreed to sell Lisa his Oldsmobile. On the phone, he quoted three hundred. However, by the time we arrived at his house, the price suddenly had risen to three hundred fifty. Lisa dug into her jeans for another fifty dollars that she knew she didn't have. Oh, hell, naw! I told her to get her damn hands out her pocket, then I told Mr. Stevens he either sell her that car at the price he quoted over the phone or he could shove that big bus up his ass. Lisa was so embarrassed she turned on her heels and headed home. I came through the door, five minutes later, with the keys to the car that I got at the original price. See, I don't play those games. If you let a mothafucka get over on you they think they can keep getting over on you.

I glanced up as the door opened and out walked Leslie. However, my eyes instantly connected with that of a tall, dark, and dangerously handsome man that followed behind. "Dayu-um!" I murmured as he moved toward the counter. He was so fine I could have jumped over the counter and licked his ass like a bomb pop. I wasn't the only one who had noticed how good he looked. All four of us stood there staring and shaking our heads.

He looked like his mama had dipped him in a pot of melted chocolate. As hungry as I was the brotha was good enough to eat. He had a bald head, large cocoa-brown eyes, a wide dimpled smile, and a body that made you want to reach out and touch somebody.

"Hello. I'm Everton. I was told you ladies are having a problem with your room rates."

I was so dazed, I was rendered speechless. His accent sounded almost British and made him even sexier. All I could do was nod my head. Thank goodness my sister stepped in.

"Yes, you are correct. My father reserved the rooms using his club membership."

His eyes brightened knowingly. "You have the club rate. That explains it. If you'd write down your father's name I can go in the back and look up the reservation."

I stood there looking like a damn fool as Lisa took the pen from his proffered hand and scribbled the information. While she wrote, Everton looked across at me and within a matter of seconds I knew he was interested in getting some of this. I ain't mad. I want some of him, too.

Everton excused himself and went back into the office while Leslie went to help another guest. Lisa hit me upside of my head and I snapped out of my fantasy.

"Damn! Why you hit me?"

"'Cause you're making a fool of yourself standing there drooling over that man."

Immediately I wiped my mouth for any signs of slobber. Just as I thought. Nothing.

Kayla and Nadine cackled.

"I wasn't slobbering."

Lisa clicked her tongue. "Girl, you might as well have been, the way you were staring down his throat."

Those two hyenas started laughing again.

I flipped them off. "Fuck y'all. You can't say that brotha wasn't fine."

Nadine licked her lips. "Oh, no doubt about it, the brotha is fine."

Kayla fanned herself with her hand. "Lord, yes."

"His ass looks barely out of high school," Lisa added with a snort.

"And what's that got to do with the price of tea in China?" I took a deep breath, rolling my eyes. "Shit, I already told y'all. I plan to enjoy myself this week. Anything is possible. Whatever happens in Jamaica—"

"Stays in Jamaica." The other three finished in unison. Then all four of us howled with laughter.

The door to the office opened and Everton returned carrying a sheet of paper.

"I want to apologize to you ladies. The discount rate should have been keyed into the computer. Let me go ahead and personally get you lovely ladies checked in."

"No big deal," I said with a grin.

I ignored the looks the others were giving me. Okay, so maybe I did get a little bent out of shape, but that's all over now.

"How would you ladies like some rum punch?" Everton was smiling like he had just offered us free hotel accommodations. Shit, the hotel was all-inclusive, which meant the drinks had already been paid for. Nevertheless, I smiled at his fine young ass like he had just handed me a hundred dollar bill.

"Sure, we would love something to drink," Lisa answered.

I glanced at the other two. Kayla declined but Nadine, like myself, was ready to get her drink on. Everton asked Leslie to go get the drinks for us while he took care of our registration. Nothing pleased me more. While he took care of Lisa and Nadine, I just stood back and stared. Damn, the negro was fine.

"You need to quit," Kayla whispered.

"Bitch, you need to quit hating," I countered.

She pinched my arm, and I flinched, then reached around and pinched her too. The entire time my eyes never strayed far from Everton.

He was dressed like all the others. He was wearing khaki slacks and a red button-down shirt that accentuated his solid frame. There was no doubt about it, he was drop-dead, make-you-want-to-scream-your-name gorgeous.

Leslie walked our way carrying a tray of drinks. "Ladies, I have punch for everyone." She reached down for the cup closest to her and offered it to me. I gazed up into her eyes, then pursed my lips and reached for a cup on the tray. How do I know she didn't spit in it? With a roll of my eyes, I carried my drink back over to the desk and waited my turn.

As soon as Lisa had her key in her hand, she swung around. "Nadine and I are going up to our room to cool off and change. We're in building two, room two-twelve, so holla at us when you're ready to go down to the beach." They moved over to a clerk who was eagerly waiting with their bags to escort them to their room.

Kayla stepped up in the line and I waited for Everton to finish checking her in. Every few seconds our eyes met. I sipped my drink and continued to watch him over the rim of my cup.

"All right, the two of you will be right across the hall from your friends, in room two-fifteen."

I frowned. "Damn, do we have to be so close?"

He offered me an apologetic smile. "I'm afraid we are completely booked this week."

Double damn. The last thing I needed was my sister's nosy ass across the hall from me. What if I wanted to get my freak on? Her ass would be watching the damn door. I heaved a heavy sigh. Oh, well, I would just have to try to keep my shit on the DL.

All-inclusive guests are issued a wrist bracelet at check-in, thereby entitling them to pretty much whatever they wanted. He snapped Kayla's around her wrist, then handed her a door key. She then swung her purse over her shoulder and stepped to the side.

I moved up to the counter and stared across at a wide smile that made me feel all jittery inside. The last thing I needed right now was an audience.

Without looking back, I gave her a dismissive wave. "Kayla, that man is waiting to carry our bags up to the room. Why don't you go on up. This might take a while," I said as an afterthought.

"You are ridiculous," she mumbled under her breath as she signaled for the clerk to follow her. I knew I would have to hear all three of their mouths later but right now none of that mattered.

Everton leaned against the counter, giving me a seductive stare. "ID, please."

I reached into my purse and removed my billfold and gave it to him. He typed in the information, stopping to look at me every few letters.

"I saw the way you were looking at me," he said low enough for only my ears.

I blinked, not sure I had heard him correctly. I glanced over at the clerks to his far left, checking in other guests; both seemed oblivious to our conversation.

"I think you were the one looking at me," I countered.

He laughed, a throaty, coochie-clenching, nipple-hardening laugh. I didn't share in his laughter because personally I don't remember saying anything that was funny.

"Am I wrong?"

He shook his head. "No, you're right. I was checking you out, but are you going to deny that you were doing the same?" he asked, his eyes never leaving the computer screen.

I dropped my hand to my waist, then said all nonchalant and shit, "okay, so I was checking you out."

He smiled, pleased with my confession. "And your friends also noticed the attraction between us."

Actually, they probably had each already come to the conclusion that I was on another dick hunt and were probably thinking, "Poor Everton, he just doesn't know what he's gotten himself into."

He handed me back my ID and met my gaze head on. "So, what do you want to do about it?"

I pursed my lips. So far I was impressed by what I saw. Everton was one of those who went after what he wanted. I ain't mad at him. "Do about what?" I asked as I gave him my wrist and he snapped my bracelet on.

"This attraction we seem to have."

My Jamaican brotha definitely has confidence, but it was time to bring his ass down a peg or two. "Isn't there some rule about the staff messing with the guests?"

My comment caused his grin to waver slightly, then he merely shrugged his shoulders and said, "Yes, but I'm not going to tell. Are you?"

Leaning closer, I shook my head. The door to the office opened and a fine light-skinned Jamaican stepped out and moved up to the counter. I half expected Everton to get all professional and shit on me, but instead he did the complete opposite.

"Casey. This is Renee."

"What a beautiful name for a beautiful woman," he replied as he licked his lips and made a sistah want to shiver. I would have pushed Everton's ass aside if Casey wasn't so damn short.

"Thank you. I might have to introduce you to one of my girls."

Lisa is faithful to her husband. Kayla is much too tall. But Nadine, if she keeps her damn mouth shut, might be a match.

"She got friends?" he asked with a heavy accent.

Everton held up three fingers. "And they're all lovely. Only this one here is the best. As soon as we saw each other, we knew we were a match."

What the fuck ever. I don't know what the hell he was talking about. All I was after was some dick.

Casey nodded. "Hopefully I'll get a chance to meet you and your friends later today."

"I'm sure you will." I followed Casey's movement as he strolled down to the end of the counter.

"Come see me later," Everton said, drawing my attention again.

"We'll see."

Everton handed me my key. "I'm here tonight until ten."

I nodded again. I was grinning so much, my jaws hurt. Finally, I forced myself to turn away from the desk and, remembering the directions he had given Kayla, walked toward the building where I would be staying for the next seven days. As I moved across the lobby, I could feel the heat of his eyes on my backside. So naturally, of course, I added a little extra swing to my sway. Jamaica was already shaping up to be one trip I would never forget.

My heart was racing so fast I almost missed the enchanting view from the back of the hotel. There was a large outdoor pool with several kids playing while parents lay around in chairs, catching rays of the sun. I stepped out of the building and followed the path toward the first building behind the main one. The lawns were thick and green and surrounded by colorful arrays of flowers and popular plants.

I stepped into the building, a little extra pep in my step. It had barely been an hour since my arrival and already I had a hook-up.

I took the stairs two at a time and found my room on the right. I reached for my key card and swiped it. Just as my luck would have it, Nadine stuck her head outside the door directly across the hall.

"About damn time."

See, didn't I tell you their nosy asses would be watching me. I didn't even bother to respond; instead I tried my key card again. Damn, the shit wasn't working.

"So, did you make plans to get you some of that this evening?" she asked, laughing, teasing.

I playfully snapped back. "None of your damn business. You need to quit hating and try to get your ass some dick while you're here." I slid the key in again and thank goodness it worked. "Matter of fact, there was a cutie down behind the desk you might want to meet."

I saw the interest that sparked her eyes. "You know I'm game. I ain't had me a man in months. Puhleeze hook a sistah up."

Lisa stuck her head out the door and glared across at me. "Do y'all have to talk about this in the hallway? Damn. Save it for later."

I rolled my eyes at her just as she yanked Nadine into the room and slammed the door. See, I told you my big sister was going to get on my last nerve.

I stepped into the room to find Kayla on the phone. I moved over to the bed closest to the balcony and fell back onto the bedspread with an exaggerated sigh.

The room was nothing to write home about. Two double beds with a nightstand between them. There was a long dresser drawer and a twenty-inch color television. The curtains and the bedspreads were peach-and-floral prints.

Kayla hung up the phone with a huff. "Did you know we have to leave a phone deposit or use a credit card to make phone calls?"

I shrugged my shoulders. "Girl, you are on vacation. Who the hell you need to call?"

She dropped her gaze to her lap. "I was going to check on the girls."

I waved my hand dismissively. "Kayla, quit tripping. They're in good hands with your mother. Believe me, the last thing I am thinking about is calling my bebe-ass kids. I have been looking forward to getting away from them for weeks. Didn't you give your mother our hotel information?"

She nodded.

"Then quit worrying. They're fine."

"I guess," she said, sounding unconvinced. "But I'm going to drop by the desk later and leave a deposit just in case."

I sat up on the bed. "Girl, relax. We're going to have a ball."

She nodded, then asked, "So, what's up with you and Everton?"

I smiled as I rose from the bed and moved toward the sliding glass door. "Nothing yet, but the night is still young."

"You never know. If you play your cards right, he might give us the hook-up the next time we come down."

I swung around to face her. Shit, I hadn't thought about that. My father's club rate expired at the end of the year, which meant if I have as good a time as I anticipate that I will, the next time I'd have to pay the full rate. Unless of course, I have myself a Jamaican connection. "Everton is starting to look better and better as we speak."

"You know how you do." She crossed her legs, smiling at me.

I smiled back at her. "Yes, I do." I took a moment to reminisce on his dimpled smile. Damn, I loved a sexy man with a beautiful body. And from what I could see, he certainly had both. Hopefully, the rumors about Jamaican men were true. If his package was the right size, my ass had definitely hit the jackpot.

I turned to face the glass again and stared out at a scene pretty enough to put on a postcard. "You should have seen his friend Casey. He was fine."

"How tall was he?"

I glanced over my shoulder and shook my head. "Too short for you."

She sucked her teeth. "The story of my life."

I gave my girl a sympathetic look, then slid open the door and stepped out onto the balcony. The view was just like the brochure. Blue-green water. Bright yellow sun. A white sandy beach with women in bathing suits and straw hats, stretched out on lounge chairs. There were books on their laps and tropical drinks in their hands. Reggae music filled the air. Directly below was a straw hut from where the smell of jerk chicken traveled directly up to my nostrils. There were people everywhere, running, laughing, just having a good time. It was beautiful. Suddenly I wanted to be down there among the excitement. I stepped back into the room with renewed energy. "Come on, Kayla, let's change and hit the beach."

For the first time, her eyes danced with anticipation.

I reached for one of my bags on the floor and tossed it across the bed. "I think I packed too much shit."

"So did I," she said as she moved over to the mirror to fix her hair.

"I wasn't sure what to bring. Lisa said it gets so hot here you change your clothes several times a day."

"I believe it."

"Personally I could just spend the entire week in my bikini." I removed the new suit and dashed into the bathroom. I came out five minutes later. "What do you think?"

Kayla turned away from the mirror and I could see the envy in her eyes. "It looks cute on you."

I stepped in front of the mirror and took in the outfit from both sides. There were faint stretch marks on both sides of my abdomen and directly above my butt, but when I tied the wrap around my waist it drew attention away from it. I had even bought a padded bikini top just to give myself an extra cup.

"Aren't you going to change?"

Kayla gave me an embarrassing look. "Girl, I am not wearing a swimsuit."

"Why not?"

"I'm too out of shape," she answered.

"You ain't never gonna see any of these mothafuckas again."

She paused for a second and I thought maybe she was giving my comment some serious consideration before she started shaking her head again. "No, that is quite all right."

You know, it is times like this her self-esteem issue wears my nerves. "Girl, you are trippin'. It is too hot to be worrying what some mothafucka is going to say. Did you see how everyone was dressed? There's a woman downstairs that has a scar running straight down the front of her stomach, yet she still had the nerve to put on a bikini." Actually, that bitch looked nasty, but I wasn't going to say that.

"That's all right. I brought some cool outfits that will do the trick."

I stared at her in silence for a few seconds, then finally spoke again. "Whatever." I tried to hide my annoyance. I moved over to my bag and removed a pair of flip-flops and slipped them over my feet. "You want me to wait for you?" I asked after a long moment of silence.

Kayla shook her head. "No, go ahead and go down. I'll meet you on the beach."

She didn't have to tell me twice. Besides, I was anxious to go outside and check out the sights before I had to be bothered with my nagging-ass sister and Nadine. I reached for a matching pair of sunglasses, then headed out the door.

Chapter 10

KAYLA

Kayla waited until Renee left the room before she strolled over to her suitcase and removed a modest red swimsuit. Leery that Renee might return and catch her in the act, she stepped into the bathroom and shut the door.

She never thought she would envy Renee, but she did. If God had given her a choice between being either fat or promiscuous, she would rather be comfortable in her skin, lying in the bed with her legs wide open. Her friend, no matter how crazy she may behave, in Kayla's book, had her stuff together. She was successful, pretty, and had enough self-confidence for two people. She would have settled for even a fourth of what Renee had. Maybe then she wouldn't mind parading around the resort in a bathing suit she had packed with no intentions of wearing.

She quickly discarded her clothes, then slipped into the suit. Stepping in front of the mirror, she glanced down at the cellulite that had taken over her vanilla-colored thighs. Her stomach made her look six months pregnant. She had brought a cover-up that would at least hide the bulge around her waist, but nothing would hide her flabby forearms.

Tears pushed to the surface. Here she was on an exotic island and she couldn't even enjoy it. She had tried to no avail to get over her self-conscious behavior. She didn't like herself. She had tried every-thing from the Atkins diet to eating cabbage soup, and nothing helped. She had a love for food that wasn't going away. What was even worse was that when she was depressed, which was most of the time, she took comfort from food and doubled her intake.

Kayla sighed, then left the bathroom and moved to her suitcase, where she removed a peach Capri outfit. She would wear it instead. The outfit was cool enough to withstand the Jamaican heat and keep her from burning.

She carried it back to the bathroom and shut the door, then slipped out of the swimsuit. She glanced down at the floor so that she wouldn't be tempted to stare at the rolls that encircled her torso. Instead, as she unzipped her pants, her eyes caught the size-twenty-four tag sewn to the waistband, reminding her that her body was nothing anyone wanted to see. Except for Leroy.

Her stomach fluttered as she thought about the first time Leroy had seen her with her clothes off. Up until that point she had always made sure the room was dark or that she was under the covers long before he was. But on one particular afternoon when they met at their spot, there was no hiding.

She had been in the hotel room barely five minutes when he pulled her onto his lap. Nervously, she tried to pull away.

"What's wrong?" he asked, eyes burning with curiosity.

She gave a nervous laugh. "I'm too heavy to sit on your lap."

He pulled her even closer. "No, you're not. You're just right."

Staring down at her hands, she tried to shield her insecurities. "You don't have to say that. I know I'm a big woman."

"You're my woman and I love you just the way you are."

She smiled at him, grateful for the kind words that she knew were far from the truth. His wife was half her size. So she knew what he was accustomed to holding, and it definitely wasn't her big behind.

Leroy rained light kisses along her cheek and neck. "You are so beautiful. Don't ever let anyone tell you otherwise." He reached up and slowly unbuttoned her shirt. Kayla tried to stop him from sliding it off her shoulders.

"Baby, look at me."

Obediently, she raised her eyelids to look up at him.

"I want to see you. All of you."

Seeing the love burning in the depths of his eyes, a tear rolled down her cheek. Finally, she nodded.

Slowly, he peeled her shirt away and gazed down at her ample breasts. Feeling slightly emboldened by the power of his loving eyes, she reached around and unhooked her bra. Then he slid it off and onto the floor. Her large forty-six double Ds hung low but her large chocolate nipples stood hard and erect. Leroy leaned forward and captured one between his teeth and a moan escaped her lips. While he continued to suckle on her, he fondled the other between his fingers. Her eyes rolled back in her head and she thought she was seconds away from fainting.

He then signaled for her to stand, then he lowered her jeans over her generous hips, followed by a pair of pink grandma panties. She was so embarrassed, but he didn't seem to notice; instead his eyes were glued to the patch of hair between her legs.

"You are beautiful." He rose, then took her hand and led her over to the bed. "Lay down," he ordered, and obediently she lowered onto the bed. "Now spread your legs so I can see."

She obeyed and opened her legs wide. Self-consciously, she tried to use her hands to cover her body but he stopped her. "Don't. I like what I see."

Lust burned from the depths of his eyes as he kneeled down in front of her. He kissed a trail up the inside of her thighs. She shook with anticipation. She couldn't believe it—he was going to finally eat her out. However, to her disappointment, he stopped only centimeters from hitting her spot, and told her to roll over and get up on all four.

Leroy then positioned himself and immediately pushed inside of her. He pumped in and out, and five minutes later collapsed beside her, and said, "I am a weak man and you are an even weaker woman. Now let's both ask the Lord for forgiveness."

Chapter II

LISA

Lisa unfastened the lock, then slid the glass door open and stepped out onto the private balcony. She took a seat in the plastic patio chair, then tipped her face into the breeze and inhaled the fresh scent. Seabirds screeched as they wheeled and dipped near the ocean. It was beautiful here, which was the reason she always requested an ocean-view room.

Taking a deep breath, she glanced down at the sandy beach and spotted Renee flirting with an islander. Her sister was a trip. She just hoped Renee didn't get herself into any trouble. Last month some woman had tried to stab Renee because she had been standing in the checkout lane at Shop & Save, flirting with her man. Luckily, an off-duty cop in the next aisle had stepped in and broken up the situation. Renee, of course, showed her appreciation by inviting the cop out for dinner. According to Nadine, the evening ended with Renee lying on her back with her legs spread.

Lisa studied her sister, trying to figure out what Renee was planning to do next. Mischief was written all over her face. Hmmm. First she was at the front desk flirting with Everton and now this. Watching a while longer, she spotted two other employees moving her way. They too stood around, obviously captivated by Renee's beauty. Lisa had to admit her sister was a beautiful woman. She had sandy brown hair and the prettiest caramel skin. Lisa remembered spending years staying out of the sun, hoping that somehow her toasted complexion would resemble her younger sister's. Renee might find it hard to believe, but there were quite a few things Lisa admired about her younger sister. She had brains, beauty, and confidence.

Even in grade school, Renee had this walk that shouted, "try me if you want to." People just didn't fuck with her sister unless they didn't know any better. She had a nasty mouth and an attitude to match, yet people still loved her despite her many ways. Especially men. They looked past the funky attitude and looked at the total package instead. Renee ran track, so she had runner's legs and a narrow waist, little breasts, and a round ass. And brothas loved it. No matter how often she tried to school her sister, she sucked that shit up.

Renee only got worse with age. She was a master at her game. That girl drew men like bees to honey and drama like it was her middle name. Lisa shook her head. One thing for certain, tonight someone would be sharing Renee's bed.

It wasn't like it came as any big surprise. For years men had been in and out of Renee's life like it had a revolving door. Lisa had tried telling Renee her ass was hot and to slow it down, but all she had ever done was blow her off, and tell her to mind her damn business. After a while Lisa just shut up and let her do what she wanted. After all, Renee was grown and she was getting sick of telling her what she should or should not do.

Lisa sighed with despair. Her sister was definitely a piece of work. She had hoped by the time she had reached thirty she would have slowed down, but apparently nothing seemed to be stopping her. Staring down at her, Lisa was glad she had asked their friends to share this week with them.

Lisa remembered when they had first met Kayla and Nadine. She had been about sixteen and her sister thirteen. They had been living in Columbia less than two months and hated it. Coming from the South Side of Chicago, she and Renee thought the little college town was country. There were possums running around out back and crickets chirping on the front porch. She remembered being afraid to come out of the house because a cricket was blocking the door.

In their small two-bedroom house, they had no central air. So she and Renee would spend many afternoons passing the time at the public library that was three blocks away.

One particular afternoon, they were sitting in the periodical section, flipping through *Teen* magazine, reading an article on Janet Jackson, when Nadine and Kayla stepped into the room. Nadine was short and petite with a long, thick ponytail, while Kayla was tall and round.

They walked over to the shelves and browsed, then Nadine cleared her throat.

"Are y'all looking at *Teen* magazine?"

"Yeah, why?" Renee answered with attitude.

Lisa had to kick her under the table. Even then she had a smart mouth.

"You mind if we look with you? I've been waiting all month to read that interview with Janet Jackson."

She signaled for them to take a seat, ignoring her sister's frowns. Renee had always been a hateful thing. It took getting to know her to discover that beneath that hard shell was a vulnerable person desperate to be loved. A friendship began that day that withstood over twenty years of ups and downs, husbands, baby's daddies, and even time and distance.

Bringing her thoughts back to the present, Lisa turned away from the view and moved back through the sliding glass door. She left the sliding door open and the sheer white curtains billowed in the wind like a sail.

"What you think?"

Lisa glanced over at Nadine, who had just changed into a swimsuit. Short and round, the black one-piece with matching cover-up was flattering to her figure. "You look nice. Where'd you find that suit?"

"I went to Penney's last weekend. They were having a sale."

"Good choice. I should have checked it out myself."

"Your suit looks nice."

Lisa glanced down at her two-piece bikini with a purple wrap tied around her waist. Never having children, her stomach was flat, her large breasts still firm and upright.

Nadine stepped out onto the balcony and gazed down below. "You know your sister is already working the beach."

Lisa gave a soft chuckle. "Yeah, I know. I don't know what to do with her crazy ass. She is out of control."

Sometimes she blamed herself that maybe if she had stood by Renee all those years and defended her maybe things would be different. But there was no way of knowing. Besides, she had been only a kid herself. What's to say if she had stood up to their stepfather, he might have rejected her also?

One thing she could say about her sister, Renee had never stopped trying to please their stepfather. No matter how much he criticized her, she never gave up. She just returned to the drawing board and started over. However, what it took Lisa years to understand was that nothing would ever have been good enough because that was the type of person he was.

Paul Perry had been a strict and heartless man. No kisses, never hugs. He rarely gave praise. For some reason he had accepted Lisa as his daughter. But Renee he never had. Lisa had wondered why for years and one day she asked Paul. He had told her simply, "Because Renee looked too much like her damn daddy."

Then, finally, five years ago, after years of being an evil bastard, Paul had given his life over to the Lord. Now he regretted the choices he had made and was trying to do everything in his power to win his youngest daughter's heart. However, Renee wasn't buying it. She didn't trust him any more than she trusted any of the other men in her life to love her. After years of rejection, Renee had learned to take what she needed from a man, then jump ship long before he had a chance to figure out where the hell she had gone.

Lisa lowered onto the bed and slipped her feet into a pair of sandals. Now if only she could find a way to get Renee to see what she was doing to herself. She needed to find a way to break the vicious cycle of self-destruction. Somehow, Lisa had to convince her sister to let go of the pain and learn to take a chance with love and life.

Lisa believed that God had given her that mission. She hoped that with the aid of a life-threatening illness she would get her sister to see that life was much too precious for games. If she could get Renee to see that, then maybe there was an underlying reason why she had been diagnosed with cancer.

Chapter 12

RENEE

It was obvious Jamaican men loved African American women, because ever since I'd left the room I'd been getting mega play. Brothas were whistling, catcalling, showing me all of their white pearly teeth, and my ass was sucking that shit up. I was looking too cute and definitely knew it.

With a rum punch in my hand, I followed the path around the resort. Bob Marley was blaring from a speaker not far from the pool. People were everywhere, laughing and totally oblivious to anything but the uplifting atmosphere. It was quite apparent I was going to like it here.

I moved along the beach, where there were over a hundred lounge chairs occupied mostly by women basting in the sun, hoping that by nightfall they might manage a tan that closely resembled my natural caramel complexion. A group on the end were laughing and sipping punch. I rolled my eyes when I noticed they were all wearing cornrows and beads.

I never could understand that shit. White folks will travel all the way to Jamaica to get their hair braided when we've got salons right in the hood that can hook their asses up. I figure they like our music, our men, but the only way they can justify wearing their hair like us is to say, "I got my hair done in Jamaica." Shit, they don't have to spend a hundred dollars to get their hair done, when they can go to my girl Kenya's shop on Twelfth Street. Shit, she's from Jamaica. So what's the difference? Not a damn thing.

After mean mugging their asses for several seconds, I quickly reminded myself that I didn't come to Jamaica to start no shit, and strolled my hateful ass over near my building to wait for the others. I smelled chicken and stopped on the path near a hut that was directly below my hotel room. One thing I can eat every day of the week is chicken. Fried, baked, barbecued—it doesn't matter. Chicken is chicken as long as it is a leg or a wing. I don't do thighs.

I saw smoke coming from behind and there were at least a dozen people standing in line. Peering over the top of my sunglasses, I noticed two ebony brothas working inside the hut. Curiosity got the better of me and I swayed my hips to the end of the line to get a closer look. From where I was standing, they both looked fine as sin.

While I waited in line, I swayed my hips to the uplifting beat of the music. They're playing that song of Janet Jackson's featuring the Elephant Man. As I continued to move to the beat, I keep my eyes trained on the brothas before me glistening with sweat. By the time I reached the front, the lanky one to the right had already been disqualified. He was too skinny and had a big jug head.

"Hey beautiful, what can I get for you?"

I was grinning like a damn fool as I moved up to lean against the counter to stare at the dark chocolate brotha who was hooking up the meat. He was buffed with long dreadlocks that hung down to the middle of his back.

"Can I have some chicken?"

"Pretty lady, you can have whatever you want."

He moved to fix me a plate. As I waited, I leaned over and gazed down at his tight ass. Nice. Very nice.

"What's your name?" he asked as he fixed my plate.

"Renee. And yours?"

"Langley, mon." He handed me a plate that smelled good, then leaned forward and kept grinning.

Langley. I liked the sound of that. "Nice to meet you." I glanced down at my plate, then frowned. "Uh-uh. Langley, I don't eat thighs."

He had the nerve to look at me like I was crazy. "But that is jerk chicken."

"I don't care what it is. I don't eat nobody's damn thighs."

"That is good meat, mon."

What part of "don't eat thighs" was he not comprehending? I handed him the plate back. "Then you eat it." I knew I was acting like a bitch. Like I've said before, it is in my nature and there ain't a damn thing I can do about that. Although I bet you a dollar Langley was probably thinking, "here we go, another spoiled-ass American woman." And, do you think I care? Hell, naw.

"How about some jerk pork?" he suggested.

I was pleased by his quick thinking. "Now, I can do pork."

He shook his head as he moved to fix me a different plate, and you know me well enough by now to know I never know how to keep my damn mouth shut.

"What are you shaking your head for?"

"You American women are so picky."

"What's wrong with being picky?"

"Nothing. But you know how that American saying goes, 'don't knock it until you try it'."

He obviously did not understand why I couldn't eat every piece of the chicken. "Tell me, Langley. Have you ever had chicken feet?"

"Chicken what?"

"Chicken feet. You know, the things they walk with that have toes?"

He chuckled. "No, mon. I've never had chicken feet."

"But would you try it?"

The way he scrunched up his face you would have thought he was about to take a shit. "No way. That's voodoo, mon."

"Well, when I was a kid my mother used to send my dad to the butcher for chicken feet." Langley's brow rose. "Yeah, I know. My mama's ass was crazy. Anyway, she would fry them and put it on our plate along with macaroni and cheese and Brussels sprouts or some other green shit. Anyway, it was considered a norm in my household like chicken thighs is obviously a norm in yours."

I could tell the exact moment when my point came across because he gave me a wide dimple smile.

"Now, if you're not even willing to try sucking on some chicken feet, how the hell you gonna get pissed off because I don't want no goddamn chicken thighs?"

He started laughing, and his boy, who obviously had been listening, started laughing also. Shit, he probably thought I had made that shit up, but I was for real. The butcher probably thought our asses was so poor we couldn't afford anything on the chicken but the damn feet. He must have felt sorry for my stepfather because he used to give him those feet for free. My sister and I used to suck between toenails looking for meat. When I think about that shit now, I wonder why I didn't realize until I was thirteen that my mother's ass was crazy. Shit, my stepfather was just as crazy for going to the store and picking up them damn feet.

Langley carried over a plate of Jamaican jerk pork. I scooted over to the last stool and grabbed a fork. The blackened meat was hot and spicy. I swallowed it down with my rum punch.

"So, what do you think?" He gave me a look that reminded me of a child after showing his mother a picture he had drawn in art class.

"Mmm, very good. Hot as shit, but good."

I glanced over at his jug-head friend, who was grinning as he prepared plates for two teenagers that came up to the hut. They looked like college students with their perfect bodies and long blond hair.

"Where's your husband?" Langley asked me. He leaned against the counter and stared down into my mouth as I ate.

I took my time chewing my food before I spoke. "Who said I got a husband? Do you see a ring on my finger?" I wiggled my hand in his face.

"No, mon. But that doesn't mean nothing in America."

I had to laugh at that because he was right, it didn't mean shit. Take me, for example. I wore my wedding ring the first year of my marriage, then suddenly I became "allergic" to gold. I'd wear it Monday through Thursday, but on Friday the sucker was itching so bad, it came off the finger. Seriously, although Lisa says it's some psychological bullshit I came up with so I could party on the weekends, ring free. I tried showing her the red irritated line but she wasn't hearing that shit. Not that it mattered. A brotha could care less. In fact, some of them consider a married woman more of a challenge.

"No husband. I'm here with my friends."

"Are they as lovely as you?" he inquired.

Now how the hell was I supposed to answer a question like that? Hell naw, they ain't as lovely as me. Instead I said, "I don't hang around with no ugly people."

I could have stood there and flirted with him all evening but the line was growing long and I already had one hook-up for the evening. I would save Langley for another time. "I'll catch you later." I wiggled my fingers, then spun on my heels and headed toward the beach.

I took a seat in a chaise that was all the way at the edge of the beach. Every time a large wave came, water spilled around my ankles and feet. That shit was refreshing, to say the least. While I sat there eating my food my thoughts drifted to my husband.

He had been so disappointed to hear that I preferred to go to Jamaica with my friends instead of him. We had just gone to the Bahamas the year before on a cruise. I spent more time in the bed with my legs up in the air than I did out on the deck enjoying the ship. I don't know why a man thinks if you go somewhere romantic all there is to do is fuck. Sure, I don't mind a little dick from time to time but not all the damn time. If I am paying good money to visit an exotic location then goddammit, I want to get my money's worth. If I wanted to fuck all day, I could have stayed home and stared at my own damn ceiling. I couldn't get John to understand that so I made sure that Lisa told him it was her idea. Sure enough, she told him she needed to spend some time alone with her sister, and he bought that shit.

I shoveled the last piece of pork in my mouth, then set my plate beside me. Glancing up from my drink, I spotted Kayla heading my way. I tried to hide the scowl on my face. I just couldn't understand why she was so ashamed of her body. I mean, I know she big, but damn, if you're that embarrassed why not do something about it. That probably sounded insensitive, because I know losing weight is no easy task. I tried many times and failed. Believe it or not, after I gave birth to Tamara, I was wearing a size fourteen for years, until one day I looked in the mirror and saw the rolls around my waist and said, "Enough with this shit!" I started running three times a week and cutting back on my sweets. It was a tough hill to climb but I did it.

Anyway, I know it takes willpower and that is one thing I know my girl is lacking. She has very low self-esteem that shows. And it's a shame, because she is so pretty.

Kayla flopped down in the chair beside me. "I should have known you'd have a drink in your hand."

I sucked my tongue. "Hell, yeah. I'm on vacation." I took another sip. "Where's Nadine and Lisa?"

"They'll be down in a few minutes."

I took a deep breath and allowed my body to completely relax. Sitting near the ocean there was a nice cool breeze.

"How's John?"

I glanced over at her, then back out onto the water. I had wondered how long it was going to take before she got around to mentioning him.

I picked up my sunglasses, slid them on, and stretched out in the chair before speaking.

"Fine . . . I guess."

"You guess? When was the last time you spoke to him?"

"A couple of weeks ago."

She shook her head. "Y'all got the weirdest marriage. So, have you decided what you're gonna do?"

I shook my head. "Nope."

"You need to just go on down to Delaware. You know that man is waiting on you."

"I know he's waiting. He bought that big old house and he's waiting for us to join him."

Kayla squinted her eyes. "So what's the problem?"

"The problem is, I don't want to be with him. But because he's so nice, I don't know how to tell him."

Kayla looked at me as if I had lost my damn mind. "Renee, he's a good man with a good job. He doesn't cheat. You don't have to work. I don't understand you."

"Because there is so much more to it than that." I inhaled deeply. "I'm so sick of people thinking I've got it made. Y'all just don't know what I have to go through."

"I'm listening."

I sighed heavily. "I just don't love him."

Kayla was thoughtful for a moment before saying, "I don't think you know what love is."

"Maybe I don't, but I know what love isn't, and it's my relationship with John. I married him for all the wrong reasons and that was my fault. I have tried so hard to love that man and look past all his faults and I can't." How can I get people to understand that I've made a mistake? What's even harder is getting myself to truly accept that I've made a mistake and then finding the strength to move on.

"What bothers me the most is that he is exactly the same man I married three years ago. I knew then that his dick was little and that he was too damn old, yet I tried to convince myself that neither of those things matter. All that mattered was that he was a good man who was willing to do anything to make me happy. Yet money and stability is not enough."

Kayla sucked her teeth. "Girl, I would love for a man to help me and the girls."

"Yeah, but at what expense? I feel that I have given up a piece of who I am to be with him. Yeah, maybe I don't have to work but that privilege comes at a cost. John wants a wife to cook his meals, clean his house, and cater to his needs. At one time I was so excited to be able to do those things because I never had the luxury. For years I had been working two jobs and going to school at night to get my degree, then I lose my job, and here comes John offering to marry me so I wouldn't have to worry about health benefits, and rushing to find another dead-end job. He put this fairy-tale life in front of me on a silver platter and I grabbed it. And as soon as the excitement wore off, I've been regretting it ever since.

"You know, my sister told me that I didn't know how to have normalcy in my life. That I live for drama and disruption, and don't you know she had my ass thinking that maybe she was right. Maybe I don't know how to have a real relationship, and because of it I keep trying to make things work between John and I."

"Does he have any idea?"

I shrugged. "I think he does, but he chooses to ignore it. He loves me so much it's scary. So many times I find myself looking for reasons to end our relationship, searching for an excuse to get out of the marriage, and can't ever seem to find one."

"Well, you can't blame the man."

"No, but I truly believe it is unfair for me to continue to stay with him. I refuse to sleep with him but once a week, and even then I feel sick to my stomach."

"Poor John."

I swung around on the seat and glared at her. "Poor John? What about me?" I asked with straight attitude. "Every time he touches me I feel like I'm being raped."

Kayla's eyes were wide. "Are you serious?"

"Yes, it is a terrible feeling. You just don't know what it feels like to have some big fat man on top of you huffing and puffing when you don't want to be touched by him. He spends almost an hour kissing and caressing every part of my body, telling me how much he loves me, and it drives me crazy. Then he makes love to me slowly, trying to savor the moment, and I want to scream. I can't even get on top and control the moment because his thing is too damn short. Doggy style is a big waste of time because he can't seem to do that shit right or maybe it's because his dick is too short to hit my spot. So instead I lie there on my back and fake an orgasm just so he'll come and get the fuck off of me." I reached for my drink, feeling tears at the back of my throat. "I can't continue like that."

"Dang, girl. I didn't know it was that bad." Kayla actually looked like she truly felt sorry for me.

"It's worse. But I also know it is unfair to him. He is a wonderful man and he deserves a chance to be happy with someone else. And I think the best thing I could ever do for him is let him go so that he has a chance to meet someone that's right for him."

"So what are you going to tell him?"

I shook my head. "I don't know. I can't tell him the truth. I've tried to come up with every possible excuse and still haven't been able to come up with shit."

"Well, it should be easier since the two of you aren't living together."

"Yeah, I know. But I just can't see telling him something like that over the phone. He's flying to Missouri in two weeks, so I guess I'll have to tell him then."

Letting go had always been easy. All I needed was a reason to justify my actions and then I could walk away. That was the case with both my first and second husband. But what I find with John is that it's not going to be that way. Because this time I don't have a legitimate reason, except that he doesn't satisfy me in bed, but I knew that long before I said "I do," only I chose to ignore it.

I have never met a nicer man. John's kind, considerate. Ever since I told him I was unhappy he has been doing everything in his power to make things better. He doesn't have a clue that nothing is going to make a difference. So far, I haven't had the heart to tell him so.

You're probably thinking, "Renee, that heartless bitch, when does she have feelings for anyone?" Well, believe it or not, I am considerate of other's feelings, especially when they've been nothing but good to me.

I look at John with a stomach as wide as his smile and the gold band shining on his left hand, and I want to cry because I wish I could be everything he wants me to be. And it hurts because I can't. Lord knows I've tried. We've been married for three years and I have been miserable for two. For one year I played the role of Suzy Homemaker, cooking, cleaning, catering to his every sexual need, and even before the twelve months were up I was asking myself what the hell was I doing trying to be someone I was not. However, I continued to try.

Every time he reached under the covers and placed his hand on my knee, I cringed. My entire body would stiffen, and I would hope that by me not responding he would leave it alone, but he never does. The last time we were together was two months ago. As soon as I brought him home from the airport he mentioned he was exhausted, so we moved to the bedroom and I lay across the bed while he took a nap. The kids were still at school so it was a good time for a little rest and relaxation. Just as my eyes began to close, I felt his hand caressing the inside of my thigh. I tried to pretend I was already asleep.

"How about giving your husband a little bit?" he whispered close to my ear.

I didn't respond, hoping he would just leave me the fuck alone, but since he hadn't had any coochie in months I should have known better.

His hand started traveling up my thigh, then, as I held my breath, he reached under my shirt. I wasn't wearing a bra, so he had easy access to my breasts. He took my nipple between his thumb and pointer finger and began to tweak it. Now I have always considered my nipples my weak spot. All it took was tweaking it just so lightly to get me turned on, but with John it became a turn-off.

He shifted on the bed and raised my shirt so that he could feast his eyes on my breasts, then as I laid there the entire time like a board, he moved his hand to my left nipple while he captured the right with his lips. Eventually feelings of arousal sailed through me, and even though I wanted to moan I didn't because with John if you responded his ass would never stop. So I continued to lay there as he suckled and tweaked one nipple and then the other over and over again until I lost the moment and was ready to scream. I held it in because I have told him many times before that my nipples were going to fall the fuck off from him playing with them so damn much. However, talking to him was like talking to a rock. He never remembered and the torture continued until he was done.

He paused long enough to slide my pants and underwear down my hips, then his lips traveled past my belly button to the patch of hair between my legs. I parted my thighs so he could have access and started counting in my head. He found my clit and suckled while his fingers continued to tweak my nipples like they were the knobs to a damn transistor radio. I tried not to think about my poor nipples and concentrated on his tongue. Beneath the hooded skin, he found my spot and suckled but I knew better to respond for long because the more you responded the harder and longer he sucked until he made me so damn mad I had to push his mouth away.

John rolled over to his side of the bed, then took my hand and guided it to his dick, which I wasn't surprised to find was still soft.

"Play with it."

I cringed inwardly before I allowed my fingers to wrap around the base of his dick and stroke it up and down. The entire time he continued to play with my damn nipples. I lay there, asking myself, "why the hell am I doing this?" I wanted to cry because his eyes were closed and he was smiling and mumbling how much he loved his wife, and all I could think about is how pitiful this mothafucka is.

Finally, when I was seconds away from giving up, his dick got hard. John quickly positioned himself between my legs and tried to find my coochie. It was so dry it took several attempts at pushing before I finally reached over and grabbed the damn K-Y Jelly and lubricated his semihard dick. It took a few minutes of stroking to bring him back to his full erection, then I guided him to my coochie and helped him find my damn hole.

He slid in quickly and lowered his three-hundred-plus body on top of me and began to pump. I rocked my hips slightly and tried to find a rhythm, which we can never find.

Finally, he lifted his weight off of me and I breathed freely until his hands found my nipples again. All I wanted was to get the shit over with. I tightened the walls of my coochie and tried rocking harder because I know moaning and faking an orgasm is the only way he is going to get the fuck off of me.

If only his dick was just a little longer, then maybe he could reach my spot. I've tried putting my legs on his shoulders but all I get is his weight slamming against my body. If he had a dick, he would be something fierce in the bedroom, but that isn't the case so there is no point in wishing.

He lowered his weight over me again and pumped faster and faster while he still had one hand plastered to my left nipple.

"Yes, baby," I moaned on cue.

"Come with me," he said.

"Uh-huh," I whispered.

I rocked my hips harder to meet each of his strokes and when he cried, I cried. When he moaned, I moaned, and when he finally came, I pretended to come with him. Then he rolled over and within seconds he fell asleep while I lay beside him and allowed the tears to fall freely.

"Here come Nadine and Lisa," Kayla said, breaking into my thoughts.

I slid my glasses on top of my head and grinned. "Check her ass out. Nadine, that suit is cute." For once she had on something that wasn't country. The one-piece was made for someone with big titties and a short torso. "Lisa, you look good, too."

"Thanks. Michael bought this for me." She took a seat at the bottom of my chair.

"Must be nice to have a man to buy you things," Kayla said with envy.

"Girl, this is a first, because most of the shit he buys me is either too big or something my damn grandma would wear."

We laughed.

"Shit. John's the same way. That's why I tell his ass to just give me the money instead."

Nadine noticed the plate beside my chair. "What you got there?"

"Jerk pork. I got it at that little hut over there. Nadine, you should check out the cutie inside."

"I will. Right now I'm hungry."

"So am I," Lisa agreed.

"Let's go eat in the dining room," Nadine suggested.

"Dressed like that?" Kayla asked.

Lisa chuckled. "Yes, like this. Girl, we can go barefoot. That's why it's right off of the pool."

We each rose and moved up the path past several vendors and two other huts. One served hamburgers and hot dogs while the other served ice cream. We stepped around a large swimming pool where a recreational director was playing water sports with a dozen or so kids. Coming up the path, three tired-looking workers tried to get our attention. Nadine flipped them off, which sent us all screaming with laughter as we moved toward the patio-style restaurant.

I moved up the wide tiled stairs into an open dining area. No windows. No doors. Just a roof to shield against the frequent rain showers and lots of open space. There were dozens of tables and chairs surrounding a large buffet. Lisa found a table closest to the pool. Directly across from the half wall was the lobby, with a clear view of the registration desk on the other side of the fountain.

I took a seat directly facing the desk. Everton wasn't around but I wanted to see him when he was. "All right, y'all go first. I'll sit here and hold our table."

"I'll sit here with you," Kayla offered. Nadine and Lisa went and joined the buffet line.

I glanced around the room. People were laughing and smiling. There were several couples lip-locking and holding hands. To my far right I spotted a group of large brothas stepping into the dining room. "Kayla, look."

There were five of them: three had women on their arms, two did not. They had to be football players. I heard you would always find them in Jamaica.

"They look like linebackers," Kayla replied.

"I think they are."

They were all gorgeous, but money could make the ugliest man handsome. However, I have to admit, in this case several of them were naturally fine.

I sat up straight on the chair and pushed out what little titties I had. As they strolled past us, a guy who was as tall as he was wide winked in our direction. I smiled, showing teeth and tongue. Kayla's grin was just as big. Our smiles weren't missed by a pretty Hispanic woman walking behind him all hugged up with a player who was a little smaller and less bulky. She gave us an I-bet-you-wish-you-were-me look as she swayed her narrow hips to a large round table in the corner.

"No, she didn't," I murmured under my breath.

"Yes, she did. And did you see the size of that ring on her finger? It had to be at least ten carats."

"Hmm, must be nice," I said, voice dripping with sarcasm.

"Yeah, some of us ain't able."

I glanced over my shoulder at the bunch and rolled my eyes. "Girl, they probably play for some overseas team we ain't never heard of."

"I know that's right. And he's probably with her today and with someone else next week."

"You know how they do." I let out an exaggerated sigh. "He ain't even cute."

"Not at all."

Kayla and I looked at each other and started laughing.

"We need to quit. 'Cause all them brothas are fine. We ain't doing nothing but sitting here hating."

"I know. I would give anything to be on that fine negro's arm," I admitted with a laugh. "And the bulky one that winked definitely had potential."

Lisa and Nadine returned with plates piled high with several succulent dishes.

"Do y'all see Clayton O'Neal?" Lisa asked as she lowered into the chair next to mine.

I glanced at her. "Is that name supposed to ring a bell?"

"Y'all never heard of him?" She looked at us with disbelief.

"Nope," Kayla answered.

She looked at both of us and we shrugged our shoulders. Lisa shook her head. "Y'all heifers live in Missouri, not me. Clayton plays for the Kansas City Chiefs." She nodded her head toward the group in the back. "The one in the green t-shirt is Clayton." Discreetly, I glanced over my shoulder to see which one she was talking about.

"He just winked at us," Kayla said.

Then it suddenly came to me. I remember reading that Clayton had just signed a ten-year 131-million-dollar deal, making him the highest paid quarterback in the NFL. "Oh shit, that's the hundred-million-dollar man!"

Nadine took a bite of baked chicken and said between chews, "Yep. And to his left, with that woman hanging all over him, that's Alex Houston," she replied, tilting her head in his direction. "He announced their engagement a couple of months ago. She's supposed to be some Central American model."

They usually are. I glanced over my shoulder again with a strong rush of envy, then rose. "Come on, Kayla. Let's eat."

We moved to the buffet line and directly on the other side of the atrium, I spotted Everton standing behind the counter watching me. He waved and I waved back. He wasn't a football player, and I knew for a fact he wasn't getting paid shit working behind a desk. But for the time being, his ass would do.

The buffet had barbecue ribs, pork, salads, desserts, and several authentic Jamaican foods. I helped myself to a serving of oxtails and rice. My grandmother used to cook them, so I know they can't be anything but good.

I moved back to the table before Kayla and slid onto my seat. I glanced over at the football group and that same woman was eyeing me down.

"I don't know why that bitch keeps looking at me."

Lisa followed the direction of my eyes then snorted rudely. "Shit, she's probably heard the rumors."

Nadine laughed. "I know that's right. She knows if she doesn't watch her man you'll be trying to fuck him before midnight."

"Fuck you," I said, then laughed because they weren't lying.

Kayla slid in across from me. "They've got cheesecake." It was her favorite.

I reached for the brochure on the table. "Have we decided what excursions we're going on?"

Lisa sipped her drink, then replied, "Definitely shopping. Maybe a sightseeing trip or something."

"I want to do that waterfall," Kayla said.

I rolled my eyes. "I'm not climbing no damn waterfall. I heard if you don't hold on your ass might fall. You know I can't swim."

"I thought you took lessons last month." I knew Lisa was going to bring that shit up.

"I did. Enough to swim in a pool, not a damn waterfall."

Kayla reached for her fork. "Well, I'm going."

"Then have fun. 'Cause my ass is going to spend the week hanging out at the hotel, drinking."

Lisa frowned. "Don't be getting drunk either. 'Cause your ass always acts like a damn fool."

"Shit. I plan to spend the week fucked up, so you might as well be prepared."

Kayla shook her head and laughed. "You are stupid."

"Hey, she can do what she wants, just as long as we don't have to carry her ass to the room." Lisa leaned back in the seat and gave me a knowing look.

Nadine started laughing like a hyena. "I know. Remember that time her ass was so drunk she passed out on the middle of the dance floor. We had to carry her ass out to the car and try to get her home."

"Girl, I was only twenty-two at the time. Them days are long gone. I can hold my liquor."

Nadine tried to come to my defense. "She ain't lying. Your sister is a damn lush."

"Fuck all y'all."

Kayla had to add her two cents. "She needs Jesus."

Nadine reached for her napkin. "Speaking of Jesus, I'm selling tickets to our church anniversary dinner we're having next week. Anyone want to buy tickets?"

Kayla nodded. "I already bought a ticket. My pastor's wife was selling them last week."

"I saw Reverend Brown and his wife last week at my GYN appointment. I can't believe they're having another baby."

I glanced over at Kayla and didn't miss the look on her face. She didn't know I knew she was fucking Reverend Leroy Brown, but I knew. Everyone around town knew, except for Lisa and Nadine, otherwise she wouldn't have said anything.

Kayla lowered her fork. "I didn't know she was pregnant."

Nadine's brow drew together in a thin line. "Girl, she's already three months. Reverend Brown brought her in for her ultrasound. He was so excited you would have thought it was their first child the way they were slobbering all over each other."

She took a drink. "Y'all, I'm not feeling too good. I'm going back to the room."

"You want me to get you something?" Lisa asked, looking concerned.

Kayla shook her head. "No, I'll be fine." Without another word, she rose from her chair and moved past the pool toward the rooms.

Lisa looked worried. "I wonder what's wrong with her?"

I gladly provided the answer. "She's fucking her minister."

Lisa choked on her chicken.

"What?" Nadine's eyes were wide as saucers.

"I ain't supposed to know, but I've seen them together."

Lisa sat back in her chair, shocked. "I can't believe this shit. When did this happen?"

I paused for dramatic effect and chewed my food first, making them wait for my answer. "One night I was pulling into the Ramada Inn in Jefferson City when I spotted her and him coming out."

Nadine's eyes danced with amusement. "What were you doing at the Ramada?"

I rolled my eyes playfully. "Don't worry about that. Now, getting back to what I was saying, I saw the two of them come out and they were lip-locking and shit. He walked to his car, then as soon as he pulled off she went to hers. Her hair was all over the place and she was smiling like a damn fool."

My sister's gaze held mine for a moment. "Did you tell her you saw her?"

"Nope. I figured she didn't want us to know, otherwise she would have told me herself."

"I think I better go check on her." Lisa rose from her chair.

"I think you need to give her a few minutes by herself."

Nadine agreed.

Lisa glanced over her shoulder, sighed, then lowered into her seat.

"I don't understand. I mean, why the hell would she be messing with her pastor? His ass ain't even cute," Nadine said.

"True."

Lisa shook her head with disbelief. "But it is so out of character for her. She's much too spiritual for that."

I snorted and almost choked on a chicken bone. "Girl, I heard that mothafucka can talk a woman out of her drawers. He used to mess with Ginger Clark."

Lisa's brow rose. "Who?"

"You know, Ryan Clark's sister. The one with the big dimples in her booty."

Nadine's eyes sparkled with recognition. "Oh, yeah. I know who you're talking about. The one that has a baby by Tony Monroe."

I nodded. "Yeah, her. Reverend was messing with her for almost a year, then suddenly he broke it off and she tried to commit suicide over him. Now she's telling everyone he ain't got no dick."

Lisa bit into a slice of chocolate cake. "Women always say that when they asses get dumped. And that nut was in a mental hospital, so I wouldn't believe shit she said."

"Nah, I know it's true because he also messed with Teresa Fox. She said as soon as he pulled that little thing out, she started cracking up laughing and said there ain't shit she could do with that little thing, and put his ass the fuck out."

Nadine sat back in her chair. "Oh, my goodness!"

We screamed with laughter.

Lisa sobered, then reached for her drink. "Well, as soon as I get done eating, I'm going to go and talk to her."

I shrugged. "Good luck. I guarantee Kayla doesn't want to hear shit we have to say."

Chapter 13

KAYLA

She rushed down the path as tears burned at her eyes. She couldn't believe what had just happened. What Nadine said couldn't possibly be true. There was no way Leroy would do her that way. No way. He loved her and planned to spend the rest of his life with her, just as soon as he asked his wife for a divorce, she told herself as she quickened her steps. Kayla was so overcome by grief she ran right smack into a wall, or at least she thought it was a wall until a large pair of hands reached out, stopping her from falling on her butt and embarrassing herself even more.

"I'm so sorry. Are you okay?"

"No, I'm . . ." her voice trailed off as soon as she gazed into his eyes.

It was Clayton O'Neal.

She gasped. All the blood rushed down to her feet. She thought she was going to faint for sure. She wobbled slightly to the left. Clayton held out his hand to her, and she grabbed it half expecting a bolt of lightning.

"Are you okay?" he asked again.

"I'm so sorry. I wasn't paying attention."

He smiled. "Feel free to bump into me anytime."

Stunned by his comment, all she could do was smile. Was he flirting with her? No, he couldn't possibly. *Girl, the impact must have scrambled your brain.*

"I'm Clayton O'Neal."

"I know. I mean, my name is Kayla Sparks."

"Nice to meet you, Kayla."

She stood there looking up into his warm, dark eyes, inhaling everything about him. She slowly took her hand back and stepped away, fearful he might try to touch her again. "I need to make a phone call. It was nice meeting you."

"The pleasure was all mine. Hopefully I'll see you around."

She suddenly felt embarrassed. Her guard had fallen down and she felt exposed. The look he gave her was as though he could read her thoughts.

"Maybe," she murmured.

She walked away feeling his gaze on her back. Sure enough, when she glanced over her shoulder, she found Clayton standing there watching her. Heat flowed through her chest and caused her nipples to become pebble hard. Quickly, she swung around and disappeared into her building. As soon as he could no longer see her, she paused and took several deep breaths, trying to calm her racing heart. *Get a grip, girl.* He was just being nice. She wasn't stupid enough to think someone like Clayton O'Neal would be interested in someone like her.

Shaking off the effects of her encounter, she walked over to the elevator, then hesitated when the doors opened and decided to take the stairs instead. She definitely could use all the exercise she could get. Huffing and puffing, she reached the top step, worn out, but pleased at her choice.

It wasn't until she slid her key in the door that she remembered why she had returned to the room in the first place. She stepped inside, reached for the phone, and asked the woman at the front desk to connect her call. As soon as she received a dial tone, she called Leroy on his cell phone. As she waited for him to pick up, she nibbled nervously on her bottom lip and prayed that he wasn't going to be angry that she had called him directly, instead of paging first.

"Reverend Brown."

"Leroy?"

There was a slight hesitation before he spoke. "Brother Barton, thank you for calling me back. Can you hold just a moment?"

It took her a few seconds to realize he was talking to her. It was obvious Darlene was around. She heard mumbling in the background before he finally came on the line again in a lower voice.

"Kayla, I'm at the movies with Darlene and the kids. Aren't you in Jamaica?"

She didn't miss the hint of annoyance that she had disturbed his family outing.

"Yes, I'm in Jamaica." She paused to take a deep breath. "But I needed to ask you a question."

"Sure, but hurry. I'm in the bathroom. If I take too long, Darlene will come looking for me."

She rolled her eyes at his response. Since when did he care what his wife thought? "Someone told me that your wife is pregnant. Is that true?" There, she'd said it. She took a deep breath and prayed that he would give her the answer that she so desperately needed to hear.

He was silent for a moment. "Baby, I was going to tell you about that when you got back."

She gasped. "I can't believe this! I thought the two of you weren't even sleeping together anymore."

"We aren't. I mean, we weren't until one night. Darlene had just gotten news that her mother had had a stroke. She was emotional and I tried to console her, then one thing led to another. I'm sorry. She's my wife, so there is no way I could tell her no."

"I can't believe this. What about us?" She felt her heart crack in two.

"There's still us. I still want to be together . . . only it's going to take a little longer."

"How much longer?"

"Until after the baby is born," he confessed, then quickly added, "What would I look like leaving my wife while's she's pregnant? I am a man of God. It just can't be done."

"Yes, it can. We can leave and move somewhere else. It doesn't matter where as long as we are together," she said, practically pleading.

He gave a strangled laugh that she felt at the pit of her stomach. "Are you crazy? I've worked too hard to get where I am today, and I am not about to lose all that because of a piece of—"

Even though he had caught himself before he'd finished the sentence, she knew what he was about to say and it hurt, really hurt. Kayla again brushed the tears away, then decided to give up as more immediately fell. It was useless to resist. She suddenly felt older than her thirty-seven years. She felt larger than her two hundred ninety-five pounds.

"Baby, I didn't mean that. I am under a lot of pressure right now. I need you in my corner." His voice broke and he paused for so long she was afraid he was crying. "Everything is going to be okay. You'll see. Please, understand."

She felt her resolve weakening. Dang, she hated the power he had over her. "I'm sorry. I do understand. I was just upset to find out this way. However, I do love you." She felt compelled to reassure him that she did love him only she felt betrayed.

There was a lot she wanted to say, but didn't. She wanted to tell him how much she loved him. How it hurt sharing him with another woman. But after what had been unveiled, she knew it was better to keep her feelings to herself for now.

"I'll call you tonight and we can talk. Okay?"

"All right." Kayla took a deep breath. She was wrong for calling and reminding Leroy of the most difficult decision of his life. It was going to be even harder, preparing to leave his wife, because now there would be another child involved. Leroy was hurting far more than she could ever feel. She couldn't wait for the day they would be together, but until then she would have to be patient and wait.

"I love you," she whispered.

He gave a long frustrated sigh. "Kayla, honey, we'll discuss everything tonight." He didn't wait for an answer. He didn't tell her he loved her. Instead, he simply hung up.

Kayla sat there for the longest time holding the phone in her hand. It wasn't until she heard the operator's voice that she also hung up.

Even though he told her he would call later, something told her he would not. Now what was she supposed to do? She had invested two years in their relationship. Was she really supposed to get over him and get on with her life? She just couldn't see it being that easy.

She was startled by a knock at the door. She rose and walked across the room.

"Who is it?"

"It's Lisa."

She reached up and quickly wiped away any traces she had been crying, although there was nothing she could do about the redness. She opened the door and was met by the concerned look on Lisa's face.

"Can I come in?"

She nodded, then turned and walked over to her bed and took a seat. Kayla had known it was just a matter of time before either Nadine or Lisa had come up to see what was really wrong. Renee was probably already at the bar, drinking and flirting.

Lisa moved around and took a seat on the opposite bed and sat directly across from her.

"Are you okay?" she heard her ask.

Kayla tried to put on a fake front. "Sure, why wouldn't I be?"

"I know you're messing around with Reverend Brown."

Her eyes grew large with alarm. "How did you find out?"

"How else?" she admitted with a sympathetic shrug.

Renee. Figures.

Lisa then told her how Renee had seen them at the hotel. She dropped her head to her hands and groaned. If Renee had seen them there was no telling who else had seen them. Although she suspected Renee had found out because she had been creeping her doggone self.

She gave a frustrated breath.

"Have you called him?"

Kayla looked over at her, then nodded. "Yeah, and he admitted it." She shook her head. "How could he treat me like this?"

Lisa looked like she wanted to comment, but remained silent. In the years that Kayla had known her, Lisa had never been one to immediately take sides. So she wasn't shocked when she heard Lisa say, "She's his wife, Kayla. She has every right to carry her husband's child."

She rapidly shook her head, refusing to believe any of it. "I want to carry his child. He swore to me that their relationship was over. That we were going to be together."

How? "Did you expect him to do this? The two of you were committing adultery. He would have had to leave the church and try to find another congregation to accept him."

"I was willing."

"Willing?" Lisa paused to shake her head. "Girl, listen to yourself. You are ready to give up your entire life and everything with it, for a man who would leave his pregnant wife and kids. What's to say he wouldn't do the same to you?"

"He loves me," she argued, defiantly tilting her chin.

"Are you sure? 'Cause it sounds to me like he has a problem." Lisa shook her head slowly from side to side, as though she were explaining right and wrong to a child. "He stands behind the pulpit, preaching to the congregation about sin and getting your life right, and shit, he's violating one of the Ten Commandments. Whatever happened to practicing what you preach?"

She simply shrugged. "He's human. Humans are weak and born sinners."

"And that's his excuse?" Lisa looked appalled. "I bet every time after y'all make love, he says to you, 'Sister Kayla, let's bow our heads and ask the Lord for forgiveness of our sins.'"

Her eyes grew large. How in the world did Lisa know that? Her blood ran warm with humiliation. Was he really playing her for a fool? No, she tossed that thought away. He loved her too much for that. No matter what she had to have faith in him. She needed to believe that what they had was real, because without him she was nothing.

Lisa leaned forward and held her shoulders. "Kayla, you are a beautiful woman. Don't settle. You deserve so much more than that."

"Look at me. I'm not the finest thing around."

"Who says you're not?"

She lowered her head and didn't bother to answer.

Lisa cupped her chin and lifted her head. "Kayla, listen to me," she said, looking fixedly into her eyes to be sure that she was really hearing her. "You are as beautiful as you believe yourself to be. If you don't think it, how the hell you expect anyone else to?"

"Leroy makes me feel so beautiful, so sexy."

"Girl, I'm not going to tell you what to do, but I know for a fact you can do so much better if you would just believe in yourself."

Kayla didn't know how to answer.

"Life is so short. I don't want you sitting back someday wishing you had done things differently. There's an entire world out there waiting to be discovered and you'll never know wasting your time with Reverend Leroy Brown."

That was easy for her to say. Lisa had always been beautiful. She had a pretty face and a shape to die for. Unlike her, she hadn't grown up fat and never fitting in. Even though she had lost five pounds in the last six months, she still felt like an eyesore, a complete replica of her mother.

Kayla had been raised by Delores Sparks, an overweight woman with low self-esteem and a dummy when it came to men. For years, her children watched her jump in and out of one relationship after another that lowered her feelings of self-worth even more. After years of seeing her repeat the cycle, her kids never understood why she just didn't have a clue.

Delores had a knack for attracting losers. Convicts, drug dealers, men without jobs, all of them wanted the same thing, her money and a chance to lay between her fat thighs. One would have thought that as a registered nurse she had some common sense. Instead, she allowed one man after the other to move in. She'd even come home to find her television missing, and still didn't have a clue. It was no wonder her daughters had no idea how to be treated by a man. The countless men they had seen in and out of their mother's life were no better than her alcoholic father. He showed up at their house whenever he needed money, banged their mother, then robbed her wallet.

The only time he spoke to Kayla, he'd say, "How're you doing, Ms. Piggy?"

When she was a child the name didn't bother her. It wasn't until she was called out by a boy in her second-grade class that Kayla first realized the name was meant to be hurtful. As her classmates laughed at her she gazed down at the shirt that kept rolling up over her stomach and realized what they said was true. From that day on she was certain everyone was watching, staring and laughing as she ate lunch, or when they were at gym class and she was always the last to complete a task. She tried to pretend that she didn't feel slighted or talked about.

She tried to pretend that she could not care less what others thought about her, that she was just like everyone else. Only no matter how hard she tried to pretend she could not. Her insecurities about herself followed her through high school, where she felt she never measured up to anyone else. By her junior year, she was wearing a size twenty-two. While all of her friends were dating and having sex and attending parties, she spent her weekends alone. And then she met Anthony.

She had been working at Burger King at the drive-through window. She had seen him several times, and when he finally asked for her number she thought he was trying to get to one of her skinny sisters through her. It wasn't until he called and actually asked to speak to her, then asked her out on her first date, that she finally believed he was serious; however, even then she thought he had ulterior motives.

They had dated for almost two months before she realized he never took her anywhere in public. They always met at his house or hers and when they went to see a movie it was never on Friday night when almost half of Hickman High could be found in the building. It was always on a school night or on Sunday at a matinee.

One evening while his parents were out to dinner, he invited her over. She knew before she arrived, he had planned to have sex. As soon as she was in his house, he ushered her up to his room and tried taking off her clothes. She stopped him because she wanted to talk about their relationship, but also because she was feeling self-conscious about her less-than-desirable body. When she told him no, then demanded to know why he never took her out around their friends, he had the nerve to say, "Be glad I'm even with your fat ass." He then broke it off with her and made her walk home alone. She cried all night and even tried swallowing a bottle of pain relievers, but all that happened was she spent most of the night throwing up. Shit, she was too fat to even OD on a bottle of pills.

She spent a week eating pastries and drinking orange soda. It took another week before Anthony came through the drive-through and over the intercom begged for her forgiveness. She forgave him of course and that night he picked her up from work and she gave him her virginity in the back seat of his mother's Buick LeSabre. It was over before she had thought it had started and was nothing like she had expected. It was painful but she was glad it was over.

She had hoped their relationship would have grown stronger, but nothing changed. They were still never seen in public together. However, she didn't dare say anything out of fear that he would dump her again. He continued to sleep with her at his convenience until she found out she was pregnant. When she told him, he had the nerve to ask, "is it mine?" even though he knew good and well he was the only man she had ever been with. When she decided to keep it, Anthony asked her why in the world did she want to bring another fat kid into the world, and stopped coming around. Kenya was born and even though she looked just like his crusty behind, Anthony still refused to acknowledge her.

Kayla swore off men for the duration of her life and everything was going just fine. For once in her life Delores stepped up to the plate and helped with Kayla's daughter while Kayla finished high school and went on to a technical school where she trained to be a certified administrative assistant. As soon as she landed a job with the University of Missouri, School of Law, she saved up her money and got her own place.

Even though her weight had escalated to a size twenty-four, life was good until Eric walked into her life. Actually, he walked into the office one afternoon. He was a fourth-year law student with an appointment with one of the professors.

She knew she wanted him the second he'd walked through the door. He was everything she wished for. He was handsome, intelligent, and had a warm sense of humor. However, she wasn't the only one in the office interested in him and other women weren't shy about showing their feelings. With all of the beautiful women after him, Kayla knew she didn't have a chance.

Then, one afternoon, he was in the office, and while he waited he struck up a conversation and she found herself relaxing and feeling at ease around him. By the time he left, he had invited her to dinner.

She went home that evening and couldn't believe her luck. She dropped her daughter off with her mother and her latest live-in, a wannabe artist, and met Eric at the steakhouse at six. This was her first date out in public.

The evening started out wonderfully. He complimented her on her pretty face and told her he had a thing for big women. At the end of the night when the waiter arrived with their bill, which included appetizers and dessert, Eric realized he had left his wallet at home. How convenient. She was too up in clouds to know he was playing her and gladly paid for the meal, which he promised to reimburse her for later. He followed her home, where the sex lasted all of three minutes. He told her being with her made him overexcited and next time would be better. A week later she again got stuck paying the bill, and that time he lasted five minutes. Within a month he had moved in after he told her his roommate up and moved out on him and there was no way he could afford the rent himself. She happily made room for him in her closet.

Kayla supported him for almost a year while he finished school, because in the back of her mind she knew her time would come after he passed the bar and found a job. Eric passed on the first try and they celebrated in Las Vegas, which she paid for, of course.

A month later she discovered she was pregnant. She came home excited to find him packing. Apparently he had gotten a job with a prestigious law firm in San Francisco.

"What about us?"

He glanced over and appeared stunned by her question. "What about us?" At her silence he continued with a small chuckle. "You couldn't possibly expect me to marry you." He then moved over toward the bed, dropped a hand to her shoulder, gazed down at her scoldingly. "As a lawyer I have an image to uphold. How could I ever expect to make partner with someone who looks like you on my arm? You do understand, don't you?"

All she could do was nod.

Months later, she found out she wasn't the first of Eric's victims.

His ex-roommate had been another overweight woman. He obviously preyed on fat women with low self-esteem.

She gave birth to Asia. The only contact she had with Eric was the less-than-sufficient check he sent every month. She had thought often about taking him to court but had chickened out.

After that, it had been the same thing: men using her for one reason or another. Finally she met Leroy and everything was different. He loved her. She was certain of that.

She briefly shut her eyes and gently rubbed her temple, trying to calm a headache that was on the verge of exploding.

Lisa wrapped her arms around her. "Girl, fuck him." She pulled back, lowered her tone, and winked. "Believe me, you might not think it now, but everything is going to work out."

Kayla took a deep breath. "Lisa, you are wrong about him. I know you don't understand, but I'm going to have to stand by my man. As soon as his wife has the baby, we're gonna be together. I just know it."

Chapter 14

RENEE

I knew as soon as I told Lisa about Kayla's affair with Columbia's favorite Baptist minister, she was going to race up to the room to talk some sense into Kayla. It was fine with me, because even though Kayla and I are closer, it's better for her to talk to Lisa than me. Lisa has compassion. Me, I would have simply told her to fuck that no-neck mothafucka.

After we finished eating, Nadine and I went to the bar for something to drink. While ordering tequila and pineapple, I spotted Everton watching me again. I waited until the bartender returned with my drink, then left Nadine at the bar, flirting, and strolled over to the front desk.

"I knew you would come." His voice seemed to get sexier every time I heard it.

I sipped my drink and gazed over at him. Everton had a lot of confidence. I have to say I like that in him.

I made a face. "That's 'cause I told you I was going to come."

"Actions speak louder than words."

"Really?" I pursed my lips playfully and leaned forward. "That remains to be seen."

He chuckled at the way I had twisted his words.

"How'd you like the food here?"

"Very good. Is it always like this?"

"Oh, it gets better. In about another hour they'll be preparing dinner."

"Good Lord! I'm going to get fat on this trip."

He perused the length of my body. "You, lovely lady, have nothing to worry about."

I smiled. His accent made even the corniest statement sound good.

"I have to be here early tomorrow morning, so I am spending the night at the hotel."

My interest was immediately peaked. "They let you stay here?"

He nodded his head toward the left. "We have rooms next door that they let us use in cases like this. One of my clerks called out sick, so I'm going to cover for him in the morning, which means I'll be here all night."

"That's nice," I said, pretending I had no idea what he was getting at.

"Are you going to come see me?"

I took another sip from my cup. "Do you want me to see you?"

"I wouldn't have said it if I didn't." He looked like he was trying to suppress a smile.

"Then I guess what you need to do is ask me."

He chuckled. "You American women have such independent spirits. That's what I love most about you." Resting his palms on the counter, he leaned forward. "I want you to come see me tonight."

I knew if I went to see him I was going to end up doing something my hot ass didn't need to be doing. But so what? I'm supposed to be on vacation, right? Like I said before, what happens in Jamaica, stays in Jamaica.

I pretended to pause like I was giving his request some serious thought before finally saying, "All right."

"Good. I'll call you in your room around ten-thirty and let you know where to find me."

Without another word, I nodded, spun on my heels, and rejoined Nadine. She seemed to be having a good time.

It was barely four o'clock and already the area was filled with guests drinking and enjoying themselves—I guess so when it doesn't cost you a damn thing.

I slid onto a bar stool and smiled over at the sexy cocoa-brown, dreadlock-wearing bartender. He wiped the area in front of me with his rag as he smiled down at me. He wasn't bad-looking.

"Pretty lady, you ready for another drink?"

I nodded. "Yeah, hook me up, and don't be so stingy with the tequila."

"No problem, mon." As soon as he turned to reach for a glass I looked down at his nice round ass. Lord, have mercy! Jamaica is turning out to be a black woman's paradise.

Nadine slapped me across the head.

I punched her in the shoulder. "Damn, you play too much!"

"You'll be all right," she replied, then gave an annoying laugh. Nadine doesn't know it, but I was about two seconds away from choking her big-titty ass.

"So, what's up with you and Everton?" Nadine asked, her curiosity obviously piqued with interest.

I shrugged, then turned away so she couldn't see the excitement that I knew was burning from my eyes. "We're going to meet tonight when he gets off, and talk."

Nadine glanced over her shoulder at him then back to me again. "He is fine. You definitely can't go wrong with him."

"No, I guess I can't."

The bartender returned and slid my drink in front of me. I took a sip and that shit was so strong, I knew I was going to be on my ass before nine if I kept this pace up. "Now, that's what's up."

He leaned over the bar and smiled, and then I smiled back. He had the prettiest teeth. I bet he's never been to a dentist in his life, while I'm in a dentist chair every six months and my shit is nowhere near as white.

"What's your name?" I asked since he wasn't wearing a name tag.

"Sylvester."

"Well, I'm Renee, and this here is my girl Nadine."

Nadine sipped her drink. "We already met."

He nodded. "Nadine here is one classy lady."

Classy? Man, he wouldn't be saying that shit if he saw her house. I simply nodded. He winked, then moved down to the other end of the bar to help a customer.

"I think he likes you," I told Nadine.

She glanced over her shoulder to find Sylvester watching her. "He is a cutie." She had a dreamy look on her face. Sylvester wasn't all that, but for Nadine, he was probably right up her alley. I decided to fuck with her a little bit.

"So, while you're in Montego Bay are you going to try and find out if the rumors are true?"

She gave me a puzzled look. "What rumors?"

"That Jamaican men have big dicks."

She gave me a dismissive wave. "Girl, you know that shit ain't no more true than the one about white men having small dicks. I know for a fact that rumor's not true."

I rolled my eyes. "I wouldn't know since I've never been with a white man."

"Well, I have, and Jason had more dick than my ex-husband."

I never could understand how she could mess with Jason. Not only was he white but he was red. No matter how much time he spent in the sun he didn't tan; instead he burned. I met Jason once. He was short and goofy just like her. She looked happy so I was happy for her, then the next thing I know, Nadine receives a call from his wife—a sistah—telling her to stay the hell away from her man. Now being played by a brotha is one thing. A white man . . . I would have run his ass over with my Camry. Not once, not twice, but three damn times.

"Well, I hope you're not looking for another white man, not with all these fine local brothas running around."

She shrugged. "I haven't decided yet. We just got here." She laughed and gave me a look that said she thought my ass was crazy.

"What the hell ever. While you're sitting around trying to decide what to do, I've got an exciting night ahead of me." I sat there sipping a drink while watching Everton. A million things ran through my mind as I thought about what was going to happen to me in his hotel room tonight. The excitement is not knowing what was ahead. However, one thing I was sure of. Tonight was going to involve some powerful sex. Once again, just the thought of him lying between my legs made my coochie wet. I raised my cup to my lips and finished it in two swallows, then gestured for the bartender. I needed another drink, then I was going back to the room to catch a quick nap.

Tonight, I'm going to need all my strength.

Chapter 15

NADINE

Long after Renee had left, Nadine sat at the bar and flirted with Sylvester. He was a nice guy, barely over thirty, and owned his own barbershop. He was cute but he didn't make her pulse race the way Arthur used to. She groaned inwardly. It was going to take more than a pretty face to get inside her panties. Unlike for Renee, sex for Nadine was as much emotional as it was physical, which was why she had never been able to manage having a one-night stand.

Sylvester brought her another drink. Was it her third or was it her fourth? In the last half hour she had sadly lost count.

While he moved to serve a couple standing at the right of the bar, Nadine twirled around on the stool and almost dropped her drink when she noticed the woman sitting at the other end of the bar.

Her long slender legs were crossed. She had short auburn hair and a beautiful butter-pecan complexion. She was definitely a cutie. Just watching the way her pink tongue darted out from between her teeth as she brought her glass to her lips caused Nadine's nipples to harden. She continued to watch her until another woman with a slightly heavier build came and took a seat beside her. After comparing their features, she came to the conclusion the two were definitely sisters. Watching the two, it took Nadine a few seconds before she realized the lovely young woman was looking in her direction.

Realizing she was staring, Nadine swung around on the stool and sighed.

She had been sitting here talking to Sylvester for the last thirty minutes, yet after five minutes, the woman had her yearning to see what was beneath her yellow sundress.

Good Lord! What the hell is my problem?

Nadine had always wondered if something was wrong with her. Even as a teenager, she found herself fascinated with watching women. One day she had even asked her mother about it. Rosie was quick to answer, "Chile, ain't nothing wrong with looking at other women. We are constantly in competition with one another. I'm always admiring the way one woman walks, wishing my boobs were as small as another. I'll even dye my hair to look like an ad that I found in a magazine. That's just the way it is. Women are naturally curious about each other and are always jealous and envious of some shit we don't have. There ain't nothing unnatural about that."

After their conversation, Nadine had felt some relief until one day she had found herself watching a woman in the bathroom change out of a pair of pantyhose with a run. She stood there washing her hands while discreetly admiring the woman's slim shapely legs and dainty feet. When the woman caught her staring, Nadine rushed out the bathroom and down the hall to the elevator. The car arrived just as the woman stepped out of the ladies' room. Nadine stepped into the empty elevator, then held the door for her. The woman thanked her when she boarded. As soon as the door closed, the woman swung around and faced Nadine.

"I saw the way you were looking at me."

Nadine didn't deny it.

"Do you like what you see?"

Her hands shook nervously. "I think you're a beautiful woman."

The woman's lips curled upward. "And so are you." She moved forward until her body was pressed firmly against hers, then she leaned forward and pressed their lips together.

Nadine shared in a hungry kiss that included tongue, while her hand roamed freely across the woman's ass. When the elevator stopped, the woman moved away and quickly exited the car. Nadine stood there frozen. She was breathing hard. Her nipples were hard and erect. Her coochie clenched, demanding some kind of relief. Quickly, she jumped out the elevator just as the doors began to close. The woman was long gone. For a moment, she thought maybe she had imagined the entire thing. However, what she was feeling was something she had never experienced in a dream.

She went home for lunch and made love to her husband, hoping to duplicate what she had felt, and could not. What she had experienced with another woman was like nothing she had ever shared with any man. The feeling scared her and she found herself crying, trying to deny what she was feeling, because she knew it was wrong to feel that way about another woman.

She hid her feelings. But after her marriage ended the feelings and desire resurfaced.

About that time, the local radio station had started a personal hotline where people could meet. Out of curiosity, she called to set up a personal mailbox, with the hope of meeting a nice man. However, while she was going through the different menus, she came across "Women Seeking Women," and she couldn't resist setting up a box. Two days later, she had four messages. Her palms sweated and her heart raced as she listened to each recording. Two were from some manly-sounding bitches, looking for some trick to turn out. The third was looking for someone to bring home to share with her husband. It was the last message that caught her attention.

"My name is Jordan. I have never done this before but I am curious, very curious, and looking for a woman who is also curious. I don't know if I can go through with this, but I want to try being friends first and possibly more later. If not, hopefully I'll have made a new friend."

By the time the message had ended, Nadine was having that same feeling again. Jordan's soft sincere voice had her coochie pulsating and her nipples so hard, she had to reach inside her shirt to massage them. It took her two days before she found the nerve to leave her a message. Then, when Jordan called again, this time she left a phone number.

Nonetheless, once again Nadine tried to deny her feelings and went out on a date with a man who had been asking her for weeks. Yet the entire time all she could do was think about Jordan. She wondered what she looked like. What she was doing now. She ended up cutting her night short. When she arrived home it was around eight on a Saturday evening. She called Jordan. She hadn't expected her to answer, figuring she was out herself.

"Hello."

"May I please speak to Jordan?"

"Is this Nadine?"

"How'd you know it was me?"

Jordan chuckled. "I listened to your message so many times I have your voice memorized in my head." There was a short pause. "I'm so glad you finally called."

"Why?"

"Because I haven't been able to get you off my mind."

Nadine gave a nervous laugh. "That's funny, because I've been feeling the same way."

They started talking like old friends. They each discussed their failed marriages. Nadine had Jordan falling out of her seat when she told her about pulling a gun on Arthur and his blond bitch.

"You are crazy!"

"So I've been told." They laughed, then Nadine sobered. "So, do I sound interesting enough to want to meet? Or am I too crazy for you?"

Jordan laughed softly. "No, I am quite intrigued. Why don't we meet right now?"

"Right now?"

"Yeah, before either of us has a chance to talk ourselves out of this. You drink coffee?"

"All the time."

"Then how about we meet at that small coffee shop on Ninth Street."

Nadine gasped. "I love their caramel latte."

"Ooh! So do I."

"All right, then. That sounds like a plan."

"How about in one hour?"

Nadine glanced over at the clock, which read nine-thirty. "All right, I'll be there. How will I know it's you?"

"You'll know." She hung up.

Nadine sat on the end of the bed, heart racing as she tried to decide if maybe she was making a big mistake.

You'll never know if you don't try.

She got up, changed into jeans and a red button-down blouse that complemented her large breasts. She pulled her long, thick hair into a simple ponytail, frowned, then yanked the rubber band from her hair and pulled out her curling iron. As she curled her hair, she couldn't believe how excited she was about meeting Jordan. She styled her hair in a simple flip that she tucked behind her ears. She reached for her purse and headed out the door.

She found parking close to the coffee shop and strode into the building. In one quick glance, she realized she was the only black female in the room. She moved to a table in the center and waited. She didn't have to wait long. As soon as the door opened she knew it was Jordan.

Peanut butter color. Short honey-blonde hair. Hazel eyes. A wide friendly smile. She was petite with a small narrow waist and generous hips and thighs. Their eyes met and Nadine felt like a teenager on her first date. Her heart banged beneath her chest and she had to put her hands in her lap because they were shaking so much.

Jordan moved to her table and smiled. "Hi."

"Hi, yourself."

Jordan dropped a hand to her waist and struck a dramatic pose. "So, what do you think?"

"I think you're beautiful."

"So are you."

They giggled like schoolgirls and spent the rest of the night sipping coffee and talking about life until the shop closed at one. The two left and when Jordan reached down and clasped Nadine's hand, Nadine curled her fingers around Jordan's and went for a stroll.

"Gosh, this feels so right."

Nadine nodded because she also felt that way. "Yes, it does."

They found a private spot at the edge of the park and Jordan asked to stop. "I want to kiss you so badly."

"Then do it."

She leaned forward and pressed her lips to hers. Once. Twice. Nadine reached out and wrapped her arms around her and pulled

her snug against her. They leaned against the tree, kissing and groping each other for what felt like forever. When they finished, they
held hands back to their cars, where they said good-bye and each
headed home.

The next morning Nadine had regrets. She ignored Jordan's
phone calls and tried denying her feelings for two weeks before she
agreed to see her again. Each visit after that was more powerful than
before, and before she knew it she had fallen in love. Now she was
afraid and embarrassed that she had fallen in love with a woman.
Jordan wanted to be public with their relationship, while she wanted
to continue to keep it behind closed doors.

She loved Jordan. That much she was sure of. Where she wanted
to go with their relationship was something she was uncertain of.
Before she had left for Jamaica she had broken things off with
Jordan, telling her she needed time and space to think about where
her life was headed.

Shaking her head, she cleared the dangerous thoughts from her
mind and returned to the present. Glancing toward the end of the
bar, she noticed the women were gone. As she stirred her watered-
down drink, she realized it was probably for the best. Not that she
had had any intentions of acting on her feelings. The last two days,
Nadine had convinced herself that time was all she needed. *I am not
a lesbian,* she told herself as she sipped her drink. She had just been
naturally curious about what it was like to be with another woman.
She had read that college girls do it all the time, yet they go on to
have healthy heterosexual relationships.

Glancing at Sylvester, she smiled. All she had to do was meet a
man that intrigued her and had the power to make her forget about
Jordan, then the rest would be easy.

Chapter 16

KAYLA

It was breezy outside, but she didn't care. She moved out toward the ocean. Wet sand and water ran between her toes. Dark shades hid her eyes, allowing her to cry in private. She passed couples kissing and holding hands, and it only made her feel worse. The second Renee had arrived in their room, she had left so she could sulk in private.

Letting go was not easy, at least not for her. Her best friend could jump from man to man without batting an eyelash, while she herself jumped in head first with her heart. Moving on was a slow, delicate process that took time. And she wasn't ready yet to let go.

All she could think about was if she hadn't come on this trip, she probably wouldn't have spoken to Nadine. After all, there were times when the two didn't speak for weeks, before one of them would pick up the phone to see what the other was doing. Which was why, if she was at home, she might have never found out about the baby. If so, then everything in her life would still be perfect. But then again, maybe she would have found out anyway. If Leroy and his wife had just gone to the doctor's, chances were they would have announced it one weekend during church services. Unless of course he had been trying to hide the pregnancy from her—then he might have convinced his wife to hold out a little while longer.

Kayla wandered down toward the dock, where there were kayaks available for renting. On the end of the pier were two chaise longues. Neither was occupied. She decided it was the perfect spot to sit and feel sorry for herself.

After Lisa left her with something to think about, Kayla sat out on the balcony, pondering everything she had said. She knew her friend meant well, but no one could begin to understand that what she felt for Leroy came only once in a lifetime. She had even been contemplating calling him back and apologizing for calling him, when Renee had returned to the room. Instead, she had quickly grabbed her glasses and high-tailed it out of there. The last thing she needed was to listen to her homegirl's big mouth.

Slowly, she moved down the pier, grateful that she had found a nice quiet spot at the edge of the beach. She stepped around one of the longue chairs and took a seat, then closed her eyes.

Kayla took a deep breath, trying to hold off the next round of tears, but found her efforts a big waste of time. She was so ready to go home and talk to Leroy in person. She needed to see his eyes when he spoke so she'd know if what he said was true. Lisa had gotten her to thinking. Maybe he was no better than the rest, but to her something was so much better than nothing at all. She wasn't like Nadine and Renee, they liked living alone. She did not. She wanted, needed, someone to make her feel good about herself. Taking a deep breath, she opened her eyes and stared ahead.

She heard movement and looked to her right in time to see a man cut through the blue water. His chocolate skin glistened. He emerged from the ocean and moved to where she was sitting, the hard muscles of his legs contracting as he walked. The red swim trunks clung to his body, emphasizing what the good Lord gave him and accenting his chiseled abdominals. He moved to the chaise beside her and reached for a large beach towel that she hadn't noticed until now and rubbed it across his face and head.

"Hi, again."

She glanced over the rim of her sunglasses at Clayton. From where she was sitting he was like a giant towering over her. "Hi."

"Do you mind if I sit here?" he asked as he wrapped the towel around his waist.

She shrugged. "You were here first."

"I guess I'll take that as a yes," he said as he lowered into the chair beside her.

Kayla gave him an apologetic smile. "Sorry, I didn't mean to be rude. I came out here to be alone."

"So did I. My roommate is entertaining."

She turned and glanced out at the ocean again, hoping if she stopped talking he would get the hint and do the same. No such luck.

"Where are your friends?"

She shrugged. "Somewhere around here. I'm typically the quiet one of the bunch."

"So am I."

She raised her brow. "You are a professional football player. I can't see you doing anything that doesn't draw attention."

"How'd you know I play football?"

She frowned as she realized she had made a mistake and had admitted to knowing who he was. The last thing she wanted was for him to get the wrong idea. "It's not that hard. Look at you."

"What about me?"

She realized where he was going. "You're wasting your time. I'm not one of your groupies. I have no intentions of blowing up your head."

He chuckled lightly as he leaned back in the chair. "You are truly genuine."

She was surprised by this choice of words. No one had ever called her genuine. "What are you doing in Jamaica?"

"My boy is getting married here on Monday."

"Wow, that's going to really be something."

"Yes, it is. I'm so proud of him. I can only hope to find someone as special. What about you? Are you married? Dating?"

She gave a painful laugh. "No, none of the above."

"That's truly a shame."

Kayla simply shrugged.

"What are you getting into tonight?"

"Partying here, I guess."

"Have dinner with me."

She swung around on her seat just to make sure she had heard him correctly. "What?"

"You heard me. There's a nice seafood restaurant not too far from here."

Why in the world would he want to be seen with me? He was staring so hard, Kayla began to feel uncomfortable. She sat up straighter, trying to draw less attention to her body, and folded her arms across her chest. She looked a mess. Why did he have to pick now to ask her out to dinner? Not that it mattered. She could have worn her best dress and she still would be inadequate in comparison. Someone like him could have anyone he wanted, so why would he ask her out to dinner unless he had other motives. "No. I don't think that's a good idea."

"Why not?"

"Because . . ."

"Because what?" He was definitely persistent.

"Because it's just not a wise choice. Lately I've been making a lot of decisions before I've had a chance to think them through clearly. I refuse to do that again. I know that going out with you is not a good idea."

"All right, maybe next time." He then opened his book and began to read.

Kayla sighed and adjusted her large body on the chair. She couldn't believe he had given up so easily. If he had asked her again, she might have considered. "Men," she mumbled before closing her eyes and getting lost in her thoughts again.

Chapter 17

RENEE

I took extra care to make sure no one saw me going into Everton's room. One reason was because I didn't want to risk him losing his job. The second reason was I might want to holler at someone else tomorrow and being seen would fuck up that chance.

I knocked once and Everton instantly opened the door. The minute I stepped into the room, I was pushed back gently against the door with his lips pressed against mine. I wrapped my arms around him as the pressure of the kiss increased. He pushed his tongue into my mouth and I willingly opened. I met him stroke for stroke. Damn, there was nothing better than a brotha that could kiss.

We then moved to the bed, where we sat and drank a pair of Red Bulls. I talked about my kids and he told me that he lived at home taking care of his disabled mother. I liked the way he stroked my arm as he spoke. The contact was really starting to turn me on. By the time we had finished our first beers, I was stroking his leg. When the beer was almost gone, Everton took the bottle from my hand and put it on top of the nightstand. He then leaned forward and pressed his lips against mine again. I welcomed the warm feeling and eagerly opened my mouth so I could feel his tongue.

As soon as I lay back on the bed, he reached down between my legs. He raised his head when he realized that I wasn't wearing any panties beneath the miniskirt. Dropping down to his knees, he wasted no time getting his eat on between my thighs. His tongue skillfully played tricks between my legs. It felt so good my eyes rolled to the back of my head. I forgot where I was and who I was with. All that mattered was what was happening now.

With his tongue deep inside my coochie, Everton reached up and caressed my sensitive nipples through the cotton of my halter top. Desperate for his fingers against my bare skin, I reached up and quickly pulled my shirt over my head. Everton immediately captured a nipple between his fingers as he continued his snack. Within minutes, he had me squirming on top of the bed. I thought I had an out-of-body experience, because I came like crazy. I couldn't believe it when I squirted all over his face.

Everton moved from teasing my clit, passed my belly button with his tongue, and started suckling my nipples. I felt his erect penis against my clit and I wiggled wildly beneath him.

"Fuck me now, dammit!"

I didn't have to tell him twice. He rose off me and lowered his pants. I slid comfortably to the center of the bed, anxious to have some of him. I slid a pillow beneath my head and watched as he lowered his boxers, then he moved to the side of the bed and put his dick in my face.

My mouth dropped.

Never again would I believe the hype about Jamaican men having big dicks, because this was not the case. Everton's dick was so little I could have used a pair of tweezers to jack his ass off. Damn! He pushed the small head against my cheek and I felt warm precum against my skin. Disgusted, I quickly rolled away.

"You got the wrong one, baby. I don't suck dick." Shit. I suck dick. I just wasn't sucking his little wiener.

"You like it back shot?"

My brow rose. "What's back shot?"

"You Americans call it 'doggy'."

I tried to keep a straight face, 'cause he sounded so much like Arnold Schwarzenegger.

As short as his dick was, doggy was probably the only way I would be able to feel anything. "Yeah, I like doggy." I glanced at his little dick again and sighed. The sooner I get this over with, the sooner I could get back to my room. "You got a condom?"

He nodded toward the side table. "In the top drawer."

I leaned over and removed a brand new pack, then ripped one open and held it out to him.

"I want you to put it on." He gave me a smile that I had thought was cute, and now was getting on my damn nerves.

Damn, the last thing I wanted to do was to touch his little-ass thing. I leaned forward and rolled it over the length with ease, which came as no surprise, considering the size. Rolling onto my stomach, I tucked a pillow beneath my lower abdomen, then reared back on my hands and knees, lifting my ass straight up in the air.

I felt him climb onto the bed behind me and position himself between my legs. He held onto my hips and entered me with ease. Unlike John, at least Everton could find my hole.

He pumped his hips and I rocked back meeting him halfway. He was stroking me slowly, gently, and I wanted to scream. I couldn't feel shit! I wanted him to fuck me. I could have laughed, but it was so sad, because I had gotten myself into this shit, and the only way to get out of it was to help him come as quickly as possible. I moved my hips back and forth to encourage him to speed up his efforts. It did the trick, because he began pumping his hips so hard against me, his balls slapped against my clit. But damn, I still couldn't feel shit.

"You've got some good stuff," he moaned.

Why me, was all I could think about as he continued to moan like some sick animal. If I'd had a gun I would have shot him and put him out of his misery.

"This is my pussy," he chanted as he continued to pump away.

Yeah, whatever. I tightened my coochie as much as I could, hoping I could feel just a little something. I could tell he was seconds away from coming.

"Whose pussy is it?" he moaned.

I rolled my eyes. "It's your pussy." I gave a few fake moans. "All yours."

"Oooh, weee!"

He yelled so loudly I was afraid someone was going to call management.

After he was done, he fell down and covered my body, raining kisses along my neck and back.

"That was wonderful. We made a connection."

What in the world did we connect?

He kissed me again. "I think your friends are going to be so jealous when they find out."

No, they won't, because I don't have any intentions of telling them shit. All I wanted was for this nightmare to be over.

I wiggled from underneath him. "I better get back."

"Why so soon? I wanted to make love to you all night."

Heaven forbid! "No, my kids are calling me in the next thirty minutes and I need to be in my room."

"Okay, I understand. Can you come back?"

"I can . . . yeah, sure." I slid out of the bed and started looking for my clothes. As I dressed, he laid there smiling like a damn fool.

"You are so beautiful."

"Thanks," I answered without even looking his way.

He slid off the bed, the used condom still on his dick, and moved toward me. I ducked and moved around him, then reached for my top.

He chuckled as he stepped into the bathroom to dispose of his load. As soon as he shut the door, I searched frantically for my shoes. As I slid them on, I heard a strange sound coming from the bathroom. I crept slowly toward the door in time to hear a grunt, followed by the sound of a turd dropping into the toilet.

I couldn't believe what I was hearing. That no-dick bastard didn't even have the decency to wait until after I had left to handle his business. Ugh! I grabbed my key card and flew out the door.

I went back to the room and was glad that Kayla was gone. Quickly, I shed my clothes, hopped in the shower and practically scrubbed my skin raw. I felt so dirty and ashamed that I started to cry.

Already I was regretting my behavior. It was times like this that I wished I had someone to talk to. All my life, all I ever had in my corner was my big sister. If I had questions about boys I asked her. When I started my period, it was she I had gone to. But there were also times like now when I couldn't go to my sister and I wished I had someone else I could turn to, like a mother or a father. As far as I'm concerned, I have neither. Physically, my parents were there, emotionally they were not.

My mother, a bipolar crackhead, has been in and out of my life since I was sixteen years old. Last week she had checked herself into a thirty-day treatment program, but I know it won't last. She has tried and failed so many times before. According to her, the crack helps her stop hearing the voices in her head.

I never knew my real father. He and my mother never married. She had Lisa at sixteen and me three years later. My father died in a car accident on his way to work one morning when I was barely two years old.

My mother married Paul Perry when I turned five. He instantly fell in love with Lisa. Me, he never liked. I never understood why. Whenever there was something broken it was my fault. Whenever something was missing, it was my fault. If I got a B, it should have been an A. If it was an A, then he said the work must have been too easy. There just wasn't any pleasing that man. Nothing I ever did was right and no matter how hard I tried, the worse it got for me. I got my ass whooped so often, my stepfather left the belt hanging on the back of my bedroom door for easy access.

I tried telling my mother, but she was never around. Instead, she was always in the streets, hanging with her friends or, as I heard my stepfather say on several occasions when I was too young to understand, "simply ho'ing."

When my little brother was born, life only got worse for me, because as far as my stepfather was concerned, Andre could do no wrong. When I was ten, I almost smothered the little darling because I had put a pillow over his face to keep my stepfather from hearing him cry. If Lisa hadn't walked in the room when she did, there is no telling what might have happened.

By the time I was thirteen, I gave up trying to make him happy and became openly defiant. I started talking back. I made up lies and told my mother so that she would get in his ass. One time he slapped me so hard I hit the wall. As soon as I realized what he had done, I kicked him so hard in his nuts, he never touched me again.

When I turned fourteen my parents divorced. On the weekends,

Paul would pick up my sister and brother, but I wasn't invited. I'd complained to my mother, who simply said, "Why do you care? It's not like you like the man anyway."

What she didn't understand was that it hurt to be rejected by him. Despite everything he was the only father I knew.

It was around this time my mother got introduced to crack. She started dating this drug dealer who tried to control her. He had found the perfect way. She stopped going to work. She would spend every night crying and all day sleeping. I tried telling my grandmother that something was wrong, but she refused to admit that her daughter was anything but perfect. We barely had food yet my mother was too proud to apply for food stamps. She'd rather starve her children than accept help. I had to forge her signature just to get free lunch at school, because she refused to complete the form.

When we were evicted from our apartment on the South Side of Chicago, my stepfather took Lisa and Andre to live with him. My mom and I moved to Missouri, across the street from my grandmother. I was the one who had to watch the woman stare off into space all day, laughing for no particular reason, crying for the littlest thing. It had gotten so bad, I stayed out on the streets as long as I could and didn't come home until it was time to go to bed, only to find my mother still sitting in the same spot she was when I had left that morning. I missed Lisa and Andre. They weren't even allowed to call me. Paul would fly them down in the summer for one week. I'd see all the nice clothes they had, when I was struggling to work on the weekends at Dairy Queen. Most of the time, I'd just sign the back of my paycheck and hand it over to my mom, just so we'd have lights and gas. When she started smoking again, I started paying the bill myself.

I was so lonely, I dated one boy after another looking for something—what, I do not know. All I wanted was to feel loved and needed for whatever length of time I could get. I lost my virginity to a senior who told me he liked my smile. All I had been was just a quick fuck. Hurt and devastated, I talked to my big sister about it when she called. She told me to let it go and move on. It was easy for her to say. She was dating Michael, the only man she'd ever been with.

The only happiness I had in my life was Mario.

I met him on my sixteenth birthday. My cousin Matthew came and got me so I could hang out with him and his crew. All his friends were either in their twenties or too busted for my taste. However, I had fun just the same. He took me to this party over in the projects and introduced me to his boy. Mario, although short, had the prettiest dark brown eyes with thick eyelashes and bushy brows. He had this beautiful white smile that lit up a room, and damn, the brotha could dress. When he asked me to dance, I eagerly said yes. He held me in his arms as we slow danced and I think in that instant, as the warmth of his body seeped into me, I fell in love.

My junior year my mama was hooked on crack again and I wouldn't see her for days at a time. I moved in with Mario, and it wasn't until then that I discovered how possessive he was. I couldn't visit my friends, participate in after-school activities or anything else teenagers did. All I could do was come straight home from school and cater to his needs. The first time he hit me, he cried afterwards like a big baby. Instead of being mad, all I could do was think, "Wow, he really must love me."

As soon as Lisa turned twenty, she had our mother committed to a mental health and drug treatment facility, then she moved to Missouri so that she could be close to me while she attended college.

Tilting my head, I allowed the spray of warm water to beat across my face as I asked myself, was that why I stayed with John for so long? Because he represented something in my life that I had never had before? Stability? Is that why it was so hard to let go? I didn't know. I just didn't know. Sometimes I feel like I am losing my mind. My psychiatrist had changed my prescriptions so many times I don't know if I am coming or going. One day I'm ADHD. Next visit I'm diagnosed with depression, and most recently, she says I am possibly bipolar, like my mother. Oh, wow, lucky me.

I shook my thoughts as I stepped out of the shower. My head was spinning from too much tequila. I hoped that when I woke up, it would have all been a dream.

Chapter 18

RENEE

"Renee, get your lazy ass up!"

"No," I muttered, then rolled over on my side, ignoring Nadine's chipper voice.

"Come on, sis, you're missing one helluva party."

Party? My sister knew exactly how to get my attention. I was instantly wide awake. Lisa and Nadine were sitting on my bed, in their pajamas.

I yawned away the last remnants of sleep and did a full body stretch before propping myself up on one elbow and glancing at the pair again. "Damn, where y'all heifers going dressed like that?"

Nadine tossed a pillow at my head. "It's a pajama party, fool."

"Dammit, Nadine, quit playing!" Annoyed, I tossed the pillow right back at her ass. She ducked and started laughing. Silly wench. "Where's Kayla?"

Lisa's face sobered. "In the bathroom. She's not going. She doesn't feel comfortable being seen in her pajamas."

I shook my head. I wished there was something I could do to boost her self-esteem.

I propped myself up on the bed. "Stand up so I can see what y'all got on."

Nadine was wearing shorts and a top with pink polka dots and pink flip-flops on her feet, while Lisa wore a short blue nightshirt.

I sprung from the bed, in panties and a sports bra, and moved over to the drawer, where I emptied the contents of my suitcase and pulled out a short skimpy green number I bought at Victoria's Secret.

As usual, my sister disapproved. "I know you're not planning to wear that."

I tossed her a look. "I don't know why not."

"You're not covering anything."

"Only the important parts. I'll even wear panties. I promise." I love to rattle my sister's chain.

Nadine crossed her legs and gave me a look of envy. "Shit, I ain't mad at her."

"I'm glad someone agrees." I stepped over and we high-fived, then I reached under my bed for a pair of white three-inch pumps to complement the look.

Kayla stepped out of the bathroom. Her head was down, but I could tell she was still upset about finding out her man was still screwing his wife.

Lisa moved to stand next to me, then mumbled close to my ear, "Renee, don't say shit about the reverend."

Yeah, yeah. "Kayla, girl, how come you're not going?"

She shook her head as she lowered onto her bed. "I really don't feel up to partying tonight."

"Girl, fuck that no-neck mothafucka!" I spat.

Lisa kicked me in the shin.

"Ow!"

"I told you to keep your damn mouth shut," she mumbled under her breath.

Lisa knows me well enough to know I don't know how to keep my mouth shut. I wouldn't have gotten as far as I have if I had. I especially couldn't stay quiet when a man's the cause of my girl's unhappiness.

Kayla shook her head again. "No, I'm going to hang out at the room. Leroy's supposed to call and I don't want to miss it."

Lisa tried to grab me, but I stepped as far away from Lisa as I could before saying, "Girl, what's it gonna take for you to realize that man is playing you?"

Kayla looked at me and I swear she gave me the meanest look I ever did see. "Renee, I'd rather you stay out of my business. What I have with Leroy is real."

"What you have is a bunch of bullshit." I was tempted to say more but Lisa looked like she was about to scratch my eyes out.

"I don't expect you to understand but I do expect you to respect my decision."

"Whatever," I mumbled as I snatched up my gown and disappeared into the bathroom. I slipped the sports bra over my head and then slipped into the sexy green gown. Tonight I was going to have fun. If Kayla wanted to spend the evening waiting by the phone like a lost puppy then that was her stupidity. I never could understand a weak woman. What was even worse was a stupid woman.

Chapter 19

KAYLA

She gets on my last nerve.

Kayla stepped out onto the balcony and lowered herself into a plastic chair, sighing with frustraton. Renee was her girl, but some days she wished she had the nerve to hit her dead in her big mouth. Her slutty ways were bad enough, but when she butted her nose where it wasn't needed, that was another story altogether.

From the balcony, she watched the three walking down the path toward the party. Renee was talking loudly and cussing up a storm, as usual. A giggle escaped Kayla's lips. Gosh, it was hard to stay mad at her. Sometimes she couldn't stand her, but other times she couldn't imagine life without her. Renee had stood by her through thick and thin. When there was no one else, there had always been Renee, standing by her side, taking the punches right along with her, and even fighting her battles for her when she had been too weak to do it herself. As she stared off into the ocean, she reminisced on the years.

What she loved most about Renee was that she was a free-spirited individual who lived her life on her own terms with no regard to what others thought or said. For years, Renee allowed her to live vicariously through her. She'd never had the guts to be freaky like her girl, but at least she got to enjoy the wild stories that Renee shared with her. Kayla actually lived for Saturday afternoons, when the two of them would go out to lunch and Renee would give her an animated play-by-play.

Kayla leaned back comfortably in the chair as she remembered the good old days. The wildest she had ever gotten was when they used to spend weekends on the highway, traveling to the NCO club to party with hundreds of lonely soldiers. That was long before she had given her life over to God. But after a broken heart that was destined to stay raw, she decided to leave the soldiers alone.

She had never been one to hang out in the club, but if Renee asked she usually tagged along. Tonight, however, Kayla wasn't in the mood for partying; instead she wanted to stay in the room, drown in self-pity, and wait for Leroy's call.

She rose and moved back into the quiet drab room and took a seat on the end of the bed. God, she missed Leroy. For two years she had spent her nights lying awake in bed, planning a life together with the man she loved. Now all she could think about was getting back home and making everything right between them. Calling him and accusing him of using her had been a mistake. And she knew that now because it was well after midnight and he still hadn't called as he had promised. Two hours ago, she tried leaving a message on his pager, and had even called his cell phone again to discover he had turned it off. With no other choice, she left him an apology, but he had yet to respond. Hopefully he could call her tonight as he had promised.

Damn, Nadine.

If she hadn't mentioned Darlene's pregnancy none of this would have happened. She curled into a ball and wondered if, before his wife had found out she was pregnant, he had ever had any intentions of telling her he was leaving her.

Kayla bit her lip and lay back staring at the ceiling and told herself not to cry. Fighting the emotions was making her sick to her stomach. A few minutes later she raced into the bathroom as fast as she could maneuver her large body. She lifted the toilet seat just in time to empty the contents of her stomach. Using the walls for support, she managed to get back in bed. She rolled onto her back, breathing hard as she tried to get her stomach to settle down. Then she lay there and considered her next move.

Five classes short of graduating, she quit attending evening classes at Columbia College so she could be readily available when Leroy called. When Darlene was "too busy" she would travel with him—in separate cars, of course—to visit surrounding churches. While he preached, she would find a seat in one of the back pews and listen proudly to her man as he ministered to the congregation. After church she would slip out and meet him at a hotel off the highway. They never went out together in public. He couldn't take that chance. Instead, she would stop and pick up something along the way, and the two would lie across the bed and feed each other before getting under the covers and having dessert.

Kayla rolled onto her side and wrapped her arms around her waist. Now what was she going to do? Go back to school? She had dropped out of school because as a preacher's wife she wouldn't need a career. Her job as the first lady of the church would have been more than sufficient. She would have been visiting the sick and shut-in, arranging programs at church, and so forth. She had every intention of giving her hundred and fifty percent, and that wouldn't have been possible with a career of her own. That was okay because she loved Leroy so much she was willing to give her life if she had to.

Now what?

She stared off into the dark star-studded sky. The girls were probably having a ball. They always had. Each one of them had something she wished she'd had.

Renee's hot tail was about to dump husband number three. However, at one time she had worked two jobs while attending college full-time. She now had a bachelor's in journalism, a master's in English, and was a best-selling author. She hadn't made any real money yet, but with her determination and conviction, Kayla knew it was only a matter of time.

Nadine was an attorney. She'd survived a nasty divorce and successfully raised her son alone. Last year, she bought a bad-ass four-bedroom house, although she didn't know a doggone thing about keeping it clean. Nevertheless, she and Renee were proof you didn't need a man to be successful.

Lisa, on the other hand, was proof that there was such a thing as happily ever after. She met Michael in high school. They went on to attend college together, where she studied to be a pastry chef. Michael owned one of the largest car lots in the city.

All three of them had something she wanted. She had been searching her entire life, and so far she still hadn't found it. Would things ever get better for her? she wondered.

The Lord helps those who help themselves.

She closed her eyes as the tears returned. "Lord, I don't know how. Please help me to find myself."

She could go back to school and finish, only her heart wasn't in it. Instead, she would rather wait for her man to make good on his promise.

Kayla scowled. Man, she was pissed by the way Leroy had held back information about his wife. However, she wasn't ready to give up hope yet. Despite his betrayal and his lies, she loved him deeply, and believed he loved her also. She was willing to wait until the baby was born. Even if it took another year, she was going to be waiting for him with open arms. She didn't care if she had to meet him across town at seedy hotels that rented by the hour. All that mattered was being together. Love made you do crazy things like that.

Now she just wasn't so sure that he'd still have her. She had possibly pissed him off. Her bold attempt at calling him might have cost her her man.

Tears streamed down her face as she feared the worse: finding herself alone again.

Chapter 20

RENEE

After my evening with Everton, I wasn't in the partying mood, but I have to admit that once I walked in the shit was off the hook. The DJ was in the corner, spinning the newest remix of "Lean Back."

"He-e-ey!" I sang as I moved through the door, gyrating my hips to the music.

Lisa laughed and shook her head at me. "Oh, Lord, she ain't even had a drink yet and already her ass is ready to party."

I whipped my body around, placing my left hand on my hip. "Shit, I've been drinking all damn day."

Nadine agreed. "Yes, she has."

I nudged her with my hip. "Bitch, your ass been drinking just as much as I have."

"That's because you're a bad influence."

I doubt that. Nadine's about the only one other than me that can hold her own.

Damn, there were so many men in here, I didn't know which side of the room to begin with. I followed my sister's lead to an empty table at the far right of the room. I barely had my ass in the chair when some brotha tapped me on the shoulder. I swung around and my mouth dropped. Damn! His head was so big I don't know how he managed to hold it up.

"Come on sexy, let's dance." He started moving toward the dance floor as if I was stupid enough to follow.

"Sorry, homey, I got to get my drink on first."

He started break dancing and roboted his ass across the floor.

Nadine and Lisa chuckled.

I gave them the finger. "Forget y'all. I'm going to go get me a drink."

"Get me one, too," Nadine called.

I wiggled my way through the crowd and stepped up to the bar and spotted Sylvester.

"St. Louis, what is up?"

"Not a damn thing except I don't have a drink in my hand."

"What can I get you, my friend?"

"You know how I do. Tequila and pineapple for me, and a rum and Coke for Nadine."

His face lit up at the mention of her name. "Nadine is here."

I tilted my head to the right. "Yeah, she's over in the corner with my sister."

"Tell her to come and holler at a brother."

I tried not to laugh at his attempt at sounding hip. He sounded the way the Prince of Wales would after spending the afternoon with Snoop Dog.

While he made the drinks, I wiggled my hips to Destiny's Child's "I Need a Soldier." Sing it, girls. They know exactly what a sistah needs in her life. Now if I could just find a soldier on this island, I just might be all right.

You would think after my earlier disaster, the last thing in the world I would be looking for is another man. I mean a sistah can take only so much disappointment in one day. However, nothing ventured, nothing gained. If I wanted to find my Mandingo prince before this trip was over, I couldn't quit looking after one flop. Hell, naw. I had to keep up the mission.

My eyes traveled around the room. Tall. Short. Fat. Skinny. And finally to the left of the room, I spotted fine.

The football players had a long table. The wives and girlfriends were there, of course. But Clayton and another player were sitting at the end of the table, unaccompanied. He was wearing boxer shorts with no shirt. Wide chiseled abs. Thick neck. At that exact moment, I knew before the night was over, I was going to ask Clayton O'Neal to dance.

Now I know what they say about ballplayers. Most of them have dicks the size of toothpicks. But there is no way in hell that could possibly be true about all of them. Why else would women be falling all over themselves to marry them? Okay, maybe the money does have a lot to do with it but, nevertheless, it's going to take a lot more than money to keep a sistah happy. Believe me. I know.

"St. Louis, here's your drinks."

"Thanks, Sylvester." When he leaned his elbow against the bar, I knew he wanted to chitchat. I was on a mission, but decided I could spare a few minutes. As a matter of fact, I could finish my drink and get a refill before I left. I tipped my cup and took a drink.

Another guy behind the bar moved over and stood beside him. Medium height. Dreadlocks. Mustache. Dimpled smile. I must say, he wasn't half bad.

"Hello," he said.

"Hello," I returned between sips.

"My name is Carlos. What's yours?"

Before I could even speak, Sylvester's cock-blocking ass intervened.

"Carlos, man, this here is Renee and she is already spoken for."

Hold up a minute. "Whadda mean I'm spoken for?"

Sylvester looked at Carlos, not me. "She and Everton are an item."

I practically choked on my drink. "The hell we are."

He was cheesing like he had a secret to tell. "He told us you are his new American babe."

I rolled my eyes and slid off the stool. "You tell Everton to kiss my black ass!"

I grabbed my drinks and stormed back to the table. I can't believe Everton's been running his damn mouth. I was tempted to leave the party and go back to his room and cuss his ass out, but decided I'd be better off staying the fuck away from his little-dick ass.

I flopped down into my seat and lowered the drinks onto the table. Nadine was on the floor, dancing and Lisa was sitting in her chair bobbing her head.

"What's wrong with you?" she asked the minute she saw my face.

I rested my elbow on the table before I spoke. "Girl, can you believe Everton has everyone thinking I'm his American babe."

She laughed. "That's what you get for sleeping with him."

I let out an exaggerated sigh. "I didn't sleep with him."

"Yeah, whatever."

"It ain't no whatever. I went to his room. We talked. I let him kiss me and cop a few feels, then I left."

"I'm your sister, and I know you better than anyone."

"If you did, then you would know I didn't sleep with him." I rose and moved out across the dance floor. My sister makes me so sick sometimes. She really thinks she knows me. Well, she doesn't. Okay, so maybe I did sleep with Everton, but how does she know that for sure? And I damn sure ain't telling her.

I moved across the room where Clayton was sitting with some Kermit-the-Frog-looking dude. Boldly, I stepped up to them.

"Damn, baby, you fine as hell!"

I glanced at his amphibian friend, smiled, then looked back at Clayton again. "Want to dance?"

"Sure." He put his drink on the table and followed me out onto the dance floor.

They were playing Usher's, "Yeah." I found us a spot in the middle of the floor. As I moved my hips to the beat, Clayton—bless his heart—swayed from side to side.

"You're not much of a dancer, are you?"

He gave me a boyish smirk. "Nah, but at least I got rhythm."

I laughed. "That you do."

"You probably already know this, but I'm Clayton O'Neal."

"I'm Renee Moore. Now why would I already know your name?"

"You don't know who I am?"

I played dumb. I learned a long time ago that athletes are challenged by women who aren't falling all over their asses. "Should I?"

He looked pleased by my answer. "No. It's a pleasure to meet you, Renee."

We danced several songs. If I could judge the way a brother moves in the bed by the way he dances, Clayton would lose. He continued to do that same tired dance. You would think with all the parties they attend that Clayton would have a little more soul. Oh, well, maybe he just needed someone to teach him. Now, dancing I don't mind giving a little assistance. Sex is a different story altogether.

My girls are always talking about you got to show a man what you like. No, I don't. Either he knows or he doesn't. I don't have time to teach a man how to fuck. Now, my brother says the problem with women is that they expect brothas to read their minds. And yes, for me, that is true. The first time, I'll try to steer you away from what I don't like, and closer to what I do. I'll moan to try to give you a hint, but if you can't catch on, your ass is history.

The music slowed down and Clayton pulled me gently into the circle of his arms, and, hallelujah, he moved like a brotha who knew what he was doing. See, that's what I'm talking about. He swayed from side to side, one-one-two, one-one-two, and I wrapped my arms around him and held on for the ride. Now that's what I call nice. I just might have to give Clayton a little something, something.

Chapter 21

NADINE

The party was held in a large multipurpose room in the main building. It was packed with guests and employees on duty, mostly the entertainment staff.

She glanced around at the men and women dressed in almost nothing. One woman said she usually slept in the nude, so she came to the party wrapped in her bedsheet.

Nadine watched Renee mimic moves she had seen on BET's *106 & Park*. She herself had two left feet and never had much rhythm. Renee, on the other hand, looked good out there in that flimsy little nightie. She looked good in everything she wore, with her small breasts and firm dancer legs. Unlike Nadine, who was top-heavy like her mother.

Everyone was gyrating their hips, looking confident half-dressed. She felt awkward in her two-piece pajamas with pink polka dots. She wished she had brought something sexy, maybe something to show off her large breasts.

She sat alone, sipping another rum and Coke, her drink of choice. Lisa was at the other end of the room, dancing with one of the entertainment coordinators, while Renee was gyrating hips with Clayton O'Neal. As she watched them, Nadine rolled her eyes. She guaranteed he'd end up in Renee's bed tonight. Renee had it like that. She would scan the room, pick out the man she planned to spend the evening with, and within an hour, had him buying her a drink.

She allowed her eyes to travel around the room and soon became entranced with a man she spotted at a table, sitting alone a couple of feet away. He was brown skinned with short jet-black curly hair and large brown eyes. She was stunned that he was sitting alone, what with all the women in the room. The man looked her way and their eyes locked. Damn, she had gotten caught staring. She was about to go over to the bar and talk to Sylvester, when the man held up a pack of gum and offered her a piece. She gave him a polite smile, then nodded.

In one fluid motion, he rose from the chair. He wore burgundy pajama bottoms and his chiseled chest was bare except for the thick herringbone chain around his neck. She definitely liked what she saw.

He held out a piece of gum and she accepted it with a thank you. Then he lowered into Lisa's seat. "You know that was just an excuse to come over and ask you to dance."

"Was it?"

"Yes, it was."

She waited. He waited.

"Care to dance?" he asked politely.

"I'd love to."

She followed him out onto the crowded dance floor. As she passed Lisa, she nudged her in the side. Her girl gave her a thumbs-up as Nadine moved to find an empty spot on the floor.

He was an excellent dancer and she didn't try to mimic his move, instead she just wiggled her hips to the beat of the music.

The music slowed down and he pulled her closer. She rested her chin on his shoulder. He smelled of Burberry. She hated Burberry. Arthur used to wear that fragrance.

The man pulled her closer. "I'm Darrius Thomas," he whispered near her ear.

"My name is Nadine Hill."

"Nice to meet you, Nadine." He had a British accent that made her simple name sound sexy.

Staring over her shoulder, she gazed at Renee dancing close with

Clayton O'Neal. She was gyrating her hips so close they might as well been in a bed somewhere fucking.

To her right, she spotted a woman who looked like she didn't want to be here. Her head rested on her partner's shoulder as she gazed over in Nadine's direction.

Nadine stared back.

Her large eyes were the focal point of her face. It took a few moments before Nadine realized that it was the lady she had seen earlier at the bar. The mystery lady mouthed, "hello."

Nadine did the same, then she watched as the woman's full lips curled into a warm smile that radiated through her body. Watching her, she felt something she didn't feel at all with Darrius. It was a feeling she could get only from another woman. Nadine stepped back abruptly as if she had touched something hot.

"Is something wrong?" he asked.

"Come on, let's get out of here."

Darrius looked puzzled, then pleased. "All right. Where are we going?"

"Wherever you want to take me."

He took her hand and guided her through the crowd and out the room. They moved down the flight of stairs and outside the building, and didn't stop until they reached the beach. When Nadine reached the sand, she kicked off her shoes and took off running. Darrius fell into step beside her. Far away from the building, she fell down on the sand, laughing, and he joined her. As soon as the laughing stopped, she pulled him against her and kissed him desperately, clawing at his clothes, wanting so badly to forget what she had been feeling only minutes ago.

"Hey, let's slow down."

"Why—you scared?" she challenged.

He sniffed. "I ain't scared of shit."

"All right, then shut up and go with the flow."

"Shit, you don't have to tell me twice." Darrius rose and lowered his pajama pants. As soon as he reached for his boxers, Nadine came to her senses. *What the hell am I doing?*

She scrambled into a sitting position. "Look—I'm sorry. This is wrong."

Darrius looked confused. "What do you mean? I thought you were down for a little harmless sex."

"I changed my mind," she said and suddenly felt bad for leading him on.

Even in the dark of the night, she could see his frown. "You ain't nothing but a dick tease."

Nadine swallowed the lump in her throat. She knew he was right. She had lured him out onto the beach, challenged him to prove his manhood, then, when he was ready to fuck, suddenly changed her mind. How else was he supposed to react? A man can't be turned on and off like that. Their dicks just don't work that way. "I said I'm sorry," she snapped in frustration. "And I'm not going to say it again."

"Fuck you." He pulled up his pants and stormed across the beach back toward the party.

Nadine lowered her head and allowed the tears to flow.

Chapter 22

RENEE

By the end of the third slow song the DJ decided to speed it up again. I was hot and sweating and was starting to feel like I was about to suffocate in the cramped space.

"You want to go out and get some air?"

Clayton smiled down at me. "Sure."

I latched onto his arm and followed him out into the hall.

"Girl, you sho know how to party."

"Hey, I've got to do me."

He smirked. "I like it in you."

"So, when's the season start?" While we were slow dancing, Clayton had told me he played for the Chiefs. I faked surprise.

"Next month I report to camp."

"It must be an exciting career."

"It has its ups and downs. What do you do?" he inquired.

"I'm an author."

"Are you published?"

"Yeah, seven novels. Two Essence bestsellers."

He looked impressed. "What name do you write under?"

"Caeramel."

"Caeramel. I can see that."

"When I was growing up my grandmother used to say, 'that chile ain't black, she's caramel.' And the name stuck. I just spell it c-a-e-r-a-m-e-l, so that people will pronounce it correctly."

"I like that." His smile was genuine.

"Thanks."

We moved outside. There was a cool breeze coming from the direction of the ocean. We took a seat on a pair of chairs near the sand. I sat across from him, slipped off my shoes, and raised my feet and lowered them across his lap. I didn't waste any time asking him personal questions. "So tell me, are the rumors about ballplayers true?"

He reached down and took my foot in his hands and gently massaged the balls of my foot. "Which rumors are those?"

"Lots of parties, drugs, fucking."

He shook his head. "I wouldn't know. I gave up the party scene three years ago. As for sex," he paused and met my gaze, "I've been celibate since I gave my life to the Lord."

My mouth dropped. "You're fucking kidding me, right?"

He shook his head. "No. I'm not."

"So I guess offering you some no-strings-attached sex is a waste of time?"

He looked stunned by my proposition before he said with a smile, "Basically."

"Damn, it's always the fine ones. You sure you're not gay?"

Clayton chuckled. "No. I love women. Believe me, back in the day, I would have been all over you. I'm just waiting to meet the right woman. I believe sex and love should go hand in hand."

I snorted rudely. Clayton had a lot to learn. "Yeah, I used to think the same thing, but three husbands later, I've learned that love is a bunch of bullshit."

He frowned. "Has anyone ever told you, you cuss like a sailor?"

"All the damn time. Oops! I'm sorry. Does it bother you?"

"If I say yes will you stop?"

"I'll try."

"Good enough. So you've had three husbands?" He looked stunned.

I chuckled. "Sorry, I didn't mean to freak you out. I'm flaky, what can I say?"

He shook his head like he thought my ass was crazy or something. Shit, I couldn't get mad, because I am crazy.

He started kneading the balls of my feet again and damn it felt good. That's what I get for trying to look cute in a pair of heels.

"I plan on getting married one time and one time only. That's why I'm waiting to meet the right woman."

"Shit, I mean, shoot, with all of your money, you should have women falling at your feet."

He sighed. "Yeah, I do, and that's the problem. There is no way for me to know if a woman is interested in me for me or for my money. It's rare when I meet a woman like you who has no idea who I am."

I lowered my eyes to my lap so he couldn't see the guilt lurking in the corners at my lie.

"You've got pretty feet."

"That ain't all that's pretty." I wiggled my eyebrows suggestively, causing Clayton to laugh. I joined in and laughed even harder.

"Renee Moore, you are truly something else."

"Yeah, so I've been told."

Chapter 23

NADINE

Nadine went back to the party. Neither Renee nor Clayton were anywhere to be found. The first thing that came to mind was that Renee had taken him somewhere to fuck. Shit, she knew she shouldn't jump to conclusions but she knew Renee too well. Renee was always talking about fucking, and lived for something new and exciting. She was probably somewhere out on the beach riding his fine ass. Renee could not care less if she had an audience. She would do it just about anywhere and lived for the moment.

For once Nadine wished she could be like her, then maybe she could find a way to get through what she needed to do. She would be able to know once and for all if she preferred a woman's touch over a man's.

After a quick glance around the room, she realized Lisa had also left. More than likely, she had retired for the night. Turning on her heels, Nadine decided she was tired and ready to call it a night. Besides, she didn't want to run the risk of bumping into Darrius.

Damn, she was embarrassed. Why in the world had she tried to do something that she knew there was no way she was going to follow through on? She had made such a fool of herself. While she walked toward the room, the incident played over and over in her mind. He had everything a woman could want in a man, but it wasn't enough. She hadn't felt the least bit aroused.

By the time she stepped into their building, Nadine had convinced herself that Darrius had been the wrong man for the job. Next time she would be ready.

Chapter 24

KAYLA

It was late, well after three o'clock in the morning, when Kayla heard Renee's key in the door. She had obviously had a good time.

Kayla pulled the covers over her head so that Renee would think she was sleep. She just wasn't in the mood to hear how many men she had met, and how much fun they'd all had while she had sat in the room, feeling sorry for herself.

Renee tiptoed across the room, grabbed something out of her bag, and disappeared into the bathroom. She was humming some doggone song, which meant she was in a good mood.

Dang, life wasn't fair. *No, it isn't,* she thought as the events of the previous day came rushing back.

Leroy.

His call never came and it was her fault.

Did you really think someone that looked like you could keep someone that looked like him?

It was her fault because in the two years they'd been together she had gained an excessive amount of weight.

You dummy. How did you expect to keep a man if you allowed yourself to look like a whale.

Leroy had asked her to start watching her carbs, but she didn't listen. It had been his way of warning her that if she didn't change he was going to leave. Only she had chosen not to listen, and look what had happened.

Part of her wondered if this point in their relationship had just been a matter of time. He had promised numerous times to end his marriage, yet something always prevented their relationship from moving to the next level. Whenever he planned to take her away for the weekend, something always came up, canceling their trip. Getting a commitment had been an impossible feat, to say the least. Now she knew why.

Countless times, Leroy told her he loved her. Last month, Kayla had asked him when he was going to buy her a ring. Caught completely off guard he stuttered for a moment, then promised to get her one as soon as he asked his wife for a divorce. He went on to explain that if he spent the amount of money that he planned to spend on her diamond, his wife would know. At first she understood. But now, after today's incident, that was no longer good enough. She needed something to prove his love, if that was even possible at this point.

What pissed her off the most was that he played with her emotions. Made her think he wanted to spend the rest of his life with her. That he was going to buy a big house for her and her girls. She had been all set to quit her job and become a traditional wife, cooking, cleaning, and catering to her man. There wasn't anything she wouldn't have done for him, yet this was the thanks she got.

She spent twenty-three months listening to him complaining and whining like a big baby about his wife. "Darlene this" and "Darlene that." Like a fool, she comforted him, then allowed him to take her to bed, where he made love to her, then left before they even had a chance to snuggle. Asking her to pray with him after every time they made love was his way of making her feel guilty and preventing her from questioning his hasty departure only minutes after each of their escapades. And she fell for it every time.

They never used protection. She told him she was on birth control, when all along she had lied. She hoped and prayed that he would bury his seed in her, and that she would find herself pregnant with his child. Only it never happened. And now she knew that it had been an act of God. Dang, she was such a fool.

Yet even though she knew all these things, regardless of how often he had played her, she still wanted him any way she could have him.

Chapter 25

RENEE

The Holiday Inn was coming alive and I was in the room, hiding from Everton. I don't know what I was smoking yesterday for me to even think that brotha was all that.

The phone had started ringing just before eight o'clock. Kayla answered it and I told her to tell that no-dick mothafucka I was sleep. Damn, he couldn't even wait until his shift had started, which wasn't until ten.

Only minutes after Kayla left for breakfast, with a promise to bring me back a plate, the phone started ringing again. Knowing Kayla, she probably went up to the desk and told Everton to call me. She would do some shit like that just to get back at me for talking stuff about her and the reverend last night. I just let the phone ring. And it rang and rang every five minutes for an hour until I knocked the damn thing off the hook. I then took a long warm shower and dressed in a pink one-piece swimsuit. I moved out onto the balcony and sipped a bottle of water. I watched the first of the beachgoers test the water and stake claim to their area of the sand. After a few minutes, I decided to read a mystery novel and tried to take my mind off of food, but it was useless.

Where the hell was Kayla? She was obviously trying to be funny. I slammed the book shut.

Enough.

Here I am, acting like I have something to be ashamed of. I'm not the one with the little dick. Damn, I wish my girl Danielle could have made the trip but she was going through some shit with her man. They call us the hoettes when we're together. Bitches just be hating. If she was here, I wouldn't even bother hiding. I would have walked right passed Everton with jokes about him being a member of the itty-bitty-dick committee. Instead, I was on my own to face him and get past the mistake I had made last night.

I slipped on a white cover-up, grabbed my room key, and headed to the dining area.

Lisa, Kayla, and Nadine were all sitting there, eating and laughing. As soon as they spotted me coming, they grew quiet.

"Renee, where have you been?" Lisa said in a mock Jamaican accent.

"Y'all bitches know where I was." I rolled my eyes. "Kayla, thanks for the plate," I murmured as I moved past the table to the buffet. I heard them laughing and held my head high and kept moving. Bitches always be hating.

The restaurant was relatively empty at ten-thirty, which meant most people had already eaten and were off starting their day. I helped myself to what was left of the food. There was cacaloo, which looked like collard greens, Ackee and saltfish, and dumplings and green bananas. I put a little of each on my plate along with the traditional eggs and bacon. I then moved back to join the others. Like a fool, I glanced over toward the registration desk and spotted Everton waving and blowing kisses at me like a damn fool. I pretended I didn't notice and moved to sit beside my sister.

Nadine looked up from her plate. "Girl, Everton has been looking for you."

"Whatever," I mumbled as I gnawed on a slice of bacon. She was trying to spoil my appetite.

Lisa arched a brow. "Why're you mad at him?"

I stared down at my plate. "I'm not mad, just not interested."

"You were interested yesterday."

"Yeah, and since then I discovered he is not my type. He reminds me too much of Bobby."

Lisa smirked. "You used to be in love with Bobby."

"Yeah, for a hot minute, until I discovered he had a little dick and then I cut his ass off."

Kayla chuckled. "Is that what happened with Everton? You discovered he wasn't working with much?"

Shit. I set myself up for that one. The last thing I wanted them to know was that I had slept with him and was pissed off because the brotha wasn't working with much. "No, I didn't sleep with his ass. He turned me off long before he pulled his dick out. He just isn't my type."

Kayla took a sip of orange juice. "Well, he thinks you're his type, 'cause he's been from behind that desk twice asking us about you."

From across the table, I glared at her. "And I guess you just happened to tell him I was in the room."

They started cracking up laughing while I rolled my eyes and continued eating. They thought his infatuation was funny. I didn't.

"So you're saying you didn't give him some?"

I stopped chewing and said, "Nope."

Lisa knew I was lying. I could see it in the look she gave me. But I wasn't in the mood to talk about my most recent mistake, so I changed the subject.

I glanced down at the bulletin on the table. "Are we going on the shopping trip today?"

Kayla nodded. "Yeah, I'm game."

Nadine glanced down at her watch. "The shuttle leaves at one."

Lisa reached for the bulletin and browsed through it. "If we want to have dinner at the restaurant upstairs tonight then we need to make reservations."

"That's cool," Kayla said.

I speared a piece of saltfish with my fork. I must admit it was quite tasty. "I want to check out that club tonight. I think they called it The Pier."

"I'm game," Nadine chimed in. "The lady at the excursion desk said tonight is Hump Night. We'll need to schedule a shuttle to transport us there and back."

Lisa nudged me in the side and tilted her head in the direction of the lobby. "Don't look, but here comes Everton."

Aw, hell! Sure enough, here he comes. Yesterday his uniform looked sexy. Today he looked a hot mess. All I could think about was that little thing he had between his legs and him taking a shit right after sex. I dropped my head to my plate and concentrated on my breakfast, wishing I could nod my head like in *I Dream of Jeannie* and blink the fuck out of here.

"Hey, Everton," Lisa greeted.

"Hello again, ladies." He stood before me. "Renee, good morning."

"Hey, whassup," I mumbled, barely making eye contact.

"I tried calling you this morning."

I ain't no coward. I glanced up at him. "I was asleep."

A smile crinkled his eyes. "Can I see you this evening?"

I stabbed my eggs with my fork. "I got plans."

His nosy ass had the nerve to ask, "What kind of plans?"

"We're going to The Pier," Kayla offered.

Big mouth.

"Oh, no! That is not a place for respectable women to hang out. I rather you not go there."

Excuse me! I must have been hearing things. Because I sure hoped Everton didn't think just because we had slept together he now had some control over my whereabouts, because if he did, he was definitely in for a rude awakening.

Nadine leaned across the table and gave Everton a smile that I knew meant her ass was up to something. "Do you dance, Everton?"

He shook his head. "No, I'm afraid I have never been very good at dancing. That's why I didn't attend the party last night. However, if I had known Renee was planning to be there I would have set my alarm so I could have joined her."

Lucky me.

Nadine shrank back in her chair. "You know, Renee's an excellent dancer. She can teach you."

I rolled my eyes at her and had to bite back laughter because they were getting a kick out of this shit, and suddenly it was kind of funny.

"I would love to have some private lessons."

My brow rose. No, he didn't go there. I rolled my eyes and reached for a slice of bacon.

Lisa joined in on the fun. "I'm sure my sister would love to give you some private lessons," she cooed.

"Look, I need to get back to work. Can we talk later?"

I wasn't promising shit. "We'll see."

As soon as he was gone, I rolled my eyes in Lisa's direction and spat, "Bitch, I'm gonna fuck you up."

The three fell out their chairs with laughter.

Chapter 26

RENEE

I don't know why we decided on shopping down at Sam Sharpe Square. As soon as the shuttle driver let us off those local vultures came down on us hard. You would have thought it was a mob. They dragged us into one store after another. There was so much begging and pleading I wanted to scream.

"Oh, come on, pretty lady, I need to feed my family."

"I'll give you special deal, very special deal."

Just to get them to shut up we ended up buying a bunch of shit we wouldn't have even dreamed of buying if we'd had the time to consider our purchases. They were good, I'll give it to them, damn good at what they do. When we finally escaped, they waved, smirking and shit at my dumb ass for blowing one hundred dollars on a bunch of shit that was going to end up on the top shelf of my closet.

After they had taken all our money, we took the walkway toward the center of the town where stood the Cage, a former jail for runaway slaves. We were fascinated by this discovery because I had no idea there had been slavery going on in Jamaica, especially since everybody in the country appeared to be black.

Afterwards we headed up Harbour Street toward the Crafts Market, snapping a roll of film along the way. Shaded storefronts displayed their treasures—coffee, souvenirs, crafts, and unique Jamaican art and jewelry, things we could have better spent our money on. We passed a kid on the curb, wearing a t-shirt with Bob Marley on it, and holding a can in his hand. We each gave him a dollar.

When we got back to the hotel we were tired and exhausted from the heat. We decided to have a drink before heading to our rooms to shower and take a quick nap.

"Renee."

I tried to ignore his voice and started walking faster across the lobby.

"Renee, Everton's calling you!" Nadine yelled from behind me.

I turned around and gave her the evil eye, then glanced over toward the desk. Everton blew me a kiss, threw me a wave. He signaled for me to come here. I groaned, then shuffled my feet toward the desk.

"Hey, I tried calling you before you left."

"I was trying to get ready so we could catch the shuttle." He was definitely a stalker.

"How was shopping?"

I rested my bag on the counter. "Horrible. Them merchants were grabbing us and shit."

"Shopping downtown is terrible. They beg and raise the prices. They're so aggressive people buy stuff just to get away."

I finally looked directly at him and smiled. "Tell me something I don't know."

"Did the one lady show you a picture of her crippled daughter?"

I nodded and started laughing.

Everton chuckled. "That's some picture she clipped out of a magazine. She's been pulling that stunt for years."

"It worked."

We laughed some more, and I had to say that Everton's dimples were quite attractive. Too bad his dick was so damn little. I smiled across the counter at him, thinking that maybe we could at least be friends, and then Everton started looking at me all hungry and shit. Damn! It was time to go.

"Look, I need to go get out of these sweaty clothes."

His expression suddenly grew serious. "Can I see you later? I could get a room again."

Hell, naw! "No, I'm going to hang with my girls tonight, but I'll drop by and talk to you later." I reached for my bag and stepped away.

"I would really like to take you to my home tomorrow so you can meet my mother."

I frowned. "Your mother?"

"I told her all about my new American lady."

What the hell could he have possibly told his mother other than the color of my naked ass? "I don't know about all that, but we can discuss it later." I turned on my heels and jogged across the lobby toward the exit.

Everton was obviously one of those Jamaicans anxious to meet and marry an American. Well, you got the wrong one, baby.

Chapter 27

KAYLA

While Renee was in the lobby with Everton, Kayla made her way back to their room. She quickly moved over to the phone, hoping to see a blinking red light, and was disappointed to discover there wasn't one.

Leroy still hadn't called.

She couldn't believe this. Yesterday he had made a promise to call her. Yet he still had not called. She sank down onto her bed and dropped her bags onto the floor. It wasn't like she was surprised. She had expected as much.

Outside the sun was shining and a beach party was going on around the pool, yet here she was sitting in her room, feeling sorry for herself.

They had spent the afternoon browsing stores and strolling through the market and she hadn't wanted to be there. No matter how much she tried not to, she dragged her depression with her. It was weighing her down and ruining her vacation. Instead of being on the exotic island, she wished she was back home in their dead-ass little town, where Leroy was only a phone call away. It was Thursday. Tonight the church had Bible study. She always sat in the front pew, where she was able to hear everything he said and see his fine tail while he did it.

Out of sight. Out of mind. She had almost canceled coming because she was afraid that if she was gone for a week he might find someone else. Then she reminded herself that he loved her. Now she was millions of miles away and had discovered that he had moved on long before she had stepped foot on that plane. He had moved on with his wife and family.

Once again tears clouded her eyes. She wiped them away, not caring that she had smeared her makeup.

She might as well face it. He wasn't going to call. In front of her friends, she looked like a damn fool. She had been played again. In her experience, with her past relationships, she already knew getting over him wasn't going to be easy.

Kayla took a deep breath, and as quickly as she blinked her eyes, she gave up her denial. Tears started running down her face and she sat there staring out at the ocean, feeling sorry for herself. The others were at the bar, drinking. Something cold sounded wonderful but right now she needed some time alone so she could cry in private. Lisa had been right. Leroy had only been using her.

Now she had to find a way to pick up the pieces and start over again. *How many times am I going to keep starting over?*

She was so stupid. By now you would think she would have recognized game, especially with her track record. But with Leroy, she had been used in the worst way. Because for once in her life she had truly believed she had finally gotten it right. She had invested more time in their relationship than she had with anyone else. Only Leroy was no better than the rest. He had used her as his little sex toy, getting her to do things his own wife would never have agreed to. Things that Kayla wouldn't have agreed to if she had known it had all just been one big game.

As Kayla stared out the sliding glass door, she remembered one evening she had met him at their spot. She had barely stepped into the room when he pulled her in his arms and kissed her until her toes curled. She loved his thick, succulent lips on hers. When he pulled back she could tell something was on his mind.

"What's wrong?" she asked, her voice filled with concern.

He hesitated. "I need to ask you a question."

She wrapped her arms tightly around him. "Sure, Leroy. Go ahead and ask me."

"Well, I . . ." He paused.

"Leroy, you're starting to scare me. What is going on?"

"I need a favor."

Her shoulders relaxed. "No problem. You know there isn't anything I wouldn't do for you."

"Do you really mean that?"

She nodded. "Of course. I love you."

"I know, but I've never asked a woman this before." He looked her directly in her eyes. "Not even Darlene."

Kayla gave him a reassuring smile. "Then I am honored that I am the first. Now ask away."

He took a deep breath. "I want to have anal sex."

"What?" she blinked twice. She couldn't have possibly heard him right.

"I want to make love to you back there." He put his hand on her butt and rubbed as to emphasize what he meant. On contact, she snatched his hand away.

"Are you serious? You want to screw me in the butt like some slut?" She was stunned. In the past, no matter how many times she had been asked to do such a thing, she had always flat out refused. Never had she considered it, but now the man she loved, the man she wanted to spend the rest of her life with, wanted her to do an act she was raised to believe was reserved for a two-dollar ho.

"Sweetheart, it's not like that. Anal sex is a beautiful thing shared by two people who love each other."

"So does that mean you're going to go down on me?"

He had the nerve to look offended. "Of course not. That is something I will do only for my wife."

"So how in the world can you expect me to allow you to screw me in the ass if you aren't even willing to perform oral sex on me?" His refusal hurt because she had sucked his penis countless times.

Leroy dropped his shoulders and gave her a pitiful look like a young boy whose mother told him no sweets before dinner. "Because my wife said she would and even after we were married she refused. I need to know that you will not do the same."

Kayla stood her ground. "I can't do it."

"Aw, come on." He tried to hold her and she moved out of his reach.

"No, so don't ask again."

"Fine! I guess you don't love me as much as you try to pretend you do." He moved and made a show of putting on his coat. "I'm glad I found out now before I wasted my time this weekend shopping for a ring."

"That's not fair. I've done everything for you."

He glared at her. "Not everything, because you're not even willing to do the one thing that no other woman has ever done for me. I'm out of here."

Kayla suddenly realized her future was walking out the door. "Wait!" She rushed over and pulled him back into the room. "Please don't go." She sighed, giving in. "I'll do it."

His eyes sparkled. "You mean it?"

"Yes, just please don't leave me," she pleaded.

Leroy leaned forward and kissed her. He then reached for his zipper and ordered her to remove her clothes.

Chapter 28

RENEE

Irushed into the room. I couldn't get away from Everton fast enough. I could have strangled Nadine and Lisa as they sat in the bar, cracking up laughing. Everton was definitely going to be a problem, and to think I was trying to be nice to his ass. I mean, after all, it wasn't his fault his dick was small. Well, regardless of the problem, Everton needed to stay out of my space, which reminded me: I still needed to get in his ass for running his mouth to Sylvester, telling everyone we were an item. I was not about to let Everton sabotage my vacation.

Tossing my bags on the table, I grumbled, "Everton is getting on my damn nerves."

I heard a strangled laugh and glancing over my shoulder. Kayla was sitting on the bed, shoulders sagged and head down. She looked like she could use a friend. I sighed. All I wanted to do was take a quick shower and sleep for the next couple of hours. But now was not the time to think of myself. Kayla needed a shoulder to cry on, and as much as I wanted to run and go get Lisa, it was my turn to give her one of mine.

I moved and took a seat beside her on the bed. "Hey, girl, what's wrong?"

She turned and looked at me. Her nose was running and her eye makeup was smudged across her cheek. "Nothing."

"Nothing? Girl, you look like shit. I hope you're not crying over Leroy's ass."

She shook her head, then looked down at her hands. "No. Just feeling a little homesick."

"Homesick for what? Leroy's lying ass?"

She started crying again and I felt like shit because, like I said before, I am not the most sensitive person on the planet. Damn. Okay, I'll try harder.

I put a hand on her shoulder. "Hey, Kayla. Come on, now. You're not the first woman to get played. Shit, look at me. I've been played lots of times."

She wiped her eyes and glanced over at me with her nose running. "When were you played?"

Damn. She would have to ask that. You know a sistah like me tries to block that kinda stuff from her memory bank. "Let me see, uh . . . oh! Shit! How in the world can you forget my second husband?"

She started laughing. "Yeah, how could I forget him."

Okay, I was sharing shit so I could be the subject of her laughter. Although the way Leroy had played her and the way Troy had played me were two different things. I didn't know he already had a wife, while everyone at Mt. Carmel knows Leroy's married. Shit, my ex was military and he had a wife in another state, only I didn't find that shit out until after we had been married six months. So, yeah, my ass got played, but that was nothing compared to what I did to his ass. However, like I said before, I'm gonna save that experience for another time. It would take too much time to share and right now I'm trying to enjoy my vacation. Well, at least I would after I got done dealing with Kayla's ass.

"Before Troy remember that Nigerian I was fucking with the big dick?"

She wiped her nose with a Kleenex and nodded. "Yeah, I remember."

"Well, I walked into K-Mart one afternoon and ran into him, his wife, and their six kids."

Her red-rimmed eyes had grown large. "Oh my God, you never told me that."

"Shit, would you?" One thing I don't like is to look bad in front of my friends, so I am selective as to what I share with them and what I don't. Damn, I don't have to tell them everything.

"So, as you can see, you ain't the only one to get played. We've all gone through it. Look at Nadine and her husband. Even Lisa's ass was played before she met Michael."

She sniffled. "I guess you right."

Of course I'm right.

She balled the snot rag in her hand. "It's just that it has happened to me too many times."

"Girl, you're gonna have to develop thicker skin. You know how I am. I hate to say it, but sometimes you've got to treat a man like shit. When you give them everything they want, when they want it, they take yo ass for granted. Why you think I act the way I act?" She gave me a look that said she was giving what I said some serious thought. "You got to start breaking a brotha down. Let them know that it's gonna take a lot to get with a sistah like you."

She gave a timid smile. "Yeah, right."

"Girl, you better recognize. That negro is not worth wasting tears over. You're letting him ruin the first vacation you've had in five years. I guarantee he ain't giving your ass a second thought since you left."

There was an awkward moment of silence, then she sighed and finally reached over and hugged me.

"Thanks, Renee, what would I do without you?"

Not much, that's for damn sure. I took a deep breath. My work was done. Now I could take my ass to sleep.

Chapter 29

NADINE

They walked down the driveway toward the main gate. The sun was already scorching. The temperatures had to be close to ninety degrees. Nadine fell into step beside Kayla. She moved at a relatively slower pace, so she adjusted her normally rapid steps to stay with her friend. Today however, Kayla was moving even more slowly. Her shoulders were slumped forward and she stared off in front of her. It was obvious to Nadine, she was still thinking about Leroy.

Nadine felt like she needed to say something. "I want to apologize for what happened the other day. If I had known you were kicking it with the reverend, I wouldn't have said anything."

Kayla snapped out of her trance. "So you're saying you wouldn't have told me he was playing me?"

Nadine shook her head, realizing how what she had said must have sounded. "No. What I mean is I would have told you in private. I wouldn't have busted you out like that in front of everyone."

Kayla chuckled. "I know what you meant. I just wanted to get you started."

"So, has he called you back yet?"

She gave her a long gloomy look. "No, and probably won't."

Nadine hesitated before she spoke again. "If he does are you going to forgive him and take him back?"

She took longer than any scorned woman would have needed to answer, which made the answer quite obvious. So she was surprised when Kayla finally said, "I don't know. I don't think so."

"Think? Girl, don't think, know. We've been friends for years. You deserve better."

"So why ain't I getting it?"

"Because you're always settling for less."

Kayla released an audible sigh. "I just want to be happy."

"Happiness is what you make it."

"Are you happy?"

Nadine gave a forced chuckle. "My husband left me for a white woman, but I've gotten on with my life. Actually started a better one." Even as she said it she knew she wasn't being completely truthful. Her life and future was still uncertain.

Kayla stared down at the pavement as she spoke. "What bothers me the most is that I can't understand how a man of the church could lie like that. He never had any intentions of leaving his wife. It was all just a game to him. He intentionally set out to hurt me. I can't understand how someone, a messenger of God, could do something like that to another person without feeling any remorse."

"Girlfriend, even a minister can be a dog, 'cause he's still a man."

"But I thought this man was going to be different."

"We always do."

Kayla had to laugh at that. "I know that's right." After a few minutes she added. "I don't need another man."

"What if it was someone like that fine Clayton O'Neal?"

"What in the world would he want with me? Renee is more his type."

Nadine had thought the same thing last night after seeing the two of them together, but Renee would have kissed and told, and today she hadn't said a damn thing. So either he had a little dick or she wasn't interested in him. Or maybe Renee wasn't Clayton's type. She smirked. Wouldn't that be something if someone had finally rejected Renee's horny ass?

"What's so funny?" Kayla asked, breaking into her thoughts.

She giggled. "Nothing important. All I have to say is that the next time a pro football player asks your crazy ass out to dinner, do not turn the brotha down. I still can't believe you did that."

Kayla increased her speed. "I knew I shouldn't have said anything. Clayton was just being nice. I looked so pitiful sitting there thinking about Leroy that he felt sorry for me."

"I doubt that. Just next time, say yes." Just in case he did decide to ask Kayla to dinner again, she wouldn't mention Renee leaving with Clayton last night. Because if Kayla knew, she wouldn't even give Clayton a chance.

They waved to the guard at the end of the driveway. He waved back and told them they would need to show their room keys in order to get back into the resort.

They moved out to the curb and Nadine frowned. "Now we've got to figure out how to get across the street." Cars were racing down the road, going in both directions.

"Girl, we are going to have to haul ass if we're gonna make it." Kayla said as a car whizzed by. "I don't know if I can move my wide ass that fast. If anything I can use it to stop traffic long enough to get you across."

Nadine cackled. "You are crazy."

"Shoot, girl. I'm serious."

They looked both ways and as soon as the last car raced around the corner, Nadine screamed, "Now!" They flew across the wide highway and Kayla moved faster than she had before. They reached the other side and stopped to catch their breath. "Damn, girl, you left my ass in the dust."

Kayla laughed between breaths. "You didn't think I could move like that, did you?"

"No, I didn't."

A car whizzed passed them and blew its horn. Then another.

Nadine glanced over at Kayla. "Kayla, girl, you're showing all ass." She was bent so far over trying to catch her breath, she was showing all ass from the back of her skirt.

She quickly stood up again and grabbed Nadine's hand. "Let's go, girl, before I cause a twenty-car pileup." They moved up the path to Holiday Village, a small craft market directly across the street from the hotel, which would have been a much better choice than the one they had made this morning.

"Kayla, look."

Kayla followed the direction of her eyes to where Clayton and another player were coming out of a small t-shirt shop.

Nadine noticed Kayla start to shy away, so she grabbed her arm and pulled her up the path toward the two.

"Hey, Clayton," Nadine said as they passed.

"Ladies." He winked and smiled at Nadine, then glanced at Kayla. "How are you?"

Nadine pinched her in the side. "Ow! I'm fine." She mumbled, then grabbed Nadine by the arm and dragged her up the path.

Nadine wiggled her arm free. "That was rude."

"No, it wasn't. I just didn't know what else to say."

"He definitely likes you."

Kayla's eyes narrowed curiously. "Why you say that?"

"It's the way he looks at you. He looked right past me and gazed directly at you."

Kayla grinned as they moved toward the shops.

"Now his boy, he was ugly."

Kayla choked on her gum, coughed it up, and spit it out on the path. "You need to quit making me laugh."

Nadine draped an arm around her waist. "I'll do whatever it takes to take your mind off that no-good reverend."

Just as they prepared to step into the t-shirt shop, she spotted Clayton and his boy heading their way. He politely looked at Nadine, then turned to face Kayla. He cleared his throat. "Can I speak to you for a moment?"

"Sure." She glanced over at Nadine, who wiggled her eyebrows suggestively as Clayton took Kayla's hand and led her away from the building. Nadine noticed that the one with the big bubble eyes was staring at her.

"Whassup, Shorty? My name is RD."

Ugh. She hated when a man called her shorty. She simply rolled her eyes and glanced over at Kayla, who was nervously shifting her weight from side to side.

"Damn, baby, you are hard. I just wanted to ask you out to dinner tonight."

He was the last person she wanted to spend the evening with. How could she possibly spend a meal sitting across from someone who looked like a toad? She was ready to tell him no when Kayla came dancing over and grabbed her arm.

"Nadine, I need a big favor," she whispered.

As Kayla dragged her into the store, Nadine noticed her eyes looked panicky.

"Whassup, girl?"

"Clayton asked me to dinner and"—she hesitated a minute—"and he wants RD to come."

"Hell, no!" Nadine frowned. "Girl, I don't want to go out with him. He looks like Kermit the Frog."

Kayla was laughing and pleading at the same time. "Please, Nadine, please. I promise not to think about Leroy once all night. Come on, you owe me from the last double date."

She pursed her lips. She was right, she did owe her. Kayla knew there was no way she would say no to that. But asking her to spend an evening with a Muppet was a bit much.

"You're going to owe me big-time for this," she whispered.

Kayla's face lit up like a lamp had been switched on beneath her beige face. "Thank you."

Nadine turned around. "All right, I'll go out with you."

Chapter 30

KAYLA

When they got back to the hotel, Nadine went up to the room while Kayla went to grab herself a hamburger. While she was walking away chewing happily on her sandwich, she spotted Renee sitting at the bar. It was barely three o'clock and she had already been going strong since this morning. She shook her head as she moved to stand beside her.

"You are going to be drunk before we even get to the club."

Renee scowled. "Quit trying to act like my mama. I'm trying to enjoy my vacation."

Kayla rolled her eyes and took a seat on the stool beside her.

"Here you go, sexy. Tequila and pineapple." Kayla glanced down at his name tag, which read THOMAS. He smiled as he sat another glass before her.

"You are too good to me." Renee blew him a kiss as she slid the drink next to another glass that was half empty.

Kayla noticed the way he looked at Renee before he moved to serve a customer at the other end of the bar. It was obvious she had spent the afternoon flirting with the cutie. Kayla slapped her knee. "Dang, Renee, I guess tonight you're going to be the one doing the serving."

Renee rolled her eyes. "Girl, ain't nothing wrong with a little harmless flirting. The more attention I give him the stronger my drinks get."

Kayla sucked her teeth. "And like any other man he's going to want something in return."

Renee swung around on the seat and glanced over in Thomas's direction, studying the strong contours of his face. "Shit, anything is possible."

"What about Everton?"

She scrunched up her lips. "Fuck him! He ain't my man."

Kayla tossed a hand in the air. "Whatever, girl. The rate you're going, tomorrow you'll be trying to screw a lifeguard."

"Bitch, don't hate," Renee snapped.

"Who's hating? Be glad I care enough to say something."

"Point taken, now leave the shit alone. If I want to fuck every employee at this resort then that's my business. I'll never see any of these mothafuckas again no way." She then raised the half-empty glass to her lips and finished the drink.

Kayla blew out a huff of breath. She was too through.

Thomas returned. "Renee, can I get your friend something?"

Kayla shook her head. "No, nothing."

"Girl, you only live once. Come on, it's my treat." She then started cracking up like she had suddenly remembered that drinks were free.

"You know I don't drink."

"You used to until you went and got all holy and shit."

"Well, I've changed."

Renee gave her a dismissive wave. "Live a little. Thomas, make her holy ass a Shirley Temple."

"One Shirley Temple coming right up." When he moved to make her a drink, Renee turned to her. "Loosen up a little."

"I am loose."

"No, you're not. You've been moping since yesterday over that no-neck mothafucka."

Kayla glanced over her shoulder, ignoring Renee.

"Fuck Rev. All the dick running around this island. You can do a whole hell of a lot better than him."

Kayla didn't bother to answer.

"Play dumb if you want to, but I ain't the one letting some man make me look like a damn fool. That man doesn't care about anybody but himself. To him you are just another piece of ass."

Kayla rolled her eyes at that last comment and was thankful Thomas had returned with her drink. Sometimes Renee could say some real hurtful shit.

Kayla remained quiet because she knew Renee was trying to comfort her in her own tactless way. All the years they had known each other Renee was loud, blunt, and lacked compassion. She had always given unwanted advice and butted her nose in where she wasn't needed. She had hurt Kayla's feelings many times but regardless of how much it hurt she had never stood up to her. Not once had she confronted her about how much her words hurt.

Like now.

However, this was one time when Renee was right. Reverend Leroy Brown had made her look like the biggest fool, and it hurt. It hurt like hell and all she wanted to do was go curl up in a corner until the pain went away. Renee expected her to just get up and move on— the same way she handled things.

She glanced at her out the side of her eyes, watching her openly flirting with the bartender, and shook her head. Renee had never been one to let anything or anyone stand in her way.

Kayla's spirits lifted slightly as she thought about her dinner date tomorrow with Clayton. Beautiful smile, gorgeous body, and he had done something that no other guy had. Instead of trying to climb into her bed, he had asked her to dinner. Maybe Renee was right. Maybe she did need to quit moping over Leroy and get on with her life.

"Ooh, Kayla. Look!"

Kayla rolled her eyes and reached for her glass. Thomas had gone to serve another customer, and without even looking in the direction of her eyes, she knew Renee had already found someone else to focus her attention on.

"Damn, that Clayton O'Neal is fine."

Clayton.

Her heart fluttered as she glanced at the pool, where Clayton and RD were standing at the side. Her mouth dropped open as she took in how good he looked in his swim shorts. Better than before. The sun was beaming down on him. His body was glistening as if he had bathed in baby oil.

Renee shook her head with appreciation. "Mmm, mmm, mmm, I'm going to get me some of that." She finished her drink in one gulp, then slid off the bar stool. "Come on Kayla, we're going swimming."

"But—"

"No buts."

Any further protests were cut off when Renee grabbed her hand and yanked her off the stool.

Reluctantly she followed her down the path, past the pool. Kayla moved fast so that Clayton wouldn't try to stop her. He waved and before she could raise her hand, Renee waved back. As soon as the two of them were out of sight, Renee started talking nonstop, with her hands flying through the air.

"Girl, did you see how good that mothafucka looked? Damn, I am going to get me some of that."

"What about Thomas?"

"Girl, fuck Thomas. I'm gonna get me some rich dick tonight. That broke-ass negro Thomas will still be there tomorrow."

She dashed into the building and up the stairs to their room before Kayla could catch her second wind. Shaking her head, she moved to wait for the elevator.

With a sigh, she realized she needed to let Renee know that the guy she was acting a fool over had asked her to dinner tomorrow night. But to be honest, Kayla was actually getting a kick out of the entire situation because for once someone was interested in her, not Renee. Between the two of them there had never been any competition, because men always preferred Renee over her, but this was one time things were different. As she boarded the elevator, Kayla giggled like a kid with a secret she was burning to tell.

By the time she made it up to the room, Renee was padding around in a yellow string bikini, hunting for her flip-flops.

"Kayla, girl, what took you so long? Hurry up and get changed."

"I'm not changing."

"Fine, don't change. Just wait until I find my shoes and we can go." She stuck her head under the bed, looking for her left shoe. Kayla lowered onto her bed.

"Girl, while I am working Clayton's fine ass, I'm going to get him to hook you up with his boy RD." She paused long enough to shake her head. "Now that brotha might resemble a frog but don't even trip. Remember that his ass is rich."

Kayla didn't say a word as she sat and watched Renee run around like a chicken with its head cut off, while talking nonstop about how she was going to coochie-whip his ass and leave him begging for more. Kayla could not resist a chuckle, although she knew she needed to tell Renee the truth, but she just couldn't seem to make her lips work.

"Found it!" Renee squealed as she slipped the shoe on her foot. "Clayton O'Neal, you are mine tonight," she said as she moved over to the mirror to take one final look. She quickly lacquered her lips and pursed them together to blot the mauve color evenly.

"All right, let's roll." She signaled for Kayla to follow and headed toward the door.

As soon as she turned the knob, she blurted, "Renee, wait!"

She swung around with her hands planted at her bare waist. "Damn, Kayla, what? Don't tell me your ass is tripping over Leroy's ass again?"

She pursed her lips. Renee was starting to get on her last nerve. "No, it's not about Leroy, it's about Clayton."

Her brow rose. "Clayton? What about Clayton?"

She took a deep breath, then said, "He's taking me out to dinner tomorrow night."

Renee's mouth dropped to the floor. Kayla wished she had pulled out her camera, because the look was priceless.

After Renee closed her mouth, she stepped away from the door. "Let me get this straight. Clayton asked you out to dinner?"

Kayla nodded her head and Renee started cracking up. Her reaction angered her.

"What's so funny?"

"Nothing, nothing at all," she replied as she moved to take a seat on her bed. "When did this happen?"

"Nadine and I ran into them across the street and he asked me then."

Her gaze narrowed, then before she could blink, Renee playfully slapped her arm. "Damn, ho. Why the hell you didn't tell me instead of getting my coochie all wet and shit."

"I tried but I couldn't get your crazy behind to shut up."

Renee crossed her legs and started laughing again. "Go head with yo bad self."

"You aren't mad?"

"Shit. Why the hell would I be mad?"

She simply shrugged.

"Girl, you can have his ass. Shit, if I wanted him, I could have jumped his bones at the party last night."

Kayla frowned. Nadine hadn't mentioned seeing Clayton at the party last night.

"Well, shit, I'm dressed now. We might as well go down to the pool and hang out with him and his butt-ugly friend."

"No-no-no!"

Renee rose. "You either bring your ass downstairs or I'm going to tell him all about you." She then dashed out the door before Kayla could stop her.

Chapter 31

RENEE

To say I was stunned would be an understatement. Not that I was hating on my girl or anything, but damn, how could Clayton have passed up an opportunity to have the best sex of his life to take my girl out to dinner? Shit, if he preferred Kool-Aid to Moët then that's his damn business. It wasn't like he was giving up any dick anyway. However, even as I say that, a part of me just couldn't give up that easily. I mean, damn, last night I thought the two of us had made a connection. We had sat out on the deck talking until he started to drift off to sleep. I leaned over and kissed both of his eyelids until he opened them again. Clayton then walked me to my room and said good night. Damn, so why didn't he ask my ass out to dinner? That's what I wanted to know. And that was exactly what I intended to find out. I love my girl, but I like a challenge. And Clayton was definitely a challenge.

Shit. Maybe he was attracted to her spiritual side and if so, that's cool. I'm only interested in his sexual side. I know you're probably thinking, this bitch is a trip, but you've got to understand I hate feeling rejected, and that is exactly how I am feeling. Besides, I am used to getting what I want, so why stop now? If I can have Clayton tonight, he will be back in time to take Kayla out to dinner tomorrow.

I took the stairs two at a time and sashayed down the path toward the pool. I knew Kayla's ass wasn't coming any time soon. So that gave me a chance to check out Clayton for myself.

I moved over to find the other players and their wives sitting around the pool. I sashayed over to where Clayton was standing and laughing with RD.

"Yo, what do we have here?" I heard RD say.

I shook my ass just a little harder.

"Whassup, Clayton?"

He smiled down at me. "Hey, Renee."

My lips curled into a generous smile. "Can I talk to you for a minute?"

I moved up as close as I could, then crossed my arms over my chest. "I hear you're taking my roommate out to dinner tomorrow."

His brow rose. "Kayla's your roommate?"

I nodded. "And my best friend. She's been through quite a bit these past couple of days so yo ass had better treat her right."

He frowned. "What did I tell you about your mouth?"

I faked innocence. "Oops. My bad."

He smiled, seeming pleased with my weak-ass apology. "Don't worry. I'ma take good care of your girl."

"You better or I am going to come looking for you." I pursed my lips seductively. He was trying not to make it obvious but I could see him checking out all my assets.

"How come you didn't ask me to dinner?" I pouted prettily. I didn't give him a chance to answer. I leaned into him and rested a palm against his moist chest. "You coulda had me for dessert," I purred. "What I've got is better than homemade apple pie."

I knew my words were affecting him because I could feel his heart pounding against my hand. Damn! Out of the corner of my eye, I spotted Kayla coming across the lawn. Slowly, I stepped away from Clayton and turned on my heels. As I moved away from the pool area, I spotted that Hispanic bitch glaring at me. I stared her down until she had no choice but to look down at her lap. With a chuckle, I moved to meet Kayla.

She shook her head disapprovingly. "I hope you didn't embarrass me."

"Nah, you know I got your back. I told Clayton he better treat you right, otherwise his ass is mine."

She groaned and we moved toward the restaurant where Lisa and Nadine were eating. Glancing over my shoulder, I spotted Clayton still standing in the same exact spot watching. My lips curled in a triumphant smile. Before this trip is over, I'm going to have that fine mothafucka in my bed.

Chapter 32

RENEE

Later that evening I called the front desk to make sure that Everton's ass had gone home. All during dinner he kept popping over to our table, staring and driving me up the wall. Everybody thought that shit was funny but me.

As soon as I was finished eating, I went back to the room to get a breath of fresh air, then decided to spend the rest of the evening working on an outline for a new PI series I was seriously considering. While working out on the balcony with my laptop, I spotted Kayla sitting near the jerk-chicken hut, talking and laughing with Clayton and his bubbled-eye friend. I discreetly watched them and decided they were the oddest looking bunch. Nevertheless, I found myself drawn to Clayton's smile. He had a pair of perfectly white teeth with a slight overbite that rested on top of his bottom lip every time he smiled. I watched him until the group moved toward the other end of the beach, then I again settled back in my chair and resumed writing.

Around eight o'clock, I woke up to find I had fallen asleep with my laptop resting on my lap. I rose and went inside and decided to take a shower and wake my ass up. As soon as I got out, I quickly dressed in a lime green knit dress that plunged deep in both the back and front. As soon as I saw the dress at Dillard's I knew I had to have it. It was scandalous, just like me.

After spraying a little perfume on my damp skin, I again slipped into those three-inch white sandals and walked over to the lobby, where they were having live entertainment. I spotted Lisa standing on the stairs, watching the native dancers below. I couldn't see the other two, so I pushed through the crowd, ascended the stairs, and moved beside her.

"Hey, girl."

Lisa glanced my way and her eyes lit up. "Hey, you've missed a good show. They just had this guy on stage that looked like 50 Cent. Girl, when he took his shirt out, I practically fell down the stairs."

I scowled. Damn you, Everton. "Where's Nadine and Kayla?"

"Nadine was in the room, taking a nap. I'm not sure where Kayla is."

I focused my attention on the women below, doing an African folk dance. The group definitely had skills. They set up to limbo under a stick ignited with fire. My mouth was wide open as I watched them move one by one beneath the flames. As the last man maneuvered his limber ass underneath the stick, I caught movement out the corner of my eyes and spotted this fine dude coming our way. He stopped and stood before me.

"Excuse me, but I think you're in my spot," he said in a deep husky tone. He smiled like he was posing at a Sears Portrait Studio. I hadn't seen him before, but had to say he was sexy as hell. The first thing that came to mind was Blair Underwood. Dark chocolate, goatee, and fine.

I glanced down at his hairy legs, then back up to his blue jeans shorts and island print t-shirt. He was standing before me just ready for me to reel his ass in.

I slowly licked my lips, then cooed, "How do I know this is your spot?"

"Because Trevor left to get me a drink."

I turned in the direction of Lisa's voice, glanced at her, then Trevor, then back at Lisa again. By the way she was smiling it was obvious the two knew each other. So in other words, Trevor hadn't been checking me out; instead, he was staring at my sister's married ass.

"Damn, my bad."

He handed my sister her drink. Lisa blushed. I dropped a hand to my waist and took a step back. Now, from the way things looked, there was something going on between the two of them. Lisa rarely blushed and right now she looked guilty as shit. I wouldn't have believed it if I ain't seen it for my own eyes. My sister was trying to get her freak on in Jamaica! Now, when I said, "whatever happens in Jamaica, stays in Jamaica," I was talking about my own ass. Who would have ever guessed Lisa's faithful behind would even think about messing around on her husband? Not that I gave a shit. I've been messing around on mine for years. Besides, she's grown and can do whatever the hell she wants to do. What gives is that her ass has been giving me shit for years when she wasn't no better. Damn. I've been sweating her ass catching me alone and drilling me about John for nothing.

"Trevor, this is my sister Renee."

I shook his hand. "The pleasure is all mine. So when did y'all meet?" I pried.

Lisa smiled up at him. "We met while snorkeling this afternoon."

"Is that so?" I started smiling and shaking my head. Lisa's eyes narrowed as she suddenly realized what I was thinking.

She gave me a disappointed look. "It ain't nothing like that."

"Gurl, whatever, your ass is grown. Just don't do anything I wouldn't do." I laughed and patted her on the arm. "Look, y'all kids have fun. I'm going to get a drink." As I pushed my way down the stairs, I started laughing again. Talk about calling the kettle black.

The entertainment had come to an end. I moved over to the bar and took a seat, then gestured for the bartender. A man I hadn't seen before took my order. He greeted me with a wide grin. He wasn't much to look at so I rolled my eyes and focused my attention to the left.

To the far right of the pool were Nadine and some brotha I couldn't see. She caught me staring and waved. I returned the gesture and swiveled on the stool. It was obvious to assume since she was nowhere around, Kayla was somewhere with Clayton.

Suddenly I started feeling sorry for myself. I don't know why I do that, but whenever I'm not the one getting attention, I feel that way. I like constant attention and to always be the main focus, yet right now I was getting neither. Instead, I was sitting all alone at the bar. Everyone had a hook-up but me. Okay, so maybe I was the first with a hook-up. How was I to know mine was going to be some no-dick fatal-attraction stalker, who, thank God, had gone home for the night? It just wasn't fair. All I have ever wanted in my life was to feel loved and return that same emotion with someone I feel is my equal. I'm a beautiful woman with a wonderful personality and a nice body, yet I can't even find a halfway-decent man. John pushed to the surface of my mind, and I groaned. Thinking about him only made matters worse.

"Mind if I sit here?"

I glanced over to my right and spotted a short round black dude with glasses standing beside me. Oh, Lord, can this night get any worse?

I shrugged. "It's a free country."

"That's not what I asked you. I asked do you mind."

I raised a brow at him. He looked like he was preparing for me to say no. However, I have to admit for an old head, he wasn't half bad. If I was my mama's age, I might have given his old ass some play. "Nah, I don't mind." Satisfied by my answer, he took a seat.

"Okay, so let's try this again." He held out his hand. "Hi, I'm Pierre."

I shook his hand. "Hello, I'm Renee."

The bartender returned with my drink and Pierre asked for a rum and Coke. I checked him out. He had a receding hairline, thick lips, and a thin mustache. His stomach sat in his lap. Good Lord, if he makes a pass at me I am going to scream.

"What brings you to Jamaica?"

I sipped my drink, then shrugged. "I'm hanging out with my girls."

"That sounds like fun. I'm here for my son's wedding. You may have heard of him—Alex Houston."

"The football player?" He nodded, beaming with pride. "Oh, no wonder there are so many players running around here."

"Yes, he and Ayanna are getting married on Monday, right in the lobby."

Ayanna must be that Hispanic chick that keeps mean-mugging

me. I had half a mind to warn Pierre to check his future daughter-in-law before I stuck my foot so far up her ass they would be forced to postpone the wedding because of possible hemorrhoid swelling.

I stirred my drink and swung around on the stool and faced him. "Their wedding sounds like a beautiful event."

While Pierre stared down at my legs, I took in the contours of his face and my eyes immediately zeroed in on the long nose hairs hanging from his right nostril. Damn. I shifted my eyes to the corner of the room and tried to focus on something else.

He slid his stool closer. "They're having karaoke tonight. You going?"

I almost fell out of my chair. Was that his breath? Damn, that shit smelled like chitterlings. "No," I said while trying not to breathe. "We're hitting the town tonight."

"Oh, yeah, where at?"

Good God Almighty! It *is* his breath. I leaned slightly back and rested a finger over my top lip, trying to shield myself from the funky smell. "I don't have the slightest idea. I'm just along for the ride." I wasn't about to tell him where we were going. The last thing I needed was for him and his funky-ass breath showing up.

The bartender returned with his drink. Pierre ordered me another. I reached into my shoulder purse and removed a stick of gum. I stuck a piece in my mouth, then offered him one. Although in this case it was going to take two or three pieces to kill that skunk.

He shook his head. "No, thanks."

"You sure?" I asked sweetly.

He chuckled. "Positively."

Damn. I lowered the pack back into my purse and scowled. I just don't understand it. Why doesn't this old head understand that if a woman offers a breath mint or a piece of gum she is trying to tell him his breath stinks? I've seen it many times before. Shit, if someone offers me a piece, they don't have to ask me twice.

"Would you like to attend the wedding with me?" I heard him say.

I met his gaze and gave him a puzzled look. "Where's your wife?"

He gave a hearty laugh. "My soon-to-be ex-wife is here with her new fella. I came alone."

"Oh." That was all I could manage because he took a deep breath and blew a cloud of stank in my direction. I almost fell off the stool.

"What's wrong?" Pierre asked.

"Nothing," I murmured as I leaned back.

His brow rose with curiosity. "Then why do you look like you're ready to run away?"

Was it that obvious? I sighed, then gave him a half-grin. "I'm fine, really."

"So, would you like to go with me?"

I looked at him like he had lost his damn mind. "You don't know anything about me."

He shrugged. "Other than you're beautiful, no, I guess I don't."

I blushed. "Thank you."

"You're welcome. So, how about it?" he asked as he reached for his drink.

"Maybe. If I see you before then I'll let you know." I mean, damn, is he desperate or what? Who in their right mind meets a woman at a bar and invites them to their son's wedding? Although, I have to admit the offer is tempting. I love weddings and would love to see Ayanna's face when I show up at her wedding. If Pierre does something about his breath, I just might consider joining him. After all, Clayton will be there.

Chapter 33

RENEE

"Are you sure you want me to leave you pretty ladies here?"
I glanced out the window of the hotel shuttle. The Pier was nothing more than a shack on the end of a raggedy-ass pier in the middle of a Jamaican ghetto. Nevertheless, I was down. The music coming from the building was hyped. Brothas in all shapes and sizes flooded the parking lot and up the ramp toward the club.

"Shit. Let's do the damn thing." I saw the skeptical looks that the other three were giving each other and rolled my eyes. "Damn, y'all, this ain't no worse than kickin it at Lou's." Lou's Lounge is our own neighborhood hole-in-the-wall.

Kayla was quick to disagree. "Uh-uh. At least we know everyone at Lou's."

Nadine clicked her tongue. "I know that's right."

They were silent for an entire minute.

"Forget y'all. I'm out." I reached for the handle and was out the door before Lisa could grab my ass. I slid my dress back down over my hips, then strutted through the crowd. I kid you not, brothas moved like Moses had parted the Red Sea. Several tried grabbing my hand and drawing my attention, but I just kept on going, walking with my head held high and my small-ass titties stuck out as I switched my wide ass.

"Ho, slow yo roll!" I heard Nadine yell.

I giggled as I pivoted on my heels to find Lisa, Nadine, and Kayla coming up behind me. They looked pissed off, but I didn't care. All three had been getting mad play all day. Now it was my turn. "I knew y'all haters wouldn't leave me here alone."

Lisa wagged a finger in my face. "That's what you get for thinking. The only reason why I got out of that shuttle was because I couldn't figure out which would be worse, this place or the ride back to the hotel."

We all laughed.

The ride over had been one hell of an experience. The driver drove like a damn fool. Thank goodness someone else was scheduled to come back to get us at one.

They fell into step beside me and we moved up the wooden ramp toward the nightclub. Below was a breakwater of massive rocks. That old-ass thing rocked so much, I even had second thoughts about turning around. "Oh shit! Hold on 'fore this bitch collapses."

We all held onto the railing and started cracking up. Obviously, we had all had too much to drink. Everyone but Kayla. I know for certain that if the other two had been sober there was no way they would have gotten out of that shuttle.

As we grew closer to the building, we came up to a small card table with two brothas sitting behind it.

"You ladies want some ganja?"

Kayla turned up her nose at the tall Rastafarian. "Ganja? That mess smells like weed."

I nudged her in the side. "That is weed, dummy."

"Want some ganja, mon?" his partner repeated.

"Hell, nah," Nadine snapped as she moved through the door.

Kayla shook her head. "Y'all need Jesus."

I have never been much of a weed smoker, but as they say, when in Rome do as the Romans do. My cousin told me you can find some of the best weed in Jamaica. Unfortunately no one else would even consider taking a hit so I decided to pass myself. I gave them an apologetic smile and followed Lisa inside.

As soon as we moved inside the building I started coughing. There was so much smoke we didn't need a hit because we were guaranteed to get high just from simply breathing. The place was packed and the music jumping. There weren't any lights. Thank goodness the back half of the building had been torn down, and the Pier was lit by moonlight. Twenty feet into the building was nothing but a pier over a large body of water. The entire shack was shaking and the wooden floor was rocking. I was too drunk to care about anything but getting my party on. Someone grabbed my hand and I allowed him to lead me out onto the dance floor.

Now I've watched enough Elephant Man and Sean Paul videos to know Jamaicans can dance their asses off. Shit, I couldn't keep up and didn't even try. I just swayed my hips and did what I do best— look good.

While I was dancing, I took a good look at my partner, who had a blunt hanging from between his lips. He offered. I declined. He stared, and even tried to touch. I kept dancing and smoothly removed his hand. And as soon as the song was over, I took the fuck off. I found Kayla standing near the bar, so I joined her.

"They sure know how to party."

"Yes, they do." I agreed as I watched Nadine try to keep up with her partner. She looked like a *Soul Train* reject. Even Kayla had to laugh at her girl.

I was wiggling my hips when I felt a hand at my waist. I swung around and my mouth fell open. It was a Taye Diggs lookalike. I did the only thing I could think of. I exhaled.

Chapter 34

LISA

As soon as they all got out of the shuttle, Lisa rolled her eyes at her sister, then stormed off through the lobby.

"Lisa, girlfriend, wait up!" Nadine fell into step beside her.

"Not now, Nadine." She waved a hand, shooing her like a fly. "I want to be alone."

"For what?"

"So I can decide how to kill my sister."

Despite her original reservations about going down to that seedy club, she had actually started to enjoy herself until Renee decided to act like a damn fool.

Renee had found a Taye Diggs lookalike and they had been bumping and grinding on the dance floor like she was some kind of bitch in heat. From the other end of the dance floor Lisa had frowned and watched, because something told her something was about to jump off. Brothas all around the room were checking out the American hoochie in the lime green dress while waiting for their chance to feel on her hot ass. Next thing she knew, the dance floor cleared and the only ones standing were Renee and some angry Jamaican chick. Lisa had quickly moved over to defuse the situation before it even got started. Over the pounding of the music, she heard the woman scream, "British bitches always trying to steal our men." By the time she had reached Renee, her sister already had her finger all in the chick's face and cussing up a storm. The girl screamed something, then three of her girls joined her. One whipped out a blade and Lisa knew if she didn't get her sister out of there, there was going to be some blood shed. Because Renee, no matter if she didn't have a chance in hell of stomping all four, didn't back down from anyone. By the time Kayla and Nadine stepped in front of her sister, Renee had already snatched off her earrings and was unstrapping her sandals. Her sister does too much Taebo and because of it thinks she's Jet Li somebody. Renee would have seized the moment and sent a series of roundhouse kicks to their Jamaican heads, and probably got her ass cut in the process. Thank goodness two of the bartenders from the hotel were there and helped them drag her sister out of the building and down the road, where they waited for the shuttle to come. She was so mad she didn't speak to her the entire ride back.

Lisa glanced over at Nadine, returning her mind to the present. "I can't believe she would act a fool in a place like that. What the hell what she thinking?"

Nadine was out of breath, trying to keep up with Lisa's powerful strides. "That's just it. Your sister wasn't thinking."

Lisa released a groan filled with frustration then slowed her steps. "I just don't understand her sometimes. She is a grown-ass woman yet she's quick to act like she's in high school. Why can't she just sit her ass down?"

"Because she wouldn't be Renee if she did."

"Yeah . . . I know. But one of these days something is going to happen to her and I'm not going to be there to save her."

Chapter 35

RENEE

Yeah, I know I showed my ass last night. But, damn, I can't help it if I look good. All those Jamaican bitches weren't doing nothing but hating. It's a damn shame, but hating is definitely universal. Women are obviously going to be women no matter where you go. And with that said you can't expect me to be any less than me, 'cause Renee is also universal. Meaning no matter where I am or who they are, white, black, or other, I might have to whoop some ass.

Now all I was doing was slow dancing. Rahsaan, that was the Taye Diggs lookalike's name, was holding me all close and feeling all good. He was thin but his body was toned. Now remember what I had said before about the way a brotha moves says a lot about the way he moves in bed? Well, there was no doubt in my mind that Rahsaan could make my toes curls.

I lay my head against his chest and closed my eyes while we swayed to the sounds of John Legend, then the next thing I know, he's telling me his girlfriend was standing across the room watching us. I eased up off him because the brotha had tried to play me. I was about to cuss his ass out for setting me up like that when I heard some ho behind me hiss, "British bitch." I turned around and quickly clarified that shit. I am an African American female, born and bred. I tried to walk away but she got slick with the tongue and then I couldn't hold my own. When she started talking about showing me how it's done in Jamaica, it was time to take the earrings off and assume the position. I told her if she wanted some of this, then go ahead and leap like a frog. Then them bitches had the nerve to pull out a knife like they gonna cut a sistah. Shit, I ain't gonna lie. I was scared as hell, especially when her girls stepped up for the challenge, but I have never been one to back down from anybody. Besides, I knew my girls had my back. Luckily, Sylvester and one of his boys dragged me out the building.

I ain't seen Lisa that pissed off in years. But, unfortunately, she is going to have to get over it because I didn't start the shit, Rahsaan's slick ass had.

I rolled out of bed and decided to get into the shower before Kayla rose. She probably wouldn't dare mention the incident. However, the look in her eyes would let me know that she was thinking about it.

Turning on the water, I let out a frustrated sigh. So far my time in Jamaica was turning out to be one big disappointment. I want what Stella found: a Jamaican brotha with skills and a great deal of potential. So far I had run into a bunch of rejects. The only man with any potential was more interested in Kayla than in me. I don't know what it is. All I can do is hope that the shit gets better.

I quickly washed my body, then stepped out the shower and reached for a towel. I moved into the room to find Kayla sitting up on her bed, reading the Bible.

"Hey," I murmured, and moved to the drawer to find something to wear.

"Good morning."

She closed the book and set it down beside her. I had hoped that she would have kept on reading so I wouldn't have to strike up a conversation, but like the way things had been going for me lately, I got no such luck.

"What are we doing today?" she asked like I was the damn tour guide or something.

I reached for a one-piece red swimsuit and stepped back into the bathroom before answering. "I think I remember hearing Nadine saying something about going out on a glass-bottom boat."

"Oh, that sounds like fun."

As soon as I pulled the straps over my shoulders, I stepped back into the room. "Don't forget you've got a date tonight." I wasn't surprised to see the smile vanish from her face. Just as I suspected, she was not looking forward to her date with Clayton. The reason was quite obvious. Leroy.

I reached for a bottle of lotion and took a seat on the bed. "What are you wearing tonight?"

Kayla shrugged. "I don't know. I'm sure I can find something."

I glanced at her and frowned. Didn't she realize how important her appearance was going to be tonight? See, this is why Clayton was better off with me, because Kayla doesn't have a clue as to how to keep a man like him. Hmmm. I guess it's up to me to help her.

"How about I arch your eyebrows for you this afternoon?"

She gave me a skeptical look. "What are you going to use?"

"A razor."

She looked relieved. "That's fine. As long as you're not plucking them. That mess hurts."

I know that's right. "You should try getting them waxed like I do."

This Nigerian guy down at the beauty shop does some of the best eyebrows around. I had gone to one of those Vietnamese at the nail salon and this old bitch in there fucked up my eyebrows. I had to draw on a new pair until they grew back.

The phone rang and I just sat there and stared at it. Kayla looked at me like I was crazy. I shook my head. "Girl, I'm not getting that phone. It might be Everton's worrisome ass."

She reached for it. It was Nadine letting us know they'd meet us downstairs for breakfast.

I tied a butt-wrap around my waist then waited until Kayla got dressed.

Walking down to the restaurant, I found it was already hot outside. I was thankful for the cool breeze coming from the ocean, because I hate feeling hot and sticky. We moved up the stairs. Lisa and Nadine were just sitting down at the table.

"Good morning," Nadine sang.

"Good morning." I went and fixed my plate and didn't speak to Lisa until I made it back to the table. "Whassup, Lisa?"

"Good morning."

I could tell she was still mad by the way she looked down at her plate when she spoke. She refused to make eye contact. Well, I was determined to get her to look at me, so I tossed some scrambled eggs at her.

Her head shot up. "Hey! Quit playing!"

"Then quit being mad." I tossed some more and they landed inside her blue halter top. She then tossed some back and started laughing.

"You make me sick," she finally said.

I smiled. "Yeah, but you love me."

Nadine snorted rudely. "Renee makes us all sick."

Who told her to add more sugar to the Kool-Aid? "Who asked you?"

"I appointed myself involved in this conversation," she said, rolling her neck like a snake.

"Yeah, whatever."

Kayla quickly changed the subject. "Are we going out on the boat today?"

Lisa smiled. "Yeah, I already signed us up."

"What's so great about a glass-bottom boat?" I asked as I chewed.

"We get to see water life."

"Whoop-de-fucking-do."

Lisa pointed her finger at me. "Ho, after last night you can't say shit. At least on this trip we don't have to worry about you bumping and grinding with some negro or some bitch trying to yank your braids out of your head."

They laughed. I joined in.

While I ate, I glanced over at the desk and was relieved to see that Everton wasn't working this morning. Good. I don't think I could have put up with him three days in a row.

Chapter 36

LISA

After breakfast Lisa went back to the room to relax before their boat trip, while the others joined a game of volleyball. She moved out onto the balcony and lowered into the seat and propped her feet up on the other chair. Closing her eyes, she allowed her mind to travel back to the day her entire life had changed.

Dr. Gaye's eyes met her as she stepped inside the doctor's office. As soon as she saw the smile vanish from the gynecologist's face, she knew something was wrong.

"Lisa, please, have a seat."

"Thanks." She took a seat in the stiff leather chair across from Dr. Gaye's desk and her eyes moved across her desk to her patient file, lying open on the desk. She had come in two weeks prior for her yearly exam and had complained of severe abdominal pain and persistent bleeding. At that time her doctor suggested running some additional tests, which included a CT scan. Yesterday Dr. Gaye called and asked her to come in.

"I've got the results back on your test."

Her hands began to shake. "Was my pap smear abnormal?"

Dr. Gaye gave her a nervous smile. "No, your pap smear was fine. It's your scan that I want to discuss."

"What about it?"

"You have a mass of cysts on both ovaries that are causing the severe bleeding and pain." She leaned forward and took a deep breath before speaking. "Your CA125 levels were extremely elevated, enough to make me suspicious of possible cancer."

Lisa gave her a stunned look. "What kind of cancer?"

"Ovarian cancer."

Lisa gave her a puzzled look. "I couldn't possibly have cancer."

Dr. Gaye folded her hands over the file. "There is still a good chance, however, that we need to consider doing surgery. Before we make any decision, I would like for you to see an oncologist and schedule you for an exploratory laparotomy."

Lisa still refused to believe what she had said. "There is no way this is happening. I come in regularly for my yearly exams."

"I wish it were that simple. It would make my job that much easier. Unfortunately, ovarian cancer is something that is rarely detected early. Most times women like yourself have no obvious signs or symptoms until the disease is in an advanced stage."

"Can it be treated?"

She paused before speaking. "There is always a chance, but it will require a total hysterectomy with bilateral salpingo-oophorectomy. That means uterus, both fallopian tubes, ovaries."

Lisa shook her head. "There is no way. Michael and I are ready to start a family. Are you telling me I will never be able to have kids?"

"I'm sorry."

Lisa shook her head. No. Somebody had made a mistake. There had to have been some kind of mix-up in radiology. Mix-ups happened all the time. Some incompetent technician wrote her name on the wrong file. That's it. No problem. There was some other poor soul out there with cancer. Not her. God wouldn't do something like that to her. She and her husband had worked too hard to get where they were. They had a four-bedroom home. Good jobs. Two cars. They traveled extensively. They were financially secure. Now it was time to start a family. Even at thirty-six she had time for at least one child to spoil. Just like they had planned it.

She gave a strangled laugh. "I'm sorry Dr. Gaye, but there appears to be some kind of mistake. We'll just have to send me down to retake my X-rays."

"Your blood work confirmed the findings; however, I'll respect your wish for a second opinion. How about I schedule you to see a gynecological oncologist before you make any decisions?"

Anger overcame her. "Why are you lying? Why would you say such terrible lies?"

"Please, Lisa, you have to remain calm."

"Fuck being calm! You're sitting here telling me that you're about to pull my entire insides out, that I will never give birth to a child, and you expect me to remain calm."

"Please, Lisa—"

"Don't 'please' me. Go to hell! I am going to get a second opinion and prove that your ass is lying!"

"Lisa, I understand your pain, but time is not on your side. I would really like to schedule you to see Dr. Watson, then we can look at your options."

Lisa sprang from her seat. "You're obviously not hearing shit I am telling you. I'm not having any surgery. I am going to find another gynecologist that is going to prove you wrong. And when I do, I am suing your ass!" Lisa turned on her heels and bolted out the office.

She denied the truth for almost two weeks before she broke down and told Michael. Then she cried for another week before she finally scheduled the exploratory surgery. Within days, Dr. Gaye's findings were confirmed. She had stage II ovarian cancer, and was immediately scheduled for a total hysterectomy. Shortly after, she started her first round of chemotherapy, which left her tired and depressed. It wasn't long before her long thick hair started to fall out. The loss hit her harder than she imagined it would. Michael shaved his head in support.

Lisa tilted her head toward the sky and took a deep cleansing breath. For a young woman who had made plans for the future, finding out she had cancer was like hitting a wall while sprinting. Now, after a two-year remission, a second-look laparotomy detected that the cancer had recurred. As soon as Lisa had realized that cancer was knocking on her door again, she was prescribed an antidepressant and began seeing a psychologist to help her cope with the future. Shortly after, she found herself back in the church, devoted to developing a closer relationship with God. Now she felt at peace and was prepared to fight until the end. In the meantime she planned to live her life to the fullest and hope only for the best.

The cancer was too aggressive for chemotherapy. Therefore, next week she was scheduled to have surgery to remove a two-centimeter pelvic mass. But before the cycle began again, she needed to find a way to prepare her friends, and especially Renee.

Chapter 37

RENEE

Around two o'clock we lined up out near the dock and waited to board the glass-bottom boat. I had my camera hanging around my neck just in case there was something—or possibly, someone—I wanted to take a picture of. It was a scorching afternoon. I was almost tempted to say to hell with the boat ride and go back to my room, but my sister was already pissed at me for yesterday, so I decided to keep my mouth closed.

"How far out are they taking us?" Nadine asked.

Lisa shrugged. "I don't know. The trip is supposed to be forty-five minutes long. So I guess as far as that boat can travel in twenty-two minutes."

I glanced out at the small boat. It was supposed to fit fifteen people comfortably. I think somebody needed to work on their math.

A tall white man came over and instructed each of us to take a life vest from a large drum at the beginning of the dock. I released a sigh of relief. I'm not the best swimmer in the world. In fact I wouldn't even call myself a swimmer since I spent more than half my life afraid of water, so the thought of the boat capsizing had crossed my mind. Just recently I had enrolled in swimming lessons at parks and recreation, but who becomes an expert after six weeks?

I slipped the orange vest on, then returned to my spot in line.

While snapping it firmly across my chest, I spotted our guide coming our way. I don't know how I knew he was our guide, I just knew.

Dayu-um!

He was the color of chestnuts roasted over an open fire. He had long dreadlocks and a thin mustache and the biggest brandy-wine-colored eyes I had ever seen. He nodded in my direction, then moved to the end of the dock and stepped into the boat.

"Oh, my goodness!" I heard Lisa say. "Renee, there's your Mandingo."

She chuckled and the other two fell out laughing. I turned and rolled my eyes, then returned my gaze to him.

Nadine lightly pinched my arm. "He is definitely a cutie."

I had to agree. "True that."

When we boarded, he held out a hand and assisted each of us down into the boat. I didn't want to let his hand go. The contact sent tingles straight down to my toes.

I took a seat on the bench across from him. He took a seat while the driver started the boat. My eyes traveled down to stare at his crotch and my eyes grew big. He had on a pair of spandex shorts and either boxers or no underwear at all because his dick was on the side of his leg.

I hit Nadine and with my eyes I signaled for her to glance between his legs. When her mouth dropped I laughed. Lisa slapped my knees and I turned and rolled my eyes at her, then looked at Nadine again and we giggled softly like two teenagers.

I whispered close to her ear. "Now if that ain't a big bamboo, then I don't know what one is." He finally closed his legs and I allowed myself to listen to his presentation.

With a heavy accent, Solomon explained the fish life in the area and talked about stingrays. Glancing down at the glass bottom we were able to see jellyfish, which he explained were dangerous. They looked so transparent I didn't know how someone could possibly see them. I have to say it was quite fascinating watching schools of fish swimming right below the surface. It wasn't until he mentioned that the water was over ninety feet deep that I suddenly realized I was in a small boat and started to panic.

Beads of sweat sprinkled my forehead as my body temperature

began to climb. "How much longer before we return to shore?" I asked anxiously.

Solomon looked over at me and winked. "We have a few minutes left."

"How about we return now?" My breath came in short, shallow gasps. "I think I am about to be sick." I stood and staggered to the other side.

"Renee, sit your ass down," Lisa hissed under her breath.

I dropped down onto the bench and started breathing even harder. "I need to get off this boat, right now!" My eyes started darting around the tiny boat. I could hear people making comments and Kayla saying how embarrassing I was. I didn't give a shit. I just couldn't believe I was stupid enough to come out this far.

"Try putting your head between your legs," I heard Solomon suggest.

I tried that, but in the vest, it only served to limit my air supply.

"I can't breathe!" I shrieked. I was sweating and felt real sick to my stomach.

"That's because you're hyperventilating." Lisa lifted my head. "Renee, take slow, deep breaths."

I tried doing what she said, but instead started breathing even faster. My breathing was choppy gasps and I was only seconds away from passing out. I heard Solomon tell the driver to head back to the dock, then he moved in front of me and gently pressed his hands on my shoulders.

"Renee, listen to me," he said in a slow, deliberate, tone. I opened my eyes to look at his concerned face. "Are you listening?"

I slowly nodded my head.

"Follow me. Breathe in through your nose then out with your mouth . . . good. In through your nose, then out through your mouth."

I followed his lead and willed myself to calm down while praying I didn't throw up. I was amazed to find that within minutes my breathing had slowed and by the time we reached the dock, I was almost completely calmed down.

"Everything is going to be okay," Solomon fixed me with a stare, making sure I was hearing what he was saying.

I was embarrassed at the loss of control. Here I was on a boat with my Mandingo and I made myself look like a damn fool.

While the boat was pulled into place and tied down, I smiled over at him.

"You look like you're feeling better," he said with a smile of his own.

I nodded. "Thank you."

He then rose and moved to help everyone off the boat.

Nadine leaned back and whispered, "I can't believe you did that to get that man's attention."

I rolled my eyes and pushed her big titties out my face. "I wasn't playing."

"Yeah, right," Kayla said as she rose and moved to get off.

"Fuck y'all! I don't give a shit if you believe me or not."

Lisa squeezed my hand, then rose. "You know I know."

Yeah, I guess my sister would know that what I had just experienced was real. She had been with me when I was twenty and decided to go canoeing. Our canoe had tipped over and I found myself kicking and screaming in the water. I had almost drowned my sister when she tried to help me. Even though I was wearing a life vest, I had been scared and refused to believe that a small orange vest had the ability to save my life. After she had forced me to open my eyes, I realized how stupid I must have looked kicking and screaming while floating on top of the water.

"Thanks, Lisa."

She rose and I then waited until everyone else had gotten off before I summoned the courage to get off myself.

I reached for Solomon's hand and allowed him to help me back onto dry land.

"How are you doing?" he asked.

I gave him a nonchalant shrug. "I'm fine, really."

"Yes, you are." My Mandingo was flirting with me.

He stared. I stared. He had to be at least six-two. Tall, lean, and sexy. When he smiled dimples dominated his cheeks.

"I could help you with your fear of water." He was still holding onto my hand.

"Oh, really?"

"Yes, I could." When he smiled his eyes twinkled in the most arousing way.

I pursed my lips and waited for him to continue. I glanced to the right and spotted the trio waiting and watching. I gave them a dismissive wave and focused on Solomon.

"I would like to see you . . . away from here. We are forbidden to date the guests of the hotel but you can come to Montego Bay to see me."

I frowned. There was no way I was running around the city with a total stranger. I shook my head. "I don't feel comfortable."

He understood my apprehension and nodded. "I understand. How about I meet you right outside the gate after the sunset? Say, nine o'clock?"

Now that was an idea I was down with. "Sounds like a plan."

Chapter 38

KAYLA

Kayla dressed carefully for her date with Clayton. She didn't want to appear too casual or too formal. After Renee raided Kayla's suitcase and frowned at everything Kayla had, Kayla allowed Renee to drag her across the street to the small marketplace, where they found several outfits created by local designers. As she faced herself in the large vanity mirror, Kayla wasn't sure if she liked what she saw.

Renee had insisted on a mauve linen Capri outfit. The shirt had capped sleeves and a floral-print top with four buttons running down the front. The pants had an elastic waistband and the same floral pattern around the bottom of the pants.

She lifted her arm and looked at the fat on her forearms and frowned. Her triceps were nothing but flab. She unbuttoned the top button, trying to draw away attention from her double chin and spotlight her large breasts instead. Renee told her the outfit would draw attention away from her thick waistline and camouflage the rolls across her back, but looking from the side, she disagreed.

Kayla dropped her head as tears sprang to the surface. There was no way she could go out with Clayton, not looking like this.

She heard the key slide into the door. Quickly, she wiped her eyes as Nadine and Lisa stepped into the room.

Nadine looked at her and smiled. "Knock, knock. Renee let me borrow her card so I could come check you out."

Kayla gave her a worried look. "Where is she?"

She sucked her teeth. "At the bar, getting drunk, as usual."

"You look great," Lisa cooed.

"This outfit makes me look bigger than I already am." She fell back on the bed, a defeated look on her face.

Lisa wagged her finger at her. "Girl, don't even start with that mess. You look great."

Nadine agreed. "Here, let me help you with your makeup." She reached for the makeup bag on the end of the dresser, and frowned when she looked inside. "Is this all you have? I'll be right back." She turned and went back across the hall.

As soon as the door shut, Lisa reached for Kayla's hand. "Girl, you have got to stop putting yourself down. If Clayton didn't want to go out with you, he wouldn't have asked."

She gave a look that said she wasn't completely convinced.

"What did I tell you? Beauty starts from within. If you don't think you're beautiful how do you expect anyone else to think so?"

"That's what Leroy says."

Fuck Leroy, she thought but she didn't say it out loud. "He's right. If you don't like the way you look, then do something about it. Go to the gym, cut back on your carbs, or quit complaining and accept yourself for who you are."

She gave a frustrated sigh. "I guess you're right."

"Girl, it ain't no guessing about it. I am right." Her statement made Kayla laugh. "Girlfriend, life is too short to be taken for granted. Love yourself for who you are. You are a cutie and you need to start thinking and feeling that way."

"I know. I know."

Lisa lowered beside her on the bed. "Remember that time we were at McDonald's and that ugly baldheaded chick walked into the restaurant, strutting like she was the shit?"

Kayla chuckled at the memories. The woman, who had to be in her late forties, had a short nappy fro and wore spandex. She stepped through the door like she was Beyoncé somebody. "She was a tired mess."

"Yeah, she was, but she thought she was the shit. You could tell by the way she walked and by the way she held her head high. Even though we thought she needed to go get a weave, the brotha that stepped to her had seen something he liked. That's how you got to be."

Kayla took a moment to think about what Lisa had said. She had low self-esteem and knew it carried over into all aspects of who she was. She was going to have to do something about that. It was not going to be easy to retrain years of thinking, but she was willing to try.

"Thanks, Lisa. I feel so much better." She wrapped her arms around her friend and gave her a hug, hoping that maybe some of Lisa's confidence would travel over her way.

"Girl, I want you to have the time of your life," Lisa began as they pulled apart. "Every woman in the room is going to be jealous of you tonight."

"You think so?"

"Girl, I know so. You're going to be out with Clayton O'Neal!"

Kayla's eyes widened. She couldn't believe it, but she was right. Women were going to be jealous of her. Suddenly she wanted to look her very best. "Now you've got me nervous and excited at once."

Lisa flashed a bright smile. "Good. And don't mention Leroy's name. Ain't nothing worse than someone talking about their ex on a date," she coached.

Kayla leaned over and hugged her again. "What would I do without you?"

"You just keep on living and carrying me in your heart. I love you girl, and don't you ever forget that."

Kayla pulled away and gave her a puzzled look. Something about her statement bothered her. She was about to ask her what she meant, when there was a knock at the door. Lisa rose and went to let Nadine in.

She waved a small bag in the air. "I've got some colors here that will look fabulous on you."

For the first time, Kayla took in Nadine's appearance. "Your outfit is slamming." She was wearing a simple black dress, but with large breasts and generous hips the dress was anything but simple.

Nadine gave her a dismissive wave. "I don't know why I went to all the trouble for RD's ugly ass."

Lisa laughed. "He doesn't look that bad. He's cute in a Kermit-the-Frog kind of way."

They all broke out in laughter.

When Kayla sobered, she said, "I'm going to make it up to you, I promise."

Nadine smirked. "Girl, don't worry about it. I plan on spending all that ugly boy's money tonight. He ain't gonna ask me out again."

Lisa took the makeup bag from Nadine's hands. "Here, I'll do her makeup while you finish getting ready."

By the time Lisa had finished, the phone rang. Kayla's heart jumped. She rose and moved over to the phone.

"Hello?"

"Please tell me you haven't changed your mind," replied a deep, sensual voice.

Kayla closed her eyes and smiled. "No, I haven't."

"Good, a brotha's heart can only take so much."

She giggled. Clayton sure knew how to make her feel relaxed. "I'll be down shortly."

"RD and I'll be in the lobby waiting."

She hung up the phone, then swung around merrily and said in a breathless whisper, "They're in the lobby."

Nadine dropped a hand to her hip and frowned. "Well, green boy is gonna have to wait a few minutes because these shoes are killing my feet."

Lisa shrugged. "Beauty hurts."

"Not this damn bad." She rolled her eyes. "Why don't you go on down and keep them company until I get there."

Kayla nodded. "All right." She faced herself in the mirror and was satisfied with what Lisa had done. She reached for her purse and headed out the door. With her heart pounding rapidly against her chest, she moved down the path and into the main building, where she found him sitting in one of the chairs that surrounded the indoor fountain.

She steeled herself and moved forward. Clayton noticed her and a lazy smile slid across his mouth. His eyes pursued her and instantly she knew that she had made the right choice.

Clayton rose to his full six feet five inches. "Wow!" he said, following with a wolf whistle. "You look fabulous."

She blushed, pleased by his compliment. "So do you."

That was an understatement. He looked handsome in a pair of gray pleated slacks and a black short-sleeved shirt that was open halfway down his chest. Expensive black leather sandals were on his feet. She was suddenly aroused by his appearance.

His dark deep-set eyes crinkled in the corners. "Ready, my dear?"

She smiled. "Yes. Nadine should be down in a moment." She glanced around. "Where's RD?"

He tilted his chin toward the bar. "He went to get a drink."

He kept smiling and suddenly she felt uncomfortable. "Why are you staring at me?" she asked.

"Because you are a beautiful woman, Ms. Sparks."

A warm feeling that she couldn't begin to explain flowed through her body. She didn't know how to respond. Luckily, she was saved from an awkward moment when she glanced to her right to find Nadine heading her way. She had changed into a pair of low strapless black mules. Lisa had done an exceptional job on her makeup as well.

"Hey, Clayton. Don't you look nice."

"Thanks, so do you."

Nadine glanced around, then gave an impatient sigh. "And where is your friend?"

"Over at the bar."

She rolled her eyes. "Couldn't he have at least waited until dinner?"

Clayton leaned forward and whispered, "I think he's a little nervous about his date."

Nadine sucked her teeth. "He should be."

Clayton chuckled openly. "How about we go out to the car and wait for him?" He held out both elbows. "Your chariot awaits." He led them out to the limo waiting in front.

Both ladies were impressed.

"Wow!" Kayla said as she climbed onto the butter-soft leather. Clayton moved beside her and Nadine sat directly across from them. "How did you manage this?" she asked curiously.

He gave a sheepish grin. "It comes with the job."

"Must be nice."

Nadine clucked her tongue. "I know that's right. Some of us ain't able."

Just then the door opened and RD stepped in, grinning with a drink in his hand. "Whassup, ladies?"

Kayla noticed how Nadine rolled her eyes and slid over close to the window as RD took a seat beside her.

"What's wrong, Shorty? I don't bite."

"You never know," she mumbled, looking totally unimpressed.

Kayla gazed over at her and gave her a look that said, "Come on, you promised."

"How about some music to lighten the mood?" Clayton suggested.

Kayla nodded and he reached up and opened an overhead compartment and pushed a button. Soft flavorful music filled the limo. As the driver pulled away from the circular drive, Kayla felt herself bubbling with excitement. She was in a limo with the hundred-million-dollar man!

"So, what brings y'all ladies to Montego Bay?" RD asked against the rim of his glass.

"R&R," Nadine replied as she crossed her legs. "I haven't had a vacation in years and decided it was time to treat myself."

RD's eyes traveled the length of her with a look of pure male appreciation. "Well, I hope I get an opportunity to make that possible for you."

Nadine gave him her first real smile, then swung around on the seat so they were facing each other. Kayla felt a light tap on her arm and glanced up at Clayton's smiling face.

"What about you? You here for a little relaxation?"

She nodded. "Yes. I need it."

"Is this your first time here?"

"Yes, yours?"

He shook his head. "I come here a least once every other year. I've been to see almost half the country, but nothing's like Jamaica."

"I can see why."

She glanced briefly over at Nadine, who was whispering quietly with RD, and released a sigh of relief. She had been worried that the evening was going to be eventful. But now that Nadine was starting to warm up to RD, the night just might have a chance after all.

Chapter 39

RENEE

"All right, little sister, it's just you and me."
I bit into my lasagna to stifle a groan. I knew with Kayla and Nadine being gone I was going to have to hang out with Lisa. There wasn't any point in trying to hide because she would have tracked my ass down. It's not that I don't like my sister, because I love her. I just don't feel like hearing her lecturing me about my life.

I hate to say this, but the best thing to ever happen to me was the day she decided to move to Texas. I was so happy I gave her ass a going-away party. Finally I no longer had to look over my shoulder to find her somewhere watching and shaking her head at me.

Lisa raised her glass to her lips and asked the question I had been dreading all week. "When are you joining John in Delaware?"

I was silent for a moment, pretending to chew my food longer than was needed. "I don't know."

"You are still planning to join him, right?"

I cut my eyes at her. "I don't remember those words ever coming out of my mouth."

"No, but I assumed you would make the right decision."

"And what is the right choice?"

"Joining your husband, of course."

"Lisa, you seem to have forgotten, but only I would know what is right for my life. Right now I don't think moving to Delaware is the thing for me to do. It would be completely unfair to him."

Lisa shook her head and gave me a pitiful look. "Unfair is that man living in that big house all alone, waiting for you to make up your mind."

"Lisa, John is a grown-ass man. He knew what type of woman I was when he married me and I'm still that same person. Only now I feel like we are moving in two completely different directions."

"That's because you keep running away from him."

"Then there must be a reason why." I raised my fork to my mouth and took another bite. "I want to have what you and Michael have."

"But you already have that."

I shook my head. "No, I don't. If I did, I wouldn't even dream of letting John go. I would fight for our relationship with everything I got. Instead, I dread his phone calls. I can't stand the sight of him naked. I want a man whose smile brightens my days. Who I just want to be close to just so I can smell the natural scent of his skin."

Lisa looked at me as if I had lost my damn mind. I knew she wouldn't understand because she's had only one man in her life. She has already found her true love.

"You know you're talking crazy. Relationships are what you make them. Don't think for a minute Michael and I don't have to work at ours, because we do. You might find this hard to believe, but I've thought about leaving him many times."

Yeah, I do find that hard to believe.

"But once I take the time to weigh the good with the bad, the good outweighs everything else. You have to be willing to fight for what you have, and I think John is worth fighting for."

"How would you know?"

"Because I know that you like to set yourself up for failure. Every relationship you have been in you've found some way to sabotage it because you are afraid that if you really try and give it your all, in the end you are going to get hurt."

I resented her trying to analyze me. "I do not!"

"Yes, you do. And I blame Daddy for that."

I was mad now. "What the hell does our stepfather have to do with my marriage?"

"Everything. He turned his back on you when you needed him most. Ever since, you've been afraid to give your heart to a man for fear of the same thing happening to you again."

I gave a humorless laugh. "You're crazy."

"No, I'm not, and you know it. Daddy wasn't there for you when you needed him most and you have never forgiven him for that. But he's truly sorry and wants to tell you himself if you'd allow him to."

I cut my eyes at her. "I'd rather not."

Lisa shook her head. "You can't keep on running away from your problems. At some point you are going to have to face them. If you don't, you will never be able to have a healthy relationship with a man."

I sat there reluctantly and listened to her lecture. Lisa really thinks she knows me. It's time like this that I can't stand my sister. Call it sibling rivalry, jealousy, or whatever floats your boat. However you want to look at it, Lisa gets on my last nerve.

For as long as I can remember she has always tried to act like my damn mama. Now I know my mother is a fruit loop and our step-father never cared much for my ass, but damn, who appointed her my guardian? Now, I know I should be grateful, but I was not. Instead I regret her trying to run my life.

I have always resented her meddling in my life, but the part that bothers me the most is that she is always acting like she knows me better than I know myself. Every time I do something wrong she is right there to correct me. Then, three years ago, right after she had a hysterectomy, everything got increasingly worse. Now, I tried being sympathetic because I know how badly she and Michael had wanted children. Unfortunately, she started having problems with fibroids and was bleeding so hard and heavy and became so anemic that she had very little choice. So when she first started on me I felt that maybe she just needed to lash her pain out at someone, so why not me. But here it is three years later and she hasn't let up yet. It was like she was determined to straighten my ass out if it was the last thing she did. Lately, I wished she'd just leave me the hell alone.

Our father is the furthest thing from my mind. Not being part of my life is his loss, not mine. I was a good kid. All I had wanted was to feel accepted by him. All I had ever wanted was his love. For years I had believed that maybe I had done something wrong, that maybe I truly was a bad child and didn't deserve to be loved.

I remember spending hours crying following one rejection after another. When I was broke, he would dangle money in my face that was mine as long as I did exactly as he said. The second I fucked up, *poof,* he and his money were gone, and I was struggling, trying to find another way. I remember mailing letters to my sister and brother that were returned unopened. I remember calling the house and being told never to call there again. In my thirty-six years, I remember every single thing that man has done and said to me. I haven't forgotten, nor will I ever forgive.

On second thought, maybe he is the reason I am the way I am today. And if he is, then he has fucked my head up. I shy away from failure. I don't set myself up for rejection. I try to control every situation and if I feel that I am losing control then I leave it alone. But my marriage with John I feel is in a separate class all of its own.

Damn, I don't want to think about this right now. Why can't Lisa just leave me the hell alone?

Chapter 40

NADINE

If she'd had any idea they were going to be sitting at separate tables she would have refused the invitation to dinner.

Nadine tossed her braids over her shoulder and stared down at her strawberry margarita. RD had been going on for the last fifteen minutes about how many tackles he had made in his last game. She was so sick of listening to him brag about himself that she was ready to scream. In the limo she had almost thought that maybe she had been too quick to judge him, but as they neared the restaurant and were quickly escorted to their tables, she realized she had been right from the start. Kermit the Frog was an arrogant self-centered jackass.

Turning her head, she tuned him out and glanced out the window, admiring the view. The restaurant was a hut surrounded by mango trees, located right off the bay. As soon as they had stepped out of the limo the tantalizing smell of island cuisines teased her nose and reminded her she had missed lunch. Food and Kayla were the only two reasons why she hadn't kicked RD's ass to the curb.

Turning away from the window, she reached for her glass and took a sip of her drink. To get through a night with RD she was going to need something much stronger.

"So, Shorty, tell me about yourself."

Her brow raised and she gave him a long hard stare because she knew good and damn well he could not care less about what she had to say. "I'm an attorney."

"Oh, damn!" he replied as he fell back against his chair. "I dated an attorney once. That crazy bitch stalked my ass. I ended up having to get a restraining order on her."

"Well, you don't have to worry about me stalking your ass." As a matter of fact, he wouldn't have to worry about seeing her the rest of the trip.

RD cocked his head to the side. "Shit, a pretty honey like you, I might enjoy you stalking me."

He gave her what she guessed he thought was his Denzel smile; instead his ass looked like Urkel somebody. Why couldn't he look like Clayton? she asked herself.

She took another sip of her drink. "I don't run after men."

He had the nerve to look offended. "Shit, I ain't just any man. I'm RD Davis, linebacker for the Kansas City Chiefs."

Whoop-de-do. "And is that supposed to mean something to me?"

He laughed. "Damn, baby, why you got to be so hard?"

"Men made me the way I am."

"What your husband do, leave you for a white woman?"

She reached for her drink again and took a long swallow. "You hit that shit right on the nail."

"Dayu-um! No wonder your ass is bitter."

She nearly slammed her glass down, causing the drink to slosh over the edge and onto her hand. "I ain't bitter. I'm mad." She paused to shrug, glad that the conversation had finally steered away from the great RD Davis, although she would rather they not discuss her failed marriage. "But I've moved on since then."

RD leaned forward. "So, you got a man in your life?"

"Nope."

He looked stunned by her answer. "Then how you get your freak on?"

"I don't need a man for that."

"Shit, don't tell me you like pussy?"

"Hell, nah!" Nadine spat all too quickly, then tried to correct her mistake. "I mean, I just haven't found a man interested in a no-strings attached relationship."

He cupped his chin and grinned. "Then I'm just what the doctor ordered."

She pursed her lips and decided not to respond to his statement. Men like him were used to women throwing themselves at them and she wasn't the one.

While he signaled their waitress for a refill, Nadine allowed her eyes to wander across the restaurant. Kayla and Clayton were sitting close and smiling across the table at one another. She smiled. She was glad to see Kayla happy. Her happiness was worth the torture of sharing a meal with RD. The last thing she wanted was for her to be sitting around moping over Reverend Brown's trifling ass. Nadine had several choice words for him the next time he came smiling down in her face.

Movement caught her eye and she glanced to the table on the other side of Kayla and spotted the woman from the club. Her heart accelerated with excitement. She was sitting with the same woman she had seen her with before. The other woman was equally beautiful, only there was something about her mystery woman that she was drawn to.

She was dressed in a short pink seersucker dress that left her long lean legs visible. On her feet were three-inch heels that laced around her legs up to her calves. Suddenly, she realized why the woman intrigued her so much. Her smile reminded her of Jordan.

Nadine wasn't sure how long she was staring before the woman turned and their eyes locked. The intensity burned right through her and she wanted so badly to get up and go over and touch her just to find out if she was real.

"Hey, Shorty, did you hear what I said?"

She shook her head, clearing her arousing thoughts, and focused on RD. "What did you say?"

"Damn, am I that boring?"

Hell, yeah. "Nah, I was thinking about something."

He leaned across the table. "I can give you something to think about."

The meaning of his words was clear but she faked ignorance. She also leaned forward and licked her lips. "Something like what?"

"Shit, a little R&R, or should I say, a little RD?" he laughed at his choice of words.

She gazed over at him trying to find something attractive about the man. He had big beady eyes and thin lips and resembled a frog—what could possibly be attractive about that? The only thing that was appealing about him was his body. He did have a body.

Out the corner of her eye, she peered over at the woman, who to Nadine's disappointment was no longer looking her way. She sighed. It was probably for the best. She had come to Jamaica to forget about Jordan and here she was staring at a woman that resembled her. She was looking for a man to prove to herself that she wasn't a lesbian, and here was one sitting right across the table from her. Leaning back in her seat she stared at the arrogant bastard and decided in that instant that RD was exactly what she needed.

Chapter 41

KAYLA

While sipping their drinks and waiting for their dinner, Clayton replied, "You've been quiet. Tell me something about Kayla Sparks."

Kayla dropped her eyes and blushed. "Well, there isn't much to tell. I am a mother of two girls. And I work as a human resource assistant."

"And what about a man in your life?"

She dropped her gaze. "Not anymore."

"What happened?"

"He was never mine to begin with."

"You care to explain?"

For the past hour Kayla had felt more relaxed with Clayton than she had ever felt with any other man. She wanted to share her dilemma with him, but something was stopping her.

She looked at him again. "I made a mistake and I don't want you to think any different of me."

Clayton reached across the table and clasped her wrist. "I may not condone what you did, but I'm definitely not here to judge you. That's the Lord's job, not mine."

She smiled. "Are you a spiritual man?"

"We're all spiritual people. How we live our lives is what makes the difference. Now, if you are asking if I am a Christian, then the answer is yes."

She knew there was something about him that attracted her to him. Now she knew.

"For the last two years I have been having an affair with my pastor."

His brow rose. "Oh, that's deep."

She sighed. "Yeah, I know."

"And it's safe to assume he's married?"

"Yep, with three kids."

He released her hand and leaned back casually in his seat. "He must be something else."

She nodded. "He had me so wrapped around his finger I didn't know if I was coming or going. I quit school so I would have free time for him. Whenever he called, I jumped like some doggone fool."

"We have all played fool at one time or another in our lives."

She gave him a grim expression. "Not like me. I was meeting this man in hotels all around the state. Waiting by the phone for it to ring, hoping it was him. On Sundays I was right there in the front pew waiting for him to smile my way."

Clayton reached for his drink. "You sound like he had you hooked."

"Like a crackhead."

They laughed, which eased some of the animosity she was feeling. "I guess we all play the fool. But I played the biggest fool. He told me he was leaving his wife and I believed him. Now I find out they have another baby on the way."

Clayton paused long enough to sip his drink. "Do you still have feelings for this man?"

"It's only natural that I still have some feelings for the man, but it is definitely over between us." Even as she said it, she knew in the back of her mind she was not being completely truthful. If he left his wife tomorrow, she would be right there.

The waiter arrived with their food. Kayla stared down eagerly at their platter, pleased with her choice. As soon as he departed, she bowed her head and said grace. Then, reaching for her fork, she dipped a piece of lobster in butter and raised it to her mouth. It was everything she had expected in such elegant surroundings.

She was impressed with the restaurant. Tropical plants filled the area and even hung from the bamboo rafters above the candlelit room. What had left her in awe was the view from the window. A full moon and twinkling stars reflected upon the water. The silhouette of ships could be seen in the distance.

As she ate her dinner, Kayla kept one arm in her lap and took small bites as they talked. She carefully chewed her food and made sure to dab her mouth every few seconds. The last thing she needed were crumbs on her face.

Clayton told her he had a degree in business and was getting ready to open an upscale nightclub in Kansas City with another player he had invested with.

"Can I ask you a personal question?" he asked after a long moment of silence.

"Sure, anything."

"After everything this man has done, would you take him back if he left his wife tomorrow?"

Kayla dropped her eyes to her plate. "Yes."

"Does he love you?"

She was about to lie, then she paused. She looked at Clayton and said with hurt in her voice, "I really don't know anymore."

"I could tell that you were hurting."

"How?"

"That day on the beach. You looked so sad. You seem to be the type of woman that when you love, you love with everything that you've got."

Her shoulders sagged. "And that's why I always get my heart broken."

He reached across the table and clasped her hand. "There is nothing wrong with loving with everything you've got. I'm the same way."

"Do you have a girlfriend?"

"No, not anymore," he said without hesitation.

She couldn't help the sigh of relief at hearing he was unattached and available. "What happened?" she asked, then felt like she had

asked something too personal. "Never mind. You don't have to answer that."

"No, I don't mind." He reassured her with a smile. "Noelle liked
to hang in the streets too much. Now hear me out: I'm not the jealous type, but when you're hanging out with your friends every
Friday and Saturday night, then I've got a problem."

"I don't blame you," she replied between chews.

"Anyway, I would mention it and she would stop for a while and
then it started again."

"Did the two of you ever do things together?"

He carved into his steak as he spoke. "Sometimes, but she used to
act like such a doggone fool if any woman came up to a brotha, that
it got to be a problem. She knew it came with the job, and she said
she could handle it, but apparently she couldn't. She started drinking too much and had a habit of making a scene."

"No, she didn't!"

"Yeah, unfortunately she did on several occasions. And after she
left with some old cat with a messed up haircut, I cut her behind
loose."

Kayla was cracking up and he joined in, and that made her feel
comfortable. The hundred-million-dollar man was as human as she
was.

When Clayton sobered, he said, "Listen to me going on and on
about my ex."

"I don't mind."

"I do." He winked. "I invited you out so I could get to know you
better." He brought her hand to his lips and kissed her and she felt
the tingle all the way down to her toes.

"So, what does Kayla like to do for fun?" Hearing this in the third
person it took her a second to realize he was talking about her. She
couldn't remember the last time a man had asked her about what
she liked to do.

"I don't know. I mean, I've never really thought about it before."

"What you mean you never thought about it?"

She shrugged. "I've been so busy, I rarely have time for myself."

"Okay. well, you have time now. So tell me," he ordered as he bit
into his steak.

She smiled. "Okay. Well, I like movies and food of course. I like traveling."

"How about joining me the day after tomorrow?"

"Where?"

"A bunch of us are going to check out Dunn's River Falls."

Her eyes lit with excitement. "Ooh! I was planning to do that but no one wanted to go with me."

He leaned in confidently to say, "Good. Then let's go."

She nodded. "I'd like that."

"And I look forward to having you all to myself."

He made her tingle like he had touched her private parts. Feeling slightly embarrassed by her feelings, she concentrated on her food. Other than reggae music, the table was quiet.

"I like the way the candlelight dances in your beautiful eyes."

She blushed and dropped her eyes before looking up again. "You really think I have beautiful eyes?"

"I think everything about is beautiful."

Kayla snorted rudely. "Yeah, right."

"I wouldn't say it if it isn't true. When I look at you, I see not only the woman on the outside, but also the beautiful woman on the inside as well."

They stared at each other and she no longer felt the urge to run and hide.

He continued to compliment her as they talked. The mood became light and animated, each smiling at the other and flirting. The time flew by and she couldn't remember the last time she'd spent so much time out to dinner.

A half hour later, the table had been cleared. Their waiter came by and brought them both cups of Blue Mountain coffee as their conversation continued. After her second cup, Kayla glanced over her shoulder at Nadine, who looked ready to kill RD at any minute.

"I think we better get out of here," she suggested.

Clayton followed the direction of her eyes and chuckled. "I agree. They are definitely not a love connection."

She agreed. "No, they're not."

He gestured for the waiter to bring their check, then reached for her hand again. "And what about us?"

Her brow rose. "What do you mean?"

"You think we're a love connection?"

She tried to swallow but her throat was suddenly dry. "I . . ." She didn't know how to answer that.

He winked. "You don't have to answer. At least not yet. However, I do expect an answer before I leave this island."

Kayla felt her body flush with heat. "You got yourself a deal."

Chapter 42

RENEE

As soon as we finished eating I dodged my sister and went up to my room to change. Solomon was meeting me outside the gate in thirty minutes.

I slipped on a pair of tight blue jean shorts and a red halter top. Since I had no idea what the brotha had planned, I slid my feet into a pair of Nike tennis shoes. I decided not to carry a purse because he could try and rob my black ass. As a matter of fact, what the hell was I even thinking, going out in a foreign country to meet a total stranger?

I took a seat on the edge of the bed and thought about it for a moment. Unfortunately I didn't give it much thought. I had always loved a challenge. Taking risk was what made life exciting. Rising from the bed, I decided to leave a note as to where I had gone and who I was with just in case something did happen to my ass.

At five minutes after nine, I strolled out the gate and found Mandingo leaning against a tree, waiting. He smiled when he spotted me.

"I didn't think you were coming," he said with an irresistible grin.

"Why not?"

He shrugged. "Because American women are picky."

"True that." I moved to stand beside him. "So, what do you want to do?"

"I want to take you for a ride on my moped."

For the first time, I noticed the small red motorbike parked near the curb. That raggedy-looking thing didn't look like it had the juice to handle both of us.

I frowned. "You sure it can handle my big ass?"

He chuckled. "Your *ass* is not big. Come on."

With skepticism, I followed him over to the curb. Solomon climbed on and I climbed on behind him.

He started the bike and it moved at about nine miles an hour. We could have walked faster than that thing traveled but if we had, I wouldn't have gotten the opportunity to lean in close to Solomon. He smelled wonderful and felt even better. I wrapped my arms loosely around his middle and rested my cheek against his back.

I watched as we left the hotel district and twenty minutes later moved into a neighborhood of small homes with clothes out back, hanging out to dry. There were children without shoes running down the streets and wearing jeans that had been cut off. A dog looked like he was thirty seconds away from keeling over. Then the city changed to small cement homes and raggedy wooden stalls. I wasn't impressed at all with this area of town, but told myself there wasn't anything to worry about as long as I stayed with Solomon.

The farther he drove the worse the scene became. As he drove high into the city, I began to see shacks that resembled the ones in the movie *Roots*. Most had tin roofs, some had flat wooden tops. There were children frolicking in the street, playing what looked like tag. They were clean, although their clothes looked shabby. Old folks were sitting in chairs out front, laughing and having a good time. I can't understand how people could be happy living like this but I guess if that's all you know, how can you know what you're missing? No wonder they say Americans are spoiled, because we are. Not one of those people seemed to mind that their hair was all over their heads. The only person that seemed to care was me.

So this was real Jamaica.

Solomon pulled in front of a red shack with a blue door and turned off the motor, then he climbed off.

I paused, giving him a puzzled look. "Where we going?"

"I want you to see how the Rastas live."

Before I could object he lifted me off the seat and onto my feet, beside him. He took my hand and led me up the raggedy steps and we entered the building. Once inside I realized we were in a small restaurant.

I glanced around at the meager surroundings and tried not to frown. Someone had tried to make the place look nice the best way they knew how. There were three round tables with mix-match chairs around them and a plastic vase with fresh yellow flowers at the center of each table. The wooden floor squeaked and was dusty. There obviously was no central air; however, there was a fan over-head. At least the building had electricity.

We took a seat and a dark-skinned woman wearing a dingy white apron and a turban wrapped around her head came out.

"Solomon, mon. Where have you been?" She wrapped her arms around him and planted a kiss to the top of his head.

"Busy working, but I thought I'd bring a friend with me. Maggie, this is Renee. She has come here from St. Louis."

She gave me a warm smile. "Nice to meet you. I am honored to have you visit my restaurant. What can I get you?"

Solomon looked over at me before answering, "You like Red Bull?"

I nodded. As hot as I was, a beer sounded good.

"I also have some good hot Jamaican food for you."

I wasn't hungry but I didn't want to hurt the nice woman's feel-ings, so I nodded. She left, then returned shortly with our beers. I immediately popped mine open and took a long thirsty drink. I was thankful to find that it was ice cold.

Solomon also took a drink, then leaned forward in his seat, his long dreads resting on the table. "What do you think of my Jamaica?"

I didn't want to offend his country in any way, so I took a moment to think about my answer. "It's nothing like the brochures."

He tossed his head back and laughed and I found I liked the loud boisterous sound. He was indeed a beautiful man in a masculine way. He stood six-one and weighed one-ninety. He had broad shoul-ders and a trim waist and hips. Tonight he looked like a typical black male between the ages of sixteen and twenty-five, although I sus-pected him to be closer to thirty. He was wearing jeans that hung low on his waist and a white sleeveless shirt that emphasized his large biceps. On his feet was a pair of Jordan's.

"Have you ever been to America?" I asked.

He shook his head. "No, and I don't care if I ever do."

"Why?"

Solomon gave me a long serious look. "Renee, not everyone wants to go to America. This is my home and I love it. So many Jamaicans go to America and come back changed. They start to look down on our people and forget our values. I love my country and I don't care to live anywhere else."

I was surprised by his answer but I could feel his pride. It was safe to assume he wasn't searching for an American wife.

Maggie came out carrying two piping-hot plates. She put one in front of me and the other near him. I glanced down at the food and was pleased to find it looked quite tasty.

"What you have is curry goat, stewed peas, rice, and pigtails. On the side is fried plantain."

"What's that?" I asked her.

"They are like bananas only sweeter."

I reached for my fork and tasted it. "Mmm, delicious." It was indeed quite good.

Looking quite pleased, Maggie left us to eat our food. While I ate, Solomon told me that he has lived with his grandmother since he was eighteen, while his parents lived in Kingston.

"How old are you?" I asked.

He reached under the table and stroked my leg. "I'm old enough for whatever you have in mind."

I was flattered by his comment and the feel of his large strong hand.

As we ate he talked about growing up in Jamaica. It sounded so much like the life of a typical child in America. He and his father never got along so when he turned eighteen his father told him there was room for only one man in their house. So he packed his bags and left to live with his ailing grandmother.

"Shit, my father and I never got along either," I said between chews. "He has grandchildren he barely even knows, and that is all right by me. I'd never subject them to the type of upbringing I endured."

He blinked as if he was coming out of a trance. "I don't have any children yet, but when I do I don't want them around my father either."

"What about your mother?"

He smiled at the mention of her. "Very sweet woman. She always has a hug and a kiss. She has lived a long life. I am the youngest of twelve."

I practically choked on my food. "You're saying your mother gave birth to twelve children?" He nodded and I shook my head. I couldn't even imagine ten more kids sliding out of my coochie.

When we finished eating, he grabbed my hand and we went for a walk down the road. There weren't any streetlights so it was dark except for the light beaming from a full moon. Children were still out playing and at the end of the road were an old man and woman sitting in front of a card table. Solomon led me up the steps and onto the wide porch.

"Grandma, I'd like you to meet Renee."

I glanced down at her smiling dark face. "Hello."

"Welcome, mon. Please have a seat."

She patted the chair beside her and I moved and took a seat.

"Can you play dominos?" she asked.

I nodded.

Leaning over she patted my hand. "Good. I need a partner."

Solomon took the seat across from me and then the game was on.

Chapter 43

NADINE

"So are we going to do this or what?"

RD was really getting on Nadine's nerves. If this wasn't important to her, Nadine would have cussed him out by now.

"I want you to know that this isn't the type of shit I do on a regular basis."

"I ain't asked you that."

Nadine looked off into the water fountain, then finally said, "Yeah, let's do this."

Next thing she knew, RD was leading her down the path to building 3 and down the hall to his ocean-view suite. As soon as the door was shut he pulled her into his arms. He kissed her and before she could respond, his hands were all over her. He pushed his tongue past her lips and entered her mouth. She met his skillful strokes as he tightened his hold on her. Thoughts of Jordan invaded her mind. She felt like she was cheating. She hadn't been with anyone else but her in over a year and never once thought about messing around. Even though they had broken up before she had left for vacation, she still felt like she was betraying her. Nadine knew she had better do something fast before it was too late, but the kiss, his lips, felt far too good to stop. Besides, wasn't her decision to sleep with RD so she would forget about Jordan?

They stood there kissing like teenagers for what felt like forever until she had to pry her mouth away just to get a breath of air.

"I've been waiting all night to stick my dick inside of you," RD murmured as he slid his tongue inside her ear. Nadine flinched and wrestled her way free of his groping hands.

"Damn, can you at least wait until I take my clothes off?" she said between gritted teeth.

He started laughing something terrible. "I see you gonna play hard to the end."

"Only if you keep acting like some horny-ass teenager. Now sit!" she ordered, and he obeyed.

She slowly slid her dress down over her hips, followed by her bra and panties.

RD reached down and stroked his crotch. "Damn, baby, just looking at you makes me want to nut."

She rolled her eyes, thankful that the room was semidark. "Now it's your turn."

She took a seat on the end of the bed and watched as he eagerly shed his clothes. Despite his arrogant attitude his body was attractive. Or at least she thought so until he lowered his boxers and she noticed what he was working with.

Damn! His dick was short, fat, and uncircumcised. Eeew!

Again she was thankful the room was dark except for the moonlight peeking through the ocean-view window, and hid her disgust.

"Come to big daddy."

Big? Where at? She asked herself. She was in no rush for what he had to offer. She was searching for a man with a dick big enough to make her forget that she preferred lying in the arms of a woman as opposed to a man.

Nadine sighed. "No, you come here."

"Shit, you ain't got to tell me twice."

She slid up farther onto the bed and RD lowered himself on top.

"Damn, these babies are lovely," he murmured as he suckled one nipple and then the other.

Nadine laid there with her eyes trained to the ceiling and felt no desire for what was happening to her. He was above her, resting his weight on his large bulky arms. RD slid on a condom and within seconds, slipped deep inside of her. He pumped between her legs and howled like a dog under a full moon while she lay there lifeless, tears flowing out of the corners of her eyes. Seconds after he rolled over, he started snoring.

Without a minute to spare, she threw on her clothes and hurried to her room.

Chapter 44

RENEE

We played cards most of the night, then Solomon and I went for a walk around the neighborhood. It was a quiet night. The kids had gone in for the evening. It was cool even though the wind was relatively still. By the time we made it back to his grandmother's house, she was on the couch, fast asleep.

"You want another beer before we head back?"

I nodded. I'd already had three, but what the hell. I wasn't the one driving.

He signaled for me to follow him to the kitchen. I was pleased to find that the house, although small, was well kept. There was a living room with two mixed-matched couches and a blue chair. Homemade blue curtains hung over a single window. Down a squeaky-floored hall were two small bedrooms and a bathroom that resembled an outhouse. Directly behind it was a small kitchen with a single sink, a small refrigerator, and an apartment-size stove. There was a square HOME SWEET HOME rug on the floor.

I was admiring the meager décor when Solomon came up behind me and whispered near my ear, "I want to fuck."

Before I could respond, he had unzipped my shorts and slid them down my hips. He then swung me around and pinned me against the sink with the weight of his body.

"I see you like it rough," I said in a breathless whisper.

"There is no better way."

"I agree," I replied, reaching down to handle—Lord, have mercy—his fully erect ten inches. The large rock-hard organ strained against his pants. I lowered his zipper, reached inside the fly of his boxers, and freed him. Damn! His dick was made for the type of action I lived for. My first impulse was to drop to my knees and bury it between my lips. But before I could make a move, Solomon swung me around and roughly pulled my thong aside.

"Wait!" I said. "What about your grandmother?"

"Don't worry about her." He bent me over the sink and without another word, grabbed my hips and pushed roughly inside of me. Oh, God! After my last disaster it was just what I needed. Everton was chopped liver; this was prime rib. My head rolled forward and I braced my hands against the counter and pushed back to meet each of his thrusts. He pumped in and out of my coochie, with his balls slapping against my clit. I bit my lower lip and tried to stifle a moan. The last thing I needed was for his grandmother to wake up and find us fucking in her kitchen. I was seconds away from coming when he started speeding up the process. I was so wet I couldn't stand it.

"Yees-s-s!" escaped between my lips at the same time I felt him explode inside of me.

Neither of us moved for the longest time, then he finally pulled out and reached for the dish towel and wiped his dick off. He grinned over at me then offered me the towel.

Yuck! I would rather go home with a sticky coochie than wipe my shit with a sour dish towel. "No thanks." I fixed my thong, then reached down for my shorts.

Solomon closed his pants, then dragged me into his arms. "You are delicious," he murmured before he captured my lips in a long wet kiss. My head was spinning with excitement. My search for the big bamboo was officially over.

Chapter 45

KAYLA

Kayla didn't think the evening could get any more perfect. There was a slight cool breeze and millions of stars painting the black sky above. She and Clayton held hands as they moved along the shore. They had kicked off their shoes and left them on a chair near the jerk chicken hut that had closed for the night.

She told him how she had never seen a beach until she was an adult and even then it had been Lake Michigan. She still had yet to visit the coast. In exchange, Clayton told her about how beautiful the beaches were on the East Coast. After a while they stopped talking altogether and just settled for listening to the sounds of the waves crashing.

"I want to thank you so much for a wonderful evening."

Clayton stopped walking and turned to her. "I should be the one thanking you. It is really a treat to go out with someone who has something to talk about for a change other than my career and themselves."

There was an uncomfortable silence for a few seconds, then it finally happened.

He leaned forward and pressed his lips against hers and she thought maybe she had heard fireworks. The brotha had skills.

He was the first to end the kiss and he stood with his feet in the wet sand, holding her against him.

Kayla took a deep breath. "No one has ever treated me this . . ." her voice trailed off as she tried to find the right words to express what she was feeling. "No one has ever made me feel this special, and I thank you."

He leaned back and stared down at her. "That's because you are special and you deserved to be treated like a princess." He kissed her again and she dove into the kiss, hands, tongue. She could feel his dick growing hard against her abdomen. It was obvious where the evening was going. But what other direction was there? He had spent hundreds on her tonight and next he would want his reward. She tried not to think about football players trying to score with as many women as they could. Deep down, she knew that Clayton was different.

"I don't want this evening to end," he murmured against her nose.

"Neither do I," she whispered as his tongue slipped inside her mouth again. *Oh, well*, she thought. Having sex on the beach might turn out to be fun. She found herself wondering if Renee had done it yet on the beach. Knowing that scandalous hoochie, she probably had, long before coming to Jamaica.

When Clayton lowered onto the cool wet sand, she followed.

"I hope you don't mind getting wet. I love the way wet sand feels against my skin," he asked.

"I don't mind."

He wrapped his arm around her and rolled her on top of him. He continued to kiss her lips, neck, and cheeks. A throbbing started at her chest and worked its way down between her legs. Clayton was making her feel so many things that having sex with him wasn't such a bad idea after all. If nothing else transpired between them at least she would have the memories of sleeping with a professional football player.

"Let's spend the night lying on the beach," he asked between kisses.

Before she could respond, his hand grazed her breast.

He rolled her over onto her back and deepened the kiss.

She turned her head. "Clayton, listen. If you want to have sex, let's go to your room."

He pulled back with a look of surprise. "What?"

Kayla swallowed. "I said let's go to your room and have sex." Then she saw his eyes change from surprise to disappointment and her stomach clenched. She had just fucked up.

Clayton sighed. He then rose and reached for her hand and helped her up from the sand. "I think it's time I walk you to your room." He led her back toward the hotel.

Panic rose up inside of her. She really had fucked up. He was pissed off because she had said no to his desire to have sex on the beach. Now he wanted to get away from her as quickly as possible. There was no way she could bear to see him tomorrow with another woman on his arm.

"Clayton, wait!" She tugged him to a halt. "Okay, I changed my mind. We can make love out here on the beach. I've never done it before and was a little scared, but I'm game. I really am."

His shook his head, then started laughing.

"What is so funny?"

He stopped laughing and leaned forward and held her for the longest time in the circle of his arms before he released her. "Kayla, I had no intention of having sex on the beach. I just met you. You're too much of a lady for me to even think such a thing. Besides, sex is the furthest thing from my mind. I wanted to spend the night lying in a chair together, holding you in my arms while we watched the sunrise. That's all."

She suddenly felt about two feet tall. "Oh, God. I feel like such a fool."

He leaned forward. "Well, you shouldn't. Come on. Let me walk you back to your room. I think maybe we both were getting just a little bit carried away."

Relief washed over her and suddenly she started laughing. That special feeling returned as he escorted her up to her door. Once again he pulled her into his arms and that warm secure feeling returned as he kissed her.

"Good night," he finally said when he pulled away.

She gave him one final smile, then turned and stepped into her room and shut the door behind her.

Glancing over at the bed, she wasn't the least bit surprised to find that Renee wasn't in the room. She had probably gotten herself into something.

She was reaching down to remove her shoes when there was a knock at her door.

"Who is it?" She thought that maybe Clayton had returned for another kiss.

"It's me, Kayla."

"Lisa, what you doing still up?" she asked as she swung open the door.

"Girl, please, there wasn't any way I was going to bed until I had a chance to speak to you." She entered the room and took a seat on the end of Kayla's bed. "Okay, I want to hear all about your night."

"Ain't you nothing." Kayla thought she would stall a few minutes and quietly moved over to Renee's bed and took a seat. "Where's your sister?"

Lisa waved her hand dismissively. "Who knows? Now quit trying to change the subject and tell me what happened," she said impatiently.

"Nothing, really. We just had a nice dinner," she replied. Her answer was obviously unconvincing, because Lisa blew out a frustrated breath.

"And?"

"And what?" Kayla gave her an innocent look.

"Kayla, you are two seconds away from getting your ass whooped."

She started to laugh. "Okay, I'll tell you."

Lisa leaned back comfortably on the bed prepared to listen.

Kayla tried to contain her excitement as she spoke. "We rode in a limo to this fancy restaurant on the water. It was so romantic. There were candles and soft music in the background."

"What did you order?"

"Lobster, of course."

Lisa sucked her teeth. "Shit, it ain't like he can't afford it."

"I know that's right."

They both laughed.

"He is the nicest guy I've ever met." She smiled as she thought about how much of a gentleman he was. "He treated me like I was someone special."

"You are special."

Kayla smiled. Lisa always knew how to say the right thing. "I guess," she said with obvious insecurity.

"There is no 'I guess'. Nobody takes a woman to dinner and spends the entire evening with her if he doesn't like her."

Kayla smirked as she spoke. "Yeah, I guess that's true."

"So, did you kiss him?"

Kayla hesitated, then nodded like a girl who'd experienced her first kiss. "Gir-r-rl, and he can kiss! Oh, my God! I could have locked lips with him all night." She tried not to sound too excited, but she couldn't help what she was feeling. "His lips were soft and gentle and he moved his tongue with skill. He didn't spit in my mouth."

Lisa frowned. "Spit in your mouth? Who the hell you've been kissing?"

She gave a dismissive wave. "No one recently. Even Leroy doesn't tongue kiss. It's been so long I'm surprised I remember."

She sucked her teeth. "Kissing is like riding a bike. You never forget."

Kayla leaned back wearing a dreamy smile. "I could get used to being held and kissed by him."

"So why don't you?"

She frowned. "He's a pro ballplayer. What in the world would he want with someone like me?"

Lisa blew out a frustrated breath. "There you go with that crap again."

"It's true. Besides, I already have a man, remember?"

Her friend looked at her like she was crazy. "Excuse me?"

"You heard me. Clayton is a nice guy, but that's it. Regardless of his wife being pregnant, I love Leroy, and I'm not ready to give up on what we have. I've got too many years invested."

Lisa sat up and leaned toward her. "If you only saw the look in your eyes when you talk about Clayton you would know that isn't true. You really like him."

Kayla rolled her eyes and lay back on the pillow. "Regardless of what you might think, I know what I have with Leroy. Clayton is a risk I just don't think I am willing to take, especially not at the risk of losing a sure thing."

Lisa snorted at her comment. For her to be one of Kayla's closest friends, she was starting to get on her nerves. Why couldn't her friends understand that even though she liked Clayton, her love for Leroy was too strong to let go?

Chapter 46

RENEE

Shortly after one, Solomon pulled his moped up in front of the Holiday Inn Sun Spree. I climbed off and he swung his leg over the side and moved to stand beside me.

"Thank you for a wonderful evening."

My lips curled into a provocative smile. "I should be thanking you."

He pulled me against him and pressed his mouth to mine. I willingly parted my lips and allowed his tongue to invade my space. He definitely had many talents.

"Can I see you again tonight?" he asked when we came up for air.

"That might be arranged." I didn't want to sound too eager, although inside I was jumping for joy.

"I'll be here, same time."

"I didn't say yes," I replied as I slowly backed away.

"You'll be here," he said confidently.

Damn skippy. I gave him a silly smirk, then turned and jogged up the circle driveway.

Oh, God! I felt like flying. The last several hours were nothing like I had ever experienced. Solomon was a rare breed and for the next couple of days he was going to be all mine!

See, this is what I have been trying to get everyone to understand.

What I felt tonight with Solomon, I have never felt with John. I'm serious.

A woman should feel proud to be on her man's arm. I should be able to stand across a crowded room and watch him interact with others and think to myself, "damn, that is one sexy mothafucka." I should be dying to get his ass home so I can ride him like a mechanical bull, then lay in his arms until morning. Now *that's* the way a wife should feel about her husband. And I honestly never felt that way.

When we first started dating I was embarrassed to introduce John to my friends because I knew what they were going to say.

I remember a week after he had proposed, my girl Danielle came over for a visit. As soon as she stepped into my house and spotted John at the table, her mouth dropped. He did look a hot mess— faded black jeans, and a t-shirt that was three sizes too small. He hadn't put in his contacts so he was wearing a pair of "birth control" glasses. You know, the thick bifocals that's guaranteed to stop you from getting any pussy.

The minute he walked out of the room, Danielle whispered, "bitch, you are wrong for that!" After that I didn't bother to introduce him to any more of my friends. Lisa had a fit when I told her I was ashamed to introduce him to anyone.

"Renee, who gives a fuck what others think about him. It's what you think that matters. I bet all them bitches wish they had some man taking care of them."

Lisa was right, and from that day on I would chant those words in my head every time I took him to meet friends and family. But instead of feeling better I would feel guilty, because who the hell has time to be going through all that each and every time. It was like— and still is—like I was forcing myself to feel something I was not. It's a bunch of bullshit, and I've been doing that for three years too long. But shit, what's a sistah to do?

On the ride back to the hotel, I had allowed myself a little time to think about my relationship with John. And I have come to the conclusion that the reason why I can't break it off with him is because I feel like I owe him something. Now, bear with me a minute. It's late and I'm tired but I know if I don't say this now, by tomorrow it will have slipped my mind.

I knew when I married John what I was getting—an older man who wanted a family. In exchange, John knew what he was getting— a woman who did not love him but needed financial stability for her family. So what has changed? Absolutely nothing, except that I don't want to do it anymore, and because of that I feel so damn guilty.

He is the exact same man I married. He has no hobbies, no friends; he lacks spontaneity, and sex is a nightmare. I settled for it in the beginning because I figured for what I was getting in return, it was a small sacrifice to pay.

John gave me the opportunity to pursue my career and he shared in the success of my first book. Now that my career is on its way, I am ready to jump ship and part of me doesn't feel that is fair. Now you would think as selfish as my ass is, I wouldn't give a fuck, but I do. I really do. With John, for the first time in my life, I have met someone who challenges my ability to make a decision.

My psychiatrist told me that I was hurting John more by staying with him because by doing that I wasn't allowing him the opportunity to find someone who would truly love him. And her old ass is right. It is unfair of me. But even knowing that doesn't make it any easier.

Damn! My ass is confused. I'm no closer to coming to a decision than I was six months ago. What's a sistah to do?

I'll have to think about it some more tomorrow, because right now I'm going to bed.

Chapter 47

NADINE

The next morning Nadine rose slowly out of the bed. The slide door was open and a gentle breeze flowed into the room.

After checking for phone messages, Lisa hung up the receiver. "Jordan called."

Nadine simply nodded and slid out from under the covers.

"You can't keep avoiding her."

"I know," she said as she reached inside the dresser for something cool to wear.

Lisa leaned back on the bed. "I'm still dying to hear about your date last night."

Nadine finally looked over at her and released a shaky sigh. "RD got on my last nerve. Then I went back to his room and let him screw me."

Lisa's eyes grew wide. "Did it work?"

Nadine made a face. "Hell no."

"Because of Jordan?"

"Yeah, because of Jordan." Not in the mood to further the discussion, Nadine turned and stepped into the bathroom. She turned on the shower, then stepped into the tub. Standing under the spray, she thought about last night. Not about RD—he had been a big waste of her time, and any thoughts of what she had done last night made her sick to her stomach. Instead, she thought about the woman who had been watching her from across the room. Just remembering her smile caused a tightening of her breasts. The tingling between her legs was not a result of RD's performance, but was a result of the beautiful woman's stares. In fact, her mind flooded with memories of the first time she and Jordan had made love.

Two weeks had passed since their first introduction and yet she still had been avoiding Jordan's calls. Then, finally, after another lonely evening, Nadine admitted to herself that she could no longer go without seeing her. She contacted Jordan and asked her to meet her at a party at her law firm.

By the time Nadine had arrived shortly after nine, conversations and music flowed throughout the room. She had arrived late, as usual, and spotted one of their criminal attorneys, Christopher Monroe, try-ing to get her attention. They were in a deep conversation about an upcoming case when she spotted Jordan coming through the door.

Something hit Nadine when she took in Jordan's thin face and large hazel eyes. The smile radiated her way and her heart fluttered. She couldn't understand what she was feeling. All she knew was that her life was about to change.

For the rest of the night no matter how much she tried to fight it she kept finding herself migrating to Jordan. They ended up spend-ing most of the evening sipping coffee in the corner while talking and discovered they had a lot more in common. They discussed men, kids, their dreams and fears, and Nadine had an intellectual conversation that she never seemed to find with a man. When it was time for the evening to end, she felt a sense of disappointment. She didn't know what it was but there was this strong need to be in her presence that she didn't even bother to try to understand. All she knew was that when Jordan asked her for a ride home, she agreed. They talked and laughed all the way to her apartment. Jordan's hand found its way to her thigh, to her arm, and even to her cheek. It seemed so natural Nadine didn't have the willpower to tell her to stop. All that kept running through her mind was that there was no denying she was attracted to this woman. A small part of her regret-ted inviting her to the party. When she pulled in front of Jordan's apartment, she felt a bit relieved.

Jordan paused before exiting her vehicle. "Would you like to come up?"

Nadine shook her head. "I don't think that's a good idea."

Jordan looked hurt, then she covered Nadine's hands with her own. "I'm sure you've realized that I like you."

"I like you too."

"No, I mean I really like you. I know why I haven't heard from you and why you've been ignoring my calls. You're scared and I understand because I'm scared too of what I am feeling for you."

Nadine gasped, unable to speak because she knew Jordan was right.

"Have you ever thought about making love to another woman?"

She dropped her eyes so she could shield her embarrassment. She couldn't bring herself to admit the nights she lay awake fantasizing about her and Jordan—caressing her breasts, running her tongue between her legs. "I've been curious," she admitted.

"So why don't you find out, with me?" Jordan reached up and stroked her cheek, sending tremors through Nadine's body. "I want to show you how good it can be."

"I don't know if I'm ready."

"I won't pressure you. I just wanted to let you know how I feel. But I won't take this a step further unless you feel the same way. We can spend the rest of the evening drinking wine and listening to music and I'll be happy just as long as I am with you."

There was a moment of silence before she heard herself agree.

They climbed out of the car and Nadine followed her up to her apartment on the second floor, a beautifully decorated room filled with African American art and rich wood furnishings.

While Jordan went to pour them both a glass of wine, Nadine strolled over to the stereo and turned on a slow jam radio station.

Jordan returned carrying two glasses of wine and a bottle of white zinfandel on a tray.

For the next several hours they talked and listened to music. Nadine allowed the wine to relax her.

Jordan would lean forward and whisper in Nadine's ear, and she found herself getting turned on again. She tried to blame the night on the wine, because she too started caressing Jordan's thigh and arm with slow lingering fingers.

Around eleven, she was totally relaxed as they sat on the couch, caressing and petting one another.

"Listen, Nadine. I want you so bad it hurts." She cupped her chin so she had no choice but to look at her. "I want you but you've got to want me too."

Nadine licked her lips, then heard herself say, "I want you too."

Jordan seized the moment and leaned forward and kissed her, a slow sensual caress that Nadine willingly accepted. She didn't even realize that her tongue was in her mouth until she moaned. She kissed with more passion than she'd ever experienced with any man. She opened her eyes and they locked gazes. She felt like the kiss would never end, and she wasn't complaining.

Jordan then rose and took her hand and led her to the bedroom.

While Nadine sat on the end, Jordan slowly removed her clothes. All her thoughts and fantasies didn't come close to what she was feeling and seeing. She was about to be made love to by a woman.

Jordan unbuttoned her shirt and peeled it away. Nadine feasted her eyes on small perky breasts with nipples that were chocolate and hard. Jordan lowered her skirt over her hips and Nadine gasped when she slipped her panties off and stood before her. Now she knew why God had created women. Now she knew why men couldn't keep their hands off women and always felt the need to be buried deep between their legs. Jordan took everything off and all that remained was black high heels.

"Now I'm going to undress you," she said, stretching her hand out to Nadine.

Nadine's response to her request was a gasp. She was aroused and she placed her hand in hers. She gently tugged her upright and brought her against her bare breasts. Her fingers ached to capture one in her hand, but instead she waited to see what would happen next.

Jordan unbuttoned Nadine's blouse and allowed it to fall to the floor. As soon as Jordan removed her bra, she cupped one of her breasts in her hand, then leaned forward and began to suckle her nipple gently. She glanced down to find Jordan staring up at her.

She then slipped her fingers down past her inner thighs, where she eased them apart. Slowly she slipped two fingers inside of her and they were doing things she had only dreamed of. Jordan urged her to lay back on the bed. Nadine willingly complied, then eased her legs open wider so that she could have plenty of room.

Jordan then kneeled down between her legs and licked the spot that only another woman would be able to find. She shivered and bucked against the bed. There was no way she could have passed up the pleasure she was receiving, and from a woman, for goodness' sake. She was powerless to fight it. It was only a matter of minutes before she felt an explosion travel though her. Afterwards, Jordan held her in her arms while her heartbeat returned to normal.

After that their relationship took off. They spent days and even nights together. Every chance she could she dashed over to Jordan's just to be in her arms and to feel her naked skin against hers. She never allowed her to stay at her house for fear that her son would find out about them. Instead, Jordan would drop by like a casual friend. After a year of living behind closed doors, she was tired of the sneaking, tired of feeling ashamed of loving another woman.

Jordan wanted them to move in together. She was ready to let the world know just how she felt about Nadine. Only Nadine wasn't ready yet to admit that she was in love with a woman. Nadine had never been completely comfortable or willing to accept her feelings and it had taken a toll on their relationship. Jordan had given her an ultimatum that had ended in a heated argument with Nadine calling off the relationship.

As she scrubbed away the memories of the night before she told herself it was for the best. Her family would never have understood.

Chapter 48

KAYLA

Kayla woke up to the sounds of reggae music coming from the jerk-chicken hut below her window. She didn't know when she had finally dozed off. The last thing she remembered hearing was a couple out in the hall, laughing near her door. She remembered glancing over at Renee's bed and finding it still empty.

She rolled over and spied the clock on the side table. It was almost ten. Renee's bed was still empty. She didn't know how she did it. Party all night, drink like a fish, then roll out the bed the next morning and start her day.

Kayla stretched her body as memories of the night before came flooding back. Her lips curled as Clayton came to mind.

She had never had a man interested in just holding her. Usually after the sex there was no moment of cuddling; instead the men she had been with broke their necks trying to get out the door. Not Clayton. He wasn't interested in sex. Instead, he had held her and kissed her with enough passion to make her feel like a beautiful and desirable woman.

However, as Kayla slipped into her clothes, doubt lurked in the corners of her mind. Was his reason for not wanting to sleep with her because he didn't find her attractive? She tried to brush that possibility aside, yet she could not help wondering if that was the case. Maybe she should have insisted that he make love to her. What man turns down sex if it's right in his face?

If he rejected her this morning she was going to cry.

Suddenly she wasn't as eager to join the others for breakfast. Yet she couldn't hide in her room forever. If Clayton was no longer interested, then at least she would know. Although being rejected by two men in one week was going to be a lot more than she could swallow.

Her thoughts suddenly shifted to Leroy. He still hadn't called her. She felt like such a fool believing that he really cared about her. She had just been another piece of ass. As stupid as she was, she had fallen for him hook, line, and sinker. Lisa was right. It was time for her to move on.

When they returned home, she intended on finding a new church and getting on with her life.

Chapter 49

RENEE

We were sitting at a booth laughing and having a good time when Kayla arrived.

"What's so funny?" she asked.

I glanced up at her as she neared our table. "Gir-r-rl, Nadine was telling us how frog boy kissed her like he was swatting flies with his tongue."

Kayla giggled and lowered onto the bench, beside Nadine. "Y'all need to stop talking about that man. He really isn't all that bad."

Nadine snorted rudely. "That's 'cause you didn't have to spend the evening with him."

"I did have to spend part of my evening with him and I have to admit he is a little arrogant, but he does have a charm about him."

We all whipped around and looked at her crazy ass at the same time, then after a long moment started laughing.

We were still laughing when I spotted Clayton moving forward in a strong, even pace. When he saw Kayla, he smiled and waved, and she finger-waved back. Then he moved and joined his friends at the other end of the room.

I swung to my right. "Dayum, Kayla, I hope you gave that brotha some last night."

"Not every man's out for sex."

Nadine snorted rudely. "Since when?"

"Since there are still a few gentlemen out there," Kayla replied with a dreamy expression on her face. Obviously she was thinking about last night.

It was my turn to add my two cents. "Believe me, no matter what bullshit lines they send your way, they all want the same thing: some ass."

Lisa looked appalled. "Renee, I know you don't really believe that shit."

"Why not? It's the truth. They might act like they value your virtue and your desire not to sleep with their asses the first night, but believe me, as soon as they drop you off at the door they are leaving to sleep in somebody else's bed and that's where their asses are until you are ready to give up the goods."

Lisa gave me a disappointed look. "Renee, you've got issues. I didn't give Michael any for an entire year."

I cackled. "My brother-in-law was a virgin his damn self, so his ass doesn't count."

They started laughing. As soon as they quieted down, I continued. "A man loves for a woman to take charge. He may be telling you no, but his dick is saying, hell yes. Shit, you gonna end up sleeping with his ass anyway. I believe it's better to find out what he's got to work with up front—that way you save yourself a lot of wasted time and efforts. Shit, you know I know."

"Yes, we know," they said in unison.

Shit, after Everton's ass I wasn't taking any more chances.

"It's obvious how Kayla's evening was. How about you, Nadine?"

"Girl, puhleeze."

Her eyes dropped to her plate. I eyed her closely and noticed the flushed tint of her cheeks and could tell Nadine was trying to hide something.

"Come on. Give us the four-one-one," I encouraged.

"Let's just say, RD needs to stay the hell away from me," she replied, flipping her wrist.

I pointed my fork at her and asked, "Did you give him some?"

"Nope."

I could tell the bitch was lying. "Yeah, right."

"Renee, everybody ain't like you," Nadine countered with a tart smirk.

"Shit, don't hate. Participate." With that said, I resumed eating my breakfast before it got cold.

Kayla leaned to the side and playfully bumped her shoulder against mine. "Where were you last night?"

"Don't worry about it."

Lisa's interest was piqued. "When did she get in?"

Kayla shrugged. "I have no idea. All I know is, when I finally drifted off to sleep your sister was nowhere to be found."

Nadine's eyes sparkled with amusement. "I bet I know where she was."

Kayla and Lisa looked in her direction and together they shouted, "Mandingo!"

I smiled, then wagged my arched eyebrows suggestively.

Nadine clapped her hands excitedly. "Oh, my God! You were with Solomon, weren't you?"

I dug into my food. "I ain't telling y'all heifers anything."

"Yes, you are." Kayla snatched my plate of food from me.

"Hey, give that back!"

She passed the plate to Lisa. "Not until you tell us."

I slumped against the seat and faked defeat. Shit, I had been dying to tell them all morning about my evening.

"Okay, I met Solomon last night."

They each shrieked. Even Lisa seemed intrigued. "And, what happened?" she asked, leaning into the table and smiling, looking for more information.

I collapsed onto the table. "I ain't never had that much dick in my life."

"Hell naw!" Nadine screamed.

Kayla grabbed my arm. "Bitch, get up and give us details."

I knew I had to make the story better than ever before. I put my elbow on the table and rested my chin in the palm of my hand, and put on a dreamy expression. "He picked me up on his moped and we rode to his neighborhoods, where he took me to an authentic Jamaican restaurant. The food was so good!"

Kayla was getting impatient. "Girl, get to the good part." We all laughed and slapped high fives.

"He ate my coochie on the kitchen table, and when I didn't think I could come anymore, he slid in all eleven inches and fucked the shit out of me."

"Hell naw!" Nadine screamed. "Are you serious? Eleven inches?"

I nodded. "And girrrls, he made sure I felt every inch."

Lisa chuckled. "Only you would find a brotha with a big dick."

"Bamboo, Lisa. Renee found her big bamboo," Nadine said with a chuckle.

"I know that's right." I picked up a napkin from the table and began fanning it across my face. "Now I see why Stella got her groove back. Solomon made me a firm believer that Jamaica is a black woman's paradise."

"So, does he have his own place?" Lisa asked.

I reached for my glass of water. "No, he lives with his grandmother."

Kayla looked appalled. "You had sex in his grandmother's house?"

I simply shrugged. "She was asleep."

Nadine practically fell out of her chair with laughter. "Oh my God! Y'all screwed with Grandma in the other room?"

Lisa and Kayla eyed me suspiciously, so I didn't bother to answer. Instead, I dropped the napkin and reached across the table and retrieved my plate.

Lisa shook her head. "I can't believe you."

"Shit, he started it, not me." I reached for my fork. "I didn't even get a chance to say no."

Kayla snorted rudely. "Not that you would have."

Memories of me leaning against the sink flashed before my eyes. "Hell naw. My coochie is wet just thinking about it."

This time Nadine fell off the bench and farted. The three of us screamed, then got as far away from her funky ass as possible.

Chapter 50

RENEE

When we finished breakfast, I returned to the room for a little private time while Kayla stopped to chat with Clayton. After my evening with Solomon, I was no longer jealous of them. As far as I was concerned, Kayla could have Clayton. Like I said before, I already found my big bamboo.

Just as I shut the door, the phone rang. I thought about ignoring it just in case it was Everton calling me again, but I was sick of running and dodging his ass. It could be important and I wouldn't even know it. I walked over to the nightstand and snatched the phone off the hook. "Yeah?"

"May I please speak to Kayla?"

My brow rose with curiosity. "May I ask who's calling?"

"Yes, a good friend."

I sucked my teeth. "Uh-huh. This must be Reverend Leroy Brown."

"Uh, no. You've got me confused with someone else. My name is Clarence."

"Clarence, my ass," I spat as I lowered onto the bed. "Reverend Brown, I know this is yo' trifling ass. You need to be ashamed of yourself."

"Who is this?" he inquired.

"Don't worry about who the fuck this is," I barked in the telephone. "What you need to be worrying about is me telling your pregnant wife about your latest escapade."

"You wouldn't do that," he said, trying to sound all bold and shit.

"The hell I won't. I love my girl and don't want to see her hurt. So I'll tell you what. You stay the fuck away from her and I won't let the church know where you spend your Wednesday afternoons."

"Now, sister, you don't—"

"I ain't your sistah. Now, I know all about you sleeping with them Campbell twins and about you going to the motel with Bonnie only to find out she was a he, so if I was you, I wouldn't fuck with me, 'cause I play for keeps."

He hesitated for a long moment. "So what is it that you want?"

"For you to stay the fuck away from Kayla, and I mean it. Let her have a chance to find someone who truly loves her, not the games you be playing."

He started laughing. "You can't stop me from seeing her."

"Oh, yes I can. Personally, I don't know what she sees in you. Now what I should be asking is what the hell she wants with you and your little shriveled-ass dick. Oh yes, I've seen the pictures."

"Pictures?"

I giggled inwardly before continuing. "Didn't you know? See, you used to mess with Shanika Martin, who is really John-John from over on Eighth Street. Anyway, one afternoon when he, oops, I mean she, had your ass tied to the bedpost, she had her older sister Ursula in the closet, taking pictures. You should be ashamed of yourself. Does your wife know you're on the DL?"

"I'm n-not on the d-down low," he stuttered nervously.

"That's what they all say."

I laughed in his face and finally I heard him sigh and say, "I do love Kayla."

"Then if you truly love her, you'll leave her alone."

"What will I tell her?"

"The truth. You never had any intention of leaving your wife."

"That's not true. I did. It's just hard when you have so many people looking up to you, and then Darlene got pregnant and everything changed."

"Yeah, yeah, save that sappy-ass story for someone who cares." I heard the knob turn so I spoke quickly. "Don't call this room again or else." I quickly hung up the phone.

"Was that Leroy?" Kayla asked as she stepped into the room.

I glanced up to find her eyes wide with anticipation. I dropped my gaze to the floor and shook my head. "Naw, that was Everton's worrisome ass. Damn, I wish I never stepped to his ass."

She cupped her mouth and giggled as she moved to the edge of her bed to remove her sandals. "That's what you get."

"So," I began as I pushed back on the bed. "How was your evening with Clayton?"

Her lips curled slightly upward. "He is a nice guy."

"Nice? Girl, he is too fine to be just nice. What were y'all talking about just now?"

She gave a dreamy smile. "He wants to see me again tonight."

"Damn! My girl hooked her a professional football player. Ain't that some shit!"

She gave me a dismissive wave. "Girl, it ain't like you don't meet anybody."

"Yeah, but Solomon ain't a ballplayer. Damn, did you ask him if he had any other friends?"

"Yes, I did, and he said they ain't nothing but a bunch of hoes."

"Shit, that's what I like."

We both started cracking up.

"Ain't you nothing."

"I'm happy for you, girl. Really I am."

She leaned back on the bed and rested her weight on her elbows. "Yeah, I just wish I knew where my relationship with Leroy was going."

"Going? Kayla, that shit has gone and died. Get over him and get on with your life."

She sat there shaking her head. "I can't until I know for sure. You sure he didn't call?"

I couldn't believe this shit. She has a fine rich brotha sweating her fat ass and all she can think about is Reverend Brown's no-neck ass. This is crazy. "Naw, his ass didn't call, and he probably won't, so get over it."

"Maybe you're right." With a weary sigh, she rose from the bed and disappeared into the bathroom.

This trip was beginning to be a trip. I just can't believe the soap opera. Kayla would rather be with some out-of-shape preacher when she could be the wife of an NFL player, and I had met my Mandingo. What could possibly happen next?

Chapter 51

NADINE

Nadine left the room certain something was wrong with Lisa. She hadn't put her finger on it but she could tell she wasn't well. She was tired all the time and when she didn't think Nadine was looking, Lisa was popping pills, lots of pills. Yesterday, while Lisa was out of the room, Nadine had pulled out the bottles and jotted down the names of the prescriptions so she could make sure to look them up when she got home. One of them she had a suspicion about but she wasn't sure she wanted to guess where her friend was concerned. She hoped she would have confided in her, and it hurt her that she had not. However, she planned to find out what it was before their trip was over.

Suddenly feeling hungry again, she went to grab a muffin and a cup of coffee. She took a seat at a table closest to the pool and stared out into the water.

Against her will, RD came to mind. Last night had been a mistake. She knew that now. RD was not at all what she needed to get Jordan off her mind. In fact, she didn't think any man was going to be able to do that.

"Do you mind if I join you?"

Nadine glanced up and almost dropped the hot coffee in her lap when she noticed it was her mystery lady. She shook her head. "Uh . . . sure have a seat."

She lowered a plate of fresh fruit onto the table, then took a seat across from her. "Hi, I'm Lavina Spencer."

Nadine wiped a damp palm on her thigh, then extended her hand. "I'm Nadine Hill. So nice to finally meet you."

The object of her erotic fantasy shook Nadine's hand, then smiled. "Me too. I've seen you so many times."

Nadine was immediately mesmerized by the dimples at Lavina's cheeks, the shine of her eyes. Knowing she was probably staring like a damn fool, she quickly searched her brain for something else to say. "Where are you from?"

"Dallas," she answered, while chewing a slice of pineapple. "And you?"

"My girls and I are from Columbia, Missouri."

"Well, it's my first time here and I am enjoying myself."

"Me too."

"Really?" Wrinkling her nose, Lavina didn't look convinced. "Every time I see you, you always look so unhappy."

Nadine wasn't sure she liked the idea of a total stranger being able to analyze her emotions. "You didn't look too happy at the party either. Man troubles?"

She paused long enough to swallow her food. "Woman troubles."

Nadine gasped, then eyed her closely.

Lavina shrugged her shoulders nonchalantly. "Don't look so surprised. I can tell you have the same problem."

"How did you . . . I mean, is it that obvious?" Nadine was shocked, and for a moment she panicked.

"To a fellow lesbian, yes. Anyone else wouldn't notice."

Her shoulders sagged with relief. "Wow." That was all she could say as she resumed eating her muffin.

Lavina reached for her water glass. "Don't look so sad. It is never that bad," she said, smiling.

"I've just got a lot on my mind these days."

"Care to talk about it?" she asked.

Before Nadine realized what she was doing she started pouring

her heart out. She started with the feelings that she had started having in her early twenties and ended with the fight she and Jordan
had before she left. "I just don't know what to do. I love her so much
but she deserves so much better."

"Jordan obviously doesn't think so. She loves you and is willing to
stand by you no matter what."

Nadine rested her chin in her hand with her elbow propped on
the table. "The problem is my family. They will disown me." She was
raised by a pediatrician and an interior decorator. Her parents were
part of a high-society social circle. Everything she said and did was a
reflection on them. She remembered when her mother's youngest
sister announced to the family at Thanksgiving dinner almost ten
years ago that she was gay. Her mother cut her completely out of her
life and has not spoken to her sister since. When Nadine divorced
her husband, her mother had a cow, because she said men naturally
messed around on their wives, but seldom do women divorce their
husbands because of it. When she shot Arthur and her name was
plastered all over the paper, her parents gave her clear instructions
not to contact them until the case was over. Even after she was
cleared of all the charges, it had taken her mother months to forgive
her.

More than anything in the world Nadine wanted her parents to
understand who she was, but deep down she knew that would never
happen.

Lavina spoke between bites. "You can't live your life for your parents. You'll never be happy if you do. My mother had a fit when I
first told her I was a lesbian, but she quickly got over it."

Nadine smiled shyly. "How long have you been . . . you know?"

"A lesbian," she chuckled. "Nadine, you are going to have to learn
to feel comfortable with that word. Until you do you'll never feel
comfortable with who you are."

She nodded.

"I've been this way since high school. I tried denying it for years
before I finally gave in to the feeling. A man could never make me
feel the way a woman does." She smiled and her eyes took on a
dreamy, faraway quality, then her expression suddenly sobered. "I
was with the same woman for almost five years. Then last month she

told me she was pregnant and that she was going to live with her baby's daddy. It hurt because we had talked about having a baby, but I never expected her to do it behind my back or fall in love with a man in the process."

"Damn."

"Damn is right." She sipped her drink. "Do your friends know that you're gay?"

Nadine shook her head. "One does, but I haven't told the other two yet."

"If they're your friends then what's the problem?"

She laughed and sighed. "Because it's too much like admitting who I really am."

"Exactly. And that's where you have to begin. You have to first admit to yourself that you're a lesbian, then the rest will be easy. Answer this." She paused to lean forward. "Do you still like dick?"

Remembering last night's fiasco, Nadine shook her head.

"Do you like eating pussy?"

Lavina's stare was so intense, Nadine blushed, then lowered her eyes to her plate. "Yeah, I guess."

"Girl, either you do or you don't. You've got to decide. Maybe you go both ways. For a while I still needed a dick stuck up in me every now and again but now there ain't nothing a dick can do that I can't get from a woman's tongue and a dildo."

Nadine smiled, then stared across with envy. Lavina was definitely comfortable with who she was, and she liked that about her.

"It's going to get easier. Trust me."

Nadine had a feeling that was easier said than done. Although she loved Jordan and missed her terribly, admitting she was gay was almost as hard as an alcoholic admitting they had a drinking problem. Somehow the latter was much easier for her to accept.

Lavina popped the last piece of watermelon into her mouth, then rose. "They're getting ready to start a volleyball game. Want to play?"

Nadine brushed her problems to the side and smiled. "Sure, why not?"

Chapter 52

RENEE

"Aren't you afraid of starting over again?" Kayla asked me as we took a seat out on the beach.

I glanced over at the group of guests playing volleyball as I thought about her questions. You wouldn't believe how many times I had asked myself the same thing. I am a thirty-six-year-old woman and I am planning to start over for the third time. "Yes, a little bit, but I really don't look at it as starting over. I already have a house full of furniture. I have the same house I bought at age twenty. I'm still living in the same town around all my friends, so other than finding a job I don't look at it as starting over. What scares me is that I have grown accustomed to living a certain lifestyle. When I leave him I'm going from first-class to coach again. Now that is going to take some adjusting to."

"How could you even consider giving all that up?"

I shrugged. "It's only material things."

"Yes, but then you're changing your name again and going in front of a judge to ask for another divorce. How does that make you feel?"

I gave a strangled laugh. "It makes me feel like shit. I can get everything else right in my life but not my marriages. But I blame myself for it."

"How so?" she inquired.

"I married for all of the wrong reasons. I don't care what anyone says, marriage has to have a foundation. If you start with nothing you're going to end up with nothing. I married a man fifteen years older than me who I have nothing in common with. We can't go to my clubs; he dresses like my grandfather."

Kayla giggled. "Then buy him some clothes."

"I do. I buy him the things I love to see a man in, and you know what? They do nothing for him. I love a man in blue jeans and Timberland boots. I'm married to a man with a size fifty waistline, who isn't even six feet tall. I can buy him a Sean Jean sweatsuit and in it he looks like a Weeble. I can buy him a Rocawear shirt and jeans, and on him it's just a shirt and jeans. It adds no character to him at all."

Kayla simply gave me a sympathetic smile.

"When I dress him, you can tell I dressed him and that he is out of his element. It just doesn't make any sense. He has always said, 'if you don't like what I wear, then buy me some clothes,' that he will wear anything I buy him, and it just doesn't work for him." I paused to shake my head. "I just don't understand what the problem is."

"You know what the problem is."

I nodded. "Yeah, I know. I write all these love stories about these women instantly falling in love with a man and I ask myself, is it all just make-believe? Because when I think I've fallen instantly in love it's been a lie." I dragged my leg to my chest. "I wonder after the book is over do these characters really live happily ever after."

"I'm sure they've got to work at it like everyone else."

"Yes, but that's the point I was getting to. They had something to begin with. If two people are truly in love and have built a life together as a team, when they find their relationship drifting apart all they have to do is rediscover what kept them together all these years. What attracted them to one another in the first place. With me and John, we never had anything."

"Oh, come on, you had to have had something if you married him in the first place," Kayla said, shaking her head with disbelief.

I shook my head because I no longer believed that. "Girl, I had blinders on. All I could see was that he was kind and willing to give me the stars. He had offered me a way of life I knew nothing about, and that excited me. A stay-at-home mom. You know how many women wish they didn't have to work."

"Shoot, I know I do."

"I know you do and so did I. And every time he hopped on top of me I kept reminding myself how lucky I was. Every time his finger reached for my breasts I kept reminding myself that I had a wonderful new career as an author because of his generosity."

"Do you think you would have begun writing even if you hadn't married him?"

I took a moment to filter that question before answering. "Yes, but it would have been quite a while later. The talent I already had. The only thing missing was time. John gave me that."

There was a long silence before either of us spoke again.

"So you're really going to let him go?"

"I have to, because if I don't he never will." I rose then, tired of talking, and raced out into the water. I knew Kayla couldn't follow because she wasn't wearing a swimsuit. Tears had pushed to the surface; I wanted to wash them away. I hate for my friends to see me being weak. Especially if the tears are for a man.

Chapter 53

LISA

Lisa told her husband for the third time she loved him, then hung up the phone. Seconds later the smile on her lips continued to linger. God, she loved that man! Michael called her every afternoon to check on her and she loved him for it. The beautiful part about it was that he had always been that way—attentive, caring, and loving, long before she had even been diagnosed with cancer.

That's the way it should be, she told herself as she moved to stare out the window, which was why she had never told her friends or family about her illness. Because she didn't want things to change. She was certain if she had told them she had cancer, they would have started treating her like she was fragile. No one would know what to say or how to act and she definitely didn't want that. If she had to battle cancer, then she wanted—correction—needed everything else in her life to remain the same. She didn't know what she would do if her entire world changed, which was why she had made the decision that she had.

Three years ago she couldn't bear to tell her sister she was having a hysterectomy as a result of ovarian cancer; instead she told Renee she had been diagnosed with endometriosis and because she was having severe bleeding and abdominal pains, she had opted for the surgery. Lisa had even gone as far as to tell her she and Michael had decided they had waited too long to start a family and having the surgery meant she no longer had to worry about birth control or periods. It had been the performance of her lifetime. It was an unfair thing to do, but at the time she thought it was for the best. Renee had just started dating John, and if she'd had any inkling her sister was sick, she would have packed her bags and headed to Texas, leaving poor John in the dust. No, she told herself countless times, she had done the right thing. Now here Renee was having marital problems and she was getting ready for surgery again. Hopefully when she finally told her sister the truth, she would turn to John for comfort and support. Something good had to come out of this experience. For all of them. She truly believed that God had given her cancer for a reason. She was certain of that. And she truly believed it was so that she could get the others to understand that life was too short for games.

Renee was about to give up a good man just so she could run the streets again. And if she did, Lisa bet a hundred dollars that by the end of the year, Renee would be swearing up and down she was in love again.

Kayla was still harboring feelings for Reverend Brown, and if she didn't come to her senses soon and realize a good thing when she had it, she was going to end up losing Clayton too.

Nadine was the easiest of the bunch. All she needed to do was realize that she couldn't live for other people and to follow her heart.

Speak of the devil. The door swung open and Nadine moved into the room, dripping with sweat.

"Hey, girl," she said with a sparkle in her eyes she hadn't seen at all during the trip. "You should have come down. I just played volleyball and my team kicked ass."

"I was watching from the window. You still got skills," she added with a smile.

Nadine pulled off her sweat-drenched t-shirt and stepped out of her shorts, then fell back in her underwear onto the bed.

Lisa took a seat on the bed. She glanced over at her bra covering a pair of double D's. She was grateful hers hadn't grown any bigger than a B. "Who was that woman I saw you talking to?" she inquired.

Nadine couldn't resist the smile. "She's a lesbian."

"Oh, really? How do you feel about that?"

"Envious."

"Why?"

She propped her arms beneath her head so she could look directly across at Lisa. "Because she is so comfortable with who she is. Why can't I be like that?"

"You can."

She frowned. "No, I can't. You know as well as I do my parents would disown me if they found out. I can't bear for my mother to turn her back on me."

Lisa was so sick of Nadine worrying about what her mother would say. As far as she was concerned Nadine's mother was a stuck-up bitch who thought the sun rose and set on her ass. Nothing or no one was ever good enough for her precious daughter. It was a surprise she even allowed the two of them to socialize. Lisa remembered one time Nadine had invited her over for a sleepover. Before she could bring her sleeping bag into the house, her mother insisted on taking it out back first and shaking it out for roaches. "Life is too short to worry about what others think. I've been telling you that for months."

"I know."

"I want to see you happy."

Nadine's expression suddenly became serious. "You've been really tired lately. Is something going on that you want to tell me about?"

Lisa hesitated a moment to consider telling her dearest friend the truth, then she changed her mind. She needed to talk to them all at the same time. Tomorrow evening after dinner would be soon enough.

"No, I'm fine, really. Just seriously anemic and guilty of not taking my supplements the way I should."

Nadine gave her a long look and for a moment she thought maybe she knew she was lying.

"Lisa, really. I'm your best friend. So quit playing and tell me what's going on with you." After a pause she added, "I saw your pill bottles."

Lisa sucked in a breath and waited for what she was about to say.

"I know you're taking antidepressants."

She released a sigh of relief. "Who doesn't take Zoloft?"

"You. Definitely not you. What the hell you got to be depressed about? Your life is perfect."

How wrong she was. "Nadine, I have problems like everyone else."

She rose from the bed. "Yeah, right," she murmured, then moved to take a shower.

Chapter 54

RENEE

Kayla and Clayton were out on the dance floor. He was trying to keep up, but my girl just doesn't have rhythm. That, coupled with her insecurities—she looked like a hot mess. I was truly embarrassed for her. Although Clayton didn't seem to notice. He was smiling down at her, holding hands and encouraging her. He seemed to really be into her. I didn't want to feel jealous, but I was.

I tore my eyes away from Clayton's fine ass and glanced over at Kermit the Frog, dancing with some big girl who had the audacity to be wearing a thong and spandex.

"Nadine, why aren't you dancing with RD?" I teased.

"Forget him."

"What's up with you? You've been acting strangely all day."

She ran a hand over her face and glared across the dance floor. "Nothing's wrong with me."

"Girl, you know you can't lie to me."

"I said nothing!" she snapped. "Damn! I'm going to go get a drink."

I watched her, trying to figure out what she was tripping off of. Maybe RD didn't give her any.

"Whassup? You want to dance?"

I glanced at the dude standing to my right. He was the best look-

ing of the last five guys who asked me to dance, and that wasn't saying much. His eyes were so crossed, I glanced up at the ceiling just to
see what the hell he was looking at.

"No, thanks," I said as nicely as I could manage.

"You know, y'all American bitches ain't shit. You come to our
country, then you want to act like you're better than us."

I squared my shoulders and said clearly, "Then stop asking our
mothafucking asses to dance."

He took a step forward but I refused to move an inch. "Fuck you!"

"Is there a problem?"

I glanced up at Clayton while the dude pushed through the
crowd.

I faked a panic. "I'm so glad you showed up. He was going off because I wouldn't dance with him."

"Well, if you have any more problems you let me know."

"Thanks, Clayton." I puckered my lips flirtatiously. "Where's
Kayla?"

He tilted his head to the right. "She went to the restroom."

"Good. Then let's dance." I grabbed his arm and dragged him out
on the floor before he could protest.

Chapter 55

LISA

"When are you planning to tell your friends?"

She glanced across the table at Trevor's kind face and smiled. "Tomorrow."

They were sitting in the hotel bar, sipping rum punch. He was a nice guy who had just recently buried his mother. For his fortieth birthday he had promised her he would take some time off from his busy construction business and go to Jamaica. A man of his word, one week after her funeral, he went to a travel agency and booked the all-inclusive vacation.

Lisa met Trevor at the pajama party. When he had told her his mother had recently died of ovarian cancer, they discovered they had something in common.

"I am still not understanding why you didn't tell your sister at dinner. The two of you were alone."

She had planned to. "My sister makes me so mad that at times I want to just strangle her," she said with disgust. "I've been protecting her for years and I am so afraid that when I am gone she is going to get herself into some shit that she is not going to be able to get herself out of."

"You can only do what you can do."

"I know. My father has been telling me that for years. I just feel so responsible for her. She has so much hate in her heart that I don't think she'll ever allow anyone to get close to her."

"Sounds to me like she needs counseling," he said seriously.

"The funny thing is, she's already seeing a psychiatrist. I think they have tried every medicine known to man. Renee takes them for a while, then decides she doesn't need them anymore."

"That's usually how it works."

Her brow crinkled. "Yeah, I know. Part of me just doesn't believe she can handle the news. That's why I invited our friends for backup. My sister acts like she's so tough, but really she is quite fragile inside."

"Regardless of what you think, you need to tell your sister soon. What if she has the same thing?"

"I know—that's what I keep telling myself. I've tried asking my mother about the diseases on her side of the family but she doesn't know. Her family doesn't believe in going to the doctor. My grandmother died of colon cancer. My father's side of the family—I don't know those people. My mother never tried to make us be a part of their lives and they had never really bothered to reach out, so I just don't bother either. However, I do need to find out what our family history is."

"That would be a smart move."

She planned to contact their paternal family when she got back home. Finding out their medical history was vital. Lisa didn't want Renee to go as long as she had without knowing she had ovarian cancer. If someone had told her it had run in her family, she would have been conscious of the signs and demanded testing years ago.

She had suffered chronic fatigue and mysterious bouts of unexplained illness and pain for two years that her doctors dismissed as "flu" or overwork. It wasn't until the heavy bleeding and abdominal pains began that she even suspected something serious was wrong with her. By the time her gynecologist decided to run some tests, the mass was already well over two centimeters. With a mass that was less than two centimeters, the patient had a seventy percent survival rate; anything larger, the rate decreased to fifty percent or less. However, Lisa had beaten the odds and had been cancer free for over two years until it decided to once again knock at her door. It was time to warn her sister and possibly save her life in more ways than one.

Lisa blinked twice and noticed that Trevor was giving her an odd look. She laughed, then reached for her drink. "Listen to me going on and on. I know you didn't come on this trip to listen to some woman's problems."

"Actually I came on this trip because I needed a break. The last year with my mother was quite rough on me. And I don't mind listening to your problems if it means I get to be in the company of a beautiful woman."

"Thanks."

Trevor reached across the bar and clasped his new friend's hand. "You are a strong woman, Mrs. Miller. You remind me so much of my mother. She fought until the end."

"You have to be." She lowered her voice to a whisper. "It's the only way I'll survive."

"And you will survive. You're physically active. You take damn good care of yourself."

She was well aware she had a fifty percent survival rate. The recurrence lessened her chances even more, but she was a survivor, and with her determination she was going to be part of that percentage.

At sixty, Trevor's mom collapsed and was found to have been suffering advanced ovarian cancer. Through nearly three years of treatment that included eight series of chemotherapy, surgery, and thirty sessions of radiation treatment, she retained her famed sense of humor. She spent her able days visiting other cancer patients, boosting their spirits. She had survived seven years before she had finally passed with her son right by her side.

"I really appreciate you listening. It's hard talking to my friends and family because they are so emotionally attached. My husband is a wonderful supporter but he loves me and can't be optimistic."

"I'm glad I could be of service."

Lisa stared at him long and hard. "I think the reason why your mother wanted you to take a trip to Jamaica was so you could find someone special to share your life with. You're not going to find her hanging out with me," she teased.

Trevor chuckled. "I have plenty of time to find love. Right now I'm trying to get over my mother's death, and I find a great deal of comfort being in your company."

Lisa squeezed his hand and shared a teary, knowing smile. She hoped and prayed someone brought Michael the same level of comfort after she was gone.

Chapter 56

NADINE

Nadine wasn't in the partying mood but Renee had insisted that she come out. She would have preferred staying in her room with Lisa, but Lisa was right, she had to make some decisions, come to terms with who she was, and accept it. She glanced out on the dance floor at Renee's nasty ass. She was dancing like she was doing a lap dance, all bent over with her ass out. Kayla had just come out of the bathroom and the expression on her face said she wasn't too happy. But she was too timid to do a damn thing about it. What Renee wants Renee gets, and right now it was Clayton. She frowned as she watched Renee grab his ass. Kayla hissed, then mumbled she was going to get a soda. Nadine shook her head. She was definitely going to have to tell Lisa about her sister's behavior when she got back to the room.

Glancing to her right, she spotted Lavina and her sister coming through the door. She smiled, glad to see her. Already she admired the young woman who was comfortable with who she was. Hopefully she could become just like her.

Lavina spotted her and waved, then pushed her way through the crowded club.

"Hey, gurl. This place is packed."

"I know. From the voices floating around the room most of them are American. I didn't know y'all were coming here."

"I wasn't at first but decided what the hell. I'm here to have fun."

The two stood there laughing and talking about people around the room. Her sister hooked up with some guy and was out on the floor. Then the music changed and 50 Cent came on.

"Oooh, girl, let's dance."

Before Nadine had a chance to decline, Lavina pulled her out onto the floor.

The two danced and gradually, Nadine began to feel relaxed and didn't care what anyone thought about her dancing with another woman. They bumped and grinded. When Lavina backed her ass up against her, Nadine latched on to her ass and gyrated her hips against her. Lavina made it seem so easy to accept who she was. By the end of the song the two were laughing and holding hands.

"I knew yo mothafucking ass was a damn dyke!"

She swung around to find RD glaring at her.

"Yeah, and what about it?" She draped her arm around Lavina's waist, feeding on her strength. Then, to her surprise, Lavina captured her chin with her hand and pressed her lips against hers. Nadine welcomed Lavina's tongue in her mouth. Lavina was an excellent kisser. When she pulled away, RD was standing there with his mouth wide open.

"Goddamn! If I knew it was like that I would have asked you to invite yo girl up to my room last night. Shit, if y'all want we can leave now."

Lavina sucked her teeth. "It ain't shit a man can do for me but kiss my ass."

"What the fuck you mean? A woman can't give you this." He grabbed his crotch.

"There's more to life than dick."

"You got life fucked up. All a woman can do is eat some pussy."

Nadine decided to step in. "Shit, and that's obviously more than I got from your ass last night." She glanced over at Lavina and the two high-fived.

"Then let's try for round two." He reached out and grabbed her around the waist and pulled her against him so she could feel how hard his dick was. Nadine pushed away, repulsed by his touch.

"What you got ain't worth a round two." She laughed and Lavina joined in.

RD got pissed off. "Fuck both y'all dykes. That's why brothas are dumping sistah for white women, 'cause y'all don't know what the hell y'all want."

"Yo, RD. What's going on?"

He glanced up to find Clayton and Renee standing beside them.

"Nothing, man. Ain't shit over here worth my time." He pushed past them and moved over toward the bar.

"Y'all ladies all right?" Clayton asked.

"Yeah, we're cool," Nadine said.

Clayton dropped a hand to Renee's shoulder. "I'm going to go get me something to drink. Nadine, you seen Kayla?"

She tilted her head to the left of the room. "Yeah, she's over there."

He excused himself. Lavina went to speak to her sister.

Nadine turned to Renee. "What you doing all up on Kayla's man?"

Renee tossed her braids over her shoulder. "Gurl, we were just dancing."

"Shit, you might as well been fucking."

"I can't help it if Kayla's ass don't know how to work it. Besides, Clayton asked me to dance. Look, I'm fin to go get me a drink."

Chapter 57

RENEE

Nadine's got a lot of nerve questioning me. What I should have did, was asked her what the hell was she doing dancing with some woman. Shit, they looked like a pair of dykes, if you ask me.

All I was doing was dancing. Nothing more. Shit, I am so over Clayton and have already moved on to something better. Okay, maybe I am lying. A part of me still finds Clayton's ass attractive and I definitely wouldn't mind getting with him, but like I said before, I'll pass. Who am I to stand in the way of his relationship with Kayla, and I must say the two of them do look happy together. Hopefully her dumb ass won't fuck it up.

It was almost eleven o'clock when I spotted Solomon coming through the door. I don't know why but my heart sped up a beat when his eyes zeroed in on me. He threw me a smile from across the crowded room.

I practically ran to meet him halfway. "I didn't know if you were going to show up."

He reached for my hand. "Why wouldn't I?"

I shrugged. "Because when I left a message with your partner at the dock, I wasn't sure if he'd give it to you."

He smiled. "Now you do."

I gave him a hug and immediately felt the pull of his sex appeal. He made my pulse race, my coochie wet.

The music changed to something slow, and taking charge of the moment, he led me out onto the floor. Together we moved to the beat and I must say the brotha has got skills. He held me tight in the circle of his arms. I closed my eyes and inhaled his masculine scent, making me more lightheaded than any glass of tequila. I felt giddy and happy. Now I knew how Cinderella felt after she met the prince.

We danced three songs before he offered me a drink. We moved over to the bar and he stood behind me and wrapped his arms around me. "I like you, Renee."

"I like you, too." Boy, did I like him. His accent was so sexy, already my nipples were getting hard just thinking about last night, and if my coochie got any wetter I was going to have to remove my panties and wring them suckers out.

Solomon ordered us each a margarita and we stood off to the right and bobbed our heads as we sipped our drinks. He moved against the wall and I leaned back against his strength. Words weren't needed. Being in his company was more than enough. I was smiling inside because I had finally met someone I really liked. Not just the sex, even though sex is important. Not to mention the brotha definitely had mad skills. But it was more than that. It was the way he looked, the way he acted, and the way he dressed.

Tonight Solomon was wearing a Rocawear shirt and jeans and Timberland boots and looked sexy as hell. I mean damn good. I didn't know Rocawear was a universal fashion, but Jamaican men dressed and acted just like my American brotha. It was the accent that separated the two.

"You look sexy tonight," he said as if he could read my mind.

"So do you."

The deejay changed to a new Sean Paul cut and the crowd went wild. These three Jamaican women were dancing their asses off. If I could move like that, damn, there would be no stopping me. We watched the others on the dance floor until we finished our drinks.

"Come on, let's go." Solomon took my hand and then he led me out of the building and down the street. When we reached his moped, he released a small green blanket that was secured to a small basket in back. He tucked it under his arm and moved back over to the sidewalk.

"Where are we going?" I asked.

"Somewhere away from the noise and the smoke."

I chuckled inwardly and quickened my pace as we moved around the block. Wherever he was taking me was close enough to walk.

Solomon draped an arm loosely around my shoulders. As we walked, he told me that tomorrow he was going to visit his younger brother, whom he was overly protective of. Once a month he tolerated his father's verbal abuse long enough to spend a couple of hours with his brother. There was something about the compassion in his voice when he spoke about his sibling relationship that made my heart swell. He asked me about my family and I told him about Lisa and Andre. I liked that he didn't interrupt nor did he try to change the subject. Instead he listened and asked intelligent questions. He was bright, with a witty sense of humor, while still managing to have a rough edge about him that drove me crazy.

At the next corner we turned and walked down a flight of steps onto a sandy beach. A little farther down the shore was the back view of Margueritaville. Even in the distance I could hear Usher's "Let It Burn."

When we reached close to the shore, Solomon dropped my hand. He unfolded the blanket and spread it out across the sand. I stood and watched as he removed his boots, then stood on top of the blanket.

"Come here."

I slipped my feet out of my shoes and moved to stand on the blanket in front of him.

I was wearing a simple spandex dress. No zippers. No buttons. He slid it up and over my head.

"Next time, don't wear any panties."

Shit, if I hadn't worn any panties, I would have had wet shit running all down between my legs.

I watched as he removed his own clothes. I gazed down at his erected package hidden behind his boxer brief and licked my lips. Didn't nothing turn me on more than a sexy mothafucka in boxer brief. Everybody isn't equipped to wear them, but Solomon definitely was.

"Have you ever made love on the beach?" he asked.

"Nope," I quickly answered. No, really, I haven't.

He smiled, looking quite pleased with my answer. "Good, then tonight will be your first time."

That's what I love about him. John always asks permission to make love to his wife, which sickens the fuck out of me, while Solomon has a dominant this-is-my-pussy-and-I'm-taking-it-whenever-the-fuck-I-want-to attitude.

He lowered me onto the blanket and commenced to suckling my nipples. He told me what he was going to do before he did it. I love a brotha that talks to me the entire time. It was a slow, teasing move that had me squirming beneath him. When he finally slid my panties down my hips and told me he was going to eat my pussy, I kid you not, I squirted all in that brotha's mouth. Solomon ate like he was a starving man. I raised my hips up so that he could get every morsel. Finally, when I could not take any more, he rose and removed his boxers. Damn, his dick was brick hard.

"Baby, open your legs wide because I'm getting ready to give you all this." He then positioned himself between my legs and paused. "How bad do you want it?"

"Bad, really bad," I whimpered.

"Then come and get it."

He didn't have to tell me twice. I raised my hips and gasped when I felt him slide all ten inches inside of me, filling my coochie to capacity.

"Now drape your legs over my shoulder."

I did as he said and he took over from there. I felt every wonderful inch. His strokes were long, deep, and powerful. Thank goodness there was no one else on the beach. I chanted his name over and over. When I finally came, I screamed so loud they could have heard my ass over at the club if the music wasn't on.

"Here it comes, baby!" Solomon snarled as he plunged even deeper and faster until he came so hard I flinched along with him. Afterwards he lay on top of me and planted light kisses to my face.

I can't remember the last time I've ever felt this at peace with a man. If I could have, I would have frozen time to this exact moment and never let it go. Solomon was something I had never found in any man in America.

"Would you come to Missouri to visit me?"

He rested his head in the palm of his hand. "Only if you'll go with me to Kingston tomorrow to meet my brother."

"It's a deal." That brotha had me cheesing like a damn fool.

Chapter 58

RENEE

We made it back to Margueritaville and danced until close, then Solomon kissed me good-bye and promised to pick me up tomorrow afternoon. After he left, I joined the others and waited for the shuttle to take us all back to the hotel.

I watched Nadine and her friend out the corner of my eye. They just looked a little too chummy to me. I knew Nadine hung around with all kinds of people but I guarantee that girl was a dyke. It was just something about the way she moved.

When we got back to the hotel, Lavina and her sister said good-bye and Nadine and I moved toward our building.

"Nadine, that girl's a dyke."

Nadine shrugged. "Yeah, so what?"

"Shit, I was just telling you just in case your ass didn't know."

"I know."

Something in the way she responded made me stop and ask, "Don't tell me you're rubbing pussy, too?"

There was a long silence before she stopped walking, turned to me, and threw her hands in the air. "Yeah, I'm a lesbian."

My chewing gum fell out my mouth. I just knew this bitch was really tripping. "Shit, you're kidding, right?"

She shook her head. "I've liked women for some time now."

I couldn't believe she was telling me this shit. "You mean every time I dressed in front of you, you were checking my ass out?"

She looked at me like I had a giant booger hanging from my nose. "Hell, naw. You are not my type."

Good, because I was going to have to punch her in her mouth.

"Does Lisa know?" I asked following a moment of silence.

She nodded.

"Kayla?"

She shook her head.

I dropped a hand to my waist. "Why the fuck you didn't tell me?"

"Because I know how you are."

Stunned wasn't even the right word. I didn't know what else to say, because I wasn't prepared for this. I always thought her ass was a little strange but I never guessed this.

I guess she sensed my discomfort, because she finally said, "Look, I'm gonna go take a walk before I call it a night. I'll see you in the morning." She then spun on her heels and headed in the direction of the beach.

Damn!

I walked toward my building, trying to figure out how the hell she could prefer coochie to dick. I mean damn, I think my stuff's the shit but I ain't trying to fuck myself. What can two women do but suck some titties and lick some clits. As I walked, I tried to imagine the two of them together. Then I stopped imagining.

I used to know this dyke. She came to Hickman my senior year of high school. She was cute. Big legs. Small chest. Long light brown hair and the biggest eyes. The boys were falling all over themselves trying to get a piece of her. You could walk down the halls and hear them horny bastards begging and shit.

"Damn, Shaunte, when you gonna let me get a piece of that."

"Come on, girl. I got the perfect job for those pretty lips of yours."

I remember one time my girl Yvette and I were heading to our next class and we spotted Shaunte inside a classroom surrounded by a group of horny-ass seniors.

She swayed her narrow hips up to the front of the class, climbed on the teacher's desk, and said, "All y'all mothafuckas listen up. Y'all need to quit sweating me. I lick pussy, not suck dicks."

My mouth was wide open. By the end of the day, every lesbian in the school was trying to get a piece of her. For the rest of the year I would see her walking and holding hands with this tiny Oriental girl, and I would ask myself what in the hell could the two of them possibly be doing?

As I entered our building, I was still thinking about Nadine's confession, so it took me a few seconds to notice the dark figure that appeared from beneath the stairwell. I flinched and almost ran into the wall. Instinctively, I balled up my fist, ready to strike. If the stranger was going to take me, I wasn't going out like some punk.

"Where have you been all night?" he hissed.

It took me a few moments to realize who was standing before me. "Everton?" I murmured, puzzled as to why he was here. I thought he was off today. "What the hell are you doing here?"

He glared at me. "Renee, I asked you a question. Where have you been? I've been calling your room for the past five hours and not once have you bothered to answer." The fool had the nerve to try and sound like he was my damn husband.

I dropped my fists; however, I kept them balled just in case he wigged out and I needed to punch him one good time in the groin.

"Why were you calling my room?" At first I thought that maybe one of his employees had called in and he had been needed to cover the shift, then I remembered seeing that light-skinned cutie Casey behind the desk before we left for the club and again when we had returned.

"I'm here because I needed to see you. I've been calling you all evening and when you didn't answer I came to find out why. I've been standing here for over an hour, but I guess you had more important things to do than spend time with me."

He stepped forward and tried to hug me. I sidestepped his grasp, then headed toward my room. "Boy, you better go on before you get hurt. Where I've been is none of your damn business."

"You're not going anywhere until you answer my questions." He jumped in front of me and had the nerve to block my path. His eyes were narrow and he was breathing hard. I have to admit, Everton was starting to scare me.

"I was at Margueritaville. Now get the hell out of my way."

"With who? Who were you with?" He was practically foaming at the mouth with jealousy.

I glanced over at the door to my room. If I could get there, I could bang on it for Kayla to open it, then I suddenly remembered she wasn't in there. She was off somewhere with Clayton. Nadine was walking the grounds, so the only choice I had left was banging on my sister's door. Nah, never mind. Then I would have had to listen to her ass tell me, "I told you so." I thought I better just take my chances.

"I was out with the girls."

"Why are you with them when you could be spending that time with me? Tonight I wanted to hold you, Renee. Make love to you again."

I cringed at the reminder.

"I wanted you to meet my mother this evening. She made dinner and everything."

"Why the hell you tell her I was coming?" This shit was like some damn soap opera.

"Because I told you I wanted you to meet my mother. She always meets the women in my life." He took a step forward. I took one back.

I shook my head. Who would believe that someone who looked that good was so doggone stupid? "There is nothing going on with us, Everton. It was an island fling. A one-night stand. It meant nothing to me."

"How can you say that?" he snarled.

"Because it's true. Everton, it's over."

He moved forward again and I once again stepped back.

"No. It will never be over. You belong to me. You told me your pussy belonged to me."

I didn't mean to, but I laughed. "I tell everyone that."

"I'm not just anybody. The other night we had a connection and I don't want that to end. I think deep down you are just scared. Scared of what we could have if you'd just give us a chance."

"The only thing I am scared of is what I will look like in the morning if I don't get some sleep. Now if you don't leave I am going to scream at the top of my lungs and send everybody running."

He froze. I know he didn't want to lose his job any more than I wanted to see him lose it, but if it came to that, then so be it.

"It's not over until I say it is." From the serious look in his eyes, I knew he was dead serious.

I tried to think of something to say to make everything better, when Kayla and Clayton exited the elevator. As soon as they stepped off, Everton made a mad dash down the steps and out the building.

Kayla asked what was going on. I turned to her and simply shrugged, then moved toward our room.

Chapter 59

NADINE

She walked along the beach for as long as she could, then found herself walking to building 3 and knocking on the door.

The door opened and she was greeted by a warm smile. "I didn't think you would come."

Lavina stepped out the way so Nadine could move into the suite. She glanced around. The room was twice the size of Nadine's. It had a bedroom and a living room.

"Please have a seat."

Nadine lowered onto the couch. "Where's your sister?"

She tilted her head toward the bedroom. "In the room with Vernon."

Vernon was some guy she had met at the club. Nadine moved and took a seat beside her.

They both curled on the couch and Lavina talked about her partner, Claudia, and then Nadine began to talk about Jordan. She was a great listener. She felt like they had been friends for years. She talked to her like she could never see herself doing with Lisa and Kayla and Renee—especially not Renee. She tried to convince herself it was strictly a casual conversation and nothing more. However, while they were talking she found herself watching the way Lavina's lips moved as she spoke. She wasn't wearing any lipstick, yet her lips were a bright, vibrant pink. Suddenly she found herself wanting to taste them again.

"Nadine?"

She blinked. "I'm sorry. Did you say something?"

Lavina giggled and reached out and placed a hand to Nadine's thigh. "Yes. I asked do you feel better now that you've admitted your feelings?"

Nadine leaned her head back against the cushions of the couch. "Oh gosh, yes. I feel like a tremendous weight has been lifted. Now I just need to finish convincing myself."

She felt her body begin to relax and she glanced down and noticed that Lavina's hand was still on her knee. At that moment Nadine knew she should leave but for some reason she didn't want to be alone. She felt so good being here with someone who understood how she thought and felt. Before she realized what she was doing, she had reached down and placed her hand over Lavina's.

"Acceptance will come as soon as you allow yourself to do so," Lavina said, smiling.

Nadine was thinking about what she said when they heard moans coming from the other room. As soon as the bed began to squeak, Nadine glanced at Lavina and the two of them started cracking up. She fell back against her and they bumped foreheads.

"Ow!"

"Sorry."

When she opened her eyes, Lavina's mouth was only inches away from her. She knew she should have pulled back and told her good night. But she couldn't. She leaned forward and met Lavina's lips halfway. She reached up and cradled Lavina's face and devoured deeper into the kiss. She pushed her tongue past her lips and met each stroke with skillful strokes of her own. Lavina pulled her against her and the two lay back on the couch kissing and touching one another.

"Lavina, this isn't a good idea," Nadine said between kisses.

Lavina's soft hands cupped Nadine's breasts. "Don't think, just feel. I need to taste you, to touch you."

Nadine groaned at her lack of willpower. Then she convinced herself that she wasn't being unfaithful to Jordan, especially since they had kinda broken up just before the trip. There wasn't time for reasoning, because the next thing she knew Lavina's hand was traveling under her shirt and unsnapping her bra. She smiled. It always amazed her the way a woman had no problem finding the hooks while a man could spend hours trying to figure it out.

Lavina lowered her mouth and captured Nadine's nipple between her teeth. Nadine squirmed beneath her and imagined what it would be like if they were both lying across a bed naked. Lavina knew just what to do to make her come apart. Suddenly she wanted, for once, to take.

She sat up and instructed Lavina to lie back on the couch, then she reached beneath Lavina's dress and slipped her panties down over her hips and ankles. She glanced up at Lavina, and when their eyes met she licked her lips, then dropped down on the carpet before Lavina. Lavina opened her legs wide, then Nadine leaned forward and buried her head between her legs. She took a deep breath. Lavina smelled so good, Nadine dived right in and feasted on what she had to offer. She alternated between probing her center with her tongue and stroking and teasing her clit with her teeth. When Nadine latched on and sucked, Lavina arched up off the couch with a gasp. Nadine's confidence in her ability soared, and she drove deeper. While she teased Lavina's clit, she slid her fingers inside of her. First one, then two, and finally three. She took slow measured strokes and moved in and out. She could feel her legs weakening.

"You like this?" Nadine asked.

"Hell, yeah, that shit feels good," she moaned as she rocked her hips to meet Nadine's hand.

Nadine smiled as she stared at the woman's eyes, which were closed in a sex-induced haze. The bed in the other room began to squeak again, and as Lavina's sister's cries increased, so did Lavina's. Nadine swore the sisters came at the same time. As soon as Lavina's body collapsed, Nadine removed her fingers, then planted light kisses up and down the inside of her thighs while her breathing returned.

Lavina's sister stepped out the room, wrapped in a sheet. "Yo, Vee . . . oh, shit!" Her eyes widened when she saw the two of them. "My bad. I didn't know you were here."

Nadine dropped her eyes and smiled. "No problem."

"I was gonna ask you to go and get us a Coke, but shit, never mind." She turned and went back into the room, shutting the door behind her.

Nadine glanced over at Lavina's smiling face and started laughing. She couldn't believe it. She didn't feel ashamed or uncomfortable. For once she felt alive because she was being who she was without fronting.

"Girl, if Jordan doesn't want your ass back, I'll take you." Lavina slipped off the couch and landed on top of Nadine. They giggled like teenagers.

Chapter 60

RENEE

I got up the next morning with Everton's threat still clear on the brain. He had taken a one-night stand to the next level. I could report him, but then I would be jeopardizing his job and that was not my intention at all. Just because I pussy-whipped his ass doesn't mean he had to lose his job behind it. He was just young and didn't understand the power of a woman and her coochie. Or should I say me and my potent coochie. Or maybe it's a Jamaican thing. Although I get the strong suspicion that they have one-night stands all over the continent. Maybe he was raised differently. Unfortunately, unlike him, Solomon knows how to please a woman.

By the time my stomach started growling, I decided not to let Everton's idle threats get the better of me and joined Kayla and the others for breakfast. I moved to the restaurant and glanced over at the registration desk and was relieved to find Leslie behind the counter. Maybe I'd get lucky and his ass wouldn't come in today.

"How was the club?" Lisa asked after we had all fixed our plates and settled down at the table.

"I had a good time." Kayla said as she sipped a glass of orange juice. "You should have come."

Nadine agreed and then I remembered her confession from the night before. My girl was a dyke. I had been so wrapped up in my problems with Everton I had almost forgotten. I couldn't help it, but I started laughing.

Nadine frowned. "What the hell is so funny?"

I pointed my fork at her. "You, ho. I still can't get over you rubbing pussies with some woman."

Kayla spit her eggs across the table and they landed on Lisa's plate. "What did you say?"

"Damn, Kayla." Lisa scooped the food onto a napkin.

"Sorry. Renee, what did you just say?"

Smiling, I reached for my mug. "Ask your girl there."

Nadine completely ignored me and chewed on a piece of toast. For several seconds no one said anything.

Kayla's eyes traveled around the table until they finally landed on me again. "Can someone please let me in on what's going on?"

I tilted my head to the right. "I'll let your girl tell you."

"Shit, I planned on telling her later, in private." Nadine looked so pissed I started laughing again.

"Now is as good a time as any," I stated avidly.

Lisa glared at me. I gave a nonchalant shrug and ignored her silent message to shut the hell up. "Fine, I'll tell her. Kayla, your girl here is a dyke."

"A what?"

Nadine flung a strawberry across the table and I ducked, barely missing it. "You are such a bitch," she hissed.

"Yeah, I know." I chuckled.

Kayla's eyes were about to fall out of her head. "I can't believe this. When did you discover this?"

Nadine shifted uncomfortably on her chair. "Some time ago and I would rather talk about this in private." She glanced around as if checking to see if anyone else was listening.

I tossed my hands in the air. "Whatchu got to hide? We're your girls. Fuck all them other mothafuckas." I know I was being a bitch but that Everton shit had me so pissed off, I wanted someone else to also be pissed. I know that's very selfish of me, but what the hell.

Kayla folded her hands on the table. "Well, I guess that explains it."

"Explains what?" I asked.

She glanced across the table at Nadine as if a lightbulb had just gone off in her head. "That's why I've never met Jordan."

I looked from one to the other. "Jordan? Who the hell is Jordan?"

Kayla somehow managed to keep a straight face when she said, "I'm assuming he's a she."

Nadine gave her a sheepish grin and the three of them started cracking up.

I was too through. Nadine had been dating a woman and had managed to keep my ass in the dark about it. "Bitch, your ass is too much. I can't believe you hid that shit from us for as long as you had."

She shrugged, then reached for her fork. "I didn't know how to tell y'all."

I rolled my eyes at her. "Shit, just like you tell us everything else. Damn, I might be a bitch but I'm a fair bitch."

"Ain't you nothing," she replied sarcastically.

"You're still my girl. Just as long as I don't wake up and find you trying to lick my coochie."

She tossed another strawberry and this time it hit me square in the forehead. I rolled my eyes. She was lucky my food looked too good to waste, otherwise I would have dotted her eye with a bagel. I reached for my coffee cup again.

"So what's up with you and Solomon?" Lisa asked, trying to change the subject. I told you my sister's ass be hating. She hates for her girl to be the subject of attention for too long, so what does she do? Switch the focus to me.

"He's taking me to Kingston today to meet his family," I mumbled against the rim of my mug.

Her brow rose. "I thought you had a fit when Everton wanted you to meet his family."

"That's 'cause Everton's ass has a little dick."

"And how do you know his dick is little?" Nadine inquired.

I rolled my eyes. She was trying to catch me in a confession. Well, you have to get up pretty early in the morning to fool my ass.

"I never said I didn't touch or see his dick. I said we didn't fuck. I was looking for an island fling and he wants a wife and kids."

"So why are you trying to meet Solomon's family?"

I couldn't resist a smile. "Because I like him. I like him a lot."

"Oh, Lord."

I'm not sure which one of them said that so I glared at all three. "What the hell is that supposed to mean?"

Lisa lowered her fork to the table. "I guess you're in love, right?"

"No-o-o. However, I do want to get to know him better. I have never met anyone like him before. He's funny, intelligent, and can fuck the shit out of a sistah; what more could a woman want?"

"Uh-huh."

I glared at Nadine. "Bitch, don't hate."

She gave me an innocent look. "Who's hating? I've just heard this song and dance before."

"We all have," Kayla added.

I couldn't believe she had the nerve to say anything, especially when I still haven't figured out what the hell Clayton sees in her.

Lisa cleared her throat. "I thought you were planning to spend the week figuring out what to do with you and John."

See, her ass is always trying to ruin my fun. "What's that got to do with me and Solomon?"

"It's got a lot to do with it. You can't focus on your future if you're trying to live for the moment."

"She's right," Nadine added.

Now that ho needs to go and lick some bitch's pussy and leave me the hell alone. I was about to cuss all their asses out when Clayton walked over to the table. Man, his ass smelled good.

"Good morning, ladies."

"Good morning," we answered in unison.

He then had eyes for no one but Kayla. He leaned over her and gently kissed her cheek and told her he'd see her later, before he turned away to join his boys. Damn, the jealousy was lurking again. I don't know why, especially now that I had Solomon in my life. Renee, shame on you. I should have been happy for her, but I wasn't. I guess because even though Solomon was fucking me right, there is still something about Clayton that I like. The money, perhaps?

I was the first to speak. "Damn! Girl, you got that negro falling all over your ass."

She blushed as she reached for her orange juice.

Lisa nudged her in the shoulder. "Kayla, honey, I'm so happy for you."

"You better grab him before someone else does." Nadine mumbled.

Do you know she had the nerve to stare at me out the corner of her eye? What the hell was she trying to imply? Okay, so maybe I was looking at Clayton, but shit, we all were. I decided that instead of getting into an argument I'd go and get myself a second helping of breakfast.

I spotted Clayton at the buffet so I rose and went over there. In my white shorts and pink halter, I knew I was looking too cute.

I moved over to the bacon and loaded my plate and swayed over to the fresh fruit, where he was helping himself to the pineapple.

He smiled when he saw me. "Whassup, Renee?"

"Nothing much, although I hear you and my girl had a good time last night."

He nodded. "Yes, we did."

"I'm glad to hear that. Although your idea of a good time and mine are two totally different things, but to each his own. I'm curious, though." I paused, then turned to face him. "Have you ever made love on a sandy beach?"

I could tell my words had a positive effect on him, because he looked like he was squirming for air. He shook his head. "No, I can't say I ever have."

"That's too bad. You just don't know what you're missing." I winked, then turned on my heels and headed back toward the table. Nadine blocked my path.

"I can't believe you said that."

I shrugged. "It's just harmless fun."

She looked like she wasn't buying it. "Nothing you do or say is harmless."

"Bitch, whatever." I purposely bumped her shoulder and moved toward the table. What was Nadine doing anyway, listening to my conversation? What her dyke ass needs to do is focus on her new woman and leave me the hell alone.

Chapter 61

KAYLA

After breakfast, Kayla returned to the room to get ready for the trip to Dunn's River Falls. The football players had chartered a bus to take them and their families to Ocho Rios for the entire day. Kayla smiled. She couldn't wait because she would have Clayton all to herself. Kayla felt a combination of nervousness and excitement.

As soon as she stepped into the room, out of habit she checked for messages and as usual there weren't any. With a sigh, she began preparing for the trip. As she packed a change of clothes for the trip, she realized how big a fool she was. Leroy never had any intentions of calling her. The minute she had made the decision to question the future of their relationship was the exact moment he had decided to call it quits, only she was too stupid and gullible to know game when it was heard. She was too stupid to know when she was being played. Instead, she sat moping around waiting for him to call and tell her he loved her.

As she tossed a pair of water shoes into a small bag, she told herself to look on the bright side. She had a wonderful man who seemed to truly like her. In fact, he had invited her to be his guest at the wedding tomorrow. Flattered, she had quickly accepted.

Kayla stepped into the bathroom to freshen up her face. She

splashed cool water across it, then patted it dry with a towel. When she caught her reflection in the large mirror, she paused.

Even as she thought about getting on with her life, she knew that it was going to take time and willpower to get over Leroy. Despite the way he had treated her, she still loved him with all her heart. And that was what made it so hard for her to move on. Luckily, she thought with a smile, she had someone like Clayton to help her. She couldn't think of a better substitute. But how could she keep someone like him happy?

Grabbing a larger towel off the rack, she moved back into the room and stuffed it into the bag with her clothes. As soon as she changed into a pair of seersucker crop pants and a matching red top, she would be all set to go.

Hearing calypso music below, she moved to the window and glanced down at the guests eager for jerk chicken. At the end of the path, she noticed Renee talking to Clayton and her jaw dropped. As usual, Renee was flirting. She could tell by the tilt of her head and the way she kept touching his arm. Panic rose up and lodged in her throat. She was going to have to do something quick or run the risk of losing him. And she couldn't bear to lose another man.

As she slipped into the cool red outfit, Kayla thought about Renee's behavior last night. Renee was supposed to be her friend, yet she had been all over him, bumping and grinding. She was envious because she wished she had the guts to be like that. At the same time she was angry because her friend had no boundaries when it came to her behavior.

At the very moment she made a promise. She was going to have to watch Renee closely.

The phone rang. Kayla practically broke her neck trying to reach it.

"Hello?"

"Good morning, beautiful."

Kayla didn't recognize the voice and frowned. "Who is this?"

There was a slight chuckle and for a moment she thought maybe Renee was downstairs playing games.

"Who else, my sweet, but the only man who truly loves you?"

She may not have spoken to Leroy in days but she definitely knew that wasn't him or Clayton either, for that matter. Besides, the mysterious voice had an accent. "I am two seconds away from hanging up."

"Renee, my love, you're breaking my heart. This is none other than your prince, Everton."

Kayla released an angry sigh. Everton had gotten her all excited for nothing. "This is Kayla. Not Renee."

"Oh, forgive me for my assumption. Is Renee there?"

She smiled, suddenly coming up with a way to get back at her roommate for pushing up on her man. "No, she's down by the beach."

"Thanks, and again I apologize for the confusion."

When Kayla finally hung up, she felt like crying. Lowering onto the bed, she forced herself to take several deep breaths. She had really thought that was Leroy finally calling her. Dang, was she ever going to learn?

Chapter 62

RENEE

How the hell are they going to tell me how I feel about someone? They don't know what I feel or what I am thinking. None of them does. I mean, it's not like I am trying to find another husband. Shit, I ain't even trying to fall in love again. All I am trying to do is have a little fun while on vacation. And that is exactly what I am having with Solomon. Lots and lots of fun. He makes me laugh. That man has a sense of humor that is all his own. He also is a wonderful conversationalist. I could listen to his accent all day. And his lips while he speaks, oh my goodness, they look so succulent, so thick and juicy, all I want to do is reach over and lick them like an ice cream cone. But the icing on the cake was the sex. That boy knew how to fuck a sistah to death. I must say, after last night my coochie was sore but there wasn't anything wrong with pleasurable pain. There was nothing better after a night of sex than to still feel the physical aftereffects the next morning. And a sistah was definitely feeling it. I woke up with a smile on my face and Solomon on the brain, and ain't shit wrong with that. So why were them bitches hating? Okay, maybe I did fuck up the first night by sleeping with Everton's worthless ass. And maybe the next night I was all over that Taye Diggs look-alike however, since I've met Solomon, I have been all about him. And that's who I planned to stick with until the end of this absolutely wonderful trip.

Another thing: what in the hell is Nadine doing questioning my motives with Clayton? I know that he and Kayla are dating. Yeah, so maybe I was flirting when I shouldn't have been, but that's just the way I am. I don't mean shit by it. Okay, maybe I am lying. I guess I do mean something by it. I'm just having a hard time trying to figure out why he passed over me for my girl. All I want to know is if he is interested and that's it, nothing more.

Before I met Solomon maybe I would have been interested in sampling the dick but now that I have my own, I don't need to. Shit, she can have him. It's not like Clayton's giving up any dick anyway.

As I moved down the beach, I shook my head. I simply don't see how women did it back in the day. They remained virgins until their wedding night. They had no idea what the mothafucka was working with until after the deal was sealed. Then it was too late to back out. I'm sorry, but there ain't no way I would even think about spending the rest of my life with some mothafucka until I had a chance to see what he was working with. And even then I'd need to take a couple of long stiff rides on his dick before I could have made the decision to spend the rest of my life with him.

Yep, the only thing appealing about Clayton was the size of his pockets. And right now money was the last thing on my mind.

"Hey, it's chicken feet!"

I glanced over at the jerk-chicken hut and waved to Langley.

"I've got some good Jamaican jerk pork, mon."

"Maybe later," I yelled, then kept on walking, feeling the heat of his gaze on my back. Damn, I love Jamaica!

I was moving down the path toward our building when I spotted Everton coming my way. Shit! Quickly, I ducked behind a bush and waited for him to pass. My heart was pounding like an African drum. I don't know why, because I wasn't scared of him. However, after last night something about him was starting to really annoy me. One more encounter with him and the rest of my day would be a total loss.

Glancing out from between two branches, I waited until he made it to the end of the path before I sprang from the bushes, dashed into the building, and climbed the stairs to the room. Kayla was in there getting ready for her outing. Clayton was taking her to Ocho Rios. How sweet! She smiled at me as I stepped into the room.

"Girl, if Everton comes in my face one more time I swear I'm going to have a long talk with his boss."

"He called looking for you. I told him you were outside." I could tell she was trying not to laugh.

"Thanks a lot." I had too good of a day ahead to be truly angry. "Girl, it's going to be a beautiful day!"

"Yes, it is," she agreed. Kayla was smiling and looking happy, and I'm glad. Anything is better than watching her moping around over Leroy's ass.

"What time are you all leaving for the falls?" I asked as I took a seat and kicked off my shoes.

"In thirty minutes. I can't wait."

I frowned. "I don't know why your ass is excited about climbing some damn waterfall."

"I heard it's a lot of fun. You climb the falls in a human chain and experience the soothing effect of the water as it cascades to the sea below. I can't wait."

That shit sounded corny as hell. "What if you fall?" Her ass is big, after all.

"Renee, it's going to be a lot of fun."

"Whatever you say." Shit, maybe spending the day under a water-fall wasn't a bad way to spend a day. It was supposed to be hot as shit today. And riding on the back of a moped was going to be torture.

I rose, moved over to my tote bag, and removed a pink bottle. "Hey, do me a favor before you leave. Rub some sunscreen on my back." The last thing I needed was for my ass to burn.

Chapter 63

LISA

"You need to check your sister," Nadine said to Lisa once they returned to their room after breakfast.

"Why do you say that?"

Frustrated, she placed a hand to her hip. "Because she is after Clayton."

Lisa shook her head. "She wouldn't do that." One thing she knew about her sister, she didn't intentionally mess with someone else's man.

Nadine gave her the eye as she spoke. "No, she won't take him, she'll wait for him to come to her. All the flirting she's doing, there is no way he's going to be able to resist too much longer. You forget he is still a man. You should have seen the way she was grinding on his ass at the club last night."

Lisa lowered onto the bed, then gave her a puzzled look. "I thought she was into Solomon."

"She is, but Clayton's a challenge, and you know how she likes a challenge."

Lisa nodded and slipped out of her sandals. Yes, she was right about that. What Renee wants, Renee gets. She knew her sister all too well. She also knew that as soon as she fucked Clayton, she was going to play him like a harmonica. As soon as she was done she was going to push him aside. She didn't want him. She wanted him because he wanted Kayla and because of it, that made him a challenge.

She and Nadine were going snorkeling this afternoon. While she reached in the drawer for a clean swimsuit, she tried to think about how to handle the situation. If she approached her sister, Renee would deny any attempt at trying to snare Clayton and would be pissed off instead.

Lisa sighed. Her sister had far too many issues; she just didn't know how to approach her anymore. Maybe bringing her to Jamaica to break the news wasn't such a good idea after all.

Don't start doubting your decisions, whispered a voice. Her conscience was right—she couldn't start second guessing her decision. Tomorrow she was going to sit all three of them down and lift a tremendous weight from her soul.

Chapter 64

RENEE

I can't believe this shit!

Solomon stood my ass up. I had been waiting at the front gate for over an hour, basting in the hot sun, and his ass still hadn't shown up. I mean, whatever happened to common courtesy? Obviously, his parents didn't teach him shit.

I have never in my life been stood up. Okay, there I go lying again. I did get stood up once but that was some pretty boy that I had met at the car wash. I knew by the way his cell phone kept popping off that he was just running game. We were supposed to meet at the movies. I told him to give me a call when he was on his way. I didn't even bother getting ready 'cause I already knew. Sure enough, he never called and I didn't give the incident a second thought.

I glanced down at my watch one last time. Five, four, three, two, one, I'm out. I stormed up the driveway past the gardeners and through the front door across the lobby.

"Renee!"

As soon as I heard Everton calling my name, I ran. Good Lord, why can't he just die and leave my ass alone? I was so pissed off with Solomon that I had made the mistake of going through the main lobby instead of cutting through the side. The last thing I wanted was for Everton to know that I was on the premises. Now he was going to bug the hell out of me.

I raced across the lobby. Once I reached the pool, I realized how stupid I must look and stopped. I couldn't believe this shit. That boy had me so upset, he had me running from his ass. This just didn't make any sense at all. And all because I gave him some. I was going to have to think of some way to get Everton off my back once and for all, because I couldn't go on like this. He was ruining my vacation.

I slid my glasses off my head and onto my eyes, then quickened my steps. I needed to make it up to the room without being spotted by Lisa and Nadine. If they knew I had gotten stood up, I would never live it down. After teasing Nadine's ass, she was definitely going to try and give me a hard time. To be honest, I just wasn't in the mood for that shit.

As I moved up the path, I passed the hamburger hut and almost plowed into Pierre.

He seemed pleased to see me. "I didn't think I would ever run into you again."

If only I could have been so lucky. Staring up at Pierre, I prayed that he had remembered to suck on a breath mint, then said, "Hello, Pierre. Ready for your son's big day?"

"Yes, tomorrow will be here soon enough. Have you thought any more about attending my son's wedding tomorrow? Everyone is going to be there."

Including Clayton and Kayla. I shrugged. "Sure, why not?" At least his breath wasn't stinking today.

"Excellent. How about dinner tonight? I made reservations at the restaurant upstairs."

The pamphlets had said the restaurant was five-star quality, with crab cakes that were so good they made you want to slap your mama. Unfortunately every time we tried to make reservations, they were already booked for the evening. Dinner with Pierre might be my only chance at getting in, then I can rub it in everybody's face. "Listen, Pierre, I might as well tell you now, I don't do old men."

"Good, then we shouldn't have any problems." He winked. "All I'm interested in is a good meal with a beautiful woman on my arm and a little conversation."

Sure, why not. Now that Solomon had stood my ass up, what else did I have to do besides dodge Everton's ass all day?

Chapter 65

NADINE

Nadine would never have believed that snorkeling was the best way to observe aquatic life if she hadn't experienced it first hand. She and Lisa and a team of ten spent the afternoon snorkeling around shallow coral reefs where marine life abounds. For someone who had never been a strong swimmer, she was delighted how easy the experience had been. She was so engrossed by the world under the sea that for almost two hours she had completely forgotten she had gotten her freak on with Lavina the night before. It wasn't until they were returning to the shore that the memories came flooding back. She closed her eyes as heat flowed through her body and settled down low. Thank goodness she was already wet between her legs, because juices were running down the insides of her thighs. Lavina had put an end to any further doubts she might have been having. She was definitely a lesbian. There was no longer any ifs, ands, or buts about it. Lavina was a skillful woman who last night shared with her the art of making love to another woman. After her sister had returned to her room, she pulled out the couch bed. She then cut off the lights and the two had gotten completely undressed and climbed beneath the sheets. From that moment on, Lavina was in complete control. She caressed every corner of Nadine's body, and with the help of a vibrating dildo, Nadine reached a level of sexual release that she had never obtained before.

As she moved out of the water she couldn't suppress the glow to her cheeks as she continued to think about how good Lavina had made her feel. However, she had made it clear that she wasn't interested in anything but a little vacation fling. Lavina agreed. Nadine had yet to share with Lisa the details of her evening.

With her partner on her mind, she glanced to her right, suddenly remembering that she was supposed to be right beside her. Only she wasn't there. Turning on her heels, Nadine spotted Lisa a short distance behind her. Nadine stopped and waited for her to catch up. As soon as she saw Lisa's face she could tell something wasn't right.

"Are you okay?" Nadine asked as she quickly moved toward Lisa.

Lisa nodded her head and tried to put on a good front, but Nadine immediately saw through it. Lisa was breathing hard and she didn't look too good. Nadine took hold of her arm and helped her the rest of the way.

"Nadine, I'm fine, really."

Nadine wasn't buying it. "Tell that to someone else. I used to be a nurse's aid, remember?"

"Yeah, and I know my body better than anyone else. I just overdid it today, that's all."

Nadine refused to argue with her, however, as soon as they got back to the room they were going to have a long talk.

They followed the rest of the group to the equipment room to return the snorkeling gear, then she and Lisa went back to their room so they could relax a little before dinner. Nadine waited until they had both showered and were lying across the bed before she mentioned the incident again.

"Lisa, I know you're hiding something," Nadine finally said.

Lisa smiled as she leaned back against her pillow. "Quit being a worrywart."

"I am not. I just know you're hiding something. I'm your best friend. Please tell me what's going on with you," she pleaded.

Before Lisa spoke she was quiet for what felt to Nadine like forever. "You're right. I have been hiding something."

"Damn. Finally the truth," she said as she swung her feet off onto the floor and sat up on the bed, giving Lisa her full attention. She watched carefully as Lisa took several deep breaths, and suddenly she got scared as she prepared for what Lisa was about to say that caused her normally happy friend to look so sad.

After several more moments of silence Lisa quietly said, "Three years ago I was diagnosed with ovarian cancer."

"What?" Nadine's hand flew involuntarily to her mouth. She couldn't possibly have heard her best friend right. "How did you . . . I mean, what happened?"

"I had been experiencing abdominal pain and constant bleeding. My doctor decided to run some tests. The results were inconclusive."

"Oh, Lisa. I'm so sorry. How come you didn't tell me?"

She shrugged. "I didn't know how to tell you. First I was mad, then I was in denial. When she told me I had to have a hysterectomy, I was devastated because I knew I would never have children."

"Wait a minute. That's why you had the surgery?" Lisa nodded. "Why did you lie?"

Tears streamed down Lisa's face as she told Nadine the truth. "I didn't want to worry any of you."

"That's what friends are for. To share burdens with." She reached over to the nightstand and handed Lisa a tissue. "Does Renee know?"

She shook her head. "Not yet."

"Damn, girl." She moved over to the bed and wrapped her arms around her best friend. There was no way she could have stopped the flow of tears even if she had tried. "How have you been? Did they get rid of all the cancer? Are you getting chemo?"

Lisa released her and sat up straight on the bed. She then told her about the surgery followed by the rounds of chemotherapy. For two years she had thought the cancer was gone, until a recent test had told her otherwise. "I'm scheduled for surgery next week."

Nadine couldn't move. She couldn't believe that something like this was happening to someone she loved. Cancer! It just wasn't fair. Lisa was such a loving and giving person. Nadine remembered when Lisa had first told her she wouldn't be able to have children. Her heart had gone out to her and Michael because she knew how badly

Lisa had wanted children. However, when Lisa had reassured Nadine that she had decided she liked her life just the way it was and was pleased about the surgery, she had actually believed her. Then she found out that it had all been one big lie.

She stared at Lisa as if she were seeing her for the first time. Physically Lisa was the same person she had known for years. Although her shoulder-length hair had been gone for over two years, Nadine had grown accustomed to the short, curly natural look. However, light radiating across her tired face, allowed her to see that the person on the inside had long since changed.

"How's Michael handling all this?"

Lisa dabbed her eyes as she spoke. "I don't know how I would have survived without his love and support."

Nadine hugged Lisa again, glad for the few seconds to shield her startled expression. While holding her, she allowed her own tears to fall freely from her face.

"I can't have you falling apart," Lisa said after she reared back.

Nadine wiped the tears away from her eyes. "I'm sorry. I know I should be giving you support, but I am just so damn mad! Why you, of all people?"

Lisa looked her in the eyes. "Things happen sometimes for reasons we can't begin to explain. I feel that God picked me for some reason. Maybe even to help save someone else's life in the process."

Nadine gasped. "Oh, my God! You're not planning to die on me, are you?"

Lisa shook her head, then chuckled. "Girl, hell no. I plan to live a long time. It's surgery, that's all. My lymph nodes are unaffected, so that's a good sign. My doctor is confident they should be able to get almost all of the cancer this time, and we should be able to shrink the rest with chemo."

Nadine tried to smile through a haze of sadness. "I hope so, because I don't know what I would do without you."

"Don't worry, girl. I'm not going anywhere. I am a survivor. Cancer is going to have to take me kicking and screaming." There was a sad little smile on her face, followed by another stream of tears.

Nadine shared a tearful laugh. When they sobered, she asked, "Is that why you asked us here?"

Lisa nodded.

"When were you planning to tell us?"

"Tomorrow. I was planning to sit down with all three of you tomorrow."

Nadine couldn't stop shaking her head. "This is so unreal. But don't you worry. We are going to get through this together. Is there anything I can do for you?"

Nodding, Lisa gave her a dead stare, then said, "Yeah, call Jordan and tell her you love her."

Chapter 66

RENEE

I was so glad to get out of that room! I can't believe I spent the entire day hiding just so I wouldn't have to run into Nadine and Lisa. And let's not forget Everton, who blew up my damn phone.

Pierre called and asked me to meet him at six. When I arrived, he hadn't made it yet. So I moved to a table in the corner of the restaurant to wait. As soon as I sat in the chair, a waitress appeared with a menu and a glass of water. I ordered my drink and was taking a sip when Everton stepped into the room. I nearly choked when I spotted him heading in my direction. I tried to hide behind my menu, but it was obvious he knew I was there when he dropped into the chair across from me.

"Hey, Renee."

I lowered the menu to the table and folded my arms on top of them. "What are you doing up here?"

"Leslie told me she saw you come up here so I thought I'd come join you."

I'd have to remember to kick her ass later. "I'm meeting someone."

"Who?"

"That's none of your business." I glanced over toward the door, expecting Pierre to arrive at any moment.

"Yes, you are my business." He reached for my hand and I snatched it back.

"No, I'm not, so go." I hadn't realized I had raised my voice until I saw the people at the next table looking our way.

Everton dropped his voice. "What's wrong? You don't want me to see who you're having dinner with?"

"No, I just don't want to see your feelings get hurt." I couldn't stop watching the door.

"Don't worry about me; I'm a big boy." He leaned back in the chair. "So I guess it's safe to assume you're meeting another man."

"Yes, now go."

He looked pissed. "You didn't even give me a chance."

Everton just wouldn't get the hint. I was two seconds away from cussing his ass out. "Listen, you are not my man and I do not appreciate you tracking me down like some damn stalker. Now I have a date coming, so I want you to go."

There was a long silence. "What did I do?"

I had to look down because he looked so sad, and the last thing I wanted to do was feel sorry for him. "Nothing. We're just not compatible."

"I think we are. We had a wonderful time and I want that again."

I didn't bother to comment. My silence said it all.

"It could be great between us if you'd just give us a chance."

I reached for my drink. "Sorry, but it's not going to work. You're just not my type. But you're a really sweet guy. Really." Suddenly I felt really bad because he was a sweet man. He just had a little-ass dick and a big-ass mouth.

"It would never work between us. We live in two different worlds. I came here to experience fantasy, not to fall in love. I'm sorry."

Everton sat there for the longest time saying nothing, and I made myself turn away and glance down at my watch.

I couldn't begin to explain how bad I felt as I watched him walk away. I could tell by the dejected slump of his shoulders that my words had hurt him.

I've done a lot of things in my life, but this is the first time I began to believe that maybe I am a bitch. I had hurt people before, but it was usually when I had been hurt first. Everton had done nothing to me but mislead me into believing he was capable of offering mind-boggling sex.

Five minutes later, Pierre walked in. He glanced in my direction and I waved at him, drawing his attention. Within minutes his old ass had me laughing and Everton was the furthest thing from my mind.

Chapter 67

NADINE

Long after Lisa had drifted off to sleep Nadine moved out onto the beach, a book in her hand and her glasses covering her red eyes.

She found a seat away from the crowd and lowered onto the chair. She then opened a book she had been trying to read for almost two months. However, ten minutes had passed and she still hadn't comprehended one word. The letters were running together and all was blurred.

It isn't fair, she screamed inwardly as she raised her hand to fiercely wipe the tears away from her cheeks. Lisa didn't deserve to have to go through the entire ordeal again. She knew how trying cancer treatments were to a person's body. She had watched her cousin battle breast cancer. Her body had dwindled away to almost nothing. She had endured months of fatigue and nausea, and some days she barely had the strength to get out of bed. Then, after six years, she lost the battle.

Dammit. She lifted the shades from her eyes and mopped fresh tears away. She was falling apart and this would not do. She had to be strong for Lisa's sake. She needed her love and support.

Gosh, she missed Jordan. Jordan would have allowed her to cry her eyes out, then would have told her to suck her bottom lip in and put a lid on it. Together she would help her help Lisa. Closing her eyes, she leaned back in the chair as she reminisced on what she loved most about Jordan.

Lisa was right; she did need to call Jordan. Jordan had a way of making her think that anything was possible.

How could she have been so stupid? She was wasting time worrying about what others thought when tomorrow wasn't promised to any of us. Lisa was right; she was making a big mistake. Jordan made her happy. And right now she needed all the happiness she could find.

As soon as she got back to the room, she was going to call Jordan and make everything right again.

Chapter 68

RENEE

I returned to the room with my stomach full. I had thoroughly enjoyed dinner. Like I said before, if I was my mama's age I might have given Pierre some play. But since we are talking fact, not fantasy, Pierre is too old and out of shape for me. At least his breath had been tolerable, and he did get me an invite to the wedding tomorrow. Speaking of, I'm going to have to make a trip across the street tomorrow and see if I can find myself something fly to wear.

I slipped out of my sandals and moved over to the drawer for a swimsuit. Shit, I ain't got shit else to do, so I might as well hang out near the pool. I had just slipped out of my shorts when the phone rang. Groaning, I ignored it because I knew it couldn't be anybody but that worrisome-ass Everton. When Pierre and I came down from dinner, he was standing behind the counter, watching. Purposely I leaned into Pierre and, I kid you not, Everton looked like he wanted to climb over that counter and kick my ass. I just laughed and kept on going. Pierre and I parted in the courtyard.

By the time I had slipped into a red bikini the phone had rung three damn times. That mothafucka is driving me insane! Okay, enough. You know I'm no punk. The phone rang again and this time I spun on my heels and went and answered it.

"I ain't gonna tell yo ass again. Leave me the fuck alone!"

"Hey, Renee, girl, whassup with you?"

"Who is this?" I had an idea who it was but I wanted to be sure.

"It's me, Solomon."

Right now I had straight attitude and was tempted to cuss his ass out, but I stopped myself because that's what the negro expects me to do and I wasn't about to give him the satisfaction. "Oh, hey, whassup?"

He sputtered with laughter. "Is that all you got to say?"

"Yeah, why, whassup?" I said, all nonchalant and shit.

"Damn, you act like you didn't even want to hear from me."

"How was Kingston?"

"I didn't go. That's what I'm trying to tell you. My grandmother forgot to tell me she had a doctor's appointment until this morning. I spent the day with her."

"Uh-huh."

"I know I should have called and I apologize. You forget I don't have a phone at home like you Americans all do."

Okay, he did have a point.

"Can I see you tonight?"

I took a moment to think about it because I didn't want to appear too eager. "Yeah, I guess so."

"Cool. Meet me outside at ten and bring an overnight bag."

I hung up the phone, screaming and hollering like a damn fool. Yes! It was on and popping again. My boo hadn't played me after all. Although I am going to have to tell his ass that the next time he needs to cancel he better find a phone even if he has to travel fifty miles to do so.

Chapter 69

RENEE

I felt like a teenager going out on her first date as I applied my makeup carefully, then searched through the drawer for something sexy to wear that night. After several wardrobe changes, I finally slipped into a white knit racer-back dress that stopped mid-thigh, and paired it with white espadrilles that laced up to my calves. As Solomon had instructed, I packed an overnight bag. Shortly after ten, I strolled away from the hotel.

Let me just say the mood was set. It was a perfect tropical evening with a slight breeze, and I was about to spend the rest of the evening with a man that made my nipples hard. What more could a girl ask for other than a good clit lick, and I was certain I would get that before the night was over.

I found Solomon waiting for me on his bike.

"What's up, beautiful?"

"Hi." I pressed my lips against his, then darted my tongue in and out of his mouth.

"Damn, baby, I can't wait to get me some." He climbed off the bike and led me around the side of the hotel. He pulled me into his arms and kissed me some more. I felt him growing hard. Suddenly feeling bold, I reached for the buckle of his pants, freed willy, and dropped to my knees.

I slipped his entire dick into my mouth without blinking. He started making all kind of noises. I then slipped just the tip of his dick inside my mouth and teased it. He moaned and precum drizzled into my mouth. I slid the head out of my mouth, then took the tip of my tongue and ran it through the slit. "Damn, baby!" he moaned as I bathed the head.

My mouth took on a rhythm of its own as it slipped his dick in and out, slowly at first, then the intensity growing with each stroke. I sucked him for a long time, licking all around the shaft, down to his balls, and back again. I love the way a man shudders when I suck him off, because that lets me know that I've got mad skills. When he finally came in my mouth, I felt triumphant.

I spit his juice into the grass, then rose and brushed the dirt from my knees.

Solomon put his dick back in his pants, then reached for his zipper. "Everton was right. You do have skills."

I stopped wiping my mouth and swung around. "Excuse me?" I know I didn't hear him right.

He gave me a disgusted look. "You heard me. Everton said you were a wonderful fuck. I really thought you were someone special."

Mothafuck. That bastard had run his damn mouth.

I sucked my teeth. "You can't believe everything you hear."

"Okay, so then tell me, mon," Solomon said as he moved all up in my face. "Were you fucking Everton?"

"Hell naw." You know I'm going to deny that shit to the end.

"So then how does he know about your strawberry?"

Oh, shit, I had forgotten about the small tattoo on my coochie. One year after partying at the club with my girl Danielle, we went to my house, shaved our coochies, and went and got matching coochie tattoos. Shit, I forgot it was even there. Damn, my ass was up a creek without a paddle.

I shrugged. "Okay, so maybe we did fuck, but it was a mistake that happened once."

He stifled a smirk and gave me a return look that dropped me lower than the soles of his shoes. "That's not the only thing that's a mistake."

I tried to laugh it off because, damn, I didn't know what to say. "Damn, it's like that?"

He spit on the ground before my feet. "I don't do whores."

Oh, hell naw! I felt like he had just slapped my ass across the face. After the shock of his comment wore off, I retorted with, "I ain't no ho."

He chuckled. "I don't know what y'all call it in America, but here in Jamaica women like you are considered whores."

Before he had a chance to react, I grabbed his balls and held them in a vice-grip hold. "If you call me a ho one more time I'm gonna break this bitch in half!"

He started to say something slick but quickly thought about it and changed his mind. "Okay, okay, I'm sorry."

I released his dick and pushed him away from me. "You ain't shit." I had enough of him. Solomon wasn't any different than the rest. I reached down for my bag.

"I can't help the way I was raised. Everton and I have been friends for years. What did you think—I wasn't going to find out?"

I glared at him. He was smiling like the shit was funny. "Fuck you, Solomon."

"You already did that and damn your lips were good."

I swung my bag and hit him dead across the side of his head.

"Hey, you crazy bitch!"

I swung at him again and he threw up his hands and blocked the blow. Instinctively, I kicked him hard between his legs, then turned and raced up the driveway. He was screaming all kinds of obscenities and calling my ass everything but a child of God.

"Renee, bring your ass back here!"

I ignored him. My back was turned and it was going to stay that way because tears were streaming down my face that I damn sure wasn't going to let him see. I felt so ashamed.

I couldn't go back to the room. The last thing I needed was for them to know I had fucked up. Tears were pouring down my face. I felt like a two-bit whore. What the hell was I doing, thinking I could screw with more than one employee at the same hotel and they would not find out about each other?

After making sure Solomon wasn't following me, I cut around the side of the building and headed toward the beach.

I had really liked Solomon. How could I have been so stupid?

I grabbed a couple of hotel towels near the pool, then moved to a chair on the beach and wrapped them around me.

I sat there feeling sorry for myself. Once again I had gotten wrapped up in a man. I really thought that Solomon and I had made a connection and that we had something that was worth holding on to long after I had returned home. Thanks to Everton the relationship was already over before I had a chance to see where we were headed. I felt cheap. I felt used. Solomon had known long before I had wrapped my lips around his dick that he had no intentions of sharing the evening together. It had just been a way to get back at me. I wouldn't be surprised to discover that someone had been hiding in the bushes videoing the whole thing.

Sleeping with Everton had been a mistake that was obviously going to continue to haunt my ass for the duration of the visit.

"Little lady, what are you doing out here?"

I glanced over my shoulder, scowled, then stared off into the ocean again. "I want to be alone."

Pierre moved to the chair beside me. "I don't believe you."

I dragged my knees up to my chest and hugged them close. "Who cares what you think?"

"I hate seeing you so unhappy. You remind me so much of my daughter Benita." When I didn't bother to answer, he added, "She once told me that I was a good listener."

"There is nothing to talk about."

"I don't believe that." He reached over and cupped my hand. "It's going to be cold tonight. I think you should go in."

Closing my eyes, I shook my head. "I can't. My roommate has company tonight."

Pierre rose. "Then come on. You can share my room. I won't bite unless you ask me to."

Chapter 70

KAYLA

Kayla took a long hot shower. Her heart was beating so hard she didn't know how she was going to pull tonight off. She asked Clayton to spend the night with her and he had said yes.

She took a deep breath and finally reached down and turned off the water. She then reached for her towel and rubbed off the excess water, then grabbed a bottle of True Star perfumed lotion and rubbed it generously across her body. If she couldn't look good at least she could smell good. She scowled. She was starting that negative mess again. What did Clayton tell her? He liked her just the way she was. All two hundred ninety-five pounds. So, then, what was the problem? The problem was she didn't like herself and as long as she felt that way there was no way she would ever believe hearing it from someone else.

Kayla, now is not the time. She had a date to prepare for and she was wasting time feeling sorry for herself. It wasn't like she was going on a blind date or something. Clayton already knew exactly what he was getting.

Still wrapped in her towel, she moved into the room and picked up a short lacy piece of lingerie she had found in one of the shops across the street. As soon as she had gotten back from her trip and told Lisa she was spending the night with Clayton, she had grabbed her arm and dragged her to find something sexy to wear. She was shocked to discover they had something not only in her size, but sexy enough that she just might be able to pull the night off.

Kayla slipped the piece of material over her head, then moved to the mirror to fix her hair. There wasn't much to do to her braids except smooth them out with a little styling gel. She then put on a little mascara and took a seat on the bed and waited. They had the entire night. Renee obviously was spending the night with Solomon because she had packed a bag and told her she'd see her in the morning.

Thank goodness for Solomon. As long as he kept Renee occupied, she wouldn't have to worry about her trying to steal her man. However, after tonight, she didn't think she'd have to worry about that possibility any longer. She was going to make sure this was a night Clayton never forgot.

She glanced over at the clock. It was almost midnight. Clayton would be arriving at any minute. Sure enough, she barely had time to relax when she heard a knock at the door. It took her a few second to get the courage to walk across the room and open that door. When she finally did, she wasn't the least bit disappointed.

"Hey." He was standing there in lightweight shorts, a Jamaican t-shirt they had gotten while at Dunn's River Falls, and a pair of flip-flops. He had the most incredible feet. She expected them to look beat-up, like most athlete's feet; instead his were nice and neat like he spent money on a pedicure.

Stepping aside she allowed him to enter, then closed the door and slowly turned around.

Clayton gave a loud wolf whistle. "Man! Baby, you look good."

"Thanks," she said, smiling bashfully.

"Come have a seat." He took her hand and led her over to her bed, where he took a seat and draped her across his lap. "I missed you." Kiss.

"I missed you, too." She said, wrapping her arms around his neck. Kiss. Kiss.

She moaned as his fingers traced her thighs. His kissing her made her all hot and bothered and her heart started pounding so hard she was afraid she was going to hyperventilate. She was spending the night with one of the finest black brothas in America. She was so excited she was shaking inside.

"Let me stop 'fore things get out of hand," he suggested. "I'm tired. What about you?"

"You? Me. That climb wore me out." They had each climbed the six hundred foot waterfall. It had been an exhilarating climb through cool waters. However, after a full day in Ocho Rios, she was worn out. She rose and moved to get her bed ready.

Clayton's eyes traveled across the room. "Where's your girl?"

Kayla shrugged. "There's no telling with Renee."

He chuckled. "That girl is a trip."

That was putting it mildly. "Yes, she is."

She reached over and turned out the lamp to hide some of her nervousness. The room was lit by the moonlight outside.

Clayton pulled the covers back, then reached down and slipped off his shirt and shorts and dropped them to the floor. Standing in front of her in red boxers, he looked like a Nubian god. Damn, she couldn't wait to get her lips on his chocolate nipples. The thought made her mouth water.

"What's wrong baby?"

"Nothing." Except she was nervous as all get-out.

He crooked a finger at her. "Then come here and gimme some."

Her coochie clenched. "Give you some?"

He chuckled. "A kiss, baby. Gimme a kiss."

She met him halfway across the bed. He wrapped his arms around her and locked her lips to his. The kiss lasted forever before they ended up on the bed, holding each other.

He just lay there holding her and dropping light kisses around her face and neck. She waited for his hand to travel under her negligee and grope her breasts. She waited for his hand to slide between his leg. But it never happened. *Is he waiting for me?* she wondered.

Kayla had never been bold in her life. She had always allowed the man to run the show. She took a deep breath. *It's now or never.*

She rolled on top of him and ran her tongue across his neck slow and sensually, the way it had been done to her. She then raised a shaky hand and rubbed it across his chest and moved down and slid her fingers inside his boxers.

Good Lord, he was hung!

Clayton grabbed her hand. "Yo, hold up."

She released him just as he flipped her over onto her back.

Kayla suddenly panicked. "I'm sorry. I must have done that wrong. Please, let me try again." She tried to reach for him again but he held her back.

She was so devastated by his actions tears pushed to the surface.

"Boo, why you crying?" He reached up and wiped her tears away.

He wasn't attracted to her, but as inadequate as she was as a woman, who could blame him. "I'm sorry. I . . . I don't know what to say," she said nervously.

Clayton stroked her cheek. "There is nothing for you to apologize for. If anyone should be apologizing it should be me."

"Why should you apologize?"

He released a frustrated sigh. "Because I should have told you the truth about me from the get-go."

Oh, boy, here it goes. Another letdown. She was shocked when he rolled over and pulled her into his arms, resting her head on his chest.

After several long seconds of silence, he finally said, "I'm celibate."

Her head flew up. "Celibate?"

"I'm afraid so."

She was confused. "But why?"

"Because I've screwed so many women in my life I've lost count."

She said "oh" like she understood, when in fact she didn't. She lowered her head back onto his chest as he continued.

"Excuse my French, but I've been getting pussy since I was thirteen years old. I tried to stick my dick in everything I could get my hands on. Then when I made pro I had women falling at my feet. Some nights I slept with two or three women at one time. Then my boy died of AIDS and I got my shit together. I realized that I was playing Russian roulette with my life. So I made a decision not to have sex again until I met a woman I was serious about."

What he said made her think. Hadn't she been doing the same thing with her own life? Sleeping with one man after another, looking for love in all of the wrong places? And where had it gotten her? Nowhere.

"I want to find my soul mate first. I got a strong feeling about you and me, Kayla."

He started touching her lightly across the arm, then down her legs and across her back while raining light kisses across her face. The tears started and she couldn't stop because no one had ever treated her like this. No one had ever taken the time to please her. It had always been about him. What he wanted. What he needed. But with Clayton it was different.

"That's it, baby. Let go."

He ran his tongue down her arm and she thought she was going to go crazy. Then he slid beneath the covers and brought her foot to his mouth. She had read about men that kissed feet, but had never experienced it. It was absolutely everything she could have imagined and more. He slipped her big toe in his mouth, sucked it until she squirmed for him to stop before he moved to the next toe and then the next until he had done all five. He then lightly lowered her leg and gently lifted the other. She felt like she had died and gone to heaven, because it had never been like this with Leroy. He had always been out for self-gratification. She sucked his dick. He never ate her out. He never asked her what pleased her because he was only interested in his own pleasure. Sex had always been about him. And when he busted a nut it was all over. If she hadn't come yet, that was her problem, not his.

But not Clayton. He paid attention to every part of her body, starting at the feet, and slowly worked his way up. He was right. There were other ways to please each other, and he introduced her to every one. When he sucked the backs of her knees she came harder than she ever had in her life. Afterwards, he held her in his arms while her heart rate returned to normal.

"Did you like that?"

She was still trying to catch her breath. "Oh my God, I've never experienced anything like that before."

"Good. I'm glad to know I was the first."

"What . . . what can I do to make you feel . . . you know?"

He planted a kiss on her forehead. "Just keep doing what you're doing."

Chapter 71

KAYLA

Kayla rose the next morning with the sun beaming down on her face. She rolled onto her back and smiled as memories of the night before came flooding back.

She could still feel Clayton's warm breath against her cheek. Every time he held her in his arms against his wide solid chest, her heart did crazy things. And when he kissed her and she felt him become aroused, it fascinated her to know that she had that kind of effect on him. *He's fine and he's mine.* Even with that said it was still hard to believe that Kansas City Chiefs' Clayton O'Neal wanted her.

Kayla hated to get up but she had to pee. She slid from under his arm and dashed to the bathroom. While on the toilet, the phone rang. She figured it was probably Renee calling to say, "Put that nigga out, so I can get my shit."

"Clayton, can you get that for me?" she called from the bathroom.

"No problem, baby." She heard the bed shift as he moved to reach for the phone. "Hello . . . yeah, just a minute. Yo, boo, telephone."

"Here I come." She flushed, quickly washed her hands, moved into the room, and lowered beside him onto the bed.

"Hello?"

"Kayla, baby." It was Leroy.

She gasped. "Leroy! What . . . I mean, how are you?"

"I'm good. Who was that answering the phone?"

She was silent. She didn't know what to say. Besides, Clayton was kissing her behind her ear and she couldn't think straight. "Um, a friend."

"Friend. What kind of friend? Are you messing around on me? Because if you are you better tell me now," he demanded.

How dare he question her? "Considering the fact you're married, I'm not going to answer that."

He was stunned by her bold retort. "Why are you talking to me this way?"

"I've accepted the fact it is over between us."

"Kayla, baby, don't talk like that. I've got so much to tell you. I've been asked to take over the congregation at First Baptist Church in Chattanooga."

She felt her heart break in two. He had gotten on with his life. "That's wonderful news. I'm sure Darlene is so happy."

"Kayla, please, listen to me," he pleaded. "I told Darlene about us."

She gasped. "What did she say?"

"She's giving me a divorce."

She couldn't believe her ears. She closed her eyes and took a deep breath, trying to quiet her heart. She had waited too long to hear those words.

"Baby, we can finally be together."

Tears fell from her eyes. She sat up on the bed and moved away from Clayton's reach.

"I love you, Kayla. I promise to make it all up to you."

She had so many things she wanted to ask him. "When are you leaving for Tennessee?"

There was a pregnant pause. "Not until after the baby is born."

Her heart stilled. "And when is that?"

He cleared his throat. "In about six months. Legally a judge won't grant me a divorce until the baby is born."

Six months and Reverend Leroy Brown would finally be hers. If only he had called her yesterday. "Why haven't you returned any of my calls?"

"I've been trying to call you all week. I left a message with your crazy roommate. You know, she threatened me never to call you again."

"She did?"

"Yes, she did, when all I wanted to do was to tell you I'd take care of everything. I love you, Kayla. I want to spend my life with you."

"Oh."

Clayton shifted on the bed and was staring down at her. "Baby, what's up?" She tried to cover the mouthpiece but didn't do it in time.

"Kayla, who the hell is that with you in your hotel room?"

She flinched. It was the first time she'd ever heard Leroy use profanity. "N-nobody."

"Nobody?" Clayton mocked.

Damn, he had obviously heard Leroy's loud voice. She pleaded with her eyes for him to understand.

"You know what? I'm out!" Clayton slid from underneath the covers and rose.

"Um, Leroy, I got to go. I'll call you back." She hung up before he had a chance to talk her out of it.

Kayla was so confused. She needed to do or say something, she just didn't know what. "Clayton, where are you going?"

"That was that preacher dude, right?" She nodded. "So, I'm nobody?"

"I didn't mean that. I . . . I just didn't know how to say . . ."

"How to say what?"

"What is going on right now in my life is confusing."

"So is it over with this guy or what?"

She stared at him blankly, knowing she had hurt his feelings. Hopefully he'd understand why she did what she did. "I don't know."

"What you mean you don't know?"

She tried to explain something that she didn't even understand. "I mean I don't know. I've got time invested in that relationship. It's not going to be that easy to just walk away."

"Now I see why you're always getting played, because you are too stupid to recognize a good man when you see him."

She was floored by his harsh tone. "Clayton, I—"

He cut her off with a frown. "You know what? You are all messed up in the head. I'm out."

After he was gone, she sat on the bed for the longest time unable to move. Had she made a mistake? She just wasn't sure. She and Leroy had been together for almost two years and during that time he had promised to spend the rest of his life with her. The problem was she didn't know how to be patient. She had prayed to the Lord on several occasions to give her strength. Yet it never came. Now after months of hoping and praying he was finally hers. So why wasn't she jumping up and down and praising the Lord?

Chapter 72

RENEE

As soon as the sun rose I took a quick shower and headed to breakfast. I didn't want anyone to know that I had spent the night with Pierre, so I made sure the coast was clear, then swung my bag over my arm and headed around to the front of the building. I wanted to walk across the lobby as if I had just returned from spending the night with Solomon.

Casey was behind the counter. I waved, then moved to the restaurant and took a seat.

Lisa and Nadine arrived shortly after. We fixed our plates and I listened to Nadine talk about how much fun she'd had snorkeling. I was thankful they didn't ask me about Solomon.

As soon as Kayla made it to the table, I could see the excitement dancing behind her eyes.

"What's up, girl? Did Clayton get them drawers?"

Nadine cracked up laughing with a mouthful of eggs. "I know that's right. Girlfriend, we want details."

Kayla lowered into the seat across from me. She didn't look like a woman who spent a night with a fine-ass brotha. Instead, she looked like she had just found out she was pregnant.

"Yo, Kayla, whassup?" I probed.

She took a deep breath and finally said, "Leroy asked his wife for a divorce."

I choked on a slice of bacon. I thought I told his faggot ass not to call back. "What the fuck are you talking about? I thought you spent the night with Clayton."

"I did. Leroy called this morning."

I couldn't believe this shit. I know this girl didn't fuck over a fine mothafucka like Clayton for Leroy's no-neck ass.

Lisa was the only one who seemed concerned. "Kayla, I thought you had decided to walk away from that relationship."

She wasn't hearing anything we had to say. "How can I walk away when I love someone as much as I love Leroy?"

Nadine snorted. "Easily, with one foot in front of the other."

I was about to be sick. This bitch was one french fry short of a Happy Meal. "Girl, that mothafucka ain't doing anything but using you."

She glared at me from across the table. "I don't appreciate you telling him not to call me anymore."

"I told him that because I'm tired of seeing the nigga using you."

"Well, he's not using me. Leroy is leaving his wife," she stated avidly.

I couldn't do anything but laugh at her stupid ass. "Don't tell me you believe that sorry-ass mothafucka!"

"It's none of your business. All I want to know is how come you didn't tell me he called?"

Lisa gave me a look that said "shut up." She knew that shit wasn't gonna happen.

"For what? So you could sit in your room tripping about your life with his little-dick ass?"

"How do you know his dick is small? You fucked him too?"

"Girl, puhleeze. It ain't shit I can do with his dick but use it to scratch my ass."

Lisa groaned. "Can we all just get along?"

Kayla leaned forward, gripping the table. "You know what? I'm so sick and tired of your sister. All week I've been listening to your mouth and watching you pop into one bed after another."

"Bitch, don't hate, 'cause you can't." Kayla was picking my last nerve, forcing me to act a damn fool. "That nigga doesn't love you."

"You've had three husbands and a different man in your bed every fifty-two weeks of the year and you want to tell me something about love. Ho, puhleeze."

I tried to keep myself under control but I was starting to get a little attitude. "And what have you done for the last two years? I'll tell you what you've done. Sat around waiting for the reverend to find five minutes in his week to break your fat ass off a piece. That's why your ass is always getting used, 'cause you are so damn stupid."

There was total silence around the table. I sat there staring, daring her to make a move. By now I was spoiling for a good fight.

She stared back at me, then when she finally dropped her eyes I smirked and looked down at my plate. Big mistake.

Kayla tossed Nadine's orange juice in my face.

"Oh, now you've done it!" I dropped my fork and sprang out of my chair and jumped across the table so fast, she fell backwards in her chair. I landed on top of her and tried to choke the shit out of her.

"Stop it!" Lisa screamed.

She and Nadine had to pull me off of her.

"Kayla, pack your shit, because you're getting the fuck out of my room."

I stepped over the mess we made and reached for my bag, then headed back to the room.

Chapter 73

KAYLA

While Renee went across the street to find a dress, Kayla moved all of her things across the hall to Nadine's room and Lisa moved in with Renee.

She still could not believe what had happened at breakfast. Renee had been only seconds away from choking her to death. She knew Renee had a temper but she had never expected her to turn on her like that. All the years she had stood by and been a good friend and this is what she got in return?

She was so pissed with Renee interfering in her life that she could scream. If Renee had told her Leroy had called she would have never spent the night with Clayton. She would have never experienced a night of unforgettable foreplay. He had made her feel things she had never felt before and it had been a big mistake, because Leroy loved her, and finally, after months of hoping and praying, he was soon going to be hers.

Suddenly, she was dying to hear Leroy's voice and was glad she had the excuse to call him to tell him she had moved across the hall. If she didn't, Renee might answer the phone and there was no telling what she might say to him. As angry as she was there was a great possibility she might even mention Clayton.

Reaching for the phone, she dialed the front desk and asked them to connect her call. As soon as she got a dial tone she punched in Leroy's number. She didn't bother paging him first. Since his wife already knew about them, what was the point?

"Hello?"

Her breath stalled. A woman had answered the phone. Her first thought was she had dialed the wrong number.

"Who is this?"

At the icy tone, she realized it was Darlene.

"Can I speak to Leroy?"

"Leroy?" She sounded stunned that someone had referred to him as something other than Reverend Brown. "Who's calling?"

"Kayla," she heard herself say. "Kayla Sparks."

"Sister Sparks, what you need to talk to my Leroy about?"

Kayla had noticed she had put an emphasis on *my*. "We have business to discuss."

"What kind of business?" Kayla noticed there was a hint of an attitude in her voice.

"None of your business." She couldn't believe what she was saying, since she was shaking inside.

Darlene started laughing. "Good Lord, don't tell me he got to your ass too."

She was floored. Never in all the years she'd known her, had she ever heard Darlene cuss. "Excuse me?"

"You heard me. My husband ain't nothing but a ho. Has been and always will be. He beds a different woman every week."

"So why are you with him?"

"Because he's the father of my children and I love him."

"He's divorcing you."

She cackled. "Is that what he told you? My husband will never leave me because he can't afford to. Besides, how many women do you know that allow their husbands to fuck around on them?" When Kayla didn't answer, she continued. "Not too many. I don't give a damn who he fucks as long as he doesn't bring home anything, 'cause then I would have to cut his dick off."

There was no way she was telling the truth. "You're wrong. Leroy and I are going to be married. He and I are leaving town together."

"Kayla, you are dumb as you look. My husband ain't going nowhere with anyone but me and his kids."

"I don't believe it."

"Well, believe it. You think you're the only one. Well, you're not. He been fucking Tisha Carroll for the last four months. Even brought her home for a ménage à trios." She chuckled. "Shit, I like to get my freak on too."

She couldn't believe her ears. He was messing with Brother Carroll's twenty-two-year-old daughter. "Let me speak to Leroy."

"He isn't home. He forgot to take his cell phone with him. More than likely he is over to Jessica Lawson's, letting her suck his dick."

Kayla felt sick to her stomach. Jessica was the church secretary.

"Listen. I got better things to be doing than wasting time on the phone with you. Leroy is never going anywhere because I allow him to do whatever the fuck he wants. With that little dick he has, better you than me." She gave a hearty laugh, then hung up the phone.

Dear God! Had she made a mistake?

Chapter 74

RENEE

The wedding was fit for a princess. Decorations, flowers, seven bridesmaids, and a satin designer gown that was worth more than my damn house.

I sat in the front with Pierre, feeling envious, wishing it was me up there getting ready to marry a millionaire.

Clayton came down the aisle with a beautiful woman on his arm. I saw the look of surprise before he smiled. I smiled back.

As Ayanna moved up to stand by the groom, the way they looked at each other was something I had written about many times in my romance novels but had never experienced myself.

Suddenly I felt cheated. I had been married three times. The first in my grandmother's living room, which I considered a shotgun wedding, since I didn't want to go through with it in the first place. The second had been in my basement. I knew I didn't love Troy. I just looked at him as an excuse to travel around the world. And the third was at the justice of the peace. The only emotion I felt was the excitement of knowing I could finally pursue my dream to become a published author.

Now, as I watched the two of them exchanging vows, I realized I wanted what Ayanna had. I wanted the big fairy-tale wedding on a tropical island with all my closest and dearest friends and family in attendance. But most of all I wanted to feel what they were feeling.

I know at this point you probably don't think someone like me would even know what love is or even appreciate it when I get it, but you're wrong. I want a man who makes my heart beat faster. A man that knows what I need even without telling him. A man who's a friend as well as a lover. And someone who has enough backbone to get in my ass when I need it. The way I behave I need someone to check my ass every now and again, which is the majority of the time. But most of all I wanted to look at a man the way Ayanna is looking at Alex. And I wanted a man to look at me the same way he was looking at her.

I've made a lot of mistakes in my life and broken a lot of hearts, but for once I would like to get it right. I believe everyone has a soul mate. I have yet to find mine.

By the time he saluted his bride, I was in tears. Pierre squeezed my hand.

"You okay?" he asked.

I nodded. He thought I was crying because the ceremony had been beautiful. Shit, I was crying because I wished it was me up there.

I was still feeling sorry for myself all through the meal. We had moved into a sparkling ballroom. It was beautifully done in pink and white. Ice swan, shrimp, caviar, and fine wines, not that cheap shit that we served at mine.

A large band on stage played soft music. The dance floor contained several dozen couples, spinning around the floor. Expensive perfume and colognes mingled in the air. Pierre escorted me out onto the floor. I have to admit, at his age he was an excellent dancer.

"Thank you for coming," he said close to my ear. "Gloria is practically foaming at the mouth."

I glanced over my shoulder at his wife, who he had introduced me to when we had first arrived. Her greeting was far from friendly. Now she was staring at us from across the dance floor. I kissed the side of Pierre's neck and gave her a triumphant smile.

"Don't start nothing you can't finish," Pierre warned.

I playfully rolled my eyes at him. "Don't get excited, old man. I did it to make your wife mad." He chuckled and I laughed with him. I knew he was just playing. Last night Pierre had been a perfect gentleman. After he took me back to his suite, we spent most of the evening talking about our failed relationships. It was so nice to have an unbiased opinion for a change. However, the way he was going on and on about Gloria, despite the fact she had cheated on him, he still loved her.

Speak of the devil. Gloria and her date moved onto the floor and fell into step. Her date had two left feet and kept stepping on her dress. Pierre and I chuckled, but despite his laughter I could tell by the way he was watching, as much as he tried to hide it, he wasn't over his wife.

The music changed to R. Kelly's "Step in the Name of Love." I stopped dancing and pulled Pierre off the floor.

"Sorry, Pierre, I'm not a stepper. Why don't you go rescue your wife?" I pointed toward her and her nondancing partner.

His eyes sparkled. "You sure?"

"Positive."

I stepped over near the crowd and watched him move over to Gloria and offer her a dance. She gladly left her partner standing there and joined her husband. As I watched the two of them move, they were like a black Ginger Rogers and Fred Astaire. They moved beautifully together.

"Care to dance?"

I swung around to find Clayton standing behind me. I smiled, then nodded. He couldn't dance so I knew I didn't have to worry about him showing me out on the floor. I stepped into the circle of his arms and together we simply swayed from side to side.

"I guess you know your girl played me."

"Yeah, I heard something about that."

"I feel like such a fool."

"We all play the fool once. Ain't no way I would have dumped you for that no-neck motha—" I stopped, remembering how he felt about my nasty mouth. "preacher."

He looked at me and grinned. "Yeah, I guess you're right." He pulled me into the circle of his arms.

I don't know what Kayla was smoking to even think about letting a man like this go. Now look at this picture. Kayla is overweight, with low self-esteem and two kids with two different baby's daddies. I mean, I have never seen her with a man that even remotely came close to what Clayton had and could offer her. Not only was he fine, but he had money. To top it off, he wasn't trying to fuck every which way; he was saving himself for someone special. You can't beat that.

In the back of my mind I'm dancing and thinking, this brotha is now free game. However, after my disappointment with Solomon, I just don't think I can deal with another upset. All I want to do is get through the next day and go the fuck home. However, just thinking about him made my stomach lurch. I was still hurting deeply from his words. I hope by saying I don't give a fuck, I will eventually believe it myself.

As Clayton held me in his arms, I realized why he had chosen Kayla over me, and I have to agree. Even though Kayla pissed me the fuck off, she is a beautiful woman inside and out. And that is what Clayton deserved. Only my girl has too many issues, so he needs to keep looking.

As much as I wanted to meet my soul mate and wished it was Clayton, I knew he was not.

The song came to an end. I thanked him and went in search of Pierre. I found him and his wife still on the dance floor, lost in each other's eyes. Smiling, I spun on my heels and headed back to my room.

Chapter 75

RENEE

The three of them had gone to Negril for the day. I was glad because that allowed me some time alone.

I took a seat out on the balcony and decided it was as good a time as any to think about my future.

I know I need to quit putting the shit off and just tell John it's over, yet I keep thinking if I just try a little harder and quit fucking around on the man everything is going to be all right.

But I know that isn't true. I can honestly say I was faithful for the entire first twelve months of our marriage. Not once did I mess around. However, as soon as summer rolled around again, I got a wild hair up my ass and decided I was ready to hit the club scene again. As soon as I saw all the fine brothas trying to holler it was downhill ever since.

Last night I think I finally realized why it has been so hard for me to tell him it's over: it's because deep down I really feel like I owe him something. Now stay with me a minute. He asked me to marry him when I was down on my luck. I had just lost my job and was having heart palpitations with no medical insurance to check it out.

Now that everything in my life is great, I don't need him anymore and I feel guilty about it.

Feeling hot and sleepy I moved back into the room and decided to take a quick shower followed by a nap. I stripped out of my shorts and top, then stepped into the shower. Tears sprang to my eyes as I thought about the look on John's face when I tell him it is over. I just can't bear to hurt him because he has been so good to me. No man has ever treated me so good and probably no one else ever will. Why can't I love him? I have asked God that question so many times over the last several years, yet I never seem to get an answer. I don't understand why the good guys always finish last. If John had been some knucklehead that was hitting me upside my head and trying to take my money, I would be crazy over that fool. The only peace I can feel is knowing that by me letting him go, I am allowing him the opportunity to meet someone who will love him the way he deserves to be loved.

I shed a few more tears, then turned off the water and wrapped my body in a towel. I was sitting on the bed rubbing lotion on my body when I heard a knock on the door.

I tightened the towel around me and opened the door.

"Clayton." I gasped as my eyes quickly roamed over his body. He was dressed in navy cotton shorts and a tight white t-shirt that showed off his body.

"Hi, is Kayla here?"

"No, she's . . . she's not here." I started to tell him that she was now staying across the hall, but fuck it, I don't owe her ass shit.

"Oh." He looked disappointed.

"Why don't you come on in and wait?"

He hesitated for less than five seconds before he moved into the room. With his back turned, I smiled, then closed the door. I took his hand and led him to the bed and told him to take a seat.

"Whassup?"

"I don't know why I came. I was just hoping to talk to Kayla."

"She and I aren't speaking."

"Why?"

"'Cause her ass is stupid. She dumped you to be with that no good preacher of hers."

"Yeah," he murmured.

"That's what you get for passing up a real sistah like me for a wet dream."

He started laughing. "You are too much."

"Yes, I am." We both laughed and got comfortable. Then everything got serious again.

The mere thought of him making love to me made my heart beat rapidly. I decided to be bold and dropped down on my knees in front of him, then leaned forward and pressed my lips to his. I half expected him to decline but was pleased when he did not. I thought about Kayla and knew what I was doing was wrong, but at this point what did it matter? She fucked him over for some no-neck mothafucka, not me. My desire for Clayton became so overwhelming nothing else mattered.

I darted my tongue in and out of his mouth, tasting him. With my tongue in his mouth, I reached inside and pulled his dick out. Yes! He was hung. I stroked him between the palms of my hand, then when I felt the first drop of precum I leaned down and captured the head in my mouth. He tried to stop me but once my lips touched the head it was all she wrote.

He gritted his teeth. "Dang, you've got skills!" He nearly came off the bed as a moan tore from his lips.

I sucked the tip of him and stroked the length of his dick, dipping my fingers inside his boxers and between his legs to caress his balls. His dick throbbed in my mouth as I sucked him long and hard. His moans became faster and he rocked against my mouth. I knew that he could come soon, so I stopped.

Slowly I dropped the towel and stood before him naked, waiting for him to make the next move.

That celibate shit went out the window the minute he rose and slipped out of his shorts. He scooped me up and lowered me onto the bed. He parted my thighs and positioned himself between them, then filled me completely and a shout tore from my lips. I wrapped my arms around his neck and pulled him down to me. He pounded into me and I moved my hips, matching each of his strokes. He pumped wildly, sending me over the edge. I closed my eyes and gave into the feeling. It was sensational, unreal. The fire came over me, stealing my breath. I dug my fingertips into his back and held on. He thrust deeper inside of me. I shuddered and convulsed and milked him with my spasms.

The brotha had skills, because I experienced the best orgasm of my life.

He then kissed me and held me in his arms. "Was it good for you?"

I was too tired to speak so I nodded. It was that wonderful feeling you get after a powerful orgasm.

A half hour passed and I could have laid there in his arms forever, and would have if I hadn't remembered that Clayton was supposed to have been Kayla's man and Lisa was my roommate and she was going to have a fit if she found out.

I was ready to send him away when I felt his dick grow hard again.

I climbed on top of him, positioned my coochie over his dick, then lowered over his hard shaft. Resting my hands on his chest, I lifted up and down again and again. He grabbed onto my waist and moved with me. It felt so good I didn't hear anything but the sound of skin slapping against skin. I was so oblivious to everything else that I didn't hear Lisa slide the key in the lock.

"Oh shit!"

My eyes snapped open and my gaze darted to the door, where Lisa was standing. A second later Nadine, followed by Kayla's head, peeked through the door.

"What's wrong?" I heard Kayla ask.

I saw the moment Kayla realized what was going on.

I jumped off of Clayton. He also jumped off the bed.

Kayla pushed her way past the other two and got all up in Clayton's face. "How could you?"

He looked scared as shit. "I . . ."

I stepped my naked ass between them and stared her down. "Excuse me, but he ain't got to answer to your ass. You played him, remember?"

"Get the hell out!" Kayla screamed.

Lisa shook her head. "Clayton, you better leave."

He quickly slipped into his clothes. Despite the problems in the room, all eyes were on Clayton's dick as he reached for boxers. The tension didn't return until he left the room.

I moved to the dresser and reached for my clothes.

"How could you fuck Clayton?"

"Shit. Your ass didn't want him," I snipped as I slipped a sundress over my head.

"And that made it all right?"

"Bitch, you decided to take Leroy's ass back. That mothafucka is screwing every fat bitch in town. You are just one of many. He plays on your insecurity, only you are too stupid to realize that."

Nadine tried to defuse the situation and dropped a hand to my shoulder. "Y'all need to quit tripping."

I pushed her hand away. "You need to shut your dyke-ass up! If you put your hands on me one more time I'm gonna fuck you up."

"You are trifling." Kayla stuck her finger in my face. I snapped my head back. No, the bitch didn't put her finger in my face.

"Bitch, you would want to get out my face before I hurt you."

Nadine, Kayla, and I all started shouting at the same time. The first one who touched me, it was on and popping.

"Stop it! Stop it!"

We all grew silent. I glanced over at my sister, who was leaning over holding her stomach.

"Stop it, all of you. This is not why I asked y'all here."

I clicked my tongue. "Why the fuck did you ask us here? That's what I want to know."

I noticed that tears were streaming down her face. After a few moments, she said, "I have cancer."

It took a moment for her words to register. "What?"

"I have cancer," she repeated as she lowered her weary body onto the bed.

This was un-fucking-believable. "I can't believe this shit! You flew me down here so you could tell me you've got cancer."

She returned her gaze to me and said, "No. I flew you down here so I could tell you I have to have surgery."

We were all stunned to silence.

Confused, I didn't blink. Kayla was the first to speak. "Cancer?" she whispered. "What kind of cancer?"

"Ovarian cancer."

There was pain on Kayla's face.

I finally found my voice. "You had me fly all the way down here just so you could tell me this shit."

"No, I flew you down here to tell you my cancer has come back and I have to have surgery again."

"Again? What do you mean again, 'cause this is the first I've heard of it?"

"I was first diagnosed three years ago. That's why I had the hysterectomy."

"Oh God!" Kayla cried. She burst out in tears, then dashed into the bathroom.

I couldn't believe this. My sister had never bothered to tell me that she had cancer.

Nadine moved next to Lisa and placed a comforting hand on her shoulders. The look in her eyes told me she was not the least bit shocked to hear of Lisa's illness.

"This is bullshit."

Nadine intervened. "Renee, listen to what she has to say."

"You stay out of this." I glanced over as she gave Lisa an I-told-you-so-look. "Wait a cotton pickin' minute. You knew?"

Nadine didn't say anything, but her silence spoke volumes. "I can't believe this shit! This dyke knew what was going on before I did."

"I just told her yesterday," Lisa wearily admitted.

"You confided in this dyke before you confided in your own sister. This is a bunch of bullshit!"

Nadine stepped in. "Renee, this is not the time."

"Bitch, fuck you. This is between me and my sister!"

"Renee, I didn't want to worry you. That's why I never said anything."

Kayla was crying so loud all of us could hear her. I wanted to scream and tell her to shut the hell up. That's not your sister who has a serious illness, it's mine. All mine.

"Who are you to decide what to tell me? I am a grown-ass woman." Tears filled my eyes. I headed for the door. Nadine stood between me and freedom.

"Renee, you need—"

"What you need to do is get out the way before I fuck you up."

"Fuck you," she spat with venom.

"No, fuck you." I quickly reached for my shoes, ignoring Lisa, who was urging me to calm the fuck down.

Kayla stepped out of the bathroom, wiping her nose.

I moved toward the door. "Kayla, move your ass so I can get out."

She shook her head. "Renee, I think you need to shut up and listen to what your sister has to say."

"No, what I need to do is get the fuck out of here because obviously Lisa doesn't need me, not when she has the two of you. Now get the fuck out of my way before I push your fat ass onto the floor!"

When she moved to the side I knew I had hurt her feelings, but so what? What about my feelings? For once someone needed to think about how I felt. As soon as I bolted through the door, I stormed out the hotel and not once looked back.

I spotted Everton as I was going through the patio area.

"Renee, I was looking for you."

I grabbed his shirt and dragged him along with me. "Good, I was looking for you, too."

"Where are we going?"

"Just shut up and come with me."

I entered the building and dragged him up to the laundry room. I didn't care who saw us or if he got in trouble. All I cared about was forgetting.

As soon as the door was shut I grabbed the buckle of his pants and whipped his dick out.

"Slow down. What's gotten into you?"

He was acting like a bitch.

I could see the shock on his face as I pushed him back onto the table, then slipped my panties down over my hips and lowered on top of him. I rode him hard. I didn't feel much of nothing but it didn't matter. It was the physical contact that I craved. That I needed. As soon as I was done I climbed off the table. He reached out and tried to grab me.

I jumped out of his reach. "Don't touch me."

"Can we talk about what just happened?"

"Everton, we ain't got shit to talk about. I don't appreciate you running your mouth to Solomon. There is no us. Not now. Not ever. All you were is a fuck, and a bad one at that."

He still kept trying to talk. I got so sick of hearing him whine like a damn baby, I fixed my dress, grabbed my panties, and headed toward the beach.

Chapter 76

RENEE

I waited at the end of the beach until I spotted the three of them leaving with their arms linked like they were the fucking Three Musketeers.

I went up to my room and shut the door, then took a seat on the bed and noticed a pamphlet on my pillow.

Ovarian cancer.

I picked it up and did not move until I had completed all twenty pages. According to the pamphlet thousands of women go years without any signs of having ovarian cancer, which is why so many, especially African Americans, don't realize they have the disease until it is too late.

Tears streamed down my face as things started to become clear for me. Lisa had a hysterectomy because of the cancer. Her short, trendy hairstyle was not a fashion statement, but a result of chemotherapy. All this time she had been hiding things from me. Why? I'm her sister. She could tell me anything. But even as I said that I know my sister all too well. She believes it is her job to protect me, not to burden me with her problems.

Dear God, I feel like ripping my hair out. All these years I have been selfish and thinking only of myself when my sister needed me.

All these years, I claimed that I hated her guts for trying to be my mama, and here she was slowly deteriorating without me even knowing it.

Why, God? Why do you have to take my sister from me? She has never done anything to hurt anyone. If anyone should be dying of cancer it should be me.

I started crying hard and couldn't stop because it wasn't fair. Lisa didn't deserve this. Not her. Me. I'm the bitch who sleeps with a total stranger without any remorse.

I must have dozed off, because I woke up to the sound of light knocking at the door. My heart jumped in my chest. I just knew it was Lisa. We needed to talk because there was so much I needed to say to her.

I rose from the bed, took a deep breath, then opened it. Everton brushed past me and entered the room.

Oh, no he didn't. "Uh, can I help you with something?"

"Renee, we need to talk."

"We ain't got shit to talk about." Before I could cuss his ass out, he pushed the door shut and grabbed me by my arm.

"Hey! Have you lost your damn mind?" He dropped my ass down onto the bed. I tried to get up but his hands were on my shoulders and he pushed me back down. I tried to swing at his chest, but he was quick and grabbed my wrist.

"Renee, I don't want to hurt you."

"Then let me go!"

"All I want to do is talk."

"Talk about what?"

"Talk about us."

"Mothafucka, there ain't no us!"

In that instant, I kid you not, I witnessed some kind of Satanism. His eyes darkened and his lips curled into a sickly smile. I gave up fighting and shut the hell up, quick.

"All I wanted to do was love you." He then reached into the waistband of his pants and removed a small knife.

"Wait a minute. Hold the fuck up. Everton, let's talk about this."

"According to you, there is nothing left to talk about."

I sat up straight on the bed. "Okay, well, maybe I was wrong. Maybe there is something I need to say to you."

"Like what?"

"Like . . . I'm sorry."

Chapter 77

LISA

Lisa decided that she had waited long enough for her sister to come and talk to her. She walked back to the room and swiped her key card. It didn't work. She swiped it again, then finally knocked.

"Go away!"

Lisa dropped her hand to her waist. "Renee, we need to talk."

"I said go away! I'm not ready to talk to you."

"Renee, you're tripping!" She was practically screaming now.

"Nah, you the one tripped, for not telling me the truth. Now go away."

She tried using her card again. "Why isn't my card working?"

"Because I told Everton to move you across the hall with your homies."

"You know, you do some stupid shit at times."

"Yeah, whatever."

"Whatever, to your ass!"

Pissed off, she stomped away from the room. How dare her sister check her out of her own room? She blinked back the tears that threatened to surface. Her sister was being a true ass about the situation. Yeah, she had been wrong about not telling her the truth, but there was no reason for her to act like that, especially at a time like this. She went back to the pool and took a seat with the others.

"Damn, you're back quick. What she say?" Kayla asked between sips.

Lisa tried to swallow a sob. "She pretty much told me to fuck off!"

"What?" Nadine exclaimed. "Your sister is trippin'. As soon as I get done eating she and I are going to have a long talk."

"It won't do any good. She even had Everton lock me out the room."

Kayla shook her head. "I am too through with that girl."

"Wait a minute," Nadine began. "She said Everton checked you out of the room? I thought Everton was off today."

Lisa glanced at them at the same time.

Kayla shrugged. "Maybe she said that because she was mad."

Nadine shook her head. "I don't think so." She rose. "I'm going to the front desk to check."

Chapter 78

RENEE

"Everton, please put the knife down."

"No. What point is living if I can't have you?"

This mothafucka is crazy and unfortunately he doesn't care if he takes me with him in the process. To say I was scared was an understatement. I was beside myself. He was pacing around the room and waving a knife like he was ready to take both of us at any time. That's why I lied to Lisa, so that she would get as far away as possible. If he had to hurt anyone I definitely didn't want it to be my sister.

"Please, Everton. This is not the way."

"Then what is it going to take for us to be together? I love you. Can't you see that?"

I tried to smile like I was flattered by his comment.

"I want you to be my wife."

"But I'm already married."

"What?"

Oops. What the hell I say that for? His body jerked. His chest rose and fell. The look on his face turned from hate to anger.

"I mean I have already been married once."

He blew air. "Now you're lying. So you're married and messing around on your husband."

"It's more complicated than that." I tried pleading with my eyes.

"So I was never any more to you than just a fuck."

I didn't bother to answer.

"You whore." He slammed his hand across the dresser and knocked the contents onto the floor.

I began to shake. For the first time I noticed how big Everton was. His eyes were glazed over and he looked like he was ready to kill me. Never before had a man made me fear for my life.

"You sucked Solomon's dick, didn't you?"

I shook my head. "No."

"You lying bitch. He told me so himself."

Something in the way he looked told me he was about to go off. I tried to dash past him except he was too quick. He grabbed me by my shirt and flung me across the room onto the bed. Before I could get up, he sprang across the floor and landed on my chest, temporarily knocking the wind out of me. While I tried to get the air back into my lungs he called me every degrading name in the book. Finally, I found the strength to scream.

"Everton, please!"

"Shut up!" He hit me in the jaw with his fist. I kept begging but it did no good. He kept hitting me and I tried to block as many blows as I could until I couldn't fight him any longer.

"I loved you so much. How could you have treated me this way?" I heard him crying like a damn baby. "Now you have to die."

I felt something sharp against my neck. I screamed and prepared myself to meet my maker. As I started to drift off, I heard a loud noise and a bunch of voices. Is that the girls? Had they come back to check on me? Before I had a chance to find out if I was dreaming, I started slipping away. Then everything went black.

Chapter 79

RENEE

"Renee, Renee, wake up." I felt someone patting my cheeks. "Get your ass up."

I opened my eyes and everything came to focus. "Lisa," I said in a breathless whisper.

"I'm here, girl. We're all here." She was sitting on the side of the bed, squeezing my hand.

I moved my head to the left to find Kayla and Nadine standing over me. Kayla was crying, of course.

"What happened?" I asked.

"Girl, Everton beat the crap out of you," Lisa replied. "Thank goodness we had his boss follow us up to the room with a key."

"Where is he now?"

"The police took him away. They want to talk to you and take you over to the hospital to be looked at."

I shook my head, regardless of how bad I felt. "No foreign hospitals. I can see a doctor when we get home tomorrow."

Nadine touched my arm. "You look like shit."

I tried to laugh. "I feel like shit."

"Bitch, I thought you could fight."

I tried to laugh but that shit made my head hurt.

Kayla started crying again and I turned my pounding head to look at her. "Girl, shut the hell up! I'm fine."

She wiped her nose as she spoke, "I was so scared when I saw you lying there. All I could think about was the way we ended things between us."

"Me too." Shit, she made me start crying. "I was so afraid I wouldn't get a chance to tell you how sorry I am. A man should never come between our friendship."

"I know you didn't mean it."

I turned to my sister. "Lisa, I'm so sorry, really I am."

She was also crying. "It's okay."

Nadine tried to cheer us all up. "We are girls, remember? Through thick and thin."

"Through thick and thin," we repeated, then engaged in a group hug.

Chapter 80

RENEE

As soon as the Jamaican police got done questioning me and realized there was no way in hell I was going to the hospital, they finally left.

I went and found my sister, who was in the room with the other two, waiting. "Can we go somewhere alone and talk?"

Lisa nodded. I laced my fingers with hers. As we moved across the beach people were pointing and staring. I know I looked jacked up, but I didn't give a damn. All that mattered right now was Lisa.

At the end of the beach, far away from everyone, I took a seat on the wet sand. I pulled my legs up to my chest and hugged them close to my body, needing the strength to get through this.

There was a long moment of silence. Neither of us knew where to begin while knowing this conversation would start a new beginning for us.

"I'm sorry," we both said at the same time.

Lisa started laughing. "Me first."

I nodded.

She rested her weight on her elbows. "I'm sorry I didn't tell you sooner."

I shook my head. There was no way I was going to allow her to take the blame. "You don't have to apologize. I know I haven't made it easy for you at all. I know I can be a pretty selfish bitch.

"It has always had to be about me. One thing I can say, as a sister you've always been there for me. I wish I could say the same." I got choked up and she tried to speak. "Please, let me finish. I know I've got a lot of problems, probably more than you know, but I plan to put my problems aside. I promise to be there for you." Tears flowed freely from my eyes and I didn't care if she saw how emotional I was.

Lisa reached out and laced our fingers together. "I know I drive you crazy, but that's because I love you and hate seeing you going around in circles."

I smiled through my sadness. "I have been fucking up a lot lately."

Lisa smirked. "Remember, you said it, not me."

We laughed, and I knew then everything was going to be okay.

I wiped my eyes. "When's your surgery?"

"Next week."

"Can I come?" I asked between sniffles.

Lisa laughed, then smiled. "I was hoping you would."

I was quiet for several long seconds, then I finally asked the question I was afraid to ask. "What are your chances of beating this?"

"Fifty percent."

My stomach dropped.

Lisa squeezed my hand. "Don't worry. I caught it in plenty of time. I've beaten it once and I'll beat it again."

"I hope so." My voice cracked. "I don't know what the hell I would do without you."

"Live life to its fullest." Lisa gave me a silly look. "Having cancer has given me a deep appreciation for life. I try to live every day like it's my last. I want you to do the same thing." Her expression suddenly became serious. "Give John a chance. I know you say the two of you aren't right for each other, but I want you to pray on it, and ask God for guidance. You're going to need his strength, like I need Mike's."

I started crying again because my sister sounded so at peace. She has accepted the fact that she might die. If it was me, I would have been in denial to the end.

Lisa hugged me close. "Quit being a big baby. I'm not going anywhere."

I wiped my eyes and pulled away. "You better not."

"I love you Nae-Nae."

"I love you too, Peanut."

We laughed, then held each other again. As I stared off into the sky, I couldn't help but feel that this moment marked a turning point for us, both headed in directions that neither would have predicted years ago.

EPILOGUE

I lay in a lounge chair with my eyes closed under the blue sky, the sun kissing everything that wasn't covered by a skimpy bikini. If Lisa were here, she would have scolded me for the provocative swimsuit.

Tears filled my eyes, I quickly brushed them away. She had left strict instructions not to mourn her death but to celebrate her life. But it wasn't always easy. Lisa had died from a blood clot to the heart a few days after surgery, surrounded by all of her loved ones.

Her last wish was that she wanted the four of us to go back to Jamaica as soon as she had recovered. We had each agreed to fulfill her request.

Lisa was right. I wouldn't have gotten through the last year if it hadn't been for John. I fed on his strength, needed his comfort.

I glanced over at Nadine, whose eyes were hidden behind dark shades, and I knew she was pretending to be asleep. She was thinking about Lisa, the same way I was. To my right was Kayla, who was openly shedding tears and blowing snot bubbles.

I reached for her hand and squeezed it. "Bitch, you need to quit. Lisa wants us to be happy."

"I am happy. Really I am." Her voice cracked. "She's with God now."

"Yes, she is," Nadine added.

Nadine and Jordan are still together. She still had a problem with sharing her personal life. I think it's because her family would kick her out of their will if they knew she was rubbing pussies. Kayla is still hanging in there with Leroy. Darlene had a baby boy and Leroy is still at home with his family, still promising to leave them soon so he and Kayla could be together. And me, well, I stayed with John. He has been so supportive that there was no way I could tell him I wanted out of the relationship. Besides, before Lisa passed she asked me to give my marriage one more chance. And I agreed. Nothing between John and me has changed, but I'm hoping if I continue to try hard enough, anything is possible.

IN THE COMPANY OF MY SISTAHS

ANGIE DANIELS

ABOUT THIS GUIDE

The suggested questions are intended to enhance
your group's reading of this book.

Discussion Questions

1. Lisa felt the best way to tell her sister she had ovarian cancer was in the company of their sistahs. How do you feel about her decision? If Renee was your sister would you have handled the situation differently?

2. Despite all her faults was Renee Moore a good friend to Kayla? What about Nadine?

3. Do you believe Renee truly liked Solomon or was she once again just caught up in the moment?

4. Renee said she was "in love with the idea of being in love." Do you agree with her personal analysis?

5. Even though Renee was not always considered a nice person, her friends were often envious of her; why do you think they felt that way?

6. Do you feel that the others were too accepting of Renee's behavior? How would you have responded to Renee's behavior?

7. Do you believe Kayla's behavior was a result of her upbringing? Do you feel sorry for Kayla? What about Nadine?

8. Why do you think Clayton told Renee he was celibate but never bothered to tell Kayla? Do you feel he was manipulated into having sex with Renee?

9. Renee justified her reason for sleeping with Clayton was because Kayla no longer wanted him. If Clayton and Kayla had been sexually active do you think that Renee would still have slept with him?

10. Do you feel that Renee played with Everton's emotions? Did Everton really want to kill Renee? Do you feel that Renee de-

served what happened to her? Did you at all sympathize with Everton?

11. Lisa had kept her illness a secret for three years because she didn't want to worry anyone. Do you feel that her decision was unfair?

12. After everything that occurred, do you see Renee changing her life in any way?

13. Of all of the characters, who do you feel had the most issues?